Serpent's Blood
The First Book of Genesys

FORTHCOMING TITLES FROM BRIAN STABLEFORD IN THIS SERIES

Salamander's Fire
Chimera's Cradle

SERPENT'S BLOOD

The First Book of Genesys

Brian Stableford

LEGEND

Published by Legend Books in 1995
20 Vauxhall Bridge Road, London SW1V 2SA

An imprint of Random House UK Limited

Random House Australia (Pty) Limited
20 Alfred Street, Milsons Point, Sydney,
New South Wales 2061, Australia

Random House New Zealand Limited
18 Poland Road, Glenfield,
Auckland 10, New Zealand

Random House South Africa (Pty) Limited
PO Box 337, Bergvlei 2012, South Africa

Random House UK Limited Reg. No. 954009

Typeset by Deltatype Ltd, Ellesmere Port, Cheshire
Printed in England by Clays Ltd, St Ives plc

ISBN 0 09 944331 7

Part One

In Xandria, linked together by chains of coincidence

Humans were made by a world other than the one they know, close kin to it but not the same. No man of the world will ever see the world which made him, and yet it can be glimpsed in dreams. No memory of the world which made the human race survives in this world, nor is there any account of it in the sacred lore, but what is written in the blood can never be wholly erased, and the flickering flame which lights the most intimate dreams can never be utterly extinguished.

No man born of this world can know what a moon or a mountain is, but there are men nevertheless who see the moon while their eyes are firmly shut, and drink of precious folly, and there are men who climb mountains while they lie abed, dizzied by sublime heights.

This world has no changing seasons, but there are seasons in the rhythm of our being. The tides which surge in our blood are greater by far than the petty tides which stir our shallow seas. The world's seas are briny, but not as briny as the blood of men. Our blood marks us children of other and unimaginably distant seas, and this is true even of those who have Serpent's blood in them. The world's seas are shallow but the water of our being is deeper by far; it marks us children of a great and unfathomable abyss, and this is true even of those whose hearts are warmed by Salamander's fire. There are seasons in the affairs of men, and always will be, despite that the men who live in the world we know were born and will be born again from Chimera's Cradle.

The Apocrypha of Genesys

I

A NDRIS MYRASOL HAD been a prince in Ferentina until he was
six years old, but now had been six years a vagabond. Exactly
half a lifetime had passed since he quit his own land, and the
anniversary was not a happy one. He had told himself a thousand
times that it was neither fear nor the fear of brotherly love turning
to hatred which had driven him away from his home. He had told
himself a thousand times what a fine thing it was to be a citizen of
the world rather than the scion of a single tiny nation, but he was
past believing it now.

Six years had taught him what it meant to be without home,
without property and without a goal in life. In six years he had
suffered every penalty of aimlessness, but he wasn't so foolish as to
imagine that things couldn't get worse.

Andris sat on a crooked chair beside a rickety table beneath the
internal staircase in a harbourside inn called the Wayfaring Tree in
the city of Xandria and cursed his miserable luck. He was alone
and friendless. The ale he was drinking was uncommonly dark and
suspiciously salty, matching his mood with uncanny precision.

The legs of the chair had become so soft and spongy by courtesy
of the corrosions of five different kinds of woodrot that it
threatened to cave in beneath his bulk – which was, admittedly,
unusually large by Xandrian standards. The surface of the table
was peppered and blotched by no less than eight kinds of rot, three
of which were unfamiliar to him, being quite unknown in milder
climes. One of these appeared to be feeding on the stain which had
been used to colour the wood, mottling the tabletop with a
strangely discomfiting pallor. Andris had no idea what kind of
wood it was, and couldn't put a name to any of the eight kinds of
rot, familiar or unfamiliar. His travels hadn't taught him a great
deal, but they had amply demonstrated the truth of the old adage

that it did no good to learn the names and habits of different kinds of rot because there would always be a new kind eating away at your possessions whenever you turned around.

That, in a nutshell, is the story of my life, he reflected. *In fact, that, in a nutshell, is the story of everybody's life, even though the vast majority of men fail to notice the fact – especially those who are privileged to live in a vast and vainglorious city like Xandria.*

Andris didn't like Xandria. He liked it even less than all the other ports which he had visited as he had made his slow way southwards across the Slithery Sea, and he was already regretting his decision to come here chasing a rumour which could hardly be expected to live up to his hopes even if it were true.

Xandria was huge, and it had a city wall – in frank defiance of what common men held to be the limits of practicability even in more temperate lands where stone had the grace to crumble at a relatively slow pace. Xandria's inhabitants thought they were the most civilised people in the world. Few of them had ever heard of Ferentina, but even those who had would undoubtedly consider it to be a stagnant backwater in the flowing stream of human history. In Ferentina, though, even tiny inns had solid chairs, tables whose four legs were all precisely the same length, and serving girls.

In Andris's view, there could be no firmer proof of the uncivilised nature of a city and its people than the fact that the city contained, and its people gladly patronised, inns which did not employ serving girls. In the Wayfaring Tree a man had to carry his own ale, which was dispensed through a hatchway of such parsimonious dimensions that merely waiting to be served could easily take ten minutes. Andris didn't know why this was, but he was prepared to assume that it had something to do with the innkeeper's fear of being mobbed, choked and beaten black and blue when his patrons tasted the ale he served.

In spite of the poor quality of the ale, the inn was crowded. Most of its patrons were sailormen from the various ships which were moored in the harbour, but there was a party of local bravos huddled about a table set in a covert on the other side of the staircase which led up to the rooms in the upper part of the house. Occasionally one or other of these bully-boys would dart a glance through one of the gaps between the slats of the stairway, as if to

4

see whether Andris was trying to listen to their whispered conversation. The implied suspicion made Andris feel direly uncomfortable, even though he had not the least interest in whatever villainy they might be plotting. He wished that he had someone to talk to, so that he could immerse himself in a conversation of his own, but none of the sailormen were from the ship that had brought him to Xandria, and his tentative enquiries regarding the possible whereabouts of one Theo Zabio had so far met with no response.

The table in the covert was not the only one from which glances were occasionally directed at Andris. At the other side of the room, close to the door which gave access to the waterfront, sat a group of ambers, whose skins were almost as pale as his own. He knew that this was mere coincidence, and that these other men were so-called darklanders from the great forest in the far south of what the Xandrians were pleased to think of as their empire. In all probability, he supposed, most of the other people in the room – who were goldens all, though some were so dark as almost to be reckoned bronze – took him for a darklander in spite of the cut of his clothes. They had been very good clothes once, but six years of mending and patching had turned them into ragged travesties.

In order to avoid the possibility of making accidental eye-contact with curious and suspicious gazes Andris studied the ceiling beams with a critical eye. In a place like this, every guest had good cause to wonder whether the ceiling of his bedroom might collapse while he was peacefully sleeping in his bunk. The beams looked solid enough, but it was easy to see where fresh paint had been applied to conceal the tell-tale blotches of softening decay. The stone pillars which supported the ends of the beams looked sturdier, with relatively few cracks and crevices, but there was clear enough evidence of patching for the informed eye to notice.

The whole lot could go at any time, Andris thought, with a silent sigh. *And there's a cellar too, subject to steady seepage if the taste of the ale's anything to go by. The whole edifice might crumble into its own soggy bowels, taking every one of us with it.* Paradoxically, the uncheerful thought made him feel slightly better. The idea that all Xandria would one day crumble into dust and slide into the every-hungry sea made his personal plight seem less remarkable.

His contemplation of the ceiling ended abruptly as his attention was caught by the unmistakable sound of trouble. Some kind of argument had started between the darklanders and the sailormen at the neighbouring table. Insults were being hurled back and forth in several different accents. Mercifully, no one was getting up to wave fists, let alone draw blades. Andris judged that it would probably die down soon enough. In any case, he was close to the bottom rung of the staircase; he could dash up to his room at a moment's notice should there be any need so to do.

He stared into the murky depths of his ale. The tankard – which was glass, albeit of a crude kind – was showing the effects of some mysterious species of blight. The vessel didn't seem likely to break, but he didn't suppose that the bloom made the ale taste any better.

His contemplation of the tankard's interior was interrupted by a sudden awareness that he was no longer alone. He jerked his head up to confront the man who was now standing beside the empty chair opposite his own. Andris would doubtless have offended the other with the fierceness of his stare had the man not been blind, but his eyes had been wrecked by some kind of disease which had turned the pupils milk-white and the whites blood-red. He was thin, and his clothes were in rags but he carried himself with a certain dignity and his ancient face was not unhandsome, apart from the terrible eyes.

'May I tell you a story,' the ancient whispered, 'for the smallest and oldest coin you have.'

Is this what I will be when I grow old? Andris thought, with a twinge of panic. The few coins which he had left were all small, and none had been minted within the last two years. 'It'd be a bad bargain,' he confessed. 'You'll find richer men elsewhere in the room.'

'I hear them,' the old man said. 'But here there is silence, and sickness of heart. Here there is a need which I might meet.' His accent was one which Andris did not know; he too must be a stranger in Xandria. Could he really judge the sickness of a heart from the quality of a pool of silence?

'Perhaps there is,' said Andris, not ungrudgingly. 'Tell me a story, then – but tell me no tales of Xandria's noble kings and valiant heroes. I'd far rather hear a tale which might remind me of my childhood in a distant land.'

'I can't promise to awaken old memories,' the ancient said, 'but I'll tell you the oldest tale I know. You might have heard it in the cradle even though you come from the far side of the world.'

'I'll settle for that,' Andris agreed.

The old man sat down. He held himself very straight although the years must have weighed heavily upon him. He was at least thirty but it was evident that he still had pride in his work. He seemed to have been thoroughly versed in his dubious Art. *When I'm old as well as destitute,* Andris thought, *I won't even have stories to trade for the coins I beg.*

'There is no destiny,' said the old man softly, in the sonorous tone of one reciting words learned in the distant past and recited many times before. 'The future cannot be foretold, but the world is pregnant with many possibilities. Some will be given birth and suckled with nourishing milk, and the strongest of these will grow to be things which are new not merely in the world but in the universe.

'What will be new cannot be foreseen, but its shadow might be glimpsed in the fertile imagination.

'There once came a Serpent into Idun, which brought the gift of a tree whose fruit had knowledge of good and evil, and the forefathers bought the tree with promises they could not fulfil. *I will make you a gift of my blood,* the Serpent said, *and hope that you will use it wisely.* The forefathers accepted the gift, and made a further promise they could not fulfil. *We shall return this gift a thousandfold,* they said, *if only we can use it wisely.*

'There also came a Salamander into Idun, which brought the gift of a tree whose fruit had knowledge of another kind, and the forefathers bought the tree with coin the Salamander could not spend. *I will make you a gift of the fire in my heart,* the Salamander said, *and hope that it might warm you.* The forefathers accepted this gift, and gave the Salamander another unspendable coin. *We shall return this gift a thousandfold,* they said, *if we can only feel its warmth.*

'Serpents die, and Salamanders too, and the people of the world brought death with them when they first descended from the sky, but if ever the world is devoid of Serpents or Salamanders men will have cause to mourn. Better by far that the promises their forefathers made might one day be fulfilled, and the coin they paid

7

might one day be spent. Milk that is given to the nourishment of Serpents and Salamanders is already owed, and does not go to waste.

'There is no destiny. The future cannot be foreknown, but the human mind is pregnant with many designs, some of which may be realised if only the necessary instruments can be devised and forged.

'We cannot know today what we might discover tomorrow, but the scheming mind should make what provision it can. Remember this, for it is a truth as vital as any in the lore.'

For a second or two, Andris didn't realise that the recitation was over. *Was that the whole of the story?* he thought. *Was it a story at all?* The blind man clearly believed that it was; he now had the manner of one who had just imparted a valuable secret.

Andris reached into the money-pouch attached to his belt, and took a coin at random. He held it out to the old man for several seconds before it dawned on him that the gesture was futile. He reached across the table to pick up the man's left hand with his own, and solemnly placed the coin in the palm. 'It's neither Xandrian nor fresh,' he admitted apologetically.

'Thank you,' said the old man. 'Was the story to your satisfaction? Had you heard it before, long ago?'

'Only the beginning and the end,' Andris told him, 'and not as parts of a story. *We cannot know today what we might discover tomorrow, but the scheming mind should make what provision it can* is a popular saying in my homeland, but the passages concerning the Serpent and the Salamander are new to me. In Ferentina, no man has ever seen a Serpent or a Salamander. I hear that Serpents, at least, can sometimes be seen in Xandria.'

'They never come to the city,' the old man said, 'but I have heard that they can sometimes be seen in the western regions of the empire.' He stressed the words *heard* and *seen* very faintly.

'If your story is from the *Lore of Genesys*,' Andris said thoughtfully, 'it's strange that I've never heard it in full. I thought the storytellers of Ferentina were thoroughly versed in that particular set of legends.'

'It's from the *Apocrypha of Genesys*,' the blind man informed him. 'We had many forefathers, and they gave us more gifts than most of us know. Goran made the lore for everyone, but his brothers took care to communicate their own wisdom to a select few.'

'Oh,' Andris said unenthusiastically. 'You mean the secret commandments and all that occult rubbish.' He regretted it immediately, realising that if the blind man could recite mock-mythology with evident respectfulness he might be a firm believer in *all that occult rubbish*. He would have apologised, but at that moment the argument between the darklanders and their neighbours erupted again, and this time there was little time wasted in mere insult.

Within a few seconds – far more quickly than Andris would have thought possible – the darklanders were on their feet, lashing out this way and that with hands and feet alike. Three tables and a dozen chairs went tumbling over, followed by a cacophony of shattering glass. Through the open doorway of the inn rushed a member of the king's guard, red-skirted and brightly helmed. He hadn't drawn his sword; his empty hands were raised in a placatory fashion, and his clear intention was to nip the trouble in the bud. Alas, he was already too late. He was immediately swallowed up by the violence.

Andris stood up, the first thought in his mind being that he ought to protect the blind man. 'Quickly,' he said. 'Up the staircase!' But the blind man didn't move – because, of course, he didn't know where the staircase was. Andris stood up and reached out his hand, intending to take the blind man by the arm and lead him away to safety, but he was rudely interrupted. Other men had their eyes on the steps and their thoughts on escape, including the bravos who had huddled about the table in the alcove beneath the slanting staircase. All of a sudden those men were jostling Andris and his companion, trying to shove them both out of the way. The blind man's chair was overturned and the table too.

The table knocked the blind man over as it fell, spilling Andris's sour ale all over his grey rags.

The insult and injury done to the meek story-teller inflamed Andris's anger rather more than the loss of the unappetising beer, but he still had sufficient presence of mind to curb his temper. When he turned to grapple with the men who were ambitious to swarm up the stairway he had no intention of hitting or hurting anyone; like the guardsman he merely wished to restore a semblance of order to the incipient chaos.

He never got the chance to speak or to take constructive action. The biggest of the conspirators – who was a little wider than Andris, though not as tall – was already intent on thrusting him out of the way. He barged forward and sent Andris spinning sideways, away from the bottom stair. Andris would probably have tripped over one of the lesser men and fallen down had it not been for the fact that he met another man coming the other way, who had apparently been hurled with even greater force. This proved to be the guardsman who had tried unsuccessfully to break up the fight as it started.

Andris grabbed hold of the guardsman and the guardsman grabbed hold of him, as both of them struggled to stay upright. Their eyes met for a moment and Andris saw – or thought he saw – a glimmer of understanding. At any rate, the guardsman made no attempt to strike Andris, and they released one another at exactly the same time. They wanted to turn in opposite directions – Andris towards the stairway and the soldier towards the area where half a dozen amber darklanders were lashing out among a crowd of thirty or forty goldens, now including at least one more guardsman – but neither of them was able to follow his intention through. The big man who had shoved Andris had picked up the table at which Andris had been seated, and he brought its heavy top across in a vicious arc aimed at the heads of the amber and the guardsman.

Andris, who had the advantage of being able to see it coming, ducked. The guardsman, who was looking the other way, took the edge of the table square on the back of his head.

The guardsman went down as if he had been pole-axed. Andris would have escaped unhurt if only the table had not had its legs still firmly attached, but one of them caught him in the ribs as he tried to shrink into an impossibly small space, and jarred him horribly. While he gasped in pain the big man turned the table sideways, lifted it up – rather inelegantly, but with considerable dexterity – and brought it crashing down on the fallen guardsman.

Had the table's edge struck the man's head again it would have killed him, but it struck his leg instead. Again, one of the table-legs – of which only two now remained attached – hit Andris, this time just beneath the hip.

The impact redoubled Andris's agony and spun him around,

with his limbs in a terrible tangle. When he fell, trying unsuccessfully to embrace his ribs with one hand and his thigh with the other, he somehow contrived to fall upon the upended tabletop, which was now sandwiched between his own body and that of the soldier. The wind had been knocked out of him, and he had to fight desperately hard to draw air into his reluctant lungs.

He was still there several minutes later, cursing his luck and nursing his injuries, when two other guardsmen seized him, and told him that he was under arrest. By this time, the men who had been fighting for access to the stairway had disappeared, having presumably made their escape. The stricken guardsman and the blind story-teller were both stretched out on the flagstoned floor, unconscious and barely breathing.

It occured to Andris, somewhat belatedly, that he might be in deep trouble.

2

THE DARKLANDER SUFFERED his fifth and final seizure shortly after the nineteenth hour. That, at least, was the time according to Ereleth's red-striped candle; a glance out of the window at the brightly shining stars suggested to her that the candle might be as much as half an hour slow, but she certainly wasn't about to summon an astronomer to make an accurate time-check. Witchery was work that required to be done in secret – preferably in a high attic with a single narrow window and a low dark-beamed ceiling, just like the room they were in.

The last seizure was by no means as spectacular as the earlier ones. The darklander had nothing left in his stomach to bring up but clotted blood, and insufficient strength in his aged muscles to sustain violent convulsions. His colour was quite ghastly. Being a darklander he had started out pale, but now his flesh was almost as white as his hair, the colour of new sailcloth. His open eyes were bulging out of their sockets, like two great glass beads with a bad case of vitric rot.

Ereleth didn't waste much time watching the dying man's convulsions. She was far more interested in watching the Princess Lucrezia's reaction to his unlovely death.

So far, Lucrezia's response had been all that could be expected, and Ereleth was not disappointed now. The expression in the young woman's eye was one of fascinated but dispassionate interest; her gaze was intense but clinical, and her lovely features were flushed with a purely intellectual excitement.

By contrast, the features of the giant who stood on the far side of the couch looked as if they had been carved out of stone; her eyes too might have been made out of glass. The giant was no longer a stranger to this room, although she had to duck under the beams every time she took a step, but she had not become used to such sights; her awe and her anxiety remained as powerful as ever. But she was only a guard, not an apprentice witch.

Lucrezia is the one, Ereleth told herself, feeling that the statement was the final confirmation of something she had known for a long time, something which had long been determined. *This is the best and truest instrument that I have forged. This is my appointed heir. She's no child of Belin's, despite that he's her father, but something wholly and exclusively mine.* The last thought brought a slight frown to her face, because Belin naturally saw things differently. According to Ereleth's spies, he had recently taken advice from his pettifogging ministers which bade him arrange a marriage for his twenty-second daughter even though she was still forty days short of her seventh birthday: a marriage to the prince of Shaminzara.

Ereleth had not the slightest idea why Sharminzara should suddenly have entered so forcefully into the ministers' calculation of the delicate balance of political power within Xandria's sphere of influence, but she had made it her business to find out what kind of place it was. According to the patient tallymen who kept count of the empire's possessions, Shaminzara was an isle fully five hundred kims distant, which measured barely sixty kims by fifty-five, so desolate as to be well-nigh treeless. It had only a single harbour and was reputed to be a favourite haunt of pirates. It wasn't the kind of place in which a young queen might be able to develop her own ambitions; nor was it the kind of place in which a young witch might find adequate scope for the exercise of her Art.

'Did I not tell you?' said Ereleth softly, lacing her fingers together and cracking her ancient knuckles. 'Dead in five hours. A small enough dosage to be easily disguised, and no known antidote. It never fails.'

The princess made a slight sound of disgust. 'It took *him* five hours,' she said warily. 'He must have been at least twenty-five, and he spent the last fifteen of them working on the wall. The only reason the seneschal released him to us was that he was no longer capable of lifting a fair-sized pebble or mixing smooth cement. He *wanted* to die. We need far better subjects if these experiments are to be reliable. If I'm ever to use the Art in earnest I need to know how to measure the effect of the poisons on men who are strong and desperate to live.'

13

'Your father has better uses for men like that,' Ereleth said wryly. 'We all have – or would have, given half the chance.' She laughed lewdly. 'In this case, believe me, the condition of the subject makes no difference.' Privately, however, she thought: *The child has a good mind. She is determined to take nothing on trust which can be tested. Not one of her sisters showed such promise – but those who have Serpent's blood have a natural aptitude for witchery.*

Ereleth, who had never borne a child herself, had been mentor to half a dozen of Lucrezia's half-sisters before her; the tricks of poisoning – and the corollary tricks of healing the poisoned – had long been considered valuable in the Xandrian royal family. Custom dictated that every king of Xandria should have at least one witch-wife, and should always let it be known – discreetly, of course – that any one of his daughters might have been trained in such skills. The alliances sealed and cemented by their marriages were just that bit stronger when tinged with a little anxiety.

Many teachers, Ereleth knew, would have construed the princess's scepticism as an insult to their teaching, and to the lore itself, but Ereleth too had never been prepared to take entirely on trust that which had been handed down to her by her own mentor. The experiments which she had undertaken in the course of a long lifetime had disclosed several significant inaccuracies in the traditional lore, which she had been careful to take aboard. She was too clever and too proud to be one of those over-devout lorekeepers who assumed that if reality would not conform with what she had been taught then reality must be at fault; she was, after all, a keeper of the secret commandments, loyal to a higher authority than the king of Xandria.

Ereleth's own mentor, in the course of *her* diplomatic career, had never had cause to use more than half a dozen of the several hundred poisons whose properties she 'knew'. She had lived in quiet times, and had not been blessed with the gift of curiosity. Ereleth had lived in quiet times too, but she had always taken care to make more liberal and varied use of what she knew, partly for art's sake but mainly to make sure that what she had been taught was actually true. It was all very well to have a profound respect for the first commandment of Goran the Forefather – 'The only sin is forgetfulness' – but the lore was no more immune to disease and decay than anything else in the world. The most insidious form of forgetfulness was surely the slow poison of cumulative error which was gradually corrupting every one of the Four Hundred Arts.

The stink of the dead darklander was becoming overpowering, but Lucrezia's fascination kept her by his side. Ereleth noted that the princess was still prepared to lean over the corpse in order to make minute inspection of the effects of the poison she had fed him. Her curiosity was indefatigable.

The giant maintained her position too, but in her case it was duty and determination that would not let her turn away. Ereleth approved of duty and determination in servants; they were qualities as valuable in their way as intelligence and curiosity in lorekeepers. This particular guard – her name was Dhalla – was the one Ereleth co-opted to help in all her quiet work. Lucrezia liked her, and the fondness seemed to be reciprocated.

'It is as well to be comfortable in the presence of death, my child,' Ereleth said approvingly. 'Ours is classified as an Art Political rather than an Art Chemical, and its exercise has as much to do with reputation and mystique as it has with healing or execution, but a poisoner must not be overwary of the fruits of her endeavours. Learn to love the stink of putrefaction, provided that you are the cause of it.'

Lucrezia straightened herself, and smiled. She had a deceptively sweet smile. Like her mother – who had died in childbed trying to bear Belin a second son, when Lucrezia was less than a year old – she was slender, with finely drawn features, but she was wiry and had a good measure of strength to support her perennial stubbornness. Her eyes were dark, almost black in the lamplight whose yellow radiance supplemented the white light of the blazing stars, but they gleamed with a moistness which a mere man might mistake for tenderness.

'Get rid of that,' Ereleth said to Dhalla, pointing to the dead man. 'He has told us all he can.'

Dhalla promptly knelt down to fold the corpse into the white shroud on which it lay. She picked it up without any evident effort. She had to set it down in order to unlock the door, and then again to close the door behind her, but she did her work with consummate efficiency.

'I need a stronger man than that for the other test,' Lucrezia said pensively, as the sound of Dhalla's footsteps on the stair died away. 'Only one of the Hyry Keshvara's seeds remains, and while the one to which I gave the dog refuses to bear flower or fruit I dare not waste the third on another diseased and enfeebled wreck of a human being. I must persuade my father to release a suitable host.'

Ereleth approved of the direction her pupil's train of thought had taken, and of the spirit that inspired her, but she could not help but feel a slight pang of anxiety about this particular experiment. Because Keshvara traded with the Apu she had long been a useful supplier of the materials Ereleth required to maintain her stock of potions, many of which originated in the darklands. Ereleth had encouraged Lucrezia's acquaintance with the woman, and had been pleased by the way in which the princess's admiration for the adventuress had nourished the discontent which inevitably afflicted the daughters of a Xandrian king as they grew to adolescence within the constricting security of the citadel's Inner Sanctum. But she had not expected Keshvara to bring gifts of an unprecedented and highly unusual kind, and strange stories with them. It was not that she could not see the possible significance of such an event, nor that she had no confidence in her own competence to respond to such a challenge, but Lucrezia's education was far from complete. One more year might make all the difference. On the other hand, if the king really were planning to send her to Shaminzara . . .

'The bush might take a year to put forth flowers,' Ereleth pointed out. 'I fear that you might not have the time to see it bloom. Rumour has it that your father has plans for you.'

'My father's plans be damned,' Lucrezia retorted carelessly. 'I've not the least intention of being shipped off to some petty island kingdom in order to be locked away in a prison narrower by far than this one, to serve as childbearer to some brutal protector of pirates. I'm worth infinitely more than that.'

Ereleth was slightly taken aback by this – not because she disapproved of the sentiment but because Lucrezia hadn't had to ask what she was talking about. The princess must have begun to cultivate her own network of spies – presumably working through her maidservent, Monalen, and Dhalla. Ereleth wondered whether she ought to caution her pupil against indiscretion. The room was secure against eavesdroppers, but such sentiments should not have been spoken aloud within the Sanctum. She decided that there were more important things which needed to be said.

'I will do what I can to persuade the king's ministers that you are too young to go to Shaminzara and might do far more for the empire in days to come if you were allowed to complete your education. All that is true – but there are other reasons why it is necessary that you and I should not be separated now. There is work for us to do.'

Lucrezia could not, of course, know what she meant – but Ereleth was nevertheless surprised by her reaction. 'I'm heartily sick of that work too,' the princess said, with defiant frankness. 'I've a burning desire to do something new, something of my own. You can have no idea of the fervour which thrills me when I listen to Hyry Keshvara telling me of her adventures in the Spangled Desert and the Forest of Absolute Night. How I envy that woman!'

'You shouldn't,' said Ereleth mildly. 'It's one thing to travel the world as a princess, with men-at-arms beside you and the implicit might of Xandria behind you, and quite another to travel as a petty trader, ever vulnerable to robbery and rape.'

'Keshvara seems to evade such fates readily enough.'

'Keshvara is by no means handsome and by no means rich,' Ereleth pointed out.

'I disagree.' Lucrezia's voice had all the stubborn authority of a princess born and bred. 'She may not dress in silks and she wears her hair uncommonly short, but she has fine, strong features – hers is not a conventional womanly beauty, I'll grant, but her face is finer by far than the one worn by that supposedly handsome popinjay of a guard-captain who persists in staring at me from his lofty coign of vantage while I work in the garden. As for riches, she has the wealth of knowledge and experience, and a desperately keen eye for precious things. Did you see the way her eyes lit up when she described how she came across the seeds from the far side of the Dragomite Hills? Did you see what a fever burned her while she spoke of gathering an expedition to find the road into the unknown?'

Ereleth had indeed seen those signs, but it was the content of Keshvara's account which had disturbed her, not the manner of its delivery.

'I believe that she was intending to serve as a recruit in someone else's expedition,' Ereleth said, thinking that it might be wise to dampen the princess's inflamed romanticism, 'and the over-whelming likelihood is that the road she intends to follow will lead nowhere but oblivion. Even if the seeds were really brought across the Dragomite Hills, that doesn't mean that any man might now cross them with impunity.'

'If anyone can do it,' Lucrezia said firmly, 'Hyry Keshvara can.'

'I wish her the very best of luck,' Ereleth said, with only the faintest hint of sarcasm, 'but you and I have a kind of wisdom which urges us to make more careful plans – and to make more extensive enquiries first. Even when time presses, the wise are patient.'

'You've led a very patient life, I know,' Lucrezia replied, obviously conscious of her rudeness in saying so but determined to say it nevertheless. 'But I hope you'll forgive me if I say that I would not like to live as you have lived. I don't want to be married off to some princeling, whether I remain my father's instrument or become a true witch-wife. I don't want to be a prisoner, condemned to rot quietly while I pass on the lore to my own daughters and step-daughters.'

Is that really how she sees me? Ereleth thought. *But then, how could she possibly see me otherwise, when she is not yet party to the deeper secrets of the lore?* 'I have not always been a prisoner,' she said aloud, rather stiffly, remembering the time when she had been free, before Belin had married her – not to bed, but to fill a space which tradition required to be filled. 'I have lived in those darklands which Keshvara merely visits. I know the Apu better than she does, although twenty years have passed since I learned their lore. I have ambition yet, for myself as well as my most precious pupil.'

'I know you have,' Lucrezia said, not ungently. 'But how will you ever escape these high walls which surround us both? I doubt that my father would ever let you go, although he might easily set one of my sisters in your place, now that you have trained so many. I wonder that you'd want to go, given that you've been here so long.'

Does she think I'm too old to cope with the world beyond the walls? Ereleth said to herself sourly. *Do I seem so feeble in body*

*and mind? Has she no imagination, to see beyond appearances to
what I really am? But how can she read signs of which she knows
nothing? How can she know secrets which I have been careful to
keep, even from her?* 'You do not know me,' she said brusquely.
'Nor do you know yourself, as yet. I have a clearer idea of what
you are and what you might be than you have yourself. You must
trust my judgment in such matters.'

In the past, her authority had always sufficed to subdue her
pupil's awkward moods, but it did not seem sufficient now.

'Must I?' she retorted. 'My whole life, it seems, is governed by
musts. I must do as my father wills; I must do what my teacher
advises; I must do what tradition demands. I must do all these
things, even when they conflict. I'd gladly trade every privilege I'm
heir to for the one which Keshvara has: the privilege of being free.'

'You don't understand,' Ereleth said, knowing how
unsatisfactory a statement it was, and how hollow it would sound
in Lucrezia's ear, even though it had the advantage of truth.

'I understand far more than you think,' the girl replied forlornly.
'I know what I am, and what I want to be.'

If only you did, Ereleth thought. *If only you could.*

Lucrezia had turned away after finishing her statement, unable
to sustain her defiance as resolutely as she might have wished. She
crossed the room to the window, and opened the casement so that
she could suck in the warm air of the summer night. Ereleth joined
her gratefully. The unpleasant odour of the corpse still lingered in
the air of the claustrophobic chamber, and had long since ceased
to serve as a useful challenge.

The sky was very clear, and the calm backcloth against which
the vivid flamestars were set scintillated with the silver dust of
fainter lights. On nights such as this it was possible to see as well as
one could in the dingy light of a cloudy winter day. Starlight had
always seemed to Ereleth to be infinitely preferable – on the
grounds of being far more intricate and far more beautiful – to the
blue curtain of daylight which danced attendance on the
imperious sun.

The chamber was set so high that they could see over the
crenellated rim of the lowest section of the citadel wall. The waters
of the great harbour were visible beyond the green-fronded
rooftops, sparkling with reflected starlight.

'On calm days and nights,' Lucrezia said, 'the open sea must be like a vast sheet of shimmering glass: a mirror to catch the image of infinity.'

It was hardly an original thought, Ereleth knew. The sea was described in similar terms in a hundred romantic tales which the young princess must have heard over and over again from her nurses, her elder sisters and her maidservants. But such ways of seeing, and the ways of thinking they reflected, were precious things which needed to be protected, and cherished, for the sake of maintaining a sense of wonder. 'It is, daughter,' she said, as softly and lovingly as she could. 'That's exactly what it is.'

3

ANDRIS STUDIED THE examining magistrate carefully while the clerk read out the charges against him. He was dark for a golden, as many Xandrians were – almost sailorman dark – although his hair and beard were going grey. He was tall, too – perhaps tall enough to resent the fact that Andris was a good three sims taller.

At least he's old, Andris thought. *My best hope is that he's experienced enough in the ways of the world to know the difference between a cultivated man from the far north and a forest savage. If only I can reason with him . . .*

He stirred restlessly. The heavy steel shackles which were clasped about his ankles always settled at an awkward angle when he stood still, and they had chafed the flesh so that any sustained pressure quickly became painful. The shackles were purely symbolic – lustrust had weakened the links of the chain strung between them to the point where at least half of them would shatter if he kicked out forcefully – but he knew better than to oppose their grip. The last thing he needed was to have attempting to escape and damaging crown property added to the list of his supposed crimes.

Apart from the magistrate, the clerk and Andris, the only other people present in the examination room were three soldiers. One had been set to guard him, and had been with him ever since he had been brought out of the cells beneath the harbourmaster's office. The other two – a sergeant and a captain – were presumably here as witnesses. The sergeant was lean and grizzled; he looked as if he had been a soldier all his life. The captain was very young and very neat; *he* looked as if he had been recruited within the tenday. Andris remembered seeing both of them when he had been arrested. He was mildly disturbed, but not unduly surprised, to find that the guardsman who had been knocked unconscious was not present.

All the other prisoners had been brought in before him; evidently they had told their stories and received their sentences. There had been eight in all – eight, at least, who had shared the harbourmaster's cells with him. Four were darklanders and four were sailors from various far-flung shores of the Slithery Sea.

The room seemed much too large for such a small gathering. There were rows of wooden benches on either side of the dock, presumably placed there for the use of onlookers as well as witnesses, but they were deserted now. The detritus of waterfront brawls were presumably of little enough public interest even at the best of times, and the hour was now uncomfortably close to the midday doldrums. The magistrate would doubtless be enthusiastic to get things over and done with, so that he might go to his bed. Andris noticed, however, that the proceedings were not entirely unobserved. A series of observation-slits had been cut into the wall behind the magistrate, so that watchers in some covert or corridor beyond could peer in without exposing more of themselves than their curious eyes. Someone was lurking behind one of the slits, quietly looking on.

Andris wished that there were more people present. He was extremely conscious of being alone and friendless, and his apprehension was heightened by the fact that he had no idea how the law-courts of Xandria functioned. According to the oft-quoted wisdom of Goran the Forefather the law was the law throughout the world, but Andris – who had reason enough to believe that he had seen but a tiny fraction of the world – had not found it so. If there ever had been a man named Goran, who really had said all the things he was supposed to have said, he must have lived a very long time ago, when the affairs of men ran far more smoothly than they did nowadays.

'What have you to say to these charges, darklander?' said the magistrate, when the clerk had finished.

'I beg your pardon, sir, but I'm not a darklander,' Andris said.

His scrupulous politeness was wasted; the magistrate frowned resentfully. 'You are the Andris Myrasol to whom the charges refer, are you not?' he said.

'That's my name,' Andris confirmed patiently. 'And to those

who know names it reveals clearly enough that I'm not a darklander. My skin is pale because I come from Ferentina in the far north, nearly two thousand kims beyond the opposite shore of the Slithery Sea. I'm a civilised man, as you are.' He added the last comment by way of diplomatic flattery, but it seemed to go to waste.

'You were arrested in the company of darklanders,' the magistrate pointed out.

'There were darklanders in the room,' Andris admitted, 'but I wasn't with them. I was sitting at a different table, and I wasn't involved in any way with the fight which broke out. I'm innocent of all the charges.'

The clerk whispered something in the magistrate's ear.

'All the men I have so far questioned say that you were involved in the fight,' the magistrate said. 'All of them have said that they saw you grappling with Guardsman Herriman, and that it was you who struck him with the table at which you had been sitting.'

With a sinking heart, Andris remembered the long hours spent in the harbourmaster's cells and all the whispered conversations that had gone on around him. The darklanders and sailors seemed to have settled their own differences by agreeing that he was the most suitable candidate to take all of the blame. He looked around at the two guardsmen, neither of whom was making any protest.

'Have you asked the guardsman who was hurt?' he said. 'Did he say I hit him?'

The magistrate looked at the officer, who stiffened slightly. 'Herriman's in the hospital, sir,' he said. 'He's unfit to attend these proceedings, having sustained a broken leg and severe concussion. He did come round for a few minutes, but he was only able to say that he was hit from behind and couldn't see who did it.'

The magistrate's dark eyes settled on Andris again.

'What about the story-teller?' Andris asked desperately. 'He was at my table.'

This time it was the sergeant who answered. 'There was another man injured, sir,' he said. 'A pauper. He was able to walk once he came round, and wasn't taken to hospital. I have no idea what happened to him, but he wouldn't be much use as a witness – he was blind.'

The magistrate turned to Andris again. 'Are you saying that all the other witnesses are lying?' he asked silkily.

'Yes,' Andris said firmly.

'I saw him grappling with Herriman myself, sir,' said the sergeant quickly. 'Just out the corner of my eye, like, while I was trying to sort things out – but I did see it.'

'Is Sergeant Purkin lying?' the magistrate asked Andris.

'No, sir,' said Andris swiftly. 'He's mistaken. The guardsman and I did collide for a moment. He was pushed towards me just as I was pushed towards him. We had to hold on to one another to keep our balance.' It sounded feeble even to him, although it was the truth, and he was quick to add: 'I'm sure that the man who was injured will confirm this, if you'll only wait until he's able to give his evidence.'

The magistrate didn't seem disposed to listen to any plea for more time. It was perfectly plain he wanted to get this over with as soon as possible.

'There was a big man,' Andris said desperately. 'Heavy-set. Almost as big as me, but not quite as tall. He and several others were desperate to get away up the staircase to the bedrooms. I just happened to be in their way – that's why they shoved me. It was the big man who picked up the table and hit us with it. He hit me as well as the guardsman – I can show you the bruises.'

'Make a note of the fact that the man has bruises,' the magistrate said to the clerk, without showing the slightest interest in inspecting them, 'even though he denies being involved in the brawl.'

'They're just trying to put the blame on me because I'm a foreigner,' Andris complained. 'They decided to say I hit the guardsman just in case someone tried to put the blame on them.'

'All of the arrested men are foreigners,' the magistrate pointed out.

'But not from as far away as me – and they all knew each other . . . at least, the darklanders knew one another and so did the men they were fighting.'

'And yet both sets of former disputants now agree that you caused Trooper Herriman's injuries,' the magistrate observed, as though it were a point of immense significance. 'You are, I suppose, a prince of your own land?'

Andris was so startled by the change of tack that he failed to notice the sarcasm in the remark.

'As a matter of fact,' he said, 'yes.'

The magistate let out a short, barking laugh. The clerk tittered. Sergeant Purkin smiled in a way that was both ironic and predatory.

'It's strange,' said the magistrate, 'that the further away visitors to Xandria hail from, the higher their rank seems to be. No matter how shabby their clothing might appear, nor how ill-supplied their purses, they always turn out to be princes.'

Or to put it another way, Andris thought dismally, *we think we just caught you out in a whopping lie, and we're not going to believe a single word you say.*

'It doesn't matter what I once was,' he said desperately. 'I arrived in Xandria a poor man, hoping to find a kinsman of mine who left my homeland many years ago. A merchant in one of the northern ports told me that he'd come here. I took a room in the Wayfaring Tree while I made my enquiries. I was just sitting by the staircase, with the story-teller, when a riot broke out. I had no quarrel with anyone . . . except, perhaps, with the man who *did* hit the guardsman, who'd already caused some injury and distress to my companion, the blind man.'

'What's the name of this kinsman for whom you're supposedly searching?' the magistrate asked.

'Theo Zabio. I understand he came south across the Slithery Sea some twelve or fifteen years ago.'

'Have you ever heard of a man named Theo Zabio, Captain Cerri?' the magistrate asked.

'Never,' said the officer, slightly unhappily.

No reason why you should, Andris thought. *You can't have been born twelve years ago.*

'I think this is all nonsense,' the magistrate said sternly. 'Whether you're a darklander or not, it seems that you behave like a darklander. I see no reason whatsoever to doubt the word of all these witnesses. I find you guilty as charged, on all counts.'

The sanctimonious bastard, Andris thought. *It's the same wherever you go. Always put the blame on the foreigner, and if you have a choice go for the big one. I should never have crossed the Slithery Sea. I should never have come south at all. What was wrong with west or east? Why should I expect Theo Zabio to be interested in me, just because he's my uncle? All my other uncles would have stabbed me in the back as soon as look at me.*

'I'm sorry, sir,' he said, keeping his voice very level in spite of the ashen taste in his mouth, 'but the witnesses are mistaken. That's understandable – it was a very confused situation. But the fact is that I didn't hit anybody, least of all the guardsman. This isn't fair. In my own land, I'd be allowed to see and hear my accusers give evidence, and I'd be allowed an advocate too.'

'This is Xandria,' the magistrate told him coldly. 'Advocates cost money, and you hadn't enough in your pouches to hire a donkey-driver. How, exactly, did you intend to make a living here? What training do you have?'

Andris wondered briefly whether he could possibly get away with a flat lie, but decided that it was best not to weave too tangled a web of deceits, even though he knew that even a half-honest answer would probably bring forth more laughter.

'My primary training is in the Arts Geographical,' he said uncomfortably. He had, indeed, been intensively educated in that subject, although his primary training – and almost all his actual experience – had been in the Arts Martial, which he thought it best not to admit in the present circumstances. Unfortunately, the Arts Geographical were held in very low esteem in these parts, because the maps which had been drummed into his memory with such great care were held by every man who sailed the Slithery Sea or knew its shores to be utterly unreliable. 'You must understand, sir,' he was quick to add, 'that insofar as they relate to the nations of the far north, the Arts Geographical are far more congruent with reality than they seem to be in these parts.'

'If that's the case,' the magistrate said, reverting to his silkily menacing tone, 'it's surprising that you've strayed so far from the lands where your education is of use to you. I ask again – how did you intend to make your living here? And how do you propose to pay the debt that you now owe His Royal Highness King Belin of Xandria?'

'It's not so very surprising, sir,' Andris said, fighting to keep calm even though he knew this was a losing battle. He tried desperately to think of a story which might be believable. 'When the maps which trading nations know are inadequate to their purposes, their noblemen become interested in making new and better maps – and who else but a mapmaker could they send forth to do such work? In Ferentina there's considerable curiosity about the Slithery Sea, the Thousand Islands and legendary Xandria. I've known the name of Xandria since infancy, sir, and have known too that the lore I learned had misplaced it. I came here in the hope that my kinsman Theo Zabio might help me to amend my faulty lore, so that I could return to Ferentina with news which might be to the benefit of our merchants – and of yours. I beg you to let me do that work.'

The magistrate's face had become stony. He was not in the least interested in the follies of foreign mapmakers. 'Have you any money, other than that which was found on your person?' he asked – displaying, Andris bitterly observed, the skill which men of justice the world over had for getting to the true heart of a matter.

'None,' he admitted, while his sinking heart attained the utmost depths of its private abyss. 'My coin amounts to three crowns, I believe – but I have my colours and brushes in my pack at the inn, and some other goods . . .'

'He had but two crowns and a quarter,' the clerk interrupted dutifully.

Andris shook his head angrily, but knew that it was useless to protest. Corrosion allowances were generous around the shores of Slithery Sea, where even gold could not be expected to last more than a few years unless a man had a very cunning purse.

'The fine for incapacitating a guardsman,' the magistrate said, 'is eight hundred crowns. The lesser charges bring the sum to nine hundred and ninety. The interest for delayed payment is one per cent per tenday.'

'But I didn't do it,' Andris said doggedly.

'Your guilt has already been determined,' the magistrate told him unceremoniously. 'Given that your education is worthless, I think it best if you pay off the debt under the supervision of the king's stonemasons.'

'I'm trained in the Arts Martial too!' Andris said swiftly – but the magistrate only favoured him with a grim smile, as if he had contradicted yet again his earlier claims to have been uninvolved in the brawl.

Anxious to find a more profitable course of action, Andris said: 'Don't I have any right of appeal? Is there no way I can delay matters until you can hear the guardsman's testimony?'

27

The magistrate sighed. 'If you decide to go to prison,' he said, 'one crown will be added to your debt for every day you spend there.'

'You mean it costs money to go to jail in Xandria?' said Andris, in genuine astonishment.

The magistate's smile broadened, albeit in a somewhat lacklustre fashion. 'Xandria,' he said unctuously, 'has been a civilised nation for a hundred thousand years. That is why its name is known even to the superstitious geographers of Ferentina. Its jails are comfortable, its prisoners well-fed – for which reason we must discourage our prisoners from staying there too long when they could be much more usefully employed in repairing the walls which secure Xandria's place as the greatest nation in the world. The rate of pay for indentured stoneworkers is three crowns a day, but the interest payable on your fine will initially take up a third of that, once you actually start. Would you like me to summon a mathematician to work out the exact time of your service?'

Andris thought of himself as a fair arithmetician, by laymen's standards, and felt in no need of a number-wise magician to tell him that the magistrate was talking in terms of four hundred days and more.

'You call this civilised?' he said, allowing his anger to show because he could no longer hold it in check. 'No wonder no one from Ferentina ever came here before – or ever went back to tell their story, if they did. Do I have the right of appeal or do I not?'

'Your only right of appeal is the right to a petition for a royal pardon,' the magistrate said, in an ominously self-satisfied fashion, 'and the administrative charge levied on a failed royal petition is a hundred crowns. I must warn you, too, that the likelihood of your petition being heard within the next few tendays is slight. The king is a very busy man.'

'Any man who keeps more than thirty wives would be!' Andris snapped – unwisely, he judged when he saw the reaction of the clerk.

The magistrate, no longer smiling in any fashion at all, said: 'I'm bound to point out that you have just committed a further offence, for which I ought to fine you another ten crowns. Given that you're a foreigner – and, clearly, a barbarian – I shall overlook the matter this time, but I urge you to show proper respect in future. Now, do you wish to go to jail in order to wait until a petition can be heard, or will you start your term of indentured labour immediately? It would be much better for you, in the long run, were you to take the latter option.'

Andris had not the slightest desire to rush into a career as a stoneworker's labourer, and he was in no mood to make complicated calculations as to the extra time he would have to spend on the wall in exchange for a few tendays in prison. 'I'll go to jail,' he said obstinately. 'I want to petition for that royal pardon – and I want the captain here to ask his man what *he* thinks about the question of who hit him.'

'We already know the answer to that,' the magistrate said icily. 'He couldn't see, because he was struck from behind, in a cowardly fashion. There's no possibility whatsoever of my verdict being overturned – and I must point out that the king has the right to increase your fine as well as imposing further administrative charges. At this rate, you'll be working on the wall for life.'

'I only want justice,' said Andris sourly, knowing even as he said it that his chances of ever receiving it – or anything like it – were vanishingly small. *I'm as good as dead,* he thought. *Dead and buried before turning thirteen – and for what? A moment's pity for a blind story-teller who hadn't anything more interesting to relate than fake sequels to the oldest and rottenest myths in the world. This is what seeing the world amounts to: a slow descent into misery and degradation, to end as a virtual slave two thousand kims from home. What a rotting city! What a rotting life!*

'Take him away,' said the magistrate.

The silent guardsman took him by the arm. Andris had no alternative but to shuffle off, dragging his absurdly corroded chains behind him.

As he paused by the door he looked back at the novice captain, who had the grace to blush slightly. Whether the blush was in sympathy for the injustice of the court's treatment of an innocent man or resentment of the angry stare with which the condemned man sought to wither him Andris didn't care to speculate.

4

'YOU DON'T SUPPOSE,' Jacom Cerri said to Sergeant Purkin, as they threaded their way through the crowded street beneath the fiery afternoon sun, 'that the amber might have been telling the truth?'

'Naw,' said Purkin, in that infuriatingly worldly wise way he had. 'All darklanders are liars. Don't even know the meaning of the word *truth*. Can't believe a word they say, sir – take my word for it.'

Jacom hated the way that the old soldier had of patronising him, always contriving to imply that he was a country-born babe in arms who desperately needed to be educated in the ways of the city and of the world. It wouldn't have been so bad had Jacom been sufficiently confident that it wasn't so, but the few short tendays he had been in the city had made him keenly aware of the sheltered nature of his upbringing.

When his father had bought him a commission in the king's guard he had fondly imagined that he would spend most of his time about the court, looking handsome and being gallant. Nobody had told him that the harbour patrol fell into the guard's jurisdiction rather than that of the constabulary or the militia, or that he would have to exert himself in such undesirable occupations as breaking up tavern brawls. The huge amber had been his very first arrest, and the mere fact of it made him feel uncomfortable and somehow dirty. The possibility that he had got it wrong *and might be found out* was too horrible to bear. He desperately wanted to prove himself – to his father, to his commanding officer, to the king . . . but most of all, at least for the moment, to Sergeant Purkin and the men in his command.

'But he isn't a darklander, is he?' Jacom persisted. 'He really is from the far north, and he really wasn't with the darklanders who actually started the fight.'

Purkin spat in the gutter, narrowly missing a pair of urchins who were intent on some game involving a reel of cotton, a handful of matches and a giant shieldbug. They didn't bother to look up. 'Came in on a ship all right,' he admitted. 'Darklanders aren't worth a bucket o' shit aboard ship, so he probably does come from t'other side o' the Slithery Sea. So what? Still a barbarian, and a fool. Should've shut up and gone to the wall right away. Might have been free again in a year or so. Damned now. Probably never get off. His own stupid fault.'

'But there were other men on that stairway, weren't there?' Jacom said. 'I saw them.' He had, in fact, arrived just in time to see a pair of heels disappearing, but he felt that it was necessary to remind Purkin that he had been in the inn while the affray was still in full flow. He didn't want anyone thinking that he had hung back while his men did all the work, because he hadn't.

'Yeah,' Purkin agreed. 'Locals – knew what a good idea it'd be to be out o' the way before we started kicking arses. Checuti's men, I think. Thieves and tricksters. I know that big bastard the amber tried to fix the blame on – Burdam Thrid, his name is. End up on the wall himself one day, that's for sure. Only hope it's some other poor sucker has to arrest him.'

'*Could* it have been him – who hit Herriman, I mean?'

'Aw, I don't know,' the sergeant complained. 'Who cares?'

It seemed to Jacom that, in the sergeant's eyes, the sin of caring was at least as bad as any others he might have committed. He wasn't sure that the sergeant was right to think so, but he didn't want to to be out of step with the whole citadel guard. It was important to fit in if he were going to build a proper career.

While they walked the last hundred mets to the hospital he directed his attention to other matters, scanning the street for signs of evildoing. He was off duty, but his commanding officer had gone to great pains to explain to him that while he was in the king's uniform he was the king's representative, bound to look after the king's interests.

The street was filled with hawkers selling a bewildering variety of fruits, vegetables and loaves of bread from carts and baskets. Competition seemed to be fierce – it appeared to be a buyers' market, in which it was impossible for anyone to make a sale without an exhaustive session of haggling.

Jacom had never been able to see the point of the kind of long-drawn-out haggling which wasted ten or fifteen minutes in making the most trivial purchases, but it seemed to be an immensely important point of pride among Xandrians never to pay a quarter-crown too much for a day's bread. He supposed that this must be what his father had been talking about in all those long lectures about efficient trade being the true basis of imperial grandeur. Personally, he had always thought of imperial grandeur in terms of armies – or, to be strictly honest, in terms of flags, military uniforms, arms and armour – but his own brand-new uniform and badges of rank seemed to carry little enough weight when it came to pushing through a crowd of serious shoppers. He was glad when they finally arrived at their destination.

The hospital was oppressively clean. The walls were white-washed every week and the floors were scrubbed every day. The constant battle that was waged about Xandria's mighty walls, in the interest of keeping them strong and impenetrable, seemed to be a cursory affair compared with the constant battle that was waged within the city's hospitals.

To Jacom Cerri, who was new to the rituals of military discipline and the ways in which they were employed to mechanise men's reflexes, the manner in which the orderlies worked seemed remarkable in its efficiency – and also in its pointlessness. He was a sceptical man, utterly uninterested in and unimpressed by all talk of the occult and the invisible. He had not an atom of faith in the 'bacteria' which were said to infest all walls and all floors – not to mention the very air itself – and which must be kept at bay at all costs in places where wounded men were laid to rest. He thought of hygiene as a matter of politeness, and felt that it was quite unnecessary to pretend that mere cleanliness was a matter of life and death.

The true purpose of all this scrubbing down with unpleasantly sharp-smelling substances, he thought, as he glanced into the wards past which he and Purkin tramped, *must be symbolic. The real idea must surely be to provide a kind of allegorical example to the patients, urging them to marshal all their inner resources to the fight against debilitation. The real medicine is in the mind, isn't that what they say?*

The psychological effect in question seemed to be working well enough on Herriman, who was looking surprisingly cheerful considering that the last time Jacom had seen him he had been unable to stay conscious for more than a few minutes at a time, and had spent most of those lost in delirium. The guardsman seemed genuinely pleased to see his sergeant and his commanding officer, and he saluted them both with some verve, although the plaster cast on his leg inhibited the initial movement of his hand and the eventual impact of his rigid fingers on his bandaged head brought a pained expression to his face.

Purkin's response was automatic but deliberately slovenly. Jacom's was much neater. An officer had to be able to salute properly, or what would people think?

'I'll be back on my feet in two tendays, they say,' Herriman told them, in response to Jacom's polite enquiry. 'I just wish the plaster cast didn't itch so much. They'll have to change it tomorrow – I just can't help trying to bend my knee, and the plaster's crumbling. They keep sluicing it with that disinfectant stuff, but it doesn't help. I keep telling them, everything crumbles, it's just the nature of things – but they don't listen. Medics, hey?'

'Medics,' Jacom echoed obligingly. 'The inquiry's concluded, by the way. We got nine of them. They all got away with trivial fines except for the big amber. He was identified as the one who hit you – he's in jail for the moment, looking for a pardon, but he'll be on the wall for a long time.'

Herriman looked puzzled for a moment or two. 'It wasn't the darklander who hit me, sir,' he said hesitantly.

Jacom's heart skipped a beat. He didn't dare look at Purkin for fear that the man might take the glance as a tacit 'I told you so', although the only thought in his mind was: *I've made a mess of this, haven't I?* Aloud, he said: 'No, it wasn't a darklander. It was the big amber by the stairway – looked almost as if he might have giant's blood in him, if that were possible. He was the one who did it. They all said so.'

'No sir,' said Herriman stubbornly. 'It definitely wasn't him.'

'You had your back to him,' said Purkin, speaking with exaggerated carefulness in order to signal to his man that this was treacherous ground. 'You couldn't see who hit you, could you? Anyway, I saw you grappling with him myself. You probably can't remember, *because you got hit on the head.*'

'He wasn't in the fight at all,' Herriman said, blithely refusing to take the hint. 'I grabbed hold of him to stop myself falling over. He *helped* me. He was just having a drink with some beggar. Some big bastard in a hurry to get up the stairs knocked his table over – the amber was only trying to stay out of trouble.'

'You didn't see it,' Purkin insisted steadfastly. To Jacom he said: 'His memory's not clear, sir. Must've been the blow on the head. He doesn't know what he's talking about.'

'It might have been the other big man, but it wasn't the amber,' the supine man insisted. 'The amber was in front of me when I was hit from behind. Whoever it was, it couldn't possibly have been him.'

'You only told me that you didn't see who hit you,' Jacom complained anxiously. 'That's what I told the magistrate. Eight witnesses all agreed that it was the big man.'

'All protecting one another, like as not,' opined the soldier – but then he caught the full glare of Purkin's disapproving eye, and a sudden expression of enlightenment dawned. 'Oh well,' he went on. 'Don't suppose it matters. The score's even. They send one of us to hospital, we send one of them to the wall. They don't care which of us they hurt, so why should we care which of them we punish? Ought to send two to the wall really – I mean, we *are* the law. We're supposed to come out ahead.'

Jacom pursed his lips. He had a strong suspicion that he ought to let the matter rest, but somehow he couldn't quite bring himself to do it. Perhaps this was an opportunity for him to demonstrate that he could be firm in a just cause.

'Are you sure it wasn't the amber?' he asked, with more unease in his tone than he would have liked. 'It was a brawl, when all's said and done. Maybe he just lost his temper and lashed out. Maybe he caught you by accident.'

'Don't worry about it, sir,' Herriman advised, with one eye still on his sergeant. 'Like I said before, I couldn't actually see who it was. Anyway, he'll be a lot more use on the wall than the other skinny bastards that were swarming around. Probably a pirate – pirates are always big. Must be all the fish they eat.' He was babbling now, trying to cover up his earlier mistake.

'That's all very well,' Jacom said slowly, although he was coming round to the opinion that his one and only priority ought to be covering up his own mistake, if indeed he had made one. 'But if you're right, it would mean that the man who did hit you has got away with it. What did you say the other man's name was, sergeant?'

'Burdam Thrid,' said Purkin, raising his eyes to the discoloured ceiling as if to say that this was all a terrible waste of time.

'Checuti's man?' the recumbent guardsman said. 'So it was! I bet it was him. If he ever tries it again I'll skewer the ugly bastard.'

'Who's Checuti?' Jacom asked.

It was Purkin who answered. 'Dealer in stolen goods,' he said contemptuously. 'Oily bastard. Getting too big for his boots. People've started calling him the prince o' thieves. He's long overdue for a fall. Needs chasing out of the city back to wherever he came from.'

'Khalorn,' said Herriman helpfully. 'Somewhere around there, anyhow. He's not exactly a foreigner, but not a real Xandrian.'

Jacom wondered whether his father's estates were far enough away from the city for its masters and labourers not to be real Xandrians, in the eyes of men like Herriman. 'Perhaps we ought to investigate this further,' he said unenthusiastically.

'We're the king's guard, sir, not the constabulary,' Purkin said pointedly. 'Keeping order is our business, not thief-taking. Checuti's nothing to do with us. No point in our pursuing this matter any further, sir. It's settled – we should let it alone.'

Jacom was uncomfortably aware of the fact that he was being lectured, in a rough and ready way. The sergeant was twice his own age, but that didn't justify his taking a pseudo-parental tone with his officer. On the other hand, Jacom had every reason to suppose that the advice was sound. If he *had* made a mistake, the best thing for all concerned – except, admittedly, the amber – was to keep quiet about it and hope nobody ever found out. He didn't like to think that the man who had really flattened one of his soldiers might have got away with it, and he felt decidedly uncomfortable about the whole affair, but he supposed that it would all blow over quickly enough. The amber had been destitute, after all – if he hadn't been picked up for this crime he'd soon have committed another.

'People shouldn't tell lies in the king's court,' he said helplessly. 'The witnesses, I mean – I don't like the idea of them ganging up to protect one of their own by accusing an innocent man. If that's really what happened . . . I mean, shouldn't we do something about it – not officially, of course, but for our own satisfaction?'

The look which Purkin gave him was withering, and even Herriman looked mildly astonished. Evidently – no matter what stories one heard about the honour of the guard and the extraordinary lengths to which good men were prepared to go in defence of that honour – that simply wasn't the way things were done around here.

'All right,' Jacom said awkwardly, after half a minute's embarrassed silence had leaked away. 'The matter's closed. Get back on your feet as fast as you can, Herriman – we need you. Mercifully, we're on citadel duty for the next three tendays. Very peaceful, I dare say, after the harbour patrol.'

'Yes sir,' said Purkin. Jacom had a paranoid suspicion that the man might be radiating contempt even though he was duty bound to provide the looked-for agreement. 'Guarding the gates and patrolling the walls is about as easy as it ever gets, in peacetime.'

'Just make sure the big amber doesn't get away while you're keeping watch on the prison, sar'nt'' said Herriman, with a chuckle which sounded wholly sincere. 'Wouldn't do to lose him now we've got him, would it?'

'No,' said Purkin dully, with a sly sideways glance at Jacom. 'It wouldn't.'

5

IN THE ENCLOSED roof-garden which was the crowning glory of the Inner Sanctum of the great citadel of Xandria Princess Lucrezia watched two servants digging up a corpse. The progress was slow; the women were used to labouring in the garden, but this was heavier work than they were usually required to do. The task was made more difficult by the fact that the upper part of the corpse was spiked with dozens of sharp and sturdy thorns, each one three or four sims long.

It was obvious that the labourers did not like their work. They were mortally afraid of the dead woman, and of the thorns which stood out from her head, arms and breasts, even though Lucrezia had assured them that they were not poisonous. Servants were prone to far too many superstitions and commonplace fears.

I should have waited for Dhalla, Lucrezia thought. *She doesn't seem to mind doing this kind of thing, even though it's not her job.*

Having given her orders, however, Lucrezia was determined to see that they were obeyed. If servants began to think they'd be let off if they made a task seem like hard work nothing would ever get done. Not until the two women had lifted the cadaver into the cart did she turn away. She was near to tears, but it wasn't pity which made her feel that way. She felt that she had lost a precious opportunity.

The dog was still alive, and the thorny shoots projecting from the upper part of its body were vividly green, but there was not the slightest sign of a bud anywhere. Lucrezia no longer had the slightest doubt that what Hyry Keshvara had told her would turn out to be true: the third and last remaining seed would reproduce if and only if she followed the instructions given by the people who had sold the seeds to the trader. She had to feed it to a human being – a strong, healthy human being – so that it might take a full

37

measure of the nourishment it needed from the human body and spirit; only then would the plant which grew inside its host put forth flowers.

In any case, she thought, a human would be able to satisfy a deeper curiosity by telling her what it felt like to undergo the fabulous process of metamorphosis, at least until the throat filled up with thorns. The dog could only whimper, in a manner which suggested puzzlement rather than pain.

If only the woman had been stronger!

Dhalla arrived while Lucrezia was still dripping water into the eager throat of the whimpering dog. The giant had to duck down very low to pass beneath the stone lintel of the gateway, moving the lustrust-stained gate very carefully lest she tear it from its hinges by accident.

'There's news that might interest you, highness,' said Dhalla, as soon as Lucrezia glanced up at her.

The princess stood up, and met the guard's eyes frankly. Dhalla immediately dropped her gaze, as she had been trained to do. Lucrezia would rather she had not done so, but understood the difficulty well enough. She liked Dhalla better than any of her personal servants and far better than any of her multitudinous sisters. The giant wasn't handsome and her conversation was limited, but she had a sense of humour, which was a rare thing in the Inner Sanctum. Her most endearing feature was that she always obeyed Lucrezia's orders with a conspicuous alacrity that she never displayed for anyone else's benefit.

'What is it?' the princess asked.

'There was a young darklander in the court today, highness. Actually, he said he wasn't a darklander, but he's an amber. He crippled a guardsman during a brawl in some harbourside drinking-den.'

'What concern is that of mine?' Lucrezia asked.

'Only that he applied for a royal pardon instead of starting work on the wall immediately. He doesn't understand the law, you see. Either that or he's too pig-headed to be sensible. If *you* were to offer him a conditional pardon . . . well, I don't think he knows enough to ask the right questions. He's very big and strong – might almost have giant's blood in him.'

Dhalla smiled as she made the last remark. She knew well

enough that all the dirty jokes and folktales about ordinary men and giants were pure fantasy. There were no male giants and no men with giant's blood in them.

'They say that I have a splash of Serpent's blood in me,' Lucrezia said. So far as she knew, that was nonsense too, but she didn't smile as she said it. There was mention of 'Serpent's blood' in ancient myths, which conferred a certain glamour on the notion even though no one Lucrezia had ever asked about it – including her mother, from whom she was supposed to have inherited the trait – had had the slightest idea what it might mean. As far as Lucrezia could tell, a mating of human and Serpent was far less likely than a mating of man and giant. Serpents were not merely unhuman but unearthly, like most of the things which grew in the Grey Waste, the Forest of Absolute Night, the fabled heartland of the Spangled Desert and the Dragomite Hills. According to rumour, the reproductive organs of Serpents were in their mouths rather than their underbellies and they were hermaphrodites; if so, it was hardly likely that sexual intercourse between their kind and human beings was possible.

'This amber sounds exactly the kind of man you'd need to grow a healthy thorn-bush, highness,' Dhalla said, although Lucrezia had already taken that inference.

'Unfortunately,' Lucrezia said pensively, 'I'd need my beloved father's permission to take him into my service, for whatever use. He won't like it – it's one thing to bring some decrepit old wallslave into the Sanctum, but quite another to import a virile tavern-brawler.'

'I could make certain that he was no trouble,' Dhalla said. 'I could break his legs before taking him from the prison. I'll watch him night and noon if necessary.'

'It's not a question of there being any real danger,' Lucrezia said, with a sigh. 'It's simply a matter of available excuses. If my father can think of any reason for refusing me, he'll probably do it. In this case, he'd have no trouble at all.'

'Sorry, highness,' Dhalla said. 'I thought . . .'

'Don't be sorry,' Lucrezia was quick to say. 'You were right. It's worth a try, given that I'm legally entitled to make the offer. If I keep on asking for favours, my father might say yes one day just to keep me quiet. I could send Monalen to see the amber right away

– then, if he's fool enough to accept the conditional pardon, I could go to father myself. If I explain it cleverly enough father might just think of it as poetic justice – too good a joke to pass up. But will the amber agree? What was his sentence?'

'He'll have to work off a fine of about a thousand crowns, plus interest accrued while he's in jail, plus whatever else they can pile on for future misbehaviour. You know how these things work – it could easily turn into a life sentence if no one offers to buy him out within the next few days. I doubt that anyone will do that; he only arrived a couple of days ago so he's unlikely to have any friends in Xandria.'

'What if someone tells him what I want him for? He's bound to be suspicious, isn't he?'

'No one would dare to interfere – and the man seems to be a complete idiot. He's an amber, after all.'

'In that case,' Lucrezia said, 'you'd better fetch Monalen.'

Dhalla bowed, and turned on her heel.

Lucrezia turned back to her garden. It was really Ereleth's garden, but Lucrezia had begun to think of it as her own, just as she had begun to think of Ereleth's wisdom as her own. She knew that she was merely the latest of a string of royal apprentices whom Ereleth had trained in the secret Arts of witchery, but she also knew that she had been trained more assiduously and more intensively than any of her sisters. She knew that Ereleth regarded her as her true heir, and she in her turn had begun to think of Ereleth as *hers*: a unique combination of substitute mother and instrument of ambition.

The garden contained more than a hundred exotic species of plants, every one of which produced – or was reputed to produce – some kind of toxic substance. Some of them had been grown here since time immemorial – Ereleth was by no means the first witch-wife to lend her knowledge to the throne of Xandria – but others were recent arrivals. Ereleth's experimental frame of mind had led her carefully to cultivate the acquaintance of certain merchants and adventurers, in the interest of increasing as well as maintaining her repertoire. Many of the 'gifts' they brought – for which the king's treasury paid high prices – did not live up to their reputations, but some did. The most reliable of these suppliers was Hyry Keshvara, whose usefulness to the king's witches was greatly enhanced by the fact that she did not need to use middlemen in her dealings with Ereleth; being female, she could pass more or less freely in and out of the Inner Sanctum.

Lucrezia had a clear memory of the day when Hyry Keshvara had brought the three seeds which grew in the flesh of living men, partly because it was the first time she had been alone with the trader for any length of time – Ereleth had been bedridden with some kind of fever – and partly because Hyry had been so obviously excited by the news she had brought along with the seeds.

'Nothing like these seeds has ever been seen in the lands with which Xandria trades, highness,' Hyry had said. 'I don't know whether the claims made on their behalf are true, but I bought other items along with these which were obviously exotic. They were offered to me not as objects of great value but as tokens of proof that the people who supplied them had achieved the impossible – that they had crossed the Dragomite Hills in safety. These seeds, they said, came from the fabled Navel of the World, which lies far beyond the Soursweet Marshes. If that is true, something of profound importance must have occurred in the lands beyond the Forest of Absolute Night, for no one who tried to cross the Dragomite Hills within the last few centuries has ever returned to tell the tale.'

Lucrezia's first instinct had been to wish as fervently as Hyry Keshvara evidently wished that this might be true – but she was Ereleth's apprentice and had been schooled in scepticism.

'Is there no other way such things could have come into Xandria?' Lucrezia had asked. 'According to Ereleth, the captain of every ship that docks in the shadow of the Great Wall swears that he brings goods never before seen within the empire, from lands so distant that no Xandrian has ever heard of them. It is all lies, she says, pandering to the thirst for travellers' tales that all sedentary city folk have.'

'I can't tell for certain,' Hyry had answered. 'Although I saved these seeds for you, highness, knowing how enthusiastic you would be to test the claims which were made on their behalf, I took the other items to a very cunning man and an uncommonly bold adventurer. They both agreed with me that the plants in question were extremely odd, and that if they did indeed originate from the lands south of the Dragomite Hills their arrival here must be reckoned a marvel. The hills stretch so far to the west and the east, and are so inconveniently bounded by the Grey Waste and the Spangled Desert, that even seeds would have difficulty surviving the journey. There were mature plants too, highness, all astonishingly free from the ravages of decay. Either they were conveyed across the hills as swiftly as a man can ride, or the people who brought them possess a powerful means of protecting their produce from corruption. In either case, highness . . .'

'Perhaps they have the secret of incorruptible stone,' Lucrezia had said, intending it as a joke – but there had been a hollow ring in Hyry Keshvara's polite laugh which suggested that the merchant did not consider it a jesting matter.

If anyone other than Hyry Keshvara had told Lucrezia that the seeds had come from the lands south of the Forest of Absolute Night, let alone that they had come from the legendary Navel of the World – of which something was said in the *Lore of Genesys,* where incorruptible stone was mentioned too – Lucrezia would not have believed it. Ereleth, when the story was repeated to her, would not believe it even from Keshvara. 'If the most honest merchant of the city swears on his firstborn's life that something is true,' Ereleth was frequently wont to say, 'you may be perfectly certain that it is a lie. If it is the richest who swears, you may be certain that it is one of the damnedest lies ever pronounced.' Hyry Keshvara was neither the most honest merchant in the city nor the richest, but there was something in her particular excitement that Lucrezia was inclined to trust . . . something which spoke not of thirst for profit but of thirst for adventure, and perhaps for glory.

Lucrezia had fallen in love with that *particular excitement*; there seemed to her to be little enough in life that was worth desiring, and she had lately developed a powerful thirst for the new and the strange. When Hyry had repeated what she had been told about the manner in which the seeds might be cultivated, Lucrezia had listened with the utmost care.

'I cannot vouch for any of this,' Hyry had said, 'and cannot easily put my trust in such a wild tale, but what I was told is that one must persuade a man or a woman to swallow the nut whole. Both his legs – I'll assume that it's a man – must then be broken in half a dozen places, but carefully, so that he doesn't bleed to death.

42

He must be buried waist deep in rich soil, left loose around his loins but packed tight about his midriff. His arms ought to be broken as well, if he's strong, to make absolutely sure that he can't uproot himself, but he mustn't be killed, for the seed will only grow in living flesh. He must be well fed while the nut germinates in his belly and begins to grow. Once the shoots are established in his flesh he'll cease to feel pain; if he hasn't gone mad before then he'll remain lucid, perhaps even cheerful, until the flowers bloom. For a hundred days and more there'll be no sign of anything amiss with him, and he may become prodigiously enamoured of his keepers and feeders, especially any comely women among them – if a woman is used, of course, the reverse would be the case.

'The first thing to emerge from his flesh will be the thorns. His legs, face and torso will sprout quills like a porcupine, but he should still be fit and well, for the plant is very ingenious in the matter of insinuating its own tissues within its host's without any considerable disruption of function. He must be very well fed during this phase, for the plant will be hungry and all its nourishment must be derived from its host's gut. A hundred and thirty days after the thorns, the flowers will begin to emerge. I'm assured that although they aren't exactly beautiful, they are fascinating in their peculiarity, resembling snakes with gaping jaws. It's the fang-like elements protecting the flower which produce the poison – it's said to be the deadliest in existence, but there are far too many substances of which that's said for the claim to be taken seriously. The flowers aren't self-fertilizing, but will exchange pollen with one another in a way which is said to be interesting to watch. Then the nuts will form anew.

'After that, the process can be repeated – but I was solemnly warned that it might not be easy to bring the plants to the point of self-reproduction, and that they cannot be grown except from seed. Some of their near cousins are adapted to grow perfectly well in animal flesh, but my informants said that these seeds cannot be relied upon to put forth flowers – or might produce sickly and sterile flowers – in any but human flesh. They said, too, that if the man in whose flesh they are growing should die, from hunger or disease or some inherent weakness, the plant will die too. There are three nuts, princess, so you have some scope for testing the truth of these statements.'

'Who sold you these seeds and told you this tale?' Lucrezia had demanded to know. 'Darklanders?'

'Certainly not, highness. Darklanders live in daily contact with much that is unearthly, but they have a powerful dislike of the unusual. The two men who brought me these things had kept them secret while they came through the forest. They were bronzes, who said they had long been homeless wanderers, and they boasted that they had drunk the water of the Lake of Colourless Blood and had seen the Silver Thorns. I think they were making a game of the whole matter, highness – but what they sold me was certainly strange, and if they *were* telling the truth about these . . .'

Lucrezia gathered from this that Hyry was very interested to know how much truth there was in what she had been told by these enigmatic merchants, and had brought the seeds to the Inner Sanctum because she fervently hoped that Ereleth – or Lucrezia – would subject them to a test which she herself dared not try.

Although the first two seeds had failed, Lucrezia, Ereleth and Hyry had all been fascinated by the manner of their failure, which bore out much of what the bronze men had said. The first had got as far as producing thorns, but the redundant slave Lucrezia had been given to use had simply not been up to the task. She had seemed sturdy enough, and was certainly not undernourished, having spent a lifetime in one of the Citadel's best kitchens, but she had shrivelled and died by slow degrees, in spite of every remedy Ereleth could prescribe. Lucrezia had no reason to think that another doctor would have fared any better.

Ereleth had been impressed by this experiment too. Initially, she had refused to believe that the plant could possibly live according to the pattern Hyry Keshvara had described, because it made no sense in terms of the theory of evolution by natural selection. The witch-queen's curiosity had been further stimulated by the second experiment with the dog, and she had then taken it upon herself to question Keshvara more carefully about the origin of the seeds.

'There's not much more I can add,' Hyry had said. 'As I told the princess, they made a game of secrecy. At the time, I thought they were merely trying to talk up the goods, but . . . Carus Fraxinus and Aulakh Phar have already chided me for missing a valuable opportunity, and they were right. There was one thing, though . . .' She hesitated, until she was commanded to go on. 'The bronzes said that if there were women in Xandria with Serpent's blood – they did say *women*, not men – they ought to be told of this, lest they mistake the restlessness within their veins. Their words, majesty – which they refused to explain.'

Lucrezia knew that Hyry must know what was whispered about her own Serpent's blood, and was annoyed that the trader had not seen fit to mention this when they had spoken before, but she understood her hesitation. Mention of such matters could be considered indelicate. Ereleth had made no criticism, though; it seemed that she simply filed the new detail away with the rest. When Lucrezia had questioned her as to what it all meant, she had confessed her ignorance with unusual frankness.

Now, as Lucrezia reached out to pet the half-buried dog, which responded to her touch with a plaintive whimper, she wondered whether there really was a special restlessness within her veins – and, if so, what it might signify.

What these people gave to Hyry was intended to serve as evidence of their power to work miracles, she thought. *She understands that, and so do those friends who are determined to investigate the possibility of crossing the Dragomite Hills. I have a part to play too, and I won't let her down. If I can only persuade my father to let me have the amber, I'll prove to her – and to him! – that the bronzes spoke the truth, and that the world is a richer and stranger place than either of them dares to imagine . . . and then, by whatever means I can devise, I'll do everything in my power to find out exactly how rich and strange it is. There has to be more to life than politics and poison.*

6

A NDRIS'S CELL WAS about as long as he was tall and so narrow
that he could easily touch both walls while standing in the
middle. The pallet which served as a mattress wasn't long enough
to allow him to stretch out full length, and the hole provided for
the expulsion of wastes was the top of a pipe which led straight
down to the sewer, with nothing but a wooden cover to keep the
stink at bay. Fortunately, it was a very long drop.

On a brighter note, some of Andris's few possessions had been
fetched from the inn where he had been lodging, so he had a
change of clothes. There was a tap over the waste-hole which
produced water with which to wash. The mattress was
surprisingly free of vermin; and the cell did have a small glazed
window. He was told that food would be served twice a day, and if
his first experience of it could be trusted it was perfectly edible,
though somewhat elementary. All in all, it wasn't as bad as some
prisons he had been in.

The jailer who installed him in the cell was a small rotund man
of perennially mournful aspect. He looked like the kind of man
who might be easily overpowered, but the doors of all the cells
were constructed in such a way as to minimise the chance of any
prisoner ever having the opportunity to overpower him. They
were made of very stout wood and had no less than three huge
bolt-beams to secure them. The top beam fitted over a spy-hole,
the bottom one over a slit some three sims deep and twenty wide,
through which food could be passed. It was never necessary to
remove more than one beam at a time – and, of course, strictly
against the rules to do so. Andris didn't doubt that the doors and
the beams were regularly checked and replaced before they
showed significant signs of weakening. He worked out that it
might be possible for a man with very strong fingers to dislodge the

top and bottom beams from inside, but there was no way he could get to the middle one even if he failed to attract attention when the top one crashed to the floor.

The ceiling seemed to be by far the weakest element in the forces of his confinement. There was a patch in the middle which was sulphurously yellow by virtue of the attentions of some ferocious local species of rot – but even Andris, who was probably the tallest man ever to have been locked up there, wasn't quite tall enough to touch it with his outstretched fingertips. In any case, it was impossible to figure out what, if anything, was beyond the stonework. The cell was set very high in one of the citadel's seven towers, and it seemed entirely possible that there might be nothing above it but empty space without any convenient egress.

Andris found the height rather dizzying the first time he looked down from the window; he had never been in a building with more than three storeys before, and this particular tower had six. Andris was no more than averagely acrophobic, but the thought of a possible collapse sent shivers down his spine as he realised how many floors he might crash through on the way down. Nor was the tower in which he was confined exceptional; he knew that the others were just as huge, and the interior of the citadel – into which his window faced – contained several erections of hardly less magnitude, including one which stood alone, unsupported by any accessory walls. The jailer informed him that this was the Inner Sanctum, in which the king kept his thirty-one wives and their households, and confirmed that there really was a walled garden set upon its roof.

'On a good day you can see the witch-wife Ereleth tending her poison apples,' the jailer said – in jest, Andris assumed. 'You also have a wonderful view of the treasury's mint, where all the coin in the realm gets freshened up at regular intervals, and you can watch the horses going back and forth from the biggest livery stable in the world, which happens to be directly below us. That's so our fall will be cushioned by straw and horseshit if ever there's a collapse. You can also see the whipping-post and the scaffold, although we don't have any whippings or hangings scheduled this tenday – not yet, at any rate.'

It was not at all difficult to obtain such information from the jailer, who was perfectly willing to stand in the corridor and chat through the spy-hole. He evidently found his job rather tedious. For the moment, he had less than thirty men in his charge, distributed about this floor and the one below. As the magistrate had observed, few men could afford to stay here for long.

'I need to send some letters,' Andris told the jailer, once he had taken stock of the possessions which had been brought to his cell, 'But I can't find my pens and paper – or my brushes and inks, come to that. I'm a mapmaker, you know.'

'Impounded,' said the jailer dolefully. 'No knick-knacks allowed in the cell. You're only allowed spare clothing.'

'But I have to try to get in touch with a kinsman of mine. He might be able to get me out of here.'

'What's the address?'

'I don't know his address. I want to write to the captain of the ship which brought me here, to ask him to make enquiries on my behalf. Surely you can let me have a piece of paper, and the use of a pen.'

'Pen *and* ink, with one piece of scrubbed parchment and the carriage charge, would add up to half a crown,' the jailer reported.

'I have my own writing materials,' Andris told him. 'I only need to be allowed to use them.'

The jailer shook his head. 'Rules,' he said stubbornly. 'Don't know how things are in the darklands, but here we do things by the rules. We're civilised, see.'

Andris sighed heavily. 'Just for the record,' he said, 'I'm not a darklander. I'm a civilised man. Are you telling me that all my tools have been confiscated? It's not that they're worth much, you understand – it's just the principle of the thing.'

'What sort of tools were they?' enquired the jailer innocently.

'Just the usual sort of thing,' Andris said. 'Scissors, skinning and gutting knives, fishhooks, eating implements . . . nothing out of the ordinary.'

'Hunter, are you?'

'All travellers have to be hunters and fishermen when the need arises,' Andris said. 'I'm a long way from home.'

'I'll check to make sure they've been safely impounded,' the jailer said. 'Maybe not – these waterfront inns are full of thieves and foreigners. Can't have 'em, though. Have to get what you need from me. Half a crown.'

Andris still had a few coins in his waist-pouch. He produced a half-crown from one of the Thousand Isles.

'No good,' said the jailer, after testing it with his teeth. 'Rotten right through. 'I'll need two like that – have to go straight to the mint at half-weight. No one in Xandria takes coin that bad. There's always plenty of fresh about – benefits of civilisation, see.'

Andris gritted his teeth as his temper rose. Had the spy-hole not been so tiny he might not have been able to resist the temptation to reach out and seize the tubby man by the throat, but his fist was too big to pass through it. Although, sadly, the law was *not* the law the world over, its keepers seemed to be much the same. He did not doubt that the jailer already knew exactly how much coin he had, and would aquire it all before the day was out.

He threw a second half-crown through the spy-hole. The jailer stooped to pick it up and ambled away. He returned, in his own good time, with a minuscule piece of old parchment and a pen whose nib was more direly in need of refreshing than the coins he had given for it. Presumably the royal metallurgists were far too busy re-minting coin to bother with mere implements of literacy. The ink was just as poor.

It took Andris ten minutes to write the letter. He would have taken a lot longer if he could, but even though he agonised over the choice of every word there simply wasn't enough space on the parchment to permit much exercise of eloquence or ingenuity. The jailer took the letter without comment, ostentatiously neglecting to read it – although Andris was certain that he would do so as soon as he was out of sight. He was welcome; the letter merely pleaded with the shipmaster to do everything he could to find one Theo Zabio and tell him that his nephew, who was confined in the citadel, had urgent news from Ferentina. In point of fact, Andris had no news from Ferentina less than six years old, and none at all concerning anyone more closely related to Theo Zabio than himself, but he felt obliged to make every effort to persuade his kinsman that it was worth taking an interest.

Andris was fairly confident that even a Ferentinan could be relied on to do something for a kinsman in trouble – assuming, of course, that he was alive, and that he was still in Xandria, and that the shipmaster could be bothered to look for him. He was painfully aware that there might be several assumptions too many in that chain of suppositions, but what could one expect for a couple of rotten half-crowns?

Later, as night was falling, the jailer returned and removed the beam covering the spy-hole.

'The ship hadn't sailed, so the letter's been delivered,' he said. 'All a waste of time, mind.'

Andris got up from the bed, where he had been trying unsuccessfully to catch up with lost sleep, and came to the spy-hole. The stars were shining brightly, but Andris's window was very narrow and the corridor without was just as gloomy as the cell. It was difficult to make out the jailer's features. 'Thanks anyway,' he said.

'Not just the letter,' the jailer said. 'This petition for a pardon you've put in. That kind of thing's not intended for the likes of you – it's for aristocrats who want to buy themselves out of trouble with big bribes. You'll just get an extra fine.'

'I suspected as much,' Andris confessed wearily, 'but that sneering magistrate annoyed me. I had to do *something*. I'm not guilty, you know – the guardsman who got hurt must know it wasn't me who hit him. I just thought that if I bought a little time, he might . . .' He stopped. He could easily imagine the pitying look that must have been on the jailer's face.

'You should never let magistrates annoy you,' the fat man advised him, in a fatherly tone. 'It's OK once in a while to lose your temper in a brawl, but never in a court of law. The guardsman won't say a word – only get himself into trouble if he did.'

Andris sighed deeply as the jailer replaced the beam and ambled away. He sat down on the mattress again, wondering how badly he had misplayed his hand, and whether there was any way out of his predicament. *I should have stayed on the other side of the Slithery Sea,* he thought glumly. *I was far enough away from home, without being too far. I should have settled down when I had the chance.* Unfortunately, he knew only too well that such slim chances as he had had to settle down wouldn't have been overly attractive even to a man without his tastes and fancies. To be an exile, unable to return to his homeland, was bad enough – to be an exile educated in early youth to the inclinations and expectations of an aristocrat was doubly problematic. Try as he might, Andris had never been able to adjust his hopes and dreams to the level of his actual prospects.

Andris had been the third and last of the sons of the king of
Ferentina – who had been the sort of king to whom tradition
allowed but a single wife. That might have been difficult in itself,
given that the city-state had been notorious for its wars of
succession for tens of thousands of years, but it was made even
more problematic by the fact that all three sons had survived and
that none of them liked the others in the least degree. In a better-
ordered world, kings of nations like Ferentina would doubtless
have refrained from having more than one son, but the only thing
likelier to cause a civil war in Ferentina than having more than one
son survive to adulthood was having *no* sons surviving to
adulthood, so every dutiful king adopted the safer course of
having more than one son, and then trying to ensure that they
would be able to avoid conflict. This could often be done, and had
been fairly easily accomplished for three generations before
Andris's time, but the pattern had to break eventually, and Andris
had spent his entire youth and adolescence surrounded by people
who expected it to break at any moment.

The situation would not have become so desperate, Andris
knew, had nature been more even-handed. If only his oldest
brother, Marc, had been taller or cleverer – or even better-looking
– than Andris, he might have felt more confident of his authority.
It would not have mattered that Andris was such a brave and bad-
tempered fighting man, if only those attributes had been counter-
balanced by dull stupidity or unquestioning loyalty or open-
hearted generosity – but even Andris had to admit that they were
not. Cruel nature really had formed him to be a dangerous rival to
his lean, sly and mean-spirited elder brothers, and by the time he
was five years old the choice before him had been stark: had he not
taken himself away he would either have been murdered, or
cynically used as a figurehead in a bitter war whose outcome he
could not control or foresee.

In the best – or perhaps worst – tradition of the romantic tales
which his nurses and tutors had been so enthusiastic to tell him
when his formal studies became too tedious, Andris had departed
to become a wanderer, a soldier of fortune, just as Uncle Theo had
a generation before.

Unfortunately, his career as a soldier of fortune had been
infinitely more difficult to manage and infinitely less rewarding

than the tales had implied. The world was every bit as large and strange as the stories had promised – and his careful education in map-making had not prepared him for its diversity half as well as he might have hoped – but it was by no means so bountiful, even to one as clearly deserving as he.

I should have been born in a nation like this one, Andris thought, *where a king may have a hundred sons and every one of them might find a proper place, and none would ever dare to take arms against his brothers. It's true, I suppose, that a prince of Xandria must have far less power and prestige than a prince of Ferentina, even at the best of times, by virtue of having to share it with so many others . . . and it's probably true that the business of keeping things in order must be far more complicated in a sea-spanning empire than in a very modestly sized kingdom, but there's the tropic sun and the warm sea, and the stars shine so very brightly four nights in every five . . . Why, oh why, couldn't I . . . ?*

His reverie was cut short by the sound of the upper beam being drawn back yet again from the door, and he saw the glimmer of lamplight through the spy-hole. He stood up, and stood close enough to the door to be seen.

'Got a visitor,' said the jailer, briefly, before dumping his lamp on the floor and stalking away.

Andris's hopes soared, as they were ever wont to do when his fortunes improved, by however small a margin – not did they sink when he saw that the visitor was a young serving-girl, whom he had never seen before.

'Have you come from Uncle Theo?' he asked hopefully.

'I have come from Princess Lucrezia,' was the reply, delivered in the automatic style of a careful recitation. 'My name is Monalen. The princess asks me to inform you that there is a law in Xandria which provides that anyone who applies for a royal pardon may be granted such a pardon by any member of the royal family, provided only that the king agrees to the release and that the person to be pardoned agrees freely to render whatever service the pardoner requires of him for a period not exceeding half a year. Princess Lucrezia has heard what happened in the court-room today, and asks whether you would be prepared to enter into such an agreement with her, if the king will permit.'

Perhaps there's justice in Xandria after all! Andris thought. *A message of hope, and from a princess! Perhaps the old tales aren't such damned lies as they've so far seemed! Perhaps my luck has changed at last, and my destiny will now be set to rights . . . and half a year is, in any case, less than three hundred days . . . and whatever service the princess has in mind must surely be less arduous than breaking stone for that huge and horrid wall.*

Aloud, he simply said: 'Yes, by all means. Tell your mistress that if the king will sanction it, I should be proud to be the princess's man for as long as she should need me.'

7

JACOM CERRI WALKED slowly down one of the many flights of stone steps which descended the inner face of the citadel wall. It led to the wide roadway which connected the City Gate to the big courtyard flanked by the main stables and the treasury. He measured his paces very carefully, not for reasons of military precision but because he wanted to make the tour of inspection last as long as possible. It was the middle of the midnight, when the citadel was at its quietest. Except for the sentries and patrols of the citadel guard the only people at work were the coiners in the treasury mint, who were working around the clock to prepare the Thanksgiving payroll.

Jacom had hoped that his second tour of citadel duty would be easier than the first, when the unaccustomed hours and the incessant tedium had proved surprisingly wearing. He had optimistically reassured himself that it was bound to be a welcome relief after the hurly-burly of the harbour patrol, but in fact the tedium seemed twice as bad now that he was repeating something he had done before. The first tenday's duty had at least been new, and he had been distracted by all kinds of trivial learning experiences; this time he knew everything he needed to know at the procedural level – the names of all his men, the distribution of his sentries, the layout of all the citadel's coverts, courtyards and alleyways – but he still lacked any kind of mental equipment for making the time fly. The passing hours seemed to have slowed to a painful degree, and no matter how he regulated his own paces he could not adjust himself to their emptiness.

His plight was not improved by the fact that the men under his command were, without exception, fully adapted to the business. Every one of them was utterly inured to all the trials and tribulations which custom imposed upon them. To the men, the routines which tested Jacom's patience were simply an opportunity to relax, even to loaf. They were forbidden to pass the time by playing cards or going to sleep, even when they were not actually posted as sentries or appointed to walk a beat, but they were experts in the business of self-distraction; they needed neither apparatus nor altered states of consciousness to attain an extraordinary aptitude in the underrated art of doing nothing.

Sergeant Purkin was, of course, a past master of this particular art. As Jacom approached his present sentry-station, at the treasury door, the greybeard seemed set in stone, perfectly still and yet perfectly relaxed. When Jacom stopped before him he saluted with mechanical precision. 'Nothin' to report, sir,' he said, as though it were the best news in the world.

'Don't you ever feel that this kind of duty is a complete waste of time, Purkin?' Jacom asked, on a confidential whim.

'Certainly not, sir,' the sergeant replied, with a certain ironic pride. 'Who knows what'd be occurrin', sir, if we weren't here?'

'Invading armies would doubtless be battering down the gates,' Jacom said, with a sceptical sigh.

'That too, like as not,' said Purkin equably. 'Though we'd probably get a few days' warning, like, so we could mobilise the regulars and the city militia. Pains me to admit it, sir, we bein' the king's guard, not thief-takers, but the real problem's petty theft. This is a big place, see – hundreds of people come back and forth through the gates on legitimate business, an' quite a lot of 'em have illegitimate business on the side. A lot o' valuable goods pass through those gates, and not all the food reaches the kitchens, if you get my meanin'. Those livery stables over there are said to be the biggest in the world, and you might be surprised by how many fine animals just disappear into thin air. Then there's this place – all that coin comin' in by the barrel to be refreshed, and the raw metal to refresh it.'

'It seems secure enough,' Jacom observed, examining the heavy door before which Purkin was standing.

'It is, sir. Locked and barred. Take a barrel of plastic to get through it. No one allowed in or out till the new issue's ready – always extra precautions when they have to pay everyone at once 'cause of the holiday. Treasury has its own guardsmen inside – real sticklers for the regs. Even so, out of every thousand coins there's always thirty or forty which somehow go missin' . . . sometimes as many as a hundred.'

'But we didn't catch a single person pilfering during our last tour,' Jacom pointed out. 'In fact, we never seem to arrest anybody at all.'

'Oh, we do, sir,' Purkin assured him. 'Last tour was unusually quiet, just like these last two days . . . which generally means, in my experience, that the evildoers're savin' themselves for a big push. As I said, though, the real point is that if we weren't here, there'd be three or four times as much stuff goin' missin'. We're a deterrent, see. Just by bein' here, we cramp the style of the thieves. They have to be twice as careful and twice as clever . . . and they try, sir, they surely try. We prevent an awful lot o' skullduggery just by doin' nothin' at all. Valuable work, sir, valuable work.'

Jacom recognised that what the sergeant said made perfect sense. He supposed that his own problem would take care of itself once he had done a few more tours of duty, because he would simply get used to being out of phase with the rest of the world, wide awake during the midday and the midnight, catching his sleep in the teen hours and the thirties. As he strode away from Purkin's post, however, this seemed small enough comfort.

He saluted the men on duty at the gate, and began to climb the steps on the further side of it, making his way upwards yet again, to the walkway that ran around the battlements. It was a long way to the top and by the time he got there his ankles were aching. He had always considered himself to be very fit, but climbing stairs in full armour – no matter how slowly and carefully he went – was an arduous business.

Once at the top, he felt a little better. His initial tendency to vertigo had quite disappeared by now, and there was something about being up so high which he found strangely exhilarating. It was an illusion, he knew, but the stars seemed so much closer here.

There was something about starlight observed from on high which was conducive to philosophical reveries, and as Jacom marched along the walkway he found himself contemplating the question of how many stars were visible in the sky. He held his hand up, ten or twelve sims from his face, made a circle with his thumb and forefinger, and tried to count the stars contained therein. It wasn't easy. There were a dozen whose brightness was quite distinct, but it was impossible to say whether there were twenty, thirty or forty fainter ones glimmering in the background.

Call it thirty altogether, he thought. *Now, how much larger than that little circle is the whole sky?*

He gave up on the problem as soon as it had been posed. He was no mathematician, and the calculation was well beyond his meagre capabilities. He began wondering instead why, if the stars really were as numerous as the lore insisted, they could not fill the night sky with a light every bit as bright as that of day.

Why, if the stars were simply distant suns, did they disappear into a sparkling blue mist when *the* sun shone?

Sometimes, Jacom regretted that his practically inclined father had not seen fit to provide him with a scholar's education. It didn't seem quite fair that the only acceptable way for him to avoid intensive schooling in the arts and practices of fruit-growing and pig-breeding had been to declare a fervent interest in the Arts Martial.

He discovered, a little belatedly, that while these thoughts had occupied his mind he had come to a complete standstill. He blushed when he realised exactly where he had stopped. He knew that it was not by coincidence that he had paused at one of the few vantage-points from which it was possible to look into the roof-garden on top of the Inner Sanctum – which was, in effect, the only part of the citadel into which a captain of the citadel guard had no right to peer, even though his men provided an outer cordon of protection around it. There was a certain dangerous significance in the fact that he had paused on this particular spot without even thinking about it.

It was, of course, impossible not to be aware of the phallic tower's presence – it was positioned at the very heart of the citadel, surrounded by an open space larger than any other courtyard, and thus had a prominence unshared by any of the other blocks and towers crammed and crowded into the available spaces of the eccentrically shaped and sprawling edifice – but that awareness ought, as a matter of duty, to be kept strictly in check. Officers in the king's guard could hardly be expected to be ignorant of all the romantic tales and obscene jokes in which the Inner Sanctum figured, but they were not supposed to let such notions preoccupy their thoughts, much less their instincts. Jacom, alas, had no more mastered the trick of that kind of indifference than he had mastered the trick of armouring himself against the tedium of night patrols.

While he was at ground level Jacom's Sanctum-inspired reveries tended to be of a fairly basic kind, along the lines of what it might be like to attempt sexual congress with a giant. To judge by the tenor of the oft-repeated jokes on the subject this was something many men thought about but few ever dared to try, on the very reasonable grounds that their equipment might be thought inadequate. When he was on the high battlements, on the other hand, his daydream fantasies tended to run on more elevated lines, involving beleaguered princesses and near-impossible feats of heroism. These might have been easier to control had he not been able to connect them up to the appearance of an actual princess, but he had – and the place where he was now standing was the very spot where he had made that connection. It was from here, on several occasions, that he had seen Princess Lucrezia in the roof-garden.

During the ten days of his first tour he had unwisely allowed such glimpses to become more and more important to him. He had begun to feel disappointed every time he found the roof-garden empty, and his heart had begun to beat a little faster every time it was not. During his ten day stint on the harbour patrol he had not given the princess a great deal of thought, but as soon as he was back inside the wall the prospect of catching brief glimpses of her had suddenly begun to seem immensely attractive – and had just as suddenly begun to seem hazardous. The fact that he could get no closer to the roof-garden than forty mets, with a yawning gulf between, made such glimpses no less exciting and no less inappropriate.

Sometimes, he had been able to watch Lucrezia working in the garden while she was unconscious of being watched, and whenever she chanced to look up it seemed easy enough to look away and feign total unconsciousness of her presence – but he could never be quite sure that his attention had gone unnoticed, and he had no way to judge how unwelcome it might be if it had not. Whenever she was absorbed in contemplation of two particularly remarkable plants – one of which bore an uncanny resemblance to a human torso, the other to the head and forepaws of a dog – she seemed utterly oblivious of all else, but he knew that the appearance might be deceptive. For a moment, during his first tour, he had almost been convinced that the strange plants actually *were* a human being and a dog, half-buried in the dark soil, but the green shoots sprouting out of them had convinced him that he had been fooled by some trick of perspective.

The bright starlight allowed him to see that the larger of the two plants had gone. Only the one resembling a dog remained. Jacom wondered whether Lucrezia would now be less inclined to linger in the garden during her waking hours.

He had heard, of course, that the roof-garden was reputed to be full of poisonous plants, kept by the witch-wife Ereleth – who was often seen in the company of Princess Lucrezia – and he had also heard that the princess was a mass-murderess perennially in the market for broken-down slaves of either sex, but he had sense enough to know that such rumours meant nothing. He knew how easily such preposterous tales could be cooked up, and how their fantastic and horrific elements tended to be amplified as they spread like wildfire within the citadel walls.

Jacom was jerked out of his reverie by the sound of a challenge emanating from the roadway far below him, echoing eerily from the wall of the Inner Sanctum. The challenge evidently went unanswered, for it was followed almost immediately by a cry of alarm.

Jacom turned on his heel and raced back to the steps which he had ascended a few minutes before. He ran full tilt, reckless of the danger involved. It was as though his feet, so long constrained to move with unnatural slowness, were intent on making the most of their sudden freedom.

It took him three minutes to get down to the roadway. By that time four or five guardsmen were running this way and that, peering into shadowy coverts in search of the fugitive. Jacom turned round, then turned again, trying to judge which way the fugitive might have gone. He saw nothing at all until one of the men suddenly shouted: 'Look out, sir!'

He turned for a third time to find a dark sihouette hurtling out of the shadowed cloister which extended from the groom's quarters behind the big stables to the side door of the main kitchen.

Convinced that he was under attack, Jacom reached for the

sword that was sheathed at his belt, but the man jinked around him, seemingly intent on scuttling into an alleyway which could take him clear of the men lumbering in his wake. Jacom immediately let go of the hilt of his weapon and hurled himself sideways. His aim was to tackle the man about the knees, but he had underestimated the effect of the breastplate he wore, and his grasping fingers closed instead about the falling man's left ankle.

Had the captain's desire to complete the capture been compromised by the slightest irresolution the fugitive would probably have pulled away, but Jacom clung on desperately, and his armoured body was far too heavy to be dragged. Thus anchored, the man's momentum carried him forward to a crashing fall, which his cartwheeling arms could not soften. By the time his other pursuers arrived he was groaning in pain, all further thought of flight having been rudely driven out.

Jacom came to his feet, feeling very pleased with himself in spite of the fact that he'd been severely shaken up in the encounter. He noticed that he had skinned both his knees on the hard flagstones. His midriff and ribs felt as if he had run full tilt into a five-barred gate.

Two guardsmen grabbed the recumbent man's arms and hauled him upright.

'What did he do?' Jacom asked, looking around for whoever had issued the first challenge.

'Nothing!' complained the victim, while a third guardsman conducted a thorough search of his clothing. He wore no belt and had no pouch of any kind. He was carrying no weapon. There was, however, a piece of parchment tucked inside his shirt. It was a pass to enter the citadel. The guardsman identified the signature as that of the senior kitchen steward, and pointed out that it was only valid until curfew. The man had long overstayed his licence to be on the premises.

'Why didn't you answer the challenge?' Jacom demanded of him.

'Because he warn't supposed to be 'ere,' answered Kirn, the guardsman who had conducted the search. 'Came in b' day, hid when the gates closed, then came out thievin'. Poor fool! 'Adn't got so much as a kitchen scrap 'fore we 'ad 'im.'

The guardsman seemed as pleased with the capture as Jacom

had been, although it did occur to Jacom that it might have been better had they caught the man in possession of stolen goods.

'It was a mistake!' the prisoner objected. 'I didn't mean to get shut in. I was just trying to clear out quietly, so as not to trouble anyone.'

'Horseshit!' said Kirn. It seemed an apt comment.

'What's your name and station?' Jacom asked.

'Sart,' the prisoner replied, promptly enough. 'Zadok Sart, bone-man.'

'You appear to have left your bone-bag behind,' Jacom observed. 'Not to mention your cart. Still – you've five hours of the midnight left to think of a good excuse, before you see the magistrate. Shackle him in the guardroom by the City Gate, for now.'

'Yes sir,' Kirn replied, with a zest which made it clear that he too was fully appreciative of a welcome break in the normal routine. 'We c'n get the truth out of 'im if'n you want us to, sir.'

'That's not our business,' Jacom said loftily. 'We're the king's guard. Our business is keeping order, not thief-taking. We can leave the sordid stuff to the constables.'

'Yes, *sir*,' the guardsmen chorused.

Jacom felt a thrill of pleasure at having demonstrated that he had learned the ropes as quickly as anyone could have expected. He tried not to limp as he strode away to resume his tour, but when he came to the stairway he decided that he'd seen quite enough of the battlements for one midnight, and went back to the guardroom instead, to inspect his cuts and bruises.

Well, he thought philosophically, as he dabbed his bloody knee with a handkerchief, *he might not be guilty of anything much, but he's definitely guilty. That's an improvement. Next time, perhaps we can arrest someone worth arresting. After that . . . who knows what possibilities the future might hold?*

8

ANDRIS LEANED ON the wall of his cell and watched a spider patiently spinning a web across the pane of the window. It was a good place to have a web because any flies which got into the gloomy cell – and somehow they did, although the possible routes of ingress were blocked most of the time – naturally headed for the beam of light the window let in.

There had, of course, been a web there before, but Andris had thoughtlessly swept it away on more than one occasion in order to peer out into the courtyard. To the spider, each such clearance must have been a catastrophe, but the creature had set about the work of reconstruction with infinite patience and care, and Andris had resolved to be more respectful in future. In fact, he had come to the conclusion that the spider was a useful resource in a situation which offered relatively few wards against boredom. He had decided to name it Belin, so that every time he looked at it he could be offering up a silent and subtle insult to the king of Xandria.

'I won't do it again,' Andris assured the spider. 'It isn't as if there's anything out there worth looking at. In all the time I've been here not a single person has been brought to the scaffold, or even to the whipping-post, and the traffic which passes in and out of the Inner Sanctum is no more interesting, seen from this height, than the comings and goings around the mint. The level of entertainment which this places provides is simply not up to scratch. I was once in a jail where my cell had a view of a crocolid pool, and I saw one poor wretch thrown in. I hadn't really believed in the logic of deterrents before that day, but I've believed in it since. I was very polite to the jailkeepers after that, even though they were complete bastards who never wasted an opportunity to wind the prisoners up. That was a busy jail, not like this one at all –

62

but they didn't make people pay to be in it. I was innocent then, too.'

The spider didn't answer, but Andris didn't mind.

'It doesn't in the least matter that you don't understand a word of what I'm saying, Belin,' he informed the indefatigable arachnid, with all due seriousness. 'I've been travelling for a long time now, always a foreigner. You get used to not being understood, or even listened to. It isn't just that I'm an amber among goldens, perennially mistaken for a darklander. It's something deeper than that – something so deep that even when my skin colour blends in nicely my foreignness still stands out and marks me as a man apart. That's strange, isn't it? I mean, given that all human beings speak the same language and are heirs to the same lore, you'd think we'd all treat one another pretty much alike, but we don't. Not everywhere's as bad as Xandria, of course. Oddly enough, the places where people pride themselves as being *civilised* tend to be the places where foreigners get the worst treatment. There's something about the frame of mind which treats anyone unlike oneself as a barbarian which is profoundly distasteful – and I say that knowing perfectly well that I come from just such a place myself. I've learned from my experiences, you see.'

Belin continued to build bridges between the strands of his web – or possibly *her* web – neatly and cleverly. Somewhere in his travels Andris had heard a tale about an imprisoned king who watched a spider making attempt after attempt to climb up a sheer wall, undeterred by constant failure. This good example had allegedly boosted the king's own morale to the point where, once released, he set about winning back his lost kingdom. It was one of those tales which was said to be *very* ancient – which probably meant that it had been invented no more than a couple of generations ago.

'In any case,' Andris told the spider, 'I have no plans to go home. A man has to have some pride. You can't let the world grind you down, no matter how often you get thrown in jail. Maybe that's what you're trying to teach me, by spinning that wonderfully intricate web. Maybe you're trying to tell me that it's cleverness and not morale that finally turns the tide of fortune. Maybe you're trying to tell me that there's a way to wealth and position, however mazy, in the Princess Lucrezia's offer to take me into her service if and when she can get your august namesake to agree. Maybe . . .'

He fell silent and spun around as the beam covering the spy-hole in the cell door was withdrawn.

' 'Nother visitor,' called the laconic jailer. 'Never knew a man so popular . . .'

Andris didn't consider two visitors in three days to be evidence of great popularity, but he was grateful to receive any attention at all. By the time he had crossed to the spy-hole the jailer was gone.

In full daylight it was easy enough to make out the features of the person who stood in the corridor. It was not, as he had half-expected, the princess's servant Monalen, nor could it possibly be Theo Zabio. It was a middle-aged and bearded golden, tall for a Xandrian, grizzled without being in the least decrepit. His brown eyes were bright but oddly melancholy. Andris could see little of the man's costume, but the cloth of his coat was of very good quality and was showing not the slightest sign of deterioration about the collar or shoulders. In Xandria, where cotton-cleaners and other linen-hungry pests were exceptionally voracious, that was telling evidence of wealth. Andris was uncomfortably aware of the fact that his own clothing was practically falling apart.

'My name is Carus Fraxinus,' the visitor said, without waiting to be asked. 'I'm a merchant. I've heard that you're a mapmaker from the far north. If that's so, I might be able to offer you employment rather more congenial than rebuilding houses and repairing the city wall.'

'I thought that the people of Xandria considered the Arts Geographical to be a joke, utterly useless in navigating the Slithery Sea and the lands about its shores,' Andris said warily.

'They do,' Fraxinus said. 'That's why the city hasn't any mapmakers of its own . . . but there's always a price to pay for the sin of forgetfulness, however venial it may seem. Is there, among the maps you memorised, one which includes a region called the Navel of the World?'

'Yes there is,' Andris said promptly. *Can I remember it after all these years?* he wondered silently. *Can I still draw and colour it, given that I haven't been required to practise for seven years and more? Better not let on that there's any doubt, though.*

'Do you have any idea whereabouts that region might be located?' the merchant asked innocently.

64

Andris knew a test when he faced one. 'Yes I do,' he said, and pointedly neglected to continue.

'You don't have to give away any secrets,' Fraxinus assured him. 'Just tell me where the region lies in relation to the Forest of Absolute Night, if you can.'

Andris closed his eyes, and tried to call the requisite image to mind. He imagined himself back in the schoolroom, labouring under the eyes of his stern mentors, drawing and drawing and drawing until his wrist cramped, dotting and stippling and colouring and labelling, driven all the while by such endlessly quoted homilies as 'There is no sin but forgetfulness' and 'A man without Art is a man without worth'.

'South,' he said eventually. 'A long way south, beyond the Soursweet Marshes. The keys to the map are the five-pointed star, the bowshot and the nest of the phoenix.' He was so glad to have been able to remember the mnemonic devices that he spilled it all out before pausing to wonder whether he might have given away something saleable.

'Can you draw the map,' Fraxinus asked, 'if I supply the requisite inks and parchment?'

'Of course,' Andris said. 'I can interpret it too, to the extent that the interpretation is part of the lore. Are you thinking of going to the Navel of the World?'

'Yes I am,' Fraxinus said frankly. 'It's long been held to be an impossible journey, but I have reason to think that it's no longer impossible. I'm trying to muster an expedition. A map would be useful – provided, of course, that it were accurate.'

'It's my belief,' Andris said, 'that the maps I was trained to draw of the Slithery Sea were accurate enough in their day – but the lore comes to us from an unimaginable antiquity, and the sea in question must have been so named because it is indeed inclined to slither. Its shores have changed over time, and so has the distribution of its lands. The map which includes the Navel of the World includes marshlands, but no sea. If my experiences in the north are any guide, it's likely to be accurate. I can offer no absolute guarantees, but for what the map may be worth, I can draw it. Would it be worth a thousand crowns to you?'

'That's a very high price,' the merchant said. 'I'd want much more than a map for a sum like that.'

'How much more?' Andris asked. He was not disheartened because he had not imagined for a moment that anyone would pay so much for a mere map.

'You're a fighting man too, I think, and a much travelled one. I might see my way to clearing your entire debt, if I could have the strength of your arms as well as the knowledge in your head. Would you be prepared to join us on this adventure, as my employee?'

The merchant seemed quite relaxed, as if he expected Andris to jump at the offer. Andris rather liked the man, but couldn't help taking a certain delight in upsetting his assumption.

'I've already had an offer which might secure my release,' he said amiably. 'I've promised to accept it, if it comes to fruition.'

Fraxinus seemed both astonished and perturbed. 'Who from?' he asked with revealing bluntness.

'Princess Lucrezia,' said Andris proudly. 'She's offered to take me into her service, if the king will give his permission. I understand that she has already submitted her petition, but that these things take time.'

'Why in the world would Princess Lucrezia want to take you into her service?' the merchant asked, maintaining a polite tone in spite of the implied insult.

'Perhaps she wants a mapmaker,' Andris retorted sarcastically.

Fraxinus's brow was deeply furrowed, and Andris realised that he was actually considering this hypothesis seriously. 'What has Keshvara started?' the merchant muttered into his beard, as he tugged at it reflexively with the fingers of his left hand. But then he looked up again and said: 'I can't believe that.'

Neither can I, Andris thought – and belatedly realised that there really was a mystery here. Why *did* the princess want to petition for his pardon, when she could easily obtain the services of any of a thousand Xandrian men? He began to regret not having made enquiries. 'I did promise,' he said weakly. 'Perhaps nothing will come of it, if the king refuses his permission . . . but have I any reason to think that I would be better off in your service than in hers?'

Carus Fraxinus was still puzzled and still hesitant. 'I'm a good master,' he said. 'Anyone in Xandria will tell you so. I'm very well known in the city. As for Princess Lucrezia . . . it's not for me to say anything at all about the lady, but . . .'

'I shouldn't need to be selling myself as a bondsman to any master,' Andris said, deciding that it might be better to steer the conversation to safer ground. 'I didn't injure the guardsman. I was simply trying to protect a blind man who was caught up in the brawl. If you have as much influence as you claim, can you not see that justice is done? Were I a free man, we could bargain on a fairer basis – and I'd have no need to sell myself for a royal pardon, for *any* purpose.'

Fraxinus stared at him contemplatively. 'How might I prove your innocence?' he enquired, seemingly taking the matter entirely seriously.

'Ask the injured man where I was when he was hit from behind. Ask the story-teller – he's blind, but neither deaf nor stupid. The man who struck the blow was almost as tall as I am, but stouter. He was part of a company of villains who seemed to be plotting something. Other people who were in the tavern might know his name. I'd be very grateful for your help, if you could do this. I'd certainly draw you a map . . . and you'd be serving the ends of Xandrian justice, which the law has not.'

'Do you know the story-teller's name?' Fraxinus asked dubiously.

'No, but if he regularly plies his trade about the harbour he shouldn't be too difficult to find. He told me a tale which he attributed to something called the *Apocrypha of Genesys*, of which I have never heard. It concerned a Serpent and a Salamander and a place called Idun. That's another name for the Navel of the World, is it not?'

Andris had assumed in saying this that tales from the so-called *Apocrypha of Genesys* must be commonplace in Xandria, but he saw in Fraxinus's expression that this was not so.

'Can you remember the tale?' the merchant asked curiously.

'Only that it had to do with gifts of trees, in return for which the forefathers made bold promises. It was dressed up very ornately with proverbs and the like, like the *Lore of Genesys* which everybody knows. It wasn't the kind of tale which has a readily discernible meaning – I doubt if the man makes an abundant living unless he knows a few which are far funnier and somewhat dirtier. Is it of any significance?'

'Probably not,' Fraxinus admitted. 'But still, I have become interested of late in hearing anything which has to do with those legendary regions. I shall try to find your story-teller, Andris Myrasol . . . and if I do, I shall see what might be done to reopen your case and prove your innocence. But I want your solemn promise that as soon as you are free you will draw me a map of the Navel of the World.'

'Prove me innocent,' Andris said, 'and I'll draw you all the maps you want – that I swear. But you'd better hurry, for I can't tell where I might be sent on the princess's service, if the king lends his blessing to the offer she has made.'

The merchant nodded, and would have turned away, but Andris interrupted him. 'By the way,' he said, 'do you know of a man named Theo Zabio – an amber from Ferentina like myself, who might have come to Xandria a long time ago?'

Fraxinus thought for a minute, then slowly shook his head. 'Was he a merchant?' he asked.

'I doubt it,' Andris said sourly. 'Like myself, he probably arrived a vagabond, although he was well enough born. If my own experience is anything to go by, I fear that he's as likely to have been enslaved to the wall, or embarked upon some criminal career, as to have become respectable and rich. Still, I had hoped . . .'

Fraxinus nodded sympathetically. 'I'll ask after Theo Zabio too,' he promised. 'If I don't hear of him in the better parts of town I'll go to Checuti, the so-called prince of thieves – who's an amiable man in spite of his vocation, and who seems to know everyone. I need that map, you see, and I'm a man to be reckoned with, even if I'm not a princess of the realm. Be cheerful, my friend – one way or another, you'll not be going to the wall.'

As the man passed out of sight, Andris permitted himself a broad and beaming smile. He did indeed feel cheerful – more cheerful than he had in many a year.

'My luck is turning,' he told the patient spider, as soon as he had regained his former position. 'I feel it in my bones. Merchants and princesses are vying for my service and fighting for my rights. The worst is over, my friend. Tomorrow, or the next day, I'll be heading for fortune and fame!'

Belin, ever the silent sceptic, didn't say a word.

9

J ACOM CERRI REMOVED his swordbelt and sank down gratefully
on to the wooden bench that ran around the guardroom wall. It
had once been upholstered with some fibrous substance but the
cushioning had long since been devoured by assiduous pests,
leaving nothing but the rotted wood to support a guardsman's
weary bones. Half an hour remained until the end of the shift,
when the men would be relieved of their posts, but captaincy had
its privileges, and he was not compelled to keep a constant eye on
his loyal watchers.

Alas, he was not to be allowed to enjoy his early retirement from
duty. There was an abrupt knock on the guardroom door, and he
sprang to his feet as it opened.

He was expecting his commanding officer, or some complaining
courtier, but the man who entered was obviously neither of those.
Jacom stared at him blankly for a few seconds, not knowing quite
what it was that made him so hesitant. The other stared at him
equally blankly. Then they realised, with a simultaneous shock of
surprise, that they knew one another.

'Carus Fraxinus!' said Jacom, who was the first to connect the
familiar face with a name. Fraxinus was the merchant to whom his
father sold the greater part of his produce. He had been a regular
visitor to the estate at one time, although he had delegated that
part of his business to his son in recent years.

Fraxinus was every bit as surprised as he was. 'Why,' he said,
'it's Arnal Cerri's boy, isn't it? I remember you when you were just
a babe in arms. So you're a guardsman now – and a captain, too!'

'Yes indeed,' Jacom agreed proudly. He knew that the merchant
must be well aware of the fact that his commission was a purchase
made by an ambitious father who wanted his favourite son to be
something other than a fruit-grower and pig-farmer, but he

nevertheless felt entitled to be proud of his position. He advanced and shook the older man's hand firmly.

'Of course,' said Fraxinus, remembering. 'You had a fencing master when I saw you last, and there were archery targets hanging from the branches of your father's plum trees. What luck! I come in search of a guard-captain, in trepidation as to how I might be received, and I find the son of an old friend.'

'Trepidation?' Jacom echoed dazedly. 'Why trepidation?'

'Because I came to ask a favour, and might have been rudely sent packing – not, of course, that I expect any favours from you because I know your father, but I dare to be confident that if you find it necessary to send me packing you'll do so politely and bear no grudge.'

'What favour?' Jacom asked, aware that he was being subtly flattered, and equally aware of his own susceptibility.

'I've just come from the prison,' Fraxinus said. 'Don't look so astonished, I beg you. I came to visit a prisoner – a man who might be of considerable use to me if I could secure his services. I wanted to pay his fine in return for his entering my employ, but he has had another offer from within the citadel, and the matter now seems much more complicated than it did before. It may be that I shall have to prove him innocent in order to get what I need from him. I wondered if perchance the guard-captain or one of his men might have useful information. The prisoner in question is the exceptionally tall man who looks like a darklander – do you perhaps know who arrested him?'

Jacom felt a dreadful sinking sensation. He needed to sit down, but didn't feel able to do so until he had invited Fraxinus to do so too – after which he seemed to have admitted the man entirely into his confidence, in spite of the fact that he didn't want to tell him anything that might make trouble for his men or himself.

'You mean Myrasol – the northerner,' Jacom said cautiously, when they were both settled on the hard bench.

'Do you know him?'

'It was my men who arrested him, and one of my men whose leg was broken in the fight which occasioned the arrest.'

'Ah!' said the merchant, immediately seeing his difficulty. 'I didn't realise that. When I spoke of his innocence, I didn't necessarily mean to imply that he actually *is* innocent. It simply seemed to be a possible avenue of exploration.'

'Of course,' said Jacom tepidly. 'As it happens, there is some doubt about it. He may well have been falsely accused by the other witnesses. The injured man wasn't well enough to testify, and neither I nor my sergeant saw the blow struck. But I'm not sure you'd be able to obtain more honest testimony than was offered to the magistrate – and in any case, wouldn't it be simpler to buy the man out than to drag the case back into court?'

'Perhaps,' Fraxinus agreed. 'At least, it would be, if Myrasol hadn't applied for a royal pardon and the Princess Lucrezia hadn't offered to get it for him.'

'Princess Lucrezia?' Jacom echoed, not trying to conceal his astonishment. 'What would she want with the amber? Male servants aren't allowed in the Sanctum, and even if they were . . .'

'I don't know,' Fraxinus said. 'I'll have to ask my associate Hyry Keshvara – she knows Lucrezia well, and she might have said something to spark the princess's interest. I *hope* the princess wants him for the same reason I do – to draw a map – but there's another possibility which . . . well, let's just say that I'd far rather she was interested in his mapmaking skills. If you happen to hear anything, I'd be grateful if you'd let me know.'

'Why should you be interested in a northern mapmaker?' Jacom asked. 'Xandrian sailormen are the only ones who know how to find their way around the Slithery Sea and its shores.'

'It's a long story,' Fraxinus said. 'Was there an old story-teller present when you arrested the amber? A blind man?'

'Yes. He was knocked out but he recovered quickly enough. What happened to him after that I don't know.'

'Had you seen him before? Do you know his name?'

'No – but he wouldn't be any use as a witness. He really was blind – it wasn't an act put on for the sake of sympathy.'

'I've another reason for being interested in him, too. I dare say there've always been story-tellers in Xandria avid to recite the *Apocrypha of Genesys* for the price of a jug of wine, and it's perfectly probable that the northern mapmakers disembark from foreign ships four or five times a year, but until now there hasn't been the slightest reason for anyone to take an interest, so I haven't. Isn't it always the way that as soon as you find out that you need something, it becomes frustratingly difficult to find? Such is life.'

'Always the way,' Jacom echoed unenthusiastically. He wondered how much trouble he might be in if the amber *were* able to prove his innocence with Fraxinus's help. Sergeant Purkin certainly wouldn't be pleased if – or when – he found out what was going on.

Fraxinus smiled, warmly enough but just a trifle wanly. 'Should you discover anything,' he said, 'I'd be most obliged if you could send a messenger – of course, if you'd be able to come yourself, I'd be very happy to open a bottle of fresh Khalornian wine so that we could enjoy ourselves a little. I'd be glad to hear news of your father and his neighbours. My son Xury will be returning from his travels in three or four days – he'll doubtless be pleased to see you, and I dare say that you'll feel much more at ease in the company of someone your own age than you can in the company of an old man like me – but if you learn anything that might interest me, please call before then. The house is on the seaward side of Torc Hill. Anyone in the neighbourhood will point you in the right direction – everyone knows me thereabouts. I really would be grateful – anything at all.'

Although he nodded in response to the invitation, Jacom felt that it might be better were he to be unable to accept it, at least for a little while. On the other hand, he knew perfectly well that there was one item of information which Fraxinus might be very glad to have. After a brief struggle, his conscience pressured him into spitting it out.

'There *was* another man nearby when Herriman was hurt,' he said slowly. 'A man named Burdam Thrid. He might have been the man responsible. I believe he works for a man named Checuti.'

'Does he indeed?' said Fraxinus.

'Everyone knows him, too, so I hear. Checuti, I mean.'

'Oh yes,' Fraxinus confirmed. 'Everybody knows Checuti, at least by reputation. Whereas my reputation works to my benefit, however, his will one day ensure his damnation. It really doesn't do to get a reputation as a prince of thieves – it's the kiss of death to a productive career. If he has any sense he'll get out of Xandria while the going's good. I must admit that I rather like him, and I can't help wishing that he'd turn his cleverness to less dubious ends. I was going to send a message to him anyway, to enquire after some relative of Myrasol's. I'll ask him about Thrid – delicately, of course. Thanks for the suggestion.'

'You're welcome,' said Jacom dolefully. An uncomfortable feeling that he needed to justify himself made him add: 'When one of my men gets hurt in a brawl, I like to see justice done and the true offender punished. I really don't have anything against the amber.'

Fraxinus raised a quizzical eyebrow. 'Of course not,' he said politely. 'Should I find out anything further, I will of course be very glad to share the information. Do come to my house, even if you don't have any news for me. It really would be pleasant to see you there. Don't leave it too long. I expect to be setting out on a long journey in the not too distant future, and I might be away for a long time.'

'That's why you need a mapmaker, no doubt,' Jacom observed, to prove that he had his wits about him.

'It is,' Fraxinus confirmed. 'We'll need a few fighting men too. Aulakh Phar will hire us a dozen darklanders, but it certainly wouldn't hurt if I could recruit a few extra men of Myrasol's impressive stature. If your sergeant knows any ex-guardsmen who are finding civilian life too dull tell him to suggest that they get in touch with me.'

'Where are you headed?' Jacom asked curiously.

'Across the Dragomite Hills and the Soursweet Marshes, to the legendary Pool of Life.'

'The Dragomite Hills are impassable,' Jacom said. 'Everybody knows that.'

'They always have been,' Fraxinus admitted. 'But it seems that some mysterious blight has starved all but a few of the dragomites, and the few that are left are too busy tearing one another apart to attack travellers. The southern limit of the empire is a limit no longer – at least until the mounds recover from the catastrophe. I never could resist a window of opportunity, Jacom – and life has become so very tedious since Xury took over all the hard work. I feel the need for one last adventure, and I'd like it to be the greatest of them all. Perhaps I ought to petition Belin for a company of guardsmen, on the grounds that the breach in the hills might have political implications. How would you like to visit all those places of which the *Lore of Genesys* speaks so enigmatically?'

Jacom was not the kind of man to place much credence in ancient myths, and he had heard all the familiar horror stories about the monstrously unearthly dragomites which had filled a vast swathe of territory with their castellate mounds. Nevertheless, he felt compelled to say: 'I wish I *could* come with you, but . . .' He left the sentence hanging because he didn't know how to finish it.

The merchant got up to leave just as the first of Jacom's men were returning from the shift, complaining in their usual ritual fashion about anything and everything. They stared after the merchant as he left, and Sergeant Purkin darted an insolently inquisitive glance in Jacom's direction.

'He's an old friend of the family,' Jacom said defensively. 'I've known him since I was a child.'

'I guess you need connections like that to become a captain,' the sergeant replied, in a carefully neutral voice. 'Still, they do say that he's the only honest man in Xandria.' The tone of his voice suggested that this was not a wholehearted compliment.

IO

B Y THE TIME Lucrezia left the Inner Sanctum it was the twenty-
eighth hour. The stars were shining brightly, illuminating the
worn stones of the courtyard but leaving the coverts and cloisters
which hugged the citadel walls in deep shadow. There were lights
in the stables and in the coinery, but the route which took her to
the place appointed for her audience with the king passed through
several unlit corridors. Because the meeting was to be in Belin's
private quarters rather than the throne room – which he usually
employed for all formally requested audiences, including those
with his wives and children – the latter part of the route was
unfamiliar to her, but Lucrezia refused to allow herself the least
feeling of discomfiture. She was an adult now, and her anxiety to
see the world beyond the world far outweighed the childish unease
of setting foot where she had never been before.

Lucrezia kept in step with the servant sent to summon her,
refusing to allow the woman to go ahead. Dhalla marched behind,
a patient and indomitable guardian. As they approached their
destination Lucrezia composed herself, reminding herself sternly
that she must not show the least hint of displeasure regarding the
time Belin had made her wait for the appointment. It was part of
the art and craft of kingship to make everyone wait; that applied
even to sons, let alone daughters.

When she stepped into the chamber, however, she could not
entirely supress her surprise at its bareness and its narrowness. She
had never before seen her father in a room that was not large and
lavishly ornamented. The throne room was commodious enough
to hold a crowd of several hundred people, its great vaulted ceiling
supported by awesome and intricately carved pillars. The throne
itself was a massive construction, and the king always sat upon it
in ceremonial garb. This room was no bigger than her own

bedroom, and the hangings which concealed its windowless walls were quite plain. The ceiling was so low that Dhalla could not stand upright. She had to squat down, in what seemed an uncomfortable and undignified position.

King Belin was reclining on a couch, reading a book by the uncommonly bright light of a tall but slender lamp. There was a low table by the couch, where there was a jug of wine and a single goblet, and three bowls of sweets, but nothing else. The king was dressed in a loose-fitting shirt and slack britches, almost as if he were an artisan. He seemed much smaller than he usually did, and the glaring lamplight showed every wrinkle in his aged face.

There was nowhere for Lucrezia to sit, so she stood. She was forced to look down at her father, but if he was trying to seem like something other than a king he did not succeed. There was a bleak hardness in his eye which Lucrezia recognised and understood. She knew full well that whatever her father was, and however he might be dressed, he was the centre of an unimaginable vast web of authority and intrigue, which extended throughout the Thousand Isles, into every port on the southern shore of the Slithery Sea, and as far south as the province of Khalorn. He was the heart and foundation-stone of the political entity which the forefathers had declared impossible. 'In this world,' Goran was reputed to have said, 'there can be no empires, and the community of men which is their strength and their glory must be preserved in other ways.' To which the ministers of Xandria were wont to add, pridefully: 'Except in Xandria, which has its own strength, and its own glory.'

'Are you well, daughter?' Belin enquired, softly, as the servant withdrew.

'Yes, thank you, majesty,' Lucrezia replied. She did not ask how the king was. The king was always well – protocol demanded that such things be taken for granted.

Belin closed his book and laid it down on the table, carefully. Lucrezia could see that it was a very old book, perhaps eight or even ten years old. The binding had been expensive, but was thoroughly rotten now. The ink on the discoloured pages would almost certainly be blurred. She wondered what point he was making by exhibiting such a wreck. Xandria had by far the greatest library in the known world – almost a thousand volumes – which employed a hundred scriveners, half of them fully occupied in copying. The strength and glory of Xandria was by no means limited to the mighty walls which enclosed city and citadel alike. Was Belin trying to imply that the empire itself was old, as direly in need of refreshment as the coins which the metallurgists were working so hard to re-cast in time for the Day of Thanksgiving? Was all this intended to inform her, subtly, that now was not a good time to plague the king with petitions?

Belin leaned forward to fill his cup and swallow a sweet. When he moved, the looseness of his shirt was inadequate to conceal the protrusion of his belly. He didn't offer the bowl or the jug to her, nor was there any other gesture of intimacy. These days, Ereleth had told her, the king did not like to be touched or approached too closely, being wont to complain that it was bad enough being public property without being handled too. According to his dutiful witch-wife, Belin had long ceased to take any pleasure in the fact of being a king; like any common man he had come to take all the advantages of his station for granted while chafing against all its constraints.

'You grow handsome,' Belin observed. 'You have the look of your mother when first I saw her — but you never knew your mother, did you?'

'No, majesty,' Lucrezia replied, wishing that he would get on with the business in hand. It was bad enough being forced to wait for days in the Sanctum, without facing further delay now.

'They said she had Serpent's blood in her. Did you know that?'

'Yes, majesty.'

'Nonsense, of course. Actual Serpents, according to the few men I've spoken to who've encountered them, are a dull lot. I prefer the ones which feature in fanciful folktales like those the darklanders tell. Darklander legend has it that some female Serpents are capable of metamorphosis into preternaturally lovely human-like creatures, in which guise they seduce hapless human males, whom they devour long before they give birth to the unnatural offspring thus conceived. You're supposed to be the remote descendant of some such creature. To the darklanders, you're a kind of demon. Did you know that?'

'Yes, majesty — but Hyry Keshvara says that the darklanders aren't as primitive or as stupid as most Xandrians think.'

'Who is this Keshvara?' Belin asked lazily — as Lucrezia had intended.

'She's the trader who brought me the seeds from the Navel of the World – the ones which are supposed to produce the most powerful poison known to man. That's why I need the amber, majesty. If I can't find a man strong enough to support the bush until it flowers, Xandria will not have the benefit of that treasure.'

'Your garden is over-full of poisons, daughter,' Belin said, with a deliberate sigh. 'I fear that Ereleth has become too determined a teacher, and you too apt a pupil. Witchcraft is supposed to be a healing art, not a murderous one. A witch-wife's true function is to protect her husband from the malice of others.'

'Has Ereleth not served you well, majesty?' Lucrezia asked, with no more than the slightest hint of sarcasm.

'She has,' Belin said gently. 'I dare say that she will continue to do so. But it is time for her to find a new apprentice.' He held up his hand before she could speak, and went on: 'I know your education is not yet complete, but the state of the world is such that nine men in ten never reach full command of their Arts before they must apply them to the vulgar business of living, and royalty has no exemption from that rule. There is a certain sector of the Thousand Islands which is becoming troublesome, and I need a new link in the great chain of obligation and affection. I need to place trusted agents and ministers in Shaminzara, and their arrival must be welcomed rather than resented. Were they to travel in the retinue of a princess of the realm destined for marriage to the prince of the island they'd have a sound basis for the execution of their duties.'

'I am not ready for marriage, majesty,' Lucrezia objected, knowing even as she said it that she ought not be quite so forthright. 'A half-formed princess is a blunt instrument in the game of diplomacy. A half-trained witch-wife would be an inefficient shield for her husband.'

'Witchery is like any other lore,' the king informed her coldly. 'All knowledge is a mere heap of memorised facts unless and until it can be ordered by practice. You have been closeted long enough, my little lamia. Xandria has an adequate supply of poisons and poisoners. Some seeds grow and others don't – that's life. Necessity, little peach, is the mother of improvisation. You will be witch-wife enough for Shaminzara – and should you ever be widowed, you'll return to Xandria a far sharper instrument than before.'

Lucrezia inferred from this remark that her duty as a witch-wife might in this instance be murderous rather than protective, but that did not affect her resolve. 'I am, of course, utterly obedient to your will, majesty,' she said, 'but I wonder if your advisors have properly judged the significance of the things which Hyry Keshvara has brought back from the far south. She believes that there is now a way to cross the land of the Dragomites which lies beyond the darklands. If so, regions which are no more distant than the isle of Shaminzara but which are utterly unknown to any man in Xandria are now accessible. To Keshvara, who is a trader, this seems an opportunity – but the king's advisors surely ought to consider the possibility that there might be danger.'

'To Xandria?'

'To the southern provinces. The way through the Dragomite Hills, if it exists, was not found by the men of Khalorn, majesty, nor by the darkland savages. It was found by bronze men from beyond the Soursweet Marshes: bold adventurers who took care to bring proof of the strangeness of the lands from which they had come. Keshvara's reaction was enthusiastic, and the expedition which she and others are mounting is motivated by curiosity and greed – but has she paused to ask *why* she was given these proofs? Has she paused to wonder what motive the men from the far south have for sending such tokens to Xandria?'

'All very well, daughter – but what has this to do with the future queen of Shaminzara? I dare say that my ministers will take an interest in Carus Fraxinus's expedition. Trade is the lifeblood of the empire, and we are ever enthusiastic to assist its expansion. Our very best agents are our merchants. But none of this is your concern, and the fact that Keshvara brought her strange seeds to the Inner Sanctum – knowing, I don't doubt, that Ereleth's garden was the one place in Xandria that such a cruel device of torture might be safely and secretly tested – does not make it your business.'

'It is in Xandria's interests that the seeds be properly examined, majesty,' Lucrezia said doggedly. 'Not merely as a source of poisons, nor as a device of torture – in which capacity they seem strangely inefficient – but as a possible weapon of war.' She was improvising as best she could, but having produced this notion out of desperation she immediately became fond of it. Perhaps, she thought, there really was a threat from the far south, not merely to Khalorn but to the rural heartland of Xandria, whose fields fed the mighty city.

'Even so, daughter,' said Belin, mildly but unyieldingly, 'I cannot see that this investigation requires a witch – and if it does, I have a perfectly good witch-wife in Ereleth. I need you to wed the prince of Shaminzara, and that is what you will do, willingly and *gladly*.'

'I need a hundred and thirty days, majesty,' Lucrezia replied, shifting her ground yet again as her last position proved untenable. 'I ask for nothing but time to complete my experiment, and I have found exactly the man I need. He's an amber, but not a darklander. He injured a guardsman in some petty dispute and was sentenced to the wall, but he's petitioned for a royal pardon. He's willing to pledge himself to my service if you will agree to release him to me.'

'Does he know what you intend to do with him, little darling?'

'Of course not, majesty – but the law is the law. Once he's consented, he's consented. The wall won't miss his services; it's stood inviolate for thousands of years. Let me have him, please. If we can bring this last bush to term, it will produce enough new seeds to ensure that Xandria will never lose this treasure. Keshvara could have sold the seeds anywhere, to any one of a thousand curious buyers, but she brought them here, not to Ereleth but to *me*. This is something rare, precious and strange, majesty, and it's mine as well as Xandria's. Give me the foreigner, majesty, and let me see this through.'

'He's a young man, daughter,' Belin observed, indicating for the first time the possibility that he might relent. 'I can't allow a young man to be brought into the Inner Sanctum.'

'His legs will be broken and his balls cut off before he's taken out of his cell, majesty,' Lucrezia assured her father. 'As long as it's done cleanly, by a good surgeon, it won't prevent his bringing the bush to flower.'

'The reason that the great wall of Xandria has endured so long while other empires have fallen into ruin,' Belin told her loftily – almost as though he were practising his speech for the Day of Thanksgiving – 'is that the people of Xandria have laboured tirelessly to maintain its solidity. *Walls rot, but great houses may abide,* as the proverb has it. There's great wisdom in proverbs, snakeling, despite that they aren't part of some sacred lore packed away into the memory of Artists and Magicians. The wisdom that everybody has to know is the greatest wisdom of all, and what that wisdom says is that a city must protect its walls as ardently as a man guards his skin. *Rare* and *strange* and *precious* are fine words, daughter mine, but *common* and *ordinary* and *useful* are finer still, to those who know the true worth of things.

'The great majority of men and women live in the everyday world, not in exotic enclosures, and everything which affects their well-being is familiar to them. Thorny bushes which grow in human flesh and produce venomous flowers might fascinate and horrify them for a fleeting moment of idle self-indulgence, but the wall which surrounds their city and preserves their civilisation is of the most urgent relevance forty hours a day, five hundred and fifty days a year – except for leap years, when there's a five hunded and fifty-first day, throughout which the wall still retains its urgent relevance. If there's ever a choice between giving a man to the stonemasons and giving him to an inquisitive witch, the wise king will always give him to the stonemasons, at least until the day comes when he can no longer lift a block or fill a mould.'

It was obvious to Lucrezia that no argument she could launch would be allowed to prevail – and yet, the very fact that her father was devoting so much time to this interview, and bothering to make lengthy speeches instead of handing down abrupt commands, implied that she was going to get at least some of what she wanted.

It dawned on her that her petition would be granted, but in such a way that she would be required to be exceedingly grateful. She suddenly understood the nature of the game she was being forced to play. On the one hand, she knew a measure of relief that she would get what she so ardently desired, but on the other, she felt seething resentment about the way in which it was being done. She hated being manipulated and manoeuvred in this fashion.

'Only give me the man I need, father,' she said sharply, deliberately setting protocol aside as a sop to her own wounded pride. 'Make me a gift of him, for the Day of Thanksgiving or in celebration of my betrothal to the prince of Shaminzara. Only give me time to see this matter through to its end, and I'll go to the end of the world thereafter, if you wish it, for Xandria's sake. I'll go *gladly,* if that is what will please your majesty.'

Belin condescended to smile. 'Your mother had a tongue like that,' he told her. 'Quick and clever, but forked. In those silly nations where even the highest of men have but one wife, a man might be seduced and strangled by a tongue like that – but this is Xandria, where a king is a king and a wife but one of thirty-and-one . . . and a daughter, for all her charm and artistry, is a mere instrument of diplomacy. I need your loyalty, my child, if not your love. If I let you have this man, it will not be a gift, for you and I are above such things. We are royal folk, who neither offer gifts nor barter favours. We are honourable folk who recognise far greater dimensions of debt. Do you understand what I am saying, little darling? Do you understand what it will mean if I send this man to your garden instead of the wall?'

It was always *little* darling, she noted, or *little* peach. In a silly, paradoxical way, she wished that she could now say no, or say yes without being able to mean it, but she did understand what she was required to understand. A year ago, she might not have been able to follow the chain of thought, but she was grown now; she had a mature brain as well as mature breasts.

'Yes, majesty,' she said meekly. 'I know what this means.'

Privately, with calculated childishness, she added in silent thought: *Perhaps I know better than you do, you fat old sot. You had but one teacher and I have had a hundred. Every sad, bored wife in the inmost tower understands her situation, because they have nothing else to do with their time and their wit but understand. If Xandria is indeed the oldest nation in the world it is not because it has a clever king who has thirty-and-one wives, but because it has thirty-and-one clever queens who have but a single king to distract them.*

All this was mere bravado, but it made her feel better to formulate the secret declaration.

'I shall send an ambassador to the prince of Shaminzara,' Belin announced. 'I think you might like the prince, and he will certainly like you, for the firmness of your flesh and that cunning snaky sheen you have learned to impose on the liquid gold of your hide. A Serpent's granddaughter for a scion of the Slithery Sea – a rare, precious and propitious union.

'In the meantime, you may have your darkland brawler, as skilfully castrated and broken in the limbs as the best of my surgeons can contrive . . . for just as long as you need him, and not a day longer.'

'Thank you, majesty,' she said insincerely. She couldn't help feeling that she had been cheated – by her father, her birth, her sex and the way of the world.

How wonderful it must be to be as free as Hyry Keshvara, she thought. *How proud one must be of honest bargains freely struck. How delightful to have a future unconfined by destiny and royal command.*

It was good to be out in the corridor again, where even a giantess could stand upright without bumping her head on a ceiling set too low.

11

SOMEWHAT TO ANDRIS'S disappointment, no word from Princess Lucrezia arrived on the day following his meeting with the merchant – nor, indeed, the day after that. Nor had any message come from Carus Fraxinus by the time night fell on the eve of the Day of Thanksgiving.

'I realise that things move very slowly in these tropic lands,' he confided to Belin the spider, who sat patiently in the corner of his – or her – reconstituted web, 'but I would have appreciated it had someone managed to secure my release before the holiday. Not that I could afford to celebrate in an appropriate style, but it would be nice to have something to give thanks for on the Day of Thanksgiving. If I were the worrying kind of man – which, on occasion, I am disposed to be – I might begin to suspect that something might have gone wrong.'

What could possibly go wrong? he imagined the spider asking.

'Good question,' he replied. 'Princess Lucrezia surely ought to be in a position to get her own way, and even the greatest of kings must be inclined towards granting petitions at Thanksgiving, however little credence they may put in the legend of the ship that sailed the infinite void or the precise date of our ancestors' arrival in the world. Even if she were to fail, the merchant seemed like a very capable kind of fellow – the sort who would make things happen, once he put his mind to it. He really did seem to think that I might be valuable . . . a prize worth going to some trouble for.'

Beware of delusions of grandeur, my huge friend counselled the cynical spider, as characterised by Andris's overactive imagination.

'I fear, my minuscule companion,' he answered mournfully, 'that I gave those up a long time ago, in spite of the fact that there's no delusion about my being a prince in exile. Grandeur is something I carry in my bones, but I no longer expect it to affect my treatment by the world. Do spiders celebrate the Day of Thanksgiving at all? I suppose you must – after all, you're not unearthly, are you? If my ancestors arrived in the world from elsewhere, so did yours – and on the very same day. I suppose you have as much – or as little – reason to be thankful for that as we have.

'Your ancestors must have made their first home in Idun alongside mine, even though they aren't mentioned in the *Lore of Genesys*. They must have been there, quietly spinning their webs about the windows and the gates, listening in when the old story-teller's Serpents and Salamanders came to call. Did my ancestors bring yours on purpose, do you suppose, or did yours just sneak a ride? Maybe the forefathers liked having your kinfolk around rather more than their decendants tend to do. Maybe you were useful for something then, but all we poor sinners have quite forgotten what it was. On the other hand, perhaps they just thought you'd be good company for all the poor fools their decendants would put in jail . . .'

Andris could have continued in this rambling vein for a long time – and, indeed, already had on more than one occasion in response to the pressure that prolonged solitude exerted upon his idle brain – but he was interrupted in full flight by the scraping of the beam which normally covered the spy-hole in the door. He shut up immediately and swung around to face the door.

The beam was not drawn back, but merely lifted for a moment and then replaced. While the spy-hole was uncovered, something small and round was flipped through it by unseen fingers. It plopped softly into the dark corner of the cell.

Andris immediately went down on his hands and knees to search for it, and eventually managed to locate it. He got to his feet again, holding it up to the window to take full advantage of the starlight.

It was a piece of soft parchment, carefully rolled up into a tiny scroll. The material was in such an advanced state of decay that it was difficult to unwrap it without inflicting any further injury, but he took great care while straightening it and finally had it spread out neatly on the windowsill.

It wasn't easy to read what was written on the parchment, but he patiently deciphered the untidily scrawled letters one by one. The ink had been intended for use on a more smoothly waxed surface, but it had not run too badly..

You are in great danger, the missive informed him. *An escape must be arranged. Keep to your cell at all costs. Help is at hand.*

Frustratingly, the only part of the message which had blurred so badly as to be ambiguous was the signature. After considering various possibilities he concluded that the second initial was certainly a Z, and that the remainder might well spell out the name *Zabio,* but that the first name couldn't possibly be *Theo,* beginning as it almost certainly did with an M.

'Now there's a thing,' said Andris to the spider, in a conspiratorial whisper. 'What on earth am I supposed to make of this? Has the shipmaster or the merchant managed to find my uncle, or some descendant of his? If so, why hasn't the person in question simply come to visit me? How is it that I'm in danger, and from whom? Why should I need to escape when I have not one but two people willing to save me from the wall – and how on earth can an escape be contrived without the aid of a small army? Even if I *were* to escape, how could a man of my stature and colouring hope to hide when all the king's horses and all the king's men were sent forth to find me? This is surely not the princess's work . . . but if it's the work of Carus Fraxinus, he's decided to go about things in a very peculiar way.'

Belin had nothing to say.

'No good asking you for advice, is it?' Andris said petulantly. 'You don't even care. You're quite content to stay here, probably imagining that you're as free as a . . . well, freer than any man, anyhow. Not that this is spider paradise, of course – the air's hardly humming with the sound of juicy flies – but it's good enough for you. You're lucky you don't know how fragile and meagre your circumstances are. Some human could come along at any time, suffering from a slight case of arachnophobia or simply a desire to clean up, and *splat!* . . . you're gone, web and all. Still, ignorance is bliss, isn't that what they say?'

Idly, he screwed up the piece of parchment and began rolling it between his warm fingers. Within minutes he had reduced it to a ball of anonymous and uninformative pulp. It could no longer be unrolled, let alone read.

Personally, he had always preferred paper to parchment; it didn't last any longer, but it was cleaner and crisper while it did last and it didn't stink as badly when it rotted down.

'Once,' he told the uncaring spider, 'that was a bit of animal hide. Then it became a medium of communication: a vessel of vital knowledge, as rich as any loreful rhyme. Now it's just crap, like fecal matter. That's the whole human life-story in an allegorical nutshell. We begin life as little parasitic worms; we grow to become the vehicles of sacred lore, carrying it over from generation to generation; and when we've handed on our precious stocks of memory to its destined recipients we become nothing but waste-matter. Like everything else, we begin to decay before we're even born, and the ink of thought and knowledge isn't very well adapted to the glossless parchment of memory and imagination. And yet we must give thanks every year to our beloved forefathers, who brought us out of the vast and empty wilderness of stars, that we might walk again upon a world, rejoicing in the sun, the soil and the silvery sea.

'Don't you wish you were human too, so that you could spin philosophy instead of silken webs?'

It seemed that the spider was no longer listening. Andris couldn't blame the creature; he wasn't really listening to himself. He was distracted by a profound unease, which arose from the suspicion that no one would go to the trouble of sending him a message like the one he had just received unless there was a very good reason. If someone were prepared to take the risk of coming into a prison in order to inform him that he was in danger, in danger he must certainly be . . . and the fact that an escape was supposedly being arranged didn't necessarily mean that the rescue attempt would be successful.

'There's been something very peculiar about this whole affair from the very beginning,' Andris told the spider. 'I should have known that it was all too good to be true, that my luck couldn't really have taken a turn for the better. For six years things have gone steadily from bad to worse, and my life has just about rotted down to pure unadulterated filth. What do princesses and merchants want with a wreck like me? What does *anyone* want with a wreck like me?'

Self-pity, observed Belin, *will get you nowhere. In my*

experience, there are only two kinds of entity in the world – those which build webs and those which get caught in them. You're just one of those who get caught in them. The question is, what are you going to do when the web-spinner comes for its supper?

'One can easily get lost in a maze of spidery metaphors,' Andris countered, dutifully setting self-pity to one side. 'The real question's much simpler than that. The real question is . . . just what the rotting filth is going on here?'

Once he'd framed the question, however, he couldn't help feeling that the spider had indeed framed it rather more elegantly. He didn't bother to wait for the answer that would never come. He sat down on the crude pallet which was all the bedding he had, wondering whether it was safe to go to sleep – or, indeed, whether he *could* go to sleep given the discomfort of his circumstances within and without.

12

J ACOM CAME AS quickly as he could in response to the summons from the jail but he found it impossible to bound up the steps with his customary easy grace. His knees were still rather sore and the unaccustomed hours he had lately been forced to keep had left him an uncomfortable legacy of lost sleep. His first impulse, on entering the jailer's room, was to curse the man for being a nuisance, but he managed to control himself.

Sergeant Purkin was already present, and so was a guardsman named Kristoforo. The latter was standing behind a thin, grey-haired man in his twenties, holding tight to both his arms. The sergeant had a hammer in his right hand, whose lumpen iron head he was thumping suggestively into the palm of his left while the jailer looked on. Jacom closed the guardroom door discreetly behind himself.

'What's the trouble, sergeant?' he asked, eyeing the hammer. The head was badly pitted and rusted, but it was still a serviceable tool. He couldn't imagine, though, that Purkin was contemplating some trivial exercise in carpentry – nor could the prisoner, who was looking distinctly fearful.

'No trouble, sir,' said the sergeant amiably, squatting down beside the prisoner. 'Except that this poor fellow might be about to stub his toe. Funny how a reluctant tongue often has that effect.'

The thin man looked nervously down at the speaker, quivering with terror.

'And why, exactly, should he be in danger of suffering such an uncomfortable effect?' Jacom asked, trying to enter into the spirit of the thing even though he didn't really feel like it.

'Passed an illicit message to one of the prisoners,' Purkin growled. 'Very reluctant to tell us what was in it, or who sent it. In my experience, sir, a crushed toe is far the best method of refreshing a bad memory. If it doesn't work the first time, doubling the dose is usually effective. Not many faulty memories can withstand two crushed toes . . . let alone ten.'

Jacom had to admire the sergeant's gruesomely laconic way with words. To judge by the thin man's face, Purkin's eloquence was not going to waste.

'What's your name?' Jacom barked at the frightened man.

'Seril Sart, sir,' the prisoner replied. 'But I didn't do anything. It's all a mistake.'

'Sart?' Jacom echoed, knowing that he knew the name.

'Brother of the man we caught in the grounds last night but one,' Purkin supplied helpfully.

'Oh,' said Jacom. 'You mean he's here.'

'Yes sir,' said the jailer. 'Convicted of trespass, fined thirty crowns. Elected to stay in jail while his family attempted to raise the money. His brother supposedly came to give him the news.'

'What's illicit about that?' Jacom asked, wondering if he had missed something.

'Nothing, sir,' said the jailer. 'But being a dutiful man, sir, I kept a surreptitious eye on him anyway, just in case. He didn't know I was watching him. Whipped up the top bar on Myrasol's cell he did, sir, and threw something in. Quick as a flash he was, sir, but I saw 'im all right.'

'Search the cell if you want to,' Seril Sart said nervously. 'You won't find anything.'

'No, we won't,' the jailer agreed. 'The message was probably written on old parchment, easily pulped as soon as read. Standard method – people take us for fools, you know, think we don't know what goes on. Only way to find out what was in it's to persuade 'im to tell us.'

'Myrasol's the big amber, isn't he?' Jacom said, although he knew perfectly well who Myrasol was. 'The one that . . . the one that's not a darklander.' He had been about to say 'The one that isn't guilty' but caught himself just in time.

'Yes sir,' said Purkin promptly. 'I always knew there was somethin' funny about that one. He's into somethin', sir – him an' Sart both. Somethin's goin' on, sir, and we're only one or two stubbed toes away from findin' out what.'

'I d-don't . . .' the thin man began, but interrupted himself with a terrific howl of pain. Kristoforo gripped him even harder, and held him in place as he tried to hop away.

'Get up, Purkin,' Jacom said tiredly. 'The poor chap might hurt himself if he trips over you again.'

'That was nothin', sir,' said the sergeant, weighing the hammer carefully in his right hand as he brought himself upright. 'Won't even leave a bruise. He ought to be careful, though. Next time, he might really hurt himself.'

'That's against the law,' Seril Sart gasped. 'This is a civilised country. There are laws . . . and lawyers. If you think I've done somethin' wrong you should charge me, lay your evidence before a court.'

'We're the king's guard,' Jacom assured the man solicitously. 'We wouldn't do anything that was against the law. Unlike you, apparently. What did the message say, Seril, and who paid you to bring it in? I don't suppose you did it out of the goodness of your heart, did you?'

'Unless, of course, you and your brother and the amber are all in this together,' Purkin suggested. 'Maybe that was why your brother was lurking around the citadel two nights ago – planning a jailbreak.'

'I don't know any ambers!' Seril Sart was quick to say. 'Zadok got shut in by accident. It's all a mistake!'

Purkin crouched down again.

Jacom put on his best predatory smile. 'Look at it this way, Seril,' he said. 'You don't have any interest in Andris Myrasol. The only reason you brought in that message was that somebody made a contribution to the fund you're trying to put together to secure your brother's release. We don't blame you for that – and we're not particularly interested in taking advantage of what we know to make it more difficult for you to get your brother out, despicable thief though he may be. All we ask of you is that you stop stubbing your toe. Now, who gave you the message?'

The thin man hesitated, but as soon as Purkin's hand moved he decided that discretion was the better part of valour. 'A g-girl,' he said, so hurriedly that he developed a distinct stammer. 'Eight maybe ten. N-never saw 'er before. Don't know her name, 'onest.' He looked down fearfully as he spoke the last sentence but Jacom suspected that if this were the truth it certainly wasn't the whole truth.

'I need more,' Jacom said. 'Tell me more.'

'I d-d— . . . she was tall . . . t-taller than me. Mannish clothes, not dirty but well-worn. Looked like a p-pirate, or m-m-maybe a smuggler.'

Jacom made a small sound of disgust. 'What's that supposed to mean?' he said – and then realised what it might mean. 'She wasn't an amber, by any chance?'

'N-not exactly,' the thin man said, as doubt caught him up. 'Not amber – but not pure g-g-gold, mind. If she'd d-darklander in 'er it was only a quarter. She warn't inlander, though. Islander or sailorman. C-could've had amber in 'er . . . certainly c-c-could've.'

'What was the message?' Jacom said quietly, tiring of the man's panic-stricken rambling.

'I d-don't . . .' Purkin raised his arm again, but he didn't have a chance to bring it down. Jacom neatly plucked the hammer out of the sergeant's hand. He was warming to his task now, and suddenly saw an opportunity to make an impression on his men.

'Don't do that, sergeant,' he said silkily. 'I know a better way to cure bad memories.'

'You do, sir?' said Purkin interestedly. It was difficult to tell whether the tone of his voice signified honest curiosity or whether he was simply trying to play his part in the pantomime.

Jacom gave the hammer back to Purkin as the sergeant stood up, and stepped past Seril Sart, brushing Kristoforo's hands away with a casual sweep of his wrist. As the guardsman stepped back, Jacom took his place. Carefully, he removed a handkerchief from his pouch and reached around to stuff it in Sart's mouth. 'Hold that in place, will you?' he said to Kristoforo. The guardsman obliged in time to stop the prisoner mumbling an objection.

'Tell me, sergeant,' said Jacom, as he took Sart's right hand in his own, and placed his left on the prisoner's shoulder. 'Have you ever seen this method of treatment?' He took a firm grip on the middle finger of Sart's hand, and twisted it in the very precise manner which he had learned from his tutor in the Arts Martial.

It was difficult to judge the exact extent of Sart's agony because the precautionary muffler stifled his scream, but Jacom noted the approving glint in Purkin's eyes.

'Interestin', that, sir,' said Purkin agreeably, as Jacom released the arm, stood the prisoner back on his feet and recovered his handkerchief. 'I've seen it done, sir, but never learned the trick of it myself. Leaves no marks, I hear, but positively excruciatin' to experience. I don't suppose you could show me again, sir – so I can try to get the hang of it, like?'

'That depends, sergeant,' Jacom said. Then he suddenly moved to transfix Sart's gaze with his own. 'Don't try to tell me that you can't read, Seril,' he said wolfishly, 'and don't try to tell me that because you were strictly forbidden to read it you daren't even look. What did the message say, Seril? Word for word, now.'

Seril Sart was no hero, and he had taken more than enough punishment for one day. 'G-g-great danger,' he ground out, through teeth clenched against the pain. 'Escape arranged. Stay p-p-put. Signed with a name begins with a z-zed. That's all, 'onest.'

This time, Jacom was inclined to believe him.

'Doesn't make sense,' opined the jailer. 'Mongrel's got people queuing up to buy him out all legal. What'd he want to escape for – even if he could?'

Jacom signalled to the jailer to be quiet.

'Thank you, Seril,' he said. 'That's all we wanted to know. You can go home now, if you want to. If anyone asks about the message, you'd be well advised to tell them you delivered it safely, and that no one was any the wiser. If you don't tell them that, I might not be pleased to see you the next time we meet. That's only one of a dozen little tricks I know, and I'd be glad of the opportunity to test the other eleven. Practice makes perfect, isn't that what they say?'

Seril Sart nodded, perhaps to confirm that that was, indeed, what they said.

Jacom watched the thin man make his exit.

'Shouldn't we have held on to him, sir?' asked the sergeant, in a pleasantly respectful tone.

'No,' said Jacom thoughtfully. This, he was sure, was a chance to get his nascent career back on the right track. 'We'd never get to the bottom of it that way. If there really is an escape planned, the sensible thing for us to do is to arrange for it to go awry. That way, we catch the would-be rescuers instead of their messenger. He must be just a messenger, don't you think?'

'But it still doesn't make sense,' the jailer complained yet again. 'The amber's as good as out. If the king won't give him to the princess, your friend Fraxinus'll buy him out.'

Jacom was uncomfortably aware of the sergeant's curious gaze studying his face. Purkin was obviously wondering whether Carus Fraxinus was behind this, but wasn't entirely sure whether it was safe to say so. Jacom, on the other hand, was wondering whether he ought to tell Fraxinus that someone seemingly had plans to liberate his precious mapmaker before anyone had the chance to get him out legally. Why, Jacom asked himself, were northern mapmakers suddenly in such demand?

'It seems that a competition is developing to claim the services of our unlucky vagabond,' he said carefully. 'When he was in court, he said he'd come to Xandria in search of a kinsman of his, by the name of Zabio. Sart's message was signed with a name beginning with a zed.'

'He wrote a letter to a shipmaster asking after a man of that name,' the jailer put in, and was swift to add: 'A legal letter, that is.'

'Perhaps this was his reply,' Jacom said. 'Carus Fraxinus is an honest man, who's exploring honest ways to take the mapmaker into his service . . . if Seril Sart is right in thinking that he was hired by a pirate lass, it's possible that this Zabio fellow is a very different sackful of prunes.'

'And that the amber isn't what he claims to be, irrespective of whether or not he clouted Herriman,' Purkin put in significantly.

'I think we ought to set a trap, sergeant,' said Jacom, who saw in this affair a golden opportunity to put the seal on his reputation, and perhaps to increase his standing in the eyes of Carus Fraxinus too. 'I think we ought to employ a full measure of cunning in getting to the bottom of this – not to mention doing the amber a favour by saving him from getting any deeper in trouble than he already is.'

Sergeant Purkin condescended to laugh at that.

'When was the last time anyone succeeded in escaping from the jail?' Jacom asked the jailer.

'Before my time,' the jailer replied stiffly. 'Twenty or thirty years, at least. Every wall and every door's solid – I'd stake my life on that. You couldn't tunnel out with a sack full of grinderworms, and he hasn't got so much as a hairpin in there. Strikes me that his friends don't have a clue about what they're letting themselves in for. *Foreigners!*'

'In that case,' Jacom said, 'I think we'll let them have a go, don't you? It might even be tonight. They probably think we'll be too busy with other matters, with the big holiday tomorrow. We'll keep a close eye on the place until they arrive, let them in . . . and stop them on the way out. Maybe we'll even have time to twist an arm or two in the interests of finding out what in corrosion's name they're playing at.'

'Suits me,' grunted the jailer. 'Done my bit. Down to you now.'

'We'll take care of it,' Jacom assured him. 'You can depend on that.'

13

IT WAS DIFFICULT to estimate Hyry Keshvara's age. Lucrezia judged that she must be at least eighteen, but she seemed amazingly fit and wiry for a woman of that age. The women of the Inner Sanctum mostly grew fat before they turned fifteen, and even those who didn't were soft, like pillows filled with featherfoam. Keshvara was by no means thin, but her flesh looked hard – harder even than Dhalla's. Lucrezia had only once had occasion to touch the older woman's arm, but she remembered vividly that she had never felt muscles so taut and flesh so firm. She imagined that the best of the king's guardsmen would feel very similar – not those like the young officer who paused to watch her from the wall while she worked in the garden, but the old veterans who had seen action in the last of the westland wars. Keshvara was surely a veteran of sorts herself – but Lucrezia had never before seen her as troubled or as hesitant as she now was, and the princess was dismayed by the sight.

Lucrezia had often urged Keshvara to visit her more frequently, but until this evening the trader had never come to see her without goods to offer for sale. When Keshvara had something to sell, she was a paragon of all the conversational virtues – polite, charming, witty and completely at ease with herself, even in the company of royalty – but she was different now. She had refused food, and she was sipping her wine in a cautious manner that might almost have been insulting, given the princess's reputation. Her gaze was moving restlessly from side to side, as though she were reluctant to look Lucrezia squarely in the eye.

Lucrezia wished that she could put the older woman at her ease. She wished she could tell her that out of all the people she knew, she envied none but Hyry Keshvara, no matter that the other women of the Sanctum – except perhaps Ereleth – would have despised her on sight. She wished she could explain that although the great majority of the queens and princesses, and even the higher-ranking servants, measured their peers according to their beauty – envying the slenderness of a waist or the curve of a breast while feeling fully entitled to sneer at a hank of grey hair or a callused hand – she, Lucrezia, was different. Alas, politeness as well as protocol forbade her to say any such thing. There was simply no diplomatic way to inform someone generally considered plain that it really did not matter that a woman had narrow eyes, a lumpen nose and hairy arms, provided that the sights those eyes had seen, the odours the nose had smelt and the objects those arms had reached out for were worthwhile.

Lucrezia studied the scar which scored Keshvara's neck and disappeared beneath the collar of her masculine blouse, where she had been caught by the teeth of a crocolid. She even envied the woman that, but knew how absurd it would be to say so. She was disappointed to discover that Hyry was capable of an altogether feminine confusion and trepidation, but she was doubly disappointed in herself for not being able to dispel that anxiety. When she groped for words, the best she could come up with was a leaden 'Are you well?' and even that came out in a formal tone quite unsuited to the asking of a sincere question.

'Yes, highness,' the trader replied. 'Very well indeed, I assure you.'

'I'm flattered that you found the time to come to see me,' Lucrezia said, trying to make up for the awkward start. 'You must be very busy with preparations for your new expedition into the southlands.'

Keshvara seemed taken aback by that observation, and her narrow eyes narrowed further, as if she were wondering whether the princess might be mocking her. 'I'm making ready for the journey,' she admitted. 'Carus Fraxinus wants me to go ahead, so I'll be setting out for Khalorn tomorrow or the day after.'

'So soon!' said Lucrezia, in mild surprise. 'I'd hoped that you'd remain here to see the culmination of our experiment.'

The trader bowed her head shamefacedly. 'Fraxinus has received news from Aulakh Phar in Khalorn,' she said. 'Phar urges us to make all possible haste – there's trouble stirring in the darklands, it seems. All kinds of strange rumours are spreading through the forest. Fraxinus thought it best to bring forward all our plans. In fact, highness, it was Fraxinus who asked me to come here tonight, to ask a small favour of you.'

'A favour!' the princess exclaimed, with a small thrill of delight. If Keshvara felt able to come here asking favours, no matter how small, that surely signified that there was more to their relationship than mere commerce. 'You have only to ask,' she added recklessly, 'and I will do whatever I can.'

Hyry Keshvara nodded, but there was no evident diminution in her uncertainty. 'It's about the tall amber who's presently held in your father's jail,' she said. 'He told Fraxinus that you had offered to secure a pardon for him if he would pledge himself to your service.'

Lucrezia tried hard to conceal her shock. 'What of it?' she said evenly.

'Do you, perchance, intend to feed him the third of the seeds I brought back from my last expedition?'

'I do,' Lucrezia said. 'It seems to me that he will make a perfect host, and my father has said that I may have him the day after Thanksgiving, although I had to strike a bargain of sorts to get him.'

Hyry's lips were very tight; it was plain that this was the answer she had anticipated – and, for some reason, feared.

'Why do you ask?' Lucrezia added. 'What has the northerner to do with you – or with Carus Fraxinus?'

'I know it's not my place to say this, highness,' Keshvara said haltingly, 'but I wish that you might see your way clear to finding a different host. Carus Fraxinus would like to buy the amber out himself.'

Lucrezia made every effort to remain calm, and to be seen to remain calm, although this request caused her some distress. 'I fear,' she said, as mildly as she could, 'that I've gone to a certain amount of trouble to secure the man's services. I've made promises in order that I might have this man, and I can't simply abandon him. With the whole realm to chose from, can't Fraxinus find a substitute?'

The trader's head was deeply bowed, concealing her expression. 'Of course, highness,' she said unhappily. 'I understand. Perhaps, though, you might order the amber to perform one brief and simple task on our behalf before you give him to the seed. We would be eternally grateful, and it shouldn't inconvenience you at all. He's a mapmaker, you see. He knows how to draw a map of the region we desire to explore.'

'Are there no other mapmakers in Xandria?' Lucrezia asked, in genuine astonishment.

The trader looked up. She was blushing, although her cheeks were so dark that they hardly showed the red. 'I fear not, highness,' she said. 'At least, none who practise openly. The Art fell into disrepute many generations ago, and although there may be patient scholars somewhere within the empire's bounds who preserve the lore on the grounds that forgetfulness is a sin, we don't know where to look for them. Carus Fraxinus has been looking for a mapmaker for some time, and when news reached him – I believe the information came from one of the clerks who serve in the king's court – that one had been found he was enthusiastic to secure his services. Alas, he discovered that his offer to buy the man out had been pre-empted . . . by your highness. When he told me, I guessed what had happened, and he asked me to come to see you, in the hope that something might be done. I knew that you were interested in the prospects of our expedition, highness, and dared to hope . . .'

'I see,' said Lucrezia, quickly taking up the conversational slack as her visitor's voice faltered. 'I really am sorry that this accidental clash of interests has arisen . . . but if the map is all you need, there'll be no problem. I'll instruct him to draw it before turning him over to the surgeon.'

'The map is all we need,' Hyry agreed, stressing the word *need* very slightly to indicate that there was a measure of compromise in the agreement. 'Fraxinus is, of course, willing to pay a fair price for it.'

Lucrezia could see that Hyry was more than willing to leave the matter there, but she wasn't prepared to release the trader so easily. She had questions of her own that required answering, and she could hardly help but remember what she had told her father regarding the political importance of the expedition that Fraxinus and Keshvara were mounting.

'Tell me more about this Carus Fraxinus,' the princess commanded.

'He's a merchant,' Hyry replied uneasily. 'One of the richest in the city – a man respected by everyone. He's not one of those who've made their fortunes by issuing usurious loans and bargaining with rapacious fervour. He's . . .'

'An adventurer like you,' Lucrezia put in, hoping that the compliment might smooth the trader's explanatory path.

'Far better and far bolder than I,' Hyry answered modestly. 'I'm glad to be his hireling in this business, although the initial inspiration for the venture was mine. He and Aulakh Phar are the ideal men to equip and undertake such an expedition.'

'Is Phar a merchant too?'

'He's more of a scholar,' Hyry said, a little uneasily. 'He makes his living as a healer but his wisdom extends far beyond any single branch of the lore. Fraxinus has often called upon his services as an agent and advisor, and thinks that his cunning will be invaluable if we can indeed cross the Dragomite Hills.'

'And you think the amber might be useful too?'

Hyry shrugged her shoulders uncomfortably. 'Fraxinus formed a good impression of him, highness. He has the look of a fighting man and he seemed to be in desperate need of a generous master . . . but the map is the main thing. If only we can obtain the map, we can hire fighting men aplenty in the darklands. At least, we can if . . .' She trailed off.

'This trouble in the darklands you mention,' Lucrezia said, quick to pick up the thread of the argument. 'What exactly are the rumours you've heard?'

'Dragomites are said to be moving out of the blighted hills into the southern regions of the forest. Humans are said to be moving with them – actually *with* them, although Phar thinks that's probably mere confusion on the part of anxious darklanders. Anyhow, the darklanders are making preparations for an all-out war – against the people as well as the dragomites. If possible, Fraxinus wants to make peaceful contact before a war starts.'

'Has all this been reported to my father's ministers?' Lucrezia asked, having heard nothing of it.

'Undoubtedly, highness,' Hyry assured her. 'Phar was unable to send a detailed report, but he has doubtless informed the governor of Khalorn of everything he has heard. The govenor will certainly include the information in his own reports.'

One of which might reach Xandria in ten or twenty days,
Lucrezia thought, *and might catch a minister's attention ten or twenty days after that. Or might not.*

'I tried to impress upon my father,' she said earnestly, 'that the existence of the seeds which you brought me was no trivial matter. I tried to make him see that it was of some importance to the realm that a way might now be open to the legendary lands beyond the Forest of Absolute Night. I even suggested that he should take an interest in your expedition himself – but he didn't take the suggestion seriously. I'm only a princess, you see . . . a mere pawn to be sacrificed in the game of diplomacy. But this *is* important, isn't it? More important than a simple experiment in witchery . . . and more important than a new trade-route. The darklanders may not be subjects of the empire, but their wars are our business nevertheless. In any case, the Navel of the World is where it all began. It's where the forefathers did their work, made their plans and issued their commandments. It's where the Pool of Life is. If the bronzes who sold you the seeds really did come from there, we don't want communication with them disrupted by darkland barbarians.'

'Yes, highness,' said the trader dutifully. 'It seems to me that this *is* important. But not everyone sees things the same way. The common view is that the *Lore of Genesys* is just a set of pretty tales, full of ringing phrases which signify nothing. It's not surprising that the king and his ministers aren't very interested by news that there's a blight in the Dragomite Hills and that its effects have spilled over into the Forest of Absolute Night. In any case . . .' Hesitancy overtook her yet again.

'You're not so sure that you want the king's agents involved in your expedition,' Lucrezia guessed. 'You don't want to have some minister's lackey or some over-polite courtier in tow, telling you what to do in the name of the crown. I don't blame you.'

'We're hoping to go farther than any man from Xandria has been for many generations,' Hyry said, carefully avoiding any direct response to Lucrezia's observation. 'We're hoping to visit places which are mentioned in the most ancient lore, but we have no reason to expect that we'll find any relics of former times. Even if the grains of truth contained in the old tales and romances haven't been corrupted in being handed down from generation to generation, the reality to which they refer must have decayed into dust long ago. We can't possibly guess what we might find there now . . . but Fraxinus thinks, even so, that myth and legend offer some reason to believe that whatever *is* there now might be of interest to scholars and traders alike.'

'You're not looking for incorruptible stone, then?' Lucrezia said teasingly. 'You don't expect to happen upon the draught of longevity or any other fabled miracles?'

'No, highness,' the trader replied soberly. 'What Carus Fraxinus is looking for is profit. I dare say that he hopes that there might be miracles — or if not miracles, wonders — but he's a hard-headed man after his own fashion. He believes that the people of today have lost much of the heritage that once was theirs, and he'd be very happy indeed were we to recover a little of that loss, but he'll gladly settle for knowledge of ordinary things if that's all there is to be had. He's not a wild-eyed treasure-hunter, highness. He's a trader.'

'That's Fraxinus,' Lucrezia observed softly. 'What about you?'

Hyry Keshvara seemed rather disconcerted by the intrusion of such a personal note into the conversation. She opened her mouth automatically, perhaps to protest that she had meant to include herself in all these judgments, but then she closed it again while she thought the matter over. Lucrezia knew that she might simply be hunting for an acceptable lie, but dared to hope that she might be trying to weigh her motives more accurately than she had ever had cause to weigh them before.

Eventually, the trader said: 'Perhaps I'm no more than a victim of silly pride. Were I to tread my accustomed pathways for a thousand years I should never be as rich as Fraxinus. Perhaps I lack the money-hunger of a true merchant. Your highness might not understand, but I've always taken a childish delight simply in being where no man of Xandria — and I use the word *man* narrowly — has ever been. I always seem to be happier in dark and dangerous places than I am when sturdy and well-maintained walls are layered about me. Perhaps I'm a barbarian at heart, or a madwoman. Either way, when Carus Fraxinus proposed that we combine forces to find a way through the Dragomite Hills my heart leapt up, because that's precisely what I had desired of him, and precisely what I hoped.'

Having finished this speech, Keshvara seemed so profoundly discomfited that Lucrezia felt sorry for her.

'I do understand,' the princess insisted, grateful for the opportunity to do so, and to do so with passion. 'Indeed I understand perfectly – and I wish with all my heart that I might go with you.'

Keshvara made no response to this, and Lucrezia continued after a brief hesitation. 'My father, alas, has other plans for me. But Fraxinus shall have his map; I can promise you that, at least. As soon as the amber is delivered into my care – before, if I can contrive it – I shall demand the very best map he can draw, in triplicate. I'll send Monalen to your house as soon as it's done – or to the house of Carus Fraxinus, if you're already on your way. All I ask in return is that you'll promise me faithfully that you'll come to me when your adventure is done, to tell me every detail of it – no matter whether I'm in Xandria, or Shaminzara, or anywhere else in the known world.'

'Yes, highness,' the trader said. 'That I'll gladly do. Thank you, highness. A thousand thanks.' It seemed that the vehemence of Lucrezia's speech had startled her, but she made no comment on it. Lucrezia would have liked to expand upon her theme, but she had no wish to torment someone she would like to be able to think of as a friend. She gave the trader permission to leave, and Keshvara accepted it with a joy which the princess tried with all her might to see as a natural relief rather than an insult.

When Keshvara had gone, escorted by the ever-patient Dhalla, Lucrezia threw herself back upon the cushions which decked her couch, and stared at the pitted ceiling of her little room. The hour at which she usually retired to her bed for the midnight had already passed, but she didn't feel at all tired. Indeed, her head was buzzing; she had never felt so vibrantly alive and alert.

What a prison this is! she thought fervently. *And what a fine, brave woman Keshvara is! How much kinder fate would have been had my birth consigned me to her vocation, instead of the rigid duties of a princess! If only . . .*

She knew, of course, that dreaming of 'if onlys' was a waste of time – but she had time enough to waste, for the present, and she was, after all, a princess.

14

ANDRIS WAS A light sleeper even at the best of times, and the citadel was home to so many slight noises that he continually drifted back and forth across the borders of unconsciousness while he lay on his bed. He was forced to shift his position constantly in the ultimately hopeless attempt to make himself comfortable upon a pallet which was too small to contain him.

These circumstances were no more distressing now than they had been when he had first been put into the cell, but on this particular night he felt frustration building up inside him like pus in a boil. It might not have been so bad if he had been certain that he was waiting, but the message thrown into his cell had not given any firm indication as to when the promised rescue attempt might take place. The awareness that he might be dangling in unwarranted suspense made the suspense itself that much harder to bear.

He tried to relax by means of all the conventional tricks, but they all failed. When he tried to rehearse his earliest and most pleasant memories of Ferentina he found that they had become flat and insipid, and that his once-beloved mother had begun to seem ineffectual and uncaring. When he tried to work up a hopeful fantasy about entering the service of a Xandrian princess, who would fall completely in love with him and launch him upon a wonderfully successful military career, the plot faltered at every step and he could not shake the suspicion that a big dagger might at any moment be plunged into his back by any one of a hundred hired assassins. When he tried to strike up a philosophical dialogue with the bugs infesting the mattress they so devastated him with their vicious logic that it was difficult to cling to the most stubbornly elementary dogma. He had no option but to wallow in his wretchedness, savouring his misery.

In spite of all this, however, he had to be rudely jerked from semi-slumber when his attention was caught by the sound of bolts being withdrawn from other doors in the corridor.

Such was his mood that his first thought was: *Why are they letting all the other prisoners out?*

His second was: *What if the others don't want to go?*

His third was: *What if I don't want to go?*

He heard muffled voices as some of the puzzled prisoners to whom release was being offered enquired as to the cause of their good fortune. Shut up, you fools! he thought, heedless of all inconsistency. *Do you want to wake the jailer and bring the guard running to the door?* None of the prisoners was completely stupid, though; those who spoke at all were wise enough to whisper.

By the time the three bars were withdrawn from his own door Andris was up on his feet, groping for the few possessions he had been allowed to retain – which he had bundled up for convenience, just in case.

The door opened and someone slipped in. The starlight which shone through the narrow window was just adequate to inform him that the person was slim and fairly tall by Xandrian standards, if not by his. He moved forward but an extended hand blocked the way.

'Not this way, cousin.'

The whispering voice was female. While he paused to consider this unexpected development she hauled one of the wooden bars through the doorway and thrust it towards him, implicitly commanding him to take it. When he had done so she brought a second one through and propped it against the wall. She was obviously strong in spite of her slimness. When the third bar was inside she shut the door again.

Having sealed them in, she laid the third bar down crosswise so that anyone who tried to open the door would have to shove hard. She took back the one Andris held, and placed it on top.

'What. . . ?' Andris began – but the woman silenced him immediately by placing a firm forefinger against his lips. She stood on tiptoe to speak softly into his ear. 'Listen! You may not know it, but if you don't get out now, you're dead. This is your only chance. The citadel guard are lying in ambush at the door we came in by. The only way out is up, along and down.'

Andris looked up at the ceiling, remembering the stains that had made him slightly anxious before he had got used to the height.

'We can't,' he muttered feebly.

'Yes we can!' she hissed fiercely. 'There's a cavity up there. Water-tanks are set in rows over the walls—there's a narrow space between them, above the middle of the ceiling. Lift me up and let me squat on your shoulders. *Now*, cousin!'

Cousin? he thought, as she said the word a second time. *Was it my letter to the shipmaster that has brought all this about, or that merchant to whom I told my troubles? One or other of them must have found my uncle, or some relict of him. But . . .* While he thought, he hesitated, and the woman quickly became impatient.

'Squat, idiot,' she said, putting her hands on his shoulders and pressing down. 'How can I reach the ceiling unless I can climb on you?'

How indeed? he thought. He gave in to the insistence of the hands and knelt. The woman — or was she merely a girl? — clambered on to his shoulders with alacrity. She was heavy in spite of her relative slenderness, by virtue of being ungirlishly tall, but Andris bore her weight easily enough.

'One step right!' she instructed impatiently, as if he should have known by instinct what to do.

Outside, the corridor was full of barely suppressed whispers and noises of movement. Andris had already figured out that a prison which charged fees to its inmates might be a useful source of revenue to a prosperous city whose courts were perpetually busy, but until now he hadn't paused to wonder what effect the privilege of paying to be in jail might have on the politics of escape. It was obvious that not everyone had been forewarned of the plan of which they were now being made part, and that he was not the only one to have doubts about the best course of action. Some of the querulous voices, moreover, were rapidly escaping their users' sense of discretion. It seemed entirely possible that a fight might break out even before the alarm was raised.

He wondered whether all the others were being told that an ambush had been laid. He also wondered why, if she knew about the ambush, the slim woman had come to save him regardless . . . and, if an ambush *had* been laid, why the would-be ambushers hadn't simply stopped her . . .

There were too many questions, none of which was easily answerable. He realised that he was completely out of his depth.

The fact that the woman wriggled somewhat as she worked on the ceiling of the cell made the task of supporting her more troublesome, but Andris stood firm, proud of his ability to do so. Had he been able to get a good look at her face and found it lovely he might have been able to derive more erotic excitement from the experience, but anxiety and ignorance combined to make that difficult.

He didn't need to ask what the woman was doing. She was smearing on some fast-acting solvent which would soak into the ceiling, loosening its solidity as it went. It would normally require an hour or two to make stone or wood crumble by any such method, but the ceiling was made out of some unnatural substance designed for the convenience of stonemasons; with the appropriate tools it could be demolished in minutes. Andris imagined a heavy tank filled with water toppling from above, but the woman obviously knew what she was talking about – and common sense dictated that the middle of a ceiling would not be subjected to such a burden.

'According to the jailer,' he whispered, 'there's no way out up there.'

'He would say that,' she observed, 'wouldn't he? Squat!'

She hopped down as he bent his knee, and grabbed the beam she had leaned against the wall. 'Hold it upright,' she said. 'Get your hands under the bottom end. When I give the word, drive it upwards with all your might. Then do what you have to do to enlarge the hole.'

He did as he was told, moving like an automaton. He expected her to give the signal almost immediately, but in fact she just stood still, listening. When a full minute had gone by, he said: 'What are we waiting for?'

'Rot needs time,' she said tersely. 'Better if we wait till the noise starts. Any second, pure chaos will break loose.'

As if on cue, pure chaos did indeed break loose. There was a sudden cacophony of shouted challenges, barked orders and howls of anguish, quickly supplemented by the urgent beating of an alarm-drum. Then – as if the drum were merely a signal for the outbreak of further mayhem – there was a series of very loud explosions. There seemed to be four in all, although they were so precisely timed as almost to fuse into a single mighty roar. Their echoes multiplied around the legendary walls like a barrage of mortar-bombs.

That must have cost a fortune! Andris thought, astounded by the economic insanity of it. *It would be cheaper by far to buy out every prisoner in the jail!*

'Now!' the woman yelled. In spite of the thunderousness of the explosions, the sudden amplification of her words from a whisper to a shout made him wince.

He got his fingertips under the end of the beam that was sitting on the floor, and drove it upwards like a vertical battering-ram. It smashed the weakened ceiling to smithereens. Bits the size of pebbles rained down on him. It was easy to move the beam back and forth, expanding the hole. He felt the top end bump against more solid objects to either side – presumably the water-tanks carefully sited above the solid walls.

'Are you crazy?' he said. 'Surely you're not releasing every prisoner in the jail and blowing up the citadel just to get *me* out!'

'Don't be silly,' she said breathlessly, as she put a hand on his right shoulder, indicating that he could put the beam down now. 'That's Checuti's people bringing off the crime of the century. We're just a sideshow to distract the guard – a diversion. You've got to go first – I'll do my best to give you a lift.'

Andris felt a sudden sinking feeling. *Crime of the century?* he thought. *What crime? What on earth have I got myself into? They'll hunt me down to the ends of the rotting earth for this!*

'Who exactly are you?' he asked, belatedly, as the woman squatted down beside him.

'Merel Zabio,' she replied, bracing herself. 'My grandfather was your uncle Theo. This is the difficult bit – don't crush me!'

Andris stared up at the gap he had made in the ceiling. It looked awkwardly narrow, in spite of all the stuff that had come tumbling down when he moved the beam about. He wasn't sure that he could fit into it, and he wasn't sure that there would be anywhere to go if he did. The ledges to either side of the hole would undoubtedly be fragile; they might well collapse under his weight as soon as he was up there.

There was now a fight going on out in the corridor, but no one was trying to get into the cell – yet. Some of the prisoners must be taking on the guards who had lain in ambush for them. Even those who were reluctant must have had little choice about getting involved. There was no sound of clashing steel – which implied that the blades the guardsmen carried were far superior to the weapons ranged against them – but the soldiers didn't seem to be winning an easy victory on that account. Sheer confusion must be making things very difficult for everyone concerned.

I'm doomed, he thought, as the woman adjusted her position, preparing herself to be used as a stepping-stone. *If they catch me now, I'm done for. It won't even be the wall this time – it'll be that rotting gibbet.*

He stepped on to his new-found cousin's back and reached up for the edges of the hole, trying to move as swiftly and as smoothly as possible so as to minimise her burden. He took a firm grip, but the moment he tried to transfer his weight from foothold to handhold the substance crumbled and he had to leap clear.

Merel Zabio moved half a met closer to the door, and made herself small again. Again he stepped on to her back and reached up for the ragged edge of the hole. This time, the edge hadn't been weakened by the gluttonous seepage of the solvent. It didn't crumble – but he still didn't dare put his whole weight on it.

'Stand up!' he commanded, as he steadied himself. 'Push!'

It couldn't have been easy for her, given that he was so nearly a giant, but she was kin to him and she was no frail flower. She heaved with all her might, gasping with the effort. He knew that she would only be able to bear him up for a few seconds, and he knew exactly what he had to do. He reached out with his two arms, groping for the edges of the water-tanks placed to either side of the hole. He knew that he had to grip them both at the same time, or risk unbalancing one of them to the extent that it came crashing into the cell – and he couldn't be certain that he wouldn't bring them *both* crashing down – but it was the best chance he had. He guessed that the tanks couldn't be so very deep, and he just had to take it on trust that their rims would be reachable.

He found one, then the other . . . and nearly slipped back as Merel Zabio collapsed under him – but when she fell away, he found himself safely suspended. He swung his legs up, groping with his feet for the edge of the hole, and found it. He sent his feet scurrying along the narrow corridor between the tanks, gaining enough support to allow him to inch his hands forward along the rims. Within thirty seconds he was lying full length along the narrow corridor between the rows of the tanks, with his head and shoulders above the hole. He had only to turn over and reach down, dangling his arms to catch his cousin.

'Take hold!' he said.

He already knew how heavy his kinswoman was, but it was still a shock when he had to bear her full weight at the end of his arms, and a momentary stab of panic threatened that the rest of the ceiling would surely come down, spilling them back on to the floor of the cell. Fortunately, she was as agile as he, and every bit as determined. As he lifted her she swung herself up, and got her legs up on the further ledge, squirming along it just as desperately as he had. When they were both up, she told him to back off, so that she could work her way past the hole, supporting herself on the two tanks to either side.

It was very dark in the space between the tanks, and there was no room to stand up. He scrambled along the narrow alleyway on his hands and knees, and the woman fell in behind him.

'Don't go too far!' she told him. 'Go to the left, between the rows of tanks.'

Mercifully, the attic space in which they found themselves was not completely dark. Starlight leaked in through a number of slender cracks in the ill-maintained roof. Once his eyes had adjusted, Andris found that it was just possible to see the silhouettes of the tanks and to pick a path between them. As soon as it could be managed, the woman squeezed past him. She evidently knew how to find the trapdoor which let workmen up into the space to carry out repairs. It wasn't possible to follow a straight path, but it didn't take long to get to the place she was aiming for.

The trapdoor was closed, bolted below, but that was no problem. She didn't have to ask him to use his superior strength – she took a heavy-bladed dagger from her belt, inserted it through the narrow gap beside the bolt so that she could use it as a lever, and exerted a steady pressure. The screws holding the bolt in place yielded easily enough.

There was a wooden stairway – little more than a ladder –

leading down to a corridor that must have been on the same level as the prison but didn't seem to be connected with it. At the far end of the corridor was a sturdier flight of stairs.

'May be a problem there,' she said, dropping her voice to a whisper again as she pointed to the downward-leading steps. 'Those take us down to a barrack-room. It ought to be empty, given that every guardsman in the citadel should be fully occupied in chasing his tail and picking his way through the rubble left by the petards, but you can't depend on anything in this place. Once we get through the barrack-room, it's still a long way to the stables. Checuti's carts will probably have gone by the time we get there, so we'll have to make our own arrangements to get through the City Gate. Our only ally is confusion, but there'll be a lot of that. Stick close to me, and for Goran's sake be careful. If we're caught, we'll *both* end up waist-deep in Princess Lucrezia's poison garden with five-sim thorns in our guts.'

'What do you . . . ?' Andris began – but he had no time to finish the question. Merel Zabio was off down the ladder, and by the time he reached the floor of the corridor he had to scurry to catch up with her.

Well, he thought, *there's no stopping now. It's full steam ahead and damn the consequences.* This was not a comforting metaphor. He had once seen a steam engine at work, and although it had not actually blown up while he was watching he had thought it the greatest folly which the human mind had ever devised, whose loss from the lore could not have been reckoned a sin by any sane man.

15

LUCREZIA'S MIND WAS so full of thoughts inspired by what Hyry Keshvara had said to her that even when she finally retired to bed she made not the slightest attempt to go to sleep. She simply lay there in the comfortable darkness, wondering what kind of magic lands might lie to the south of the Forest of Absolute Night. In spite of what Ereleth had often said about the *Lore of Genesys* being no less vulnerable to corruption than any other aspect of traditional wisdom she could not help but consider it the best place to look for guidance, and in the deepest midnight she lit a lamp so that she could consult a written version she had borrowed from the king's library.

The book was not old – no more than a year – but there was no way of knowing how many times the words within it had been copied by faithful scribes. Rumour spoke in terms of hundreds of thousands, but she knew well enough what inflationary tendencies rumour had. It was probable, she judged, that the figure could be cut by a considerable order of magnitude – but even if one thought in terms of tens of thousands, each reproduction carried out at intervals of a year or two, the words themselves must be unimaginably ancient. The majority of civilised men believed that the whole thing was a set of fictions, invented by the men of old to explain an origin of which they had no true memory or record, but even if that were not so Hyry Keshvara was surely right to argue that no relic of what was described there could possibly have survived into the world of today. And yet the words somehow retained their magic, even after all this time.

Lucrezia found the passage she wanted easily enough, and read it through. She had read it before and had often heard it read by others, but she had not been trained in the Art of Remembrance, and could not remember it well enough to recite it aloud without the aid of the written page.

The place where humans first came into the world, the text read, *was named Idun by the people of the ship, in memory of a place which never was but was remembered and revered nevertheless. The people of the ship built a city there, but their sons and daughters were not permitted to live long in the city.*

'*You must go forth into the world and multiply,*' *the forefathers said to the people of the world.* '*You must go to every region which will support you: to every forest, every plain and every seashore. You must build cities of your own wherever you can, and protect them as best you can against corrosion and corruption. Where you cannot build cities you must follow other ways of life, but you must leave no land alone, even in the farthest reaches of the world, for the purpose of human life is to fight evil wherever it may be found.*'

When the city of Idun crumbled into dust, as the cities of the world are ever wont to do, the forefathers made no attempt to rebuild it. To their remaining sons and daughters they said: '*Go follow your brothers and sisters into the regions of the world, for we have other work to do here before we leave. Where there was a city we shall make a garden, but it will be a garden of poisons. Do not forbid your descendants to visit this garden, but bid them beware of it, for they will be wise to avoid it for many generations.*'

The garden of Idun became the source of many evil and dangerous things, for which reason the people of the world called it Chimera's Cradle, but they also named it the Navel of the World, to remind themselves that they too were chimerical beings. The best of the new chimeras spawned and cradled in the garden followed the people of the world as they dispersed themselves through the forests and the plains, but the worst of them tainted the region around the garden. The people of the world complained of this injustice, but to no avail. '*Even that which has never been known before may yet be created,*' *the loremasters said,* '*but it cannot be designed. The cradle in which it will be hatched and nourished must give birth to evils too, but in the end evil will be defeated and Order will prevail.*'

The people of the ship gave what earthly gifts they could to the people of the world, but the most precious gift of all was one they did not have to give and that was an incorruptible stone. Aboard the ship, there were many kinds of stone that had been incorruptible there, but corruption had no dominion aboard the ship and incorruptibility was easily achieved. In the world, alas, corruption reigned supreme.

'The war against evil will be hard fought in the world,' the loremasters told theirs sons and their daughters, 'but war is the mother of all weapons, and the war against evil is the mother of the weapons by which evil shall one day be defeated. There is as yet no incorruptible stone in all the world, but it will not always be so. We have planted the garden of Idun so that the incorruptible stone might one day be born from the Pool of Life, nourished by milk and blood. When that day comes, your children's children must seize and use the stone, and turn the evil of corrosion to the good of inscription.'

'That is what Carus Fraxinus and Hyry Keshvara hope to find,' Lucrezia whispered aloud. 'They may deny it – they may not even know it – but this is the lure which attracts them. They are setting forth in search of the garden of Idun itself, of Chimera's Cradle and the Pool of Life. They do not know the meaning of what is written here, any more than I do, but they know that it means *something*.'

When she had closed the book Lucrezia dressed herself fully. She clasped her many-pouched belt about her waist – not because she had any need of it, but because Ereleth had told her a thousand times that it was too dangerous a thing to leave aside.

She tiptoed down the long stairway as quietly as she could, and came eventually to the room beside the door of the tower, from which the night-guard kept watch. Dhalla was by the window, as she was honour-bound to be, intently staring out into the darkness.

When the giant heard the door opened she turned swiftly around, her huge hand reaching out for the spear that was propped up against the wall. As soon as she saw who it was, though, her hand dropped away again.

'Highness,' she said, politely inclining her head. She did not seem surprised; she was accustomed to Lucrezia's nocturnal wanderings.

'Is all well?' Lucrezia asked, as she crossed the room to join Dhalla at the window. She did not doubt for a moment that all *was* well, but she felt obliged to ask.

'I don't know, highness,' the giant replied uneasily.

Lucrezia started in astonishment. 'What's wrong?' she said.

'Perhaps nothing – but there are two sentries missing from their posts, and the patrol is taking three times as long as normal to complete its round. I called out to the guardsmen to ask them what was happening, but they told me I must be silent, because they had some secret operation in progress. After that, I heard someone moving in the darkness, but I dared not sound a challenge. I've seen men moving stealthily, over by the stables. They're probably just playing their usual boys' games, but I don't like it. At least three of the lamps which usually stay lit all night have gone out, and there's no sign of the lamplighter.'

Boys' games was Dhalla's term for almost everything the king's guard did: their ceremonies, their drill and their occasional training exercises. Lucrezia was profoundly uninterested in *boys' games* of every shape and form, but she didn't like to see the giantess so anxious. 'It's probably nothing,' she assured her.

'True,' Dhalla agreed. 'But I wish the captain would pass by, so that I could ask him what's happenng. There's never any sense to be had from his boorish men.'

'I've been thinking about what Hyry Keshvara said,' the princess told the giant. 'About the amber being a mapmaker. If he really can draw a map to guide Keshvara and her friends to the place where Chimera's Cradle once was, we have to make sure he does it. We'll have to handle the matter carefully, though – we don't want him to think that he's in a position to strike bargains, or to realise how desperately he might need to.'

Dhalla said nothing in reply to this. Whether that was because she thought it was nonsense or simply because she was preoccupied by her own anxieties there was no way to tell.

'What Keshvara really wants, of course,' Lucrezia added, 'is for me to hand the amber over to Fraxinus – but I can't do that. I'd like to help her, of course, but I can't go back on the agreement I made with my father.'

Dhalla continued staring out into the shadows.

'What do you see out there?' the princess asked, rather petulantly.

'I *see* nothing,' Dhalla replied uneasily. 'It's what I hear that troubles me. I'm almost sure that someone was at the door – and something's going on in the stables. If the guardsmen are playing practical jokes again . . .'

'Practical jokes aren't important,' Lucrezia said firmly. 'What I'm trying to talk to you about is. Please listen to me, Dhalla.'

In any normal circumstances, Dhalla would never have disobeyed such a direct command, but all she did was hold up her hand. Her whole body had stiffened.

'Go, highness, I beg you,' she said. 'You should not be here. Please, highness!'

Lucrezia had not the slightest intention of going anywhere. If something really was about to happen, she wanted to have the best possible view.

'Something's wrong,' Dhalla said, more positively than before. 'The guardsmen should have gone past by now. I'm sure something's happening in the stables.'

'It's just part of their secret operation,' Lucrezia said, hoping now that it might not be true and feeling a thrill of excitement at the thought. 'Boys' games.'

'No,' Dhalla said. 'It can't be. I ought to raise the alarm . . . I ought at least to find out what's happening.'

'Find out what's happening,' Lucrezia advised. 'That's best. Look before you leap.'

'Please, highness,' Dhalla said, moving back from the window, 'I wish you would rouse my sisters while I go to see. Tell them that they must guard the door.'

'I will, if you think it necessary,' the princess said, savouring another sharp thrill of excitement at the thought that Dhalla surely must be right. 'Be careful.'

The giant moved swiftly from the room and Lucrezia followed her. As Dhalla went down to the door the princess turned the other way, rounding the corner to go along the corridor which led to the barrack-room where the giants were lodged. She had no need to rouse anyone – two of them were in the antechamber, wide awake but utterly engrossed in a game of cards. When the princess looked in they both stood up.

'Dhalla's gone over to the stables,' Lucrezia said. 'She thinks something's happened to the guardsmen who should be patrolling the inner court. She says that you should . . .'

She was abruptly interrupted by the sound of an explosion. The floor beneath her feet shuddered.

While the princess stood still, rooted to the spot by astonishment, the two giants reached for their spears. They had not completed the action when a second explosion followed the first, much louder and much closer at hand.

This time the floor leapt instead of shuddering, and Lucrezia put her hands to her ears. She had not been able to tell the direction of the first explosion, but she knew immediately that the second one must have been at the very door of the Inner Sanctum: the door through which Dhalla had passed – or had tried to pass – only seconds before.

The second explosion was instantly followed by a third and a fourth, and the princess was seized by the terrifying thought that the whole tower might be coming down. Panic-stricken, she turned to run for the door. The corridor was already filling up with thick, choking smoke. From the floors above she could hear the sound of screaming, which grew in a stridulant crescendo as more and more voices joined in.

The damage was not as bad as she had expected, although the wooden doors had been blown open, sagging from their hinges. Ignoring the thickening smoke, Lucrezia ran out through the gap. She looked wildly about for Dhalla's body, but it was nowhere to be seen.

She must have got through in time! Lucrezia thought. *She must have been clear before the charge went off! Thank Goran she didn't catch sight of it and stop to see what it was!*

Without pausing for further thought, Lucrezia raced off in the direction of the stables. The one thought in her head was to make sure that the giant was all right, and the stables seemed the obvious place to look for her. The other two giants stayed behind, clearing the debris from the doorway. Their first duty was to see to the safety of the occupants of the tower.

Although the stars were bright the shadows gathered about the fringes of the Great Courtyard deep and dark. There should have been lighted lamps set to either side of the stable doors, but these were among the three which had reportedly gone out – or, as now seemed likely, had been deliberately doused. It was not until she was almost there that Lucrezia could see that one of the huge doors had been drawn back, and that a cart was waiting within with a team of horses ready hitched.

The horses had evidently been disturbed by the explosions, and the princess's precipitate arrival set them to whinnying wildly, but the beasts were making far less noise than the women in the Sanctum, who were creating enough racket by now to drown the sounds of even the most strenuous boys' games.

Lucrezia barely had time to dance aside as the horses hitched to the cart were started forward by a whipcrack, but she evaded them gracefully enough and did not fall. 'Dhalla!' she shouted, seeing no reason why she shouldn't add her own voice to the gathering cacophony, since she at least had a good reason for shouting.

As soon as the cart was gone Lucrezia moved once again towards the open doorway, but saw her mistake immediately. This time it wasn't possible to be graceful about the business of evasion. She had to dive sideways, and surely would have fallen had not strong arms reached out to catch her and put her upright again.

There was no mistaking those arms, and Lucrezia cried out in wordless relief – but the giant did not hold on to her for long. As soon as she was out of the way the giantess let go of her, and moved past her.

As the cart swept by, Dhalla leapt up behind, vaulting over the backboard without any apparent effort or difficulty. Lucrezia heard the sound of a violent scuffle, and knew that the giant must have landed among men eager to thrust her back again.

Lucrezia was quite certain that her friend did not have her spear with her, for her hands had been empty when she reached out to steady her stumbling mistress. Indeed, as the princess took another step back her foot fell upon the abandoned weapon. Lucrezia immediately knelt down to grope for it with her hands – and was glad that she did so, for it became obvious almost immediately that there was a third cart yet to come, and a company of men gathered on top of it. There were other men coming on the scene too, hurrying from every direction, and Lucrezia was certain that she would be trampled if she stayed where she was.

The third cart didn't move forward quite as precipitately as the others, and Lucrezia had time enough to run towards it, casting the spear as she ran. She hurled the weapon as hard as she could, but it was too heavy for her unpractised arm, and she could not raise it high enough into the air to make it fly as she had intended.

It fell low, clattering along the ground – but its head went between the spokes of the leading wheel of the cart, and it was carried around by the turning wheel so that its head smashed against the underside of the cart.

With better luck the spear might have broken the wheel, but the wheel was stronger than the shaft of the weapon, and it was the spear which broke as the cart lurched and rocked, temporarily interrupted as the horses were gathering pace. The interruption was time enough for Lucrezia to leap nimbly up on to the step that gave access to the driver's bench, and in a trice she was beside him, reaching out as though to dispossess him of his whip. There was no thought in her head to tell her how foolish and how reckless she was; she was entirely possessed by wrath and determination.

The carter did not even deign to glance at her. He simply swept his arm back in a short and brutal arc, so that his forearm cannoned into her upper body, catching her just beneath the neck.

She had no chance of riding the blow. The impact tumbled the princess backwards, and she fell into the body of the cart. Already off-balance, she had no way to cushion or interrupt her fall.

She felt a sudden wave of dizziness . . .

16

FROM THE TINY window in the south-west tower Jacom Cerri watched the two stealthy figures sidle along the deserted walkway to the door of the jail. They moved through the shadows as if darkness were their natural habitat, but they had to come out into the starlight when they came close to the door. Even so, it was impossible to tell whether they were young or old, male or female.

Jacom presumed that the two had come into the citadel in much the same way as Zadok Sart, using legitimate passes. It was obvious that the issuing of such passes had become reckless, and that the places of legitimate tradesmen and their hirelings were being taken by dubious characters. If two men could get in that way, then so could half a hundred ... but Jacom smiled as he thought of the difficulties these two would face in getting out again.

The door of the jail was barred on the inside, as it always was, but the two felons were prepared for that. The door itself was very sturdy, being renewed at regular intervals, but the glazed loophole let into it at eye height was a weak point. Jacom deduced from their actions that they had pushed aside the shield which protected the spy-hole, removed the glass, and let a pair of threads through the grille. The threads would doubtless carry hooks which could be used as miniature grappling-irons to lift the bar securing the door.

It seemed impossible that they could lift the bar free and lower it without sending it crashing to the floor, but they managed it. The two were obviously highly skilled practitioners of the black arts of thievery. Jacom couldn't even be sure that the jailer and the men he had set to lie low in the jailer's anteroom would have heard the bar fall – but someone would have an eye glued to a tiny peep-hole drilled through the anteroom door, and there was a lantern just inside the jail door whose light the intruders would have to occlude in order to get to the darker corridors beyond.

Jacom had given his men strict instructions to lie low and let the invaders through; he wanted to catch them in the company of the prisoner they had come to release, so that they would have little or no scope for invention when the time came to question them.

When the two were safely inside Jacom signalled to four more of his men, indicating that they should move along the walkway and take up a position outside the door to the prison. He was confident that the trap was now sealed tight.

Jacom stayed where he was. To Guardsman Aaron, the one man who remained by his side, he said: 'That's it. Signed, sealed and delivered.' He was smugly confident that the prisoner and his would-be rescuers would surrender rather than risk a fall from the unrailed walkway, even if they were armed.

'Should be,' Aaron admitted unexcitedly.

As the seconds dragged by, though, Jacom began to grow impatient. What on earth could be taking so long?

When he heard the sound of a challenge, his heart leapt with exultation – but it lurched sickeningly as he realised that the challenge had not been sounded inside the jail, but had come from far below. Someone somewhere began beating an alarm-drum very fervently, but he wasn't sure exactly where the sound was coming from and had not the slightest idea why anyone should think it necessary to rouse the whole citadel.

'What the . . . ?' he began – but the rest of the question was drowned out by an almighty explosion which stunned his ear-drums. He felt the tower shake beneath his feet – and then there followed three more explosions in very rapid succession, each one seemingly louder than the last. Bright flashes blinded his eyes for a moment, although he could not have caught more than the merest glimpse of the explosions.

The first petard, he knew, must have been placed at the City Gate. As his sight readjusted it became horribly clear that one of the others had been set against the doors of the coinery, and one against the doors of the Inner Sanctum. Flickering flames and thick black smoke were billowing about in both doorways, and from his lofty station Jacom could see running figures hurdling the wreckage in both directions.

His first thought was that such things couldn't happen, and never did. What sort of man would take the enormous risks involved in handling so much explosive material? And what sort of man could possibly be mad enough to smuggle such stuff into the citadel of Xandria?

It occurred to him that he had removed half a dozen of the sentries whose purpose was to ensure that such things never happened. The terrible possibility that he had been tricked and manipulated was suddenly all too clear.

'They've blown the gate!' said Aaron disbelievingly. 'They've only gone and blown the rotting gate!'

Jacom calculated, with icy lucidity, that the four men he had left on guard at the City Gate were highly likely to have been injured, perhaps killed, and that he had removed the men who would normally have been first to run to their aid.

The alarm-drum would rouse a hundred and fifty extra guardsmen from their various barrack-rooms – plus another hundred constables and servants authorised to bear arms – and twenty officers to yell orders at them, but *he* was the commander of the watch: the one man who was supposed to be able to judge what ought to be done, and by whom, in immediate answer to this carefully sown havoc. With this thought in mind he ran full tilt from the room, ignoring the residual pain of his bruises, taking the steps three at a time as he headed for the City Gate, forgetting all about the jail and the men he had stationed there.

'Assemble by the gate!' he howled to anyone within earshot. 'Keep the bastards out at all costs!'

There seemed little point in the alarm-drum continuing its urgent throb, given that no one within the walls could possibly have slept through the explosions, but the boy whose task it was clung to his duty regardless. The sound laid down an ominous undercurrent to the screams of panic which were emanating from the Inner Sanctum and the cries of anguish which were rising from the mint.

There were four men waiting at the foot of the stairway, not knowing which way to run.

'The gate!' Jacom yelled again, only realising as his words were drowned out how difficult it was to make himself heard. He raised his arm and stabbed the index finger in the direction of the City

Gate. One of the men saluted him, and all four ran alongside him.

As they arrived at the gatehouse a guardsman staggered back from the doorway, evidently having been expelled by force. He collapsed to the ground in front of them. Jacom leapt over the prostrate body and two of the men who had accompanied him hurled themselves through the open doorway, intent on punishing the invisible assailants. Jacom did not follow them – instead he went to the great gate himself, which had been blown apart.

The huge and gaping hole which was still belching forth thick clouds of acrid smoke was more than wide enough to drive a horse and cart through, but nothing of that size was coming through as yet. Indeed, nobody seemed to be coming in at all – although there were several figures hanging back within the gate, waiting to run out as soon as the smoke cleared. For a moment Jacom thought that they must be with the attackers, but they were liveried as servants, and he realised that they simply wanted to get away. He understood why they were in such a hurry. Xandria's citadel might be famed for the awesome strength of its walls, but everyone who lived within it knew full well that rot worked in its heart, just as it worked in the heart of every other structure. The instinct of every man and woman said that no edifice was to be trusted in the face of such sudden violence. In theory, the walls of the citadel had been built to withstand the shock of any and all explosions, but if a chain reaction of cracking and crumbling got to work on the stone, anything might happen. No one now alive in Xandria had ever been forced to withstand siege or bombardment, and Jacom knew that untested courage usually proved fragile.

The crowd about the gate was swelling rapidly. Half a hundred servants were quartered in the lower levels of the towers to either side of the City Gate, and all of them had leapt out of their beds, grabbing whatever came conveniently to hand as they made their exits. Not one in five of those authorised to bear arms had bothered to seize anything which might be used as a weapon, and even those who had taken up cudgels seemed bent on self-defence rather than the apprehension of whoever had set the explosives, but Jacom knew that he had to impose some order on the gathering confusion.

'Form a cordon across the gateway!' Jacom yelled, relying on his own men to take notice and set an example. 'What's without, for Goran's sake?'

'No enemy in sight!' came back the cry.

What's happening here? Jacom asked himself silently. *What kind of corruption is this?*

It was then, and only then, that he guessed the truth. No secret army waited beyond the gate, eager to take the citadel by storm. The marauders within were not an advance guard but a whole expeditionary force, whose target could only be . . . the royal treasury.

As the smoke cleared Jacom fought his way through the milling throng to stand within the arch of the shattered gate. He was relieved to see that there were no corpses mingled with the wreckage. His men were barely holding a formation while the panic-stricken servants began to flock past them and spill out into the square beyond. It was obvious that the guardsmen could not hold the yawning gap against any substantial assault. Those who had so far gathered only carried swords; they had not a single pike between them.

Jacom joined the line and began yelling at the crowd, telling the servants to be calm. He might as well have tried to howl down the wind.

He looked out into the open concourse outside the gate. There were plenty of people about, hundreds having hurried from the nearby houses and the wooden shanties erected along the wall to see what was afoot, and the mob was swelling by the minute, its members eagerly receiving·the refugees from the citadel, plying them with urgent questions as to what was going on. Jacom suppressed an impulse to wave his arms about and order the crowd back. *Let them stay,* he thought. *Let them all stay, to form a barrier with their bodies even though they have no weapons.*

'Hold the line solid!' he cried out to his men. 'Let no one pass, inwards or outwards. Hold the line!'

He had no idea what was happening inside the gatehouse, and no idea how long it would take for an adequate number of reinforcements to gather. He supposed that help must be on its way but asked himself anxiously whether it would come in time.

The answer, it seemed, was no.

A large cart pulled by four horses came hurtling towards the gate from the direction of the Great Courtyard, scattering the crowd before it.

Jacom's hope that an impenetrable wall of human flesh might build up spontaneously before his thin line of armed defenders was instantly dashed. The panic-stricken people were entirely ready to respond to any threat, and they scattered with awesome alacrity before the juggernaut of fevered horseflesh and seasoned hardwood, whose clattering hooves and thundering steel-rimmed wheels struck sparks from the stones. The driver was standing up, plying a huge whip with considerable vigour, and Jacom had not the slightest doubt that a two-deep rank of tight-wedged pikes inscribing a line of steel before the horses would not have been adequate to turn them back. A single line of swordsmen had no chance at all.

'Look out!' he howled at his men – a quite unnecessary order, given that they knew only too well that anyone who tried to block the passage would be ridden down and crushed. They were already scattering in disarray. Four or five missiles were hurled at the cart-driver as he passed by, but he did not flinch and did not fall.

As the horses blasted their way through Jacom caught the edge of the driver's bench with both his hands and tried to vault up on to it, but the cart was travelling so fast that the wrench nearly dislocated his shoulders, and he could not complete the daring manoeuvre. The force of the impact threw him sideways and he sprawled full length on the cobblestones. His quilted armour provided some cushioning but the crash jarred him very painfully, awakening all his old bruises and inflicting dozens more.

Aaron and Kirn attempted to catch hold of the back of the cart, evidently hoping to leap up behind. They might have succeeded where Jacom had failed, but there were half a dozen men on the back of the heavily laden cart, and one of them was quick to bring down a club of some kind to break Aaron's grip, while Kirn simply could not get a firm hold. Aaron fell back upon the merciless stones, howling with pain, while Kirn spun away.

Jacom looked in vain for a company of mounted guardsmen to pour forth in hot pursuit. 'Get horses!' he yelled from where he lay. 'Get after them!' But it was not clear to whom the order was addressed, and the men who had tried to block the gateway made no attempt to run for the stables. All but a few formed up again as a second cart came into view, while the remainder went to help their fallen comrade – but none of them, it was clear, had any real stomach for the task of smiting the king's enemies.

Jacom struggled to his feet unaided, but he could see well enough that there was no scope for constructive heroics. Had there been a javelin to hand he might have been able to knock the second driver from his perch, but there was no convenient missile within reach. He staggered to the line and drew two men away. They were not at all reluctant to be drawn.

'Commandeer some horses!' he gasped, pointing at the still-swelling crowd outside the gate, which had parted to let the cart through as easily as the crowd within. 'Get after that cart! At least find out where it's gone! Alert the constables and the harbour patrol! Oh, *no*!'

The final cry of anguish was occasioned by the fact that the second cart which was driving forward at the gateway was accompanied by half a dozen galloping horses – not one of which had a rider. The chaos which had claimed the citadel evidently extended to the stables.

'*Cut the horses' legs!*' someone yelled – meaning the horses which were drawing the cart. Jacom would have tried it had he had a blade to hand, and one or two of the men whose swords were drawn did hack out half-heartedly as they dodged aside, but the second cart scattered the gate's defenders even more easily than the first. The loose horses bowled one or two people over, but the guardsmen had by now been left in sole charge of their territory, free to discharge their duty unhelped and unhindered by panicking civilians.

No one tried to jump aboard the second cart, the risk and costs of such heroics having been all too obviously demonstrated.

Helplessly, Jacom watched the cart sail past him and out into the streets of the city. He tapped two other men on the shoulder, and looked wildly about in the hope that one or more of the loose horses might have baulked and stopped. None had. 'Get out there!' he shouted. 'Find horses – get after that rotting cart!'

He was not in the least surprised when a third cart followed the second. He had few companions left by now, but this time the vehicle was pursued. Three mounted guardsmen were coming after it, and dozens more were flocking to the gate on foot. They were not Jacom's men, but he yelled at them anyway, telling the horsemen to split up and mark the progress of all three carts – but he could do no more to slow the third cart than the others.

When the third cart had gone, a kind of lull seemed to descend, although the air was still full of riotous sound. Jacom sagged back against the wall, feeling utterly defeated. He knew that what had happened tonight had never happened before, and the knowledge that it had happened during *his* watch, in the course of his second turn of duty, seemed monumentally misfortunate. His bruises seemed to be setting his entire body afire, and he had to close his eyes against the pain, but it was another kind of hurt which made him sick to his stomach.

Why me? he complained. *Why me?*

He had to open his eyes again as another of his men, Pavel, ran towards him.

'It's the tower, sir!' said Pavel urgently. 'Come quickly. The Inner Sanctum!'

'Has it fallen?' Jacom asked, immediately jumping to the worst of all possible conclusions. 'Are they all dead?'

'Oh, no, sir!' the guardsman answered, blinking hard and pulling at his sleeve. 'But the women are terrified! The door was blasted open and they're everywhere running blind with panic. Some of them are hurt, sir – queens and maidservants alike! It's terrible, sir!'

Jacom suppressed an urge to laugh. *The Inner Sanctum violated! The women of the royal household driven to panic! What unimaginable horror!* When the smoke cleared, he knew full well, the king would be far more anxious for his newly refreshed coins than his thirty-and-one wives and their hysterical ladies-in-waiting.

'Go back!' he told Pavel. 'Above all else, *we must secure the gate.* Do you understand me?'

'But you *must* come, sir!' the man wailed. 'You must!'

Corrosion and corruption! Jacom thought. *There are a thousand places I must be, a thousand stations I must hold, a thousand orders I must give – and what will it all count for, when morning dawns? I'm as good as dead and damned . . . perhaps better off dead and damned.*

'It's the women, sir,' Pavel said again, plaintively. 'You have to come, sir, to keep order. All chaos is breaking loose, sir! Someone will pay for this!'

'Not in ready money, soldier,' Jacom told him, revelling in the grim humour of it. 'You can be sure of that much.'

His private thoughts, alas, could not raise quite as much sardonic bravado as his spoken words. *Damn that amber and his filthy friends!* he raged inwardly. *I'll pay them out for this foul trick if it's the last thing I ever do!* Even as he thought it, though, he felt utterly impotent to do any such thing . . . or anything else that might save him from ruination.

17

THE BARRACK-ROOM at the bottom of the long stairway was ill-lit, although there were half a dozen narrow windows emitting starlight and a few tallow candles burning. Having come from the dark crawlspace above the cells, though, Andris had no difficulty adapting his eyes. The room held more than forty beds, most of which gave every evidence of having been quit in a desperate hurry; blankets, bolsters and items of clothing had been scattered in every direction. Merel Zabio, who was still holding the door ajar while peeping through it, indicated with the briefest of nods that she was satisfied that it was safe to proceed, and moved hurriedly on.

She had only taken three steps into the room – with Andris two paces behind her – when one of the bundles of blankets suddenly stirred, and a man sat up in one of the bunks, pointing at the newcomers.

'Halt!' he commanded. 'Who goes there?' He must have realised immediately what the answer was, because he didn't hesitate for an instant before following the challenge with a cry of 'Here, mates! To me! To me! Escapers!'

Andris fully expected the guardsman to leap out of bed and seize the swordbelt which hung from a hook above the bed, and made ready to fight – but the challenger remained where he was, in a sitting position, pointing his accusative finger. Andris realised why when he saw that the soldier's eyes had grown wide with excited recognition. It was the guardsman who had been hurt in the brawl at the Wayfaring Tree – the man whose injury had landed him in prison in the first place. The soldier was still sitting down with his legs outstretched because he couldn't get up. His leg was still in plaster.

'Run for it!' said Merel Zabio, following her own advice without the slightest hesitation.

The barrack-room was long and narrow, and the door at the far end seemed a very long way away – but no one had as yet come through it in response to the guardsman's cry. The noise in the Great Courtyard was so tempestuous that the probability of anyone having heard was virtually negligible. Andris picked up pace so quickly that he was able to draw level with his cousin within a few strides. This was the first opportunity he had had to see her clearly, and he realised – somewhat to his surprise – that her skin was so dark that she might almost have passed for a pure-bred golden. Had he seen her at a distance, dressed as she was, he would have taken her for a boy rather than a girl. Her hair was cut very short and any feminine curves she might have had were concealed by her loose-fitting jacket and trousers. She was younger than he but not by much, and her skin had the weatherbeaten look of a sailorman. He guessed that she might have been a deckhand on one of the wide-hulled galleys which traded between Xandria and the Thousand Isles.

Something heavy sailed through the air after them, landing less than a met behind Andris's flying heels. Andris winced as he half-turned to see what it was, imagining that he had just avoided being transfixed by a javelin, but in fact it was only a water-jug, which would not have done any substantial damage even if it had clipped his heels. He could not resist the temptation to look back at the angry guardsman and grin.

'Come back, you bastard!' shouted the wounded soldier optimistically.

'It wasn't me!' Andris shouted over his shoulder, as Merel paused to snatch something from one of the beds. 'I'm not the one who broke your leg!'

The guardsman had now managed to get down from the bed, and was standing awkwardly beside it with one leg rigid, but he had no spear within reach, nor anything else which would serve as a deadly missile. He could do nothing but shake his fist at the fleeing pair, shouting: 'That doesn't mean you can just run away!'

Still no one came in response to the guardsman's shouts, and they were able to bound down another stairway to an open door which let them out into a shadowed corner of the Great Courtyard.

There was uproar in the stables, with people running in every direction, shouting madly at one another. Twenty or thirty loose horses were galloping hither and yon across the courtyard, frightened by the racket and the clouds of smoke that were drifting from the Inner Sanctum and the coinery. The half-dressed grooms and soldiers who were chasing the beasts were adding to their panic. Half a dozen lantern-bearing servants milling about the stable doors were being shouted at from every direction by at least thirty others ardently desirous of light. Those horses still within were in a state of high excitement. No doubt they had been trained to remain steady under battle conditions – including all kinds of fireworks – but the present situation was quite unlike any they would ever have faced before, if only because of the astonishing number of frightened women who were spilling out of the central tower, wailing in terror and anguish. It was well-nigh impossible to tell the queens from the lowliest maidservants.

Merel pulled Andris into a quiet covert from which they could see everything.

'Wow!' she said. 'Checuti certainly knows how to put on a show. He said it'd be worth watching.'

'But how the rotting hell do we get out?' Andris wanted to know. 'It's three hundred mets to the City Gate and there's at least five hundred people in the way.'

'This is the most difficult part,' she admitted. 'The carts Checuti's men were sent to steal have long gone, and every guardsman and groom who can ride will be saddling up for the pursuit. On the other hand, nobody's got a thought to spare for the likes of us. If we can just cover up that big pale face of yours no one'll give us a second glance. Can you ride?'

'Of course I can ride!' he told her.

'OK – no need to take offence, *prince*. In that case, we either grab a couple of saddles and rig up our own chargers, or we go for ones that've been kitted out already and dispossess whoever's on top. I vote for number two, provided you're up to it. Are you?' The way she said it implied another insult, but he knew that was just a tactical ploy.

'I'm up to it,' he assured her, 'but I can't do much about the colour of my face.'

'Stick this on,' Merel said, handing him a guardsman's helmet. He realised that it must have been what she paused to pick up in the barrack-room. He took it. It fitted tightly, but it did cover his forehead and the sides of his face.

'What about. . . ?' he began, but shut up very abruptly as Merel, who had crouched down while he was donning the helmet, splashed something wet and sticky over his chin and cheeks. It was mostly mud, but not entirely; he dared not open his mouth to protest until she had finished smearing it.

'It's not much,' she said, 'but whatever you look like, it isn't a darklander. Go get a horse, cousin. And when you've got yours, get another one for me.'

Andris didn't have to look far for a likely target. Providence was obviously taking his side for once. Not fifteen mets away two young grooms had grabbed the reins of a bucking mare and were doing everything possible to quiet her while a guardsman tried to put a saddle on her back. The task completely absorbed the attention of all three, and Andris was able to come up behind the guardsman as soon as the girth-strap was fastened and tightened.

Everything fell into place perfectly. The horse consented to be calm and the guardsman put his left foot into the stirrup. Andris tapped him on the right shoulder and he turned reflexively, just in time to line up his chin with a vicious right hook. Fortunately, the unlucky guardsman's foot slipped smoothly out of the stirrup, and Andris slipped his own in its place while the two stable-lads stood gawping.

'Privilege of rank,' he assured them, as he swung himself up. 'I'm the ambassador from Ferentina.'

The mare tossed her head, but seemed to find his weight reassuring, and the lads surrendered the reins without objection or alarm. While he looked around for another horse to steal, Merel hurried out of the covert carrying what looked like an axe-handle. 'Sorry,' she said, as she passed it up. 'It's all I could find.'

As Andris turned away, lifting the makeshift weapon like a mace, Merel knelt beside the guardsman he had knocked over. The man was already sitting up, dazed but not unconscious. She put out a hand as if to help him up and he took it – but while he was only halfway up, still reliant on her support, she let go, and hit him in the face with her other fist as he fought for balance. Then she grabbed at the sword he wore at his waist, and managed to pull it free from its scabbard.

By this time the stable-boys had finally reached the conclusion that something was amiss, and moved as if to tackle her, but now the sword was in her hand she had only to scowl at them to make them change their minds.

Andris would have hauled his cousin up behind him, but their combined weights would have put far too much strain on the poor mare, and Andris wanted to be sure of getting well away from the citadel before his mount ran out of strength. He looked around again, and this time saw a fast-approaching problem. Another mounted guardsman had noticed Merel's ploy, and had leapt to the conclusion that anyone laying low one of his comrades was likely to be one of the perpetrators of the dire chain of events which had brought chaos to the citadel. He was already charging, yelling for support as he came. The weapon he was wielding was no axe-handle but a very solid sabre.

Andris, somewhat to his own astonishment, was not in the least intimidated. Almost five years had passed since he had last been in the saddle, and it was nearly seven since he had been tutored in the skills of fighting from horseback, but he suddenly felt very much at home. He tweaked the reins, hoping that the lore of horse-training was more consistently universal than the law or the making of maps, and was glad when the mare did exactly as she was bid, turning to put him in the right position to receive and counter the assault. As the point of the sabre thrust for his heart he swept the blade aside with the axe-handle.

There was no time for a riposte, but the attacker unwisely tried to check his horse's momentum rather than carrying through so that he could win space on which to turn. While the guardsman was still reining back Andris urged the mare after him, and by the time his adversary had everything back in balance Andris was all but on top of him. Using the axe-handle exactly as if it were a sabre Andris thrust with all his might, driving the head of his weapon into the other's ribs.

If the axe-handle really had been a blade it would have gone clean through. The head was hardly less broad than a fist, and the awesome weight of the blow catapulted the guardsman clean out of the saddle and over the rump of his mount. The horse reared up, but Andris had already dropped his weapon and he leaned sideways, groping at full stretch for the trailing rein. He was fortunate enough to touch it with his fingers, and he clutched it with gleeful tenacity.

Merel Zabio let out a mighty cheer – mighty enough to have brought a horde of avengers hurtling towards them had there not been so many other voices trying to out-scream one another. Within ten seconds he had brought the horse back to her. She thrust the captured sword into his hand as she took the reins, then clambered up into the saddle in a most ungainly fashion.

'Can *you* ride?' he shouted, as she settled herself rather uncomfortably.

She did not deign to answer. Instead, she said: 'Go for the City Gate, and don't stop for anything!'

The advice was far easier to offer than to take. The crowd in the courtyard was so dense that it was well-nigh impossible to force the horse into a gallop, and now that they were in plain sight others were beginning to realise that they were enemies. Another guardsman ran towards them on foot, but had to turn aside when Andris raised the sword to strike at him, and Merel saw him in plenty of time to keep out of harm's way. The soldier cried out an alarm, but the cry was wordless and half-strangled, and would not have been heard or heeded even in far better circumstances.

Another man – presumably a servant – grabbed at the mare's bridle as Andris went by, and actually caught it for a moment, but he was no hero and he let go rather than risk being trampled or stabbed. By now Andris was gathering momentum, and the clatter of the mare's hooves seemed to have a marvellous magical ability to cause the crowd to melt away from the animal's course. The great majority of the people in the crowd were so well used to dodging horses that it had become a kind of second nature – they may not have been consciously aware of hearing the hoofbeats, but they could pick them out from the general cacophony well enough to take the appropriate action.

Now that she had picked up speed the mare changed her paces with remarkable alacrity, and her battle training stood her in good stead. Andris was soon able to fall in behind three other riders, who were also heading full tilt for the City Gate, letting their mounts help to clear the way. None was in uniform but all were bearing arms – whether they were servants of sufficient rank to be so entitled or guardsmen roused precipitately from their beds there was no way to tell, but no one could doubt their determination or their authority. As they moved out of the Great Courtyard the crowd thinned and the noise abated slightly, but this only gave the three riders the chance to shout at their comrades to clear the way – and the way was, indeed, cleared. There were a dozen armed men at the City Gate, but they were not making the slightest attempt to stop anyone riding out. Indeed, they were waving riders through, shouting something about the need to catch carts before they could be unloaded.

As the three men ahead galloped under the arch of the gate Andris lowered his head, hoping that the gleam of starlight on his stolen helmet would be signal enough to obtain free passage. He pressed so hard on the heels of the three horses that he became the rearmost element in a diamond shaped wedge. Neither of the men to either side looked back – they dared not take their eyes off the route ahead – and the man in front must have been well known to the guardsmen at the gate, for they yelled encouragement to him as he raised his arm in salute.

Had the soldiers on foot had their way all four of the horses would have galloped on unimpeded, but there was a crowd outside the gate as well as one within, and its members were pressing forward with eager curiosity. They probably had no intention of blocking the pursuit of the carts which were carrying away the contents of the king's coinery, and certainly had no intention of exposing themselves to danger, but the leading rider in the diamond had to snatch up as he faced a wall of faces, cursing loudly. Andris hauled on his own reins, and bumped the horse to his right, which nearly came down. There was a moment's awful hesitation, when everything gained might have been lost, but the sheer momentum of the horses carried them through in spite of the narrowness of the gap, tumbling citizens of Xandria to the left and to the right as they tried, unsuccessfully, to get out of the way.

The horse to Andris's right veered off as soon as it was clear of the crush, and Andris veered too, taking his own mount out of the tight formation. As he came away he was seen clearly for the first time, and he heard a shout of 'Darklander!' from way behind him. Others must have heard the shout too, but none could have known for certain which way to look, and the people around him now were unarmed, with not a red skirt in sight. He ducked low over the mare's neck again and rode for dear life across the open square and into the first street that yawned invitingly before him. He looked round as he moved into the star-shadow of the houses, and saw that Merel Zabio was right behind him.

Unfortunately, she was not alone.

A guardsman with a spear was riding after her, and was almost alongside. She must have known he was there but she was staring dead ahead, concentrating all her efforts on the guidance of her horse. The pursuing rider was already raising the spear, trying to get into a position from which he could contrive a mortal thrust.

Andris reined in hard. The mare couldn't stop, and certainly couldn't turn, but she slowed dramatically, and that was enough to bring the other two horses rapidly up behind. Andris caught Merel's eye, and knew that although there was no time to signal she knew what to do. She steered her mount so that it came to Andris's left, while the guardsman found himself forced to choose between going to the right or cannoning into Andris.

Unfortunately, the guardsman was cast in the heroic mould. He looked Andris full in the face, aimed the spear at the gap between his shoulder-blades, and drove straight forward, heedless of the danger of taking a fall.

Andris yanked hard on the rein and pulled his own mount sideways, but all the advantage was now with the man behind and the point of the spear hurtled towards the middle of his back.

Andris ducked as low as he possibly could and suppressed the anticipatory scream that swelled in his lungs. He felt the head of the spear glide along the bumpy line of his backbone, slicing cloth and flesh, but he knew immediately that he had escaped death.

The point of the spear caught the rim of the stolen helmet and flipped it clear of Andris's head. Andris lashed out sideways with his right hand – which had somehow lost the sword it had been clutching but a moment before – smashing his fist upon the nose of the guardsman's horse just as it ran into the mare's heels. Both horses could easily have come down, but the mare was both agile and courageous. She danced away from the bump while the other took a crashing fall.

Andris couldn't look back to see whether the rider or his unlucky mount had been seriously injured. As he tried to straighten up he experienced the strangest sensation, as if his back were on fire from waistline to neck. He could feel the two halves of his divided shirt flapping wetly in the wind.

'Follow me!' Merel shouted to him, having by now taken the lead. Her voice seemed unnecessarily loud, and the command unreasonably difficult. Andris felt very sick and exceedingly giddy, and every fall of the mare's hooves seemed to reverberate through his body. His back now felt as though all the elements of his spine had suddenly fused together, so that the least jar was like the scalding strike of a whip.

He heard himself moaning piteously, like a lovesick cat, and wondered why he had not the breath to howl like a man.

The sound of the vast crowd gathered outside the citadel died away in the distance, but Andris no longer knew where he was or where he might be going. The mare was making her own way now, but she was slowing down. He was grateful for that.

The mare went slower and slower, but she had not quite stopped when he heard a voice saying: 'Andris! Let me take the reins!'

He would have surrendered the reins gladly enough had he only known how, but he no longer seemed to be connected to his own arms. He hardly seemed to be connected to the world at all . . . and such connection as he retained was rapidly unravelling.

He heard a voice saying 'Rot! Rot! Rot!' – but the obscenity was spoken in a very strange way, more anguished than angered. Then he heard the same voice saying: 'You can't die on me, you bastard. After I went through all that, *you can't rotting die on me!*'

Andris summoned up every vestige of his strength, reminding himself that he was big enough to be thought half-giant.

'I'm alive!' he whispered. 'Ride! Ride! I'll follow to the Navel of the World, if that's what's needed.' It was all bravado, but saying it – and having his valiant cousin believe it – was all that was required to make it true.

She rode on, and he followed, with no scope in his throbbing head for any thought at all save a defiant determination that he mustn't lose consciousness lest he fall off his horse and die.

18

KING BELIN OF Xandria sat on his uncomfortable throne in his dismal throne room – it seemed dismal even by daylight nowadays, despite the heroic efforts invested in the maintenance of the carpet and wall-hangings – and listened with gritted teeth to report after report on the magnitude of the tragedy which had struck his realm. He was flanked to the left by the Prince-Commander of the Armed Forces and the Chief of the Secret Police, while the Chief Steward of the citadel and the Lord High Treasurer stood to his right. All four of these worthies were aghast and angry, not to mention desperate and determined; they wailed and they shouted and they blustered, and would doubtless have gnashed their teeth if they had been slightly less well bred.

Belin, by contrast, was calm and diffident. He knew that this would be taken as evidence of regal composure, and was perfectly content to let that interpretation stand, but the truth of the matter was that he simply didn't care enough to get excited.

He was past caring about the loss of twelve barrels of newly refreshed coin. He was past caring about the laxity of citadel security or the evident readiness of trusted servants to take bribes. He was past caring about the violation of the Inner Sanctum. He couldn't even bring himself to care about the injury done to his household or the insult to his reputation.

He had to pretend to care, of course, about all of it – and more – but at least he had a reputation for regal composure to help him pretend with the minimum of effort. When he simply nodded his head at each new item in the long catalogue of atrocities and catastrophes, he could be confident that the observers would only admire him all the more for his awesome dignity and self-control. Privately, he was hardly bothering to listen.

It would have been far better, of course, if none of this had happened; Belin liked life to be uneventful. Given that it *had* happened, though, the scrupulous accumulation of details seemed to him to be ineffably tedious and inconsequential. He would rather have shrugged his shoulders and forgotten about it – but that, alas, was out of the question. A king had his obligations.

The trouble is, Belin thought, as the Chief Steward interviewed yet another lackey as to the precise extent of the damage done by the petards, *that a king has far too many obligations. There are people in the world who envy me my thirty-and-one wives, my ninety-and-nine children, my boundless wealth and my glorious empire. Every man who takes pleasure in one wife – and perhaps a mistress or two on the side – imagines that I enjoy that pleasure multiplied many times. Every man who takes pride in three or four children imagines that I possess that pride exaggerated to its limit. Every man who has more than enough wealth to live in the manner to which he is accustomed imagines that I experience his every appetite greatly magnified and yet fully satisfied. Every man who has authority over a household and half a dozen servants imagines that I exert such power over a space which extends from horizon to horizon and far beyond . . .*

And yet, a man who has thirty-and-one wives has no intimates at all, merely a flock of laying hens whose furious clucking is all envy and pride; and a man who has ninety-and-nine children has no true heirs at all, merely a herd of fattened pigs whose snuffling and snorting is all ambition and greed; and a man who has far more wealth than he could ever spend can take satisfaction in nothing; and a man who rules the greatest empire in the world is nothing but the bulkiest and most tortuous knot in a huge net, whose one and only privilege is to be pulled this way and that . . . and that . . . and that . . . until his every sinew and sensation is strained to the limit of human endurance . . .

The king had immersed himself so completely in this reverie that the Prince-Commander of the Armed Forces actually had to touch him on the arm to reclaim his attention. He was sufficiently skilled in such matters not to start. He raised his arm in reflexively negligent acknowledgement.

A young man had been brought to stand before the throne. He was, to judge by his face, an extremely unhappy young man. He seemed horribly conscious of the fact that he was weary, dishevelled and unwashed. Presumably, like almost everyone else in the citadel, he had been awake for more than forty hours, twenty of which had been spent in furious – if ultimately hopeless – action. Like everyone else, he would doubtless have done his utmost to salvage something from the disaster unfolding around him, and like everyone else he would doubtless have failed dismally in every possible respect.

'Captain Cerri, majesty,' the Prince-Commander explained. 'The officer in command of the night-watch.' The Prince-Commander clearly didn't want his august father to miss any part of this particular episode; it was to be a climax of sorts.

'Of course,' Belin said, looking down at the damned man.

Captain Cerri clearly knew that he was damned, but did not seem inclined to resist his fate. He was probably not much concerned about the magnitude of the punishment likely to be visited upon him, because he knew how thoroughly he deserved it and was bitterly ashamed of himself. He was all the more ashamed because he had to face his accusers looking like something which had crawled out of the gutter.

Belin, who had lately made stern efforts to cultivate a taste for perversity, instantly took a liking to the young man.

'How do your men fare, Captain Cerri?' asked the Prince-Commander, immediately taking the initiative. He was fully entitled so to do, by virtue of the fact that he was the man ultimately in charge of the king's guard.

'None dead, sir,' the young man reported dully. 'Several struck down by the darts which the darklanders fired. Two trampled by horses, two wounded in the arms by knife-thrusts, one with a broken head. All will recover, according to the doctors.'

'No worse, then, than the injuries suffered by the other companies which came rushing to your aid,' observed the Prince-Commander. It was obvious that he didn't mean the judgment as a compliment.

'No sir,' the young man admitted.

'*None dead*,' the Prince-Commander repeated, emphasising the words with ominous force. 'The citadel is invaded, the wall breached for the first time in a thousand years, and every single man set to guard it is so enthusiastic to protect his own skin that the intruders get clean away. Clean away!'

The young man winced at the unfairness of the judgment, but knew better than to protest. Belin raised his hand to put a temporary stop to the torture.

'How did they get past the men you had stationed at the City Gate, captain?' the king asked, in a much milder tone – although the young man did not seem in the least reassured by its softness.

'My men were felled by anaesthetic darts, majesty,' he said. 'While the petard was being set against the gate a dozen men or more must have come through the gatehouse – but the men who set the other petards were already inside, having entered during the day and secreted themselves. Others must already have been in the stables.' He did not add that they must have had considerable help from within the citadel – from grooms and kitchen servants, perhaps even members of the royal household. It was not his place to make such accusations, no matter how obviously warranted they were.

'Why did your sentries and patrols fail to see or intercept these men?' Belin asked, although he already knew the answer.

The young officer cringed. 'I'd withdrawn some of the sentries, majesty,' he said, as evenly as he could, 'and halved the patrols. I had to set a trap in the prison, because I had information regarding an escape attempt.'

'Which you did not report,' the Prince-Commander put in.

Belin raised his hand again. The officer was no more than a boy, and a country boy at that: the son of some provincial lordling sent to make his fortune in the great city, with the aid of a commission expensively bought with hard-earned coin – fully trained in the Arts Martial, though not at the expense of the State, but otherwise utterly naïve.

'Tell us how you came by the information, captain,' Belin said, trying not to let his weariness become too obvious.

'The jailer saw a man pass a message into one of the cells, majesty. He was there visiting his brother, shortly before the gates were due to be closed, and took the opportunity to drop a piece of parchment into another man's cell. I . . . persuaded the man to tell me what the message said. I would have reported the matter had it occurred earlier in the shift, or if the night had passed without incident, but . . . it seemed best to take precautions.'

'Imbecile,' said the Prince-Commander.

The young man lifted his head for the first time, but there was nothing heated about his response. 'I now see, majesty, that I was intended to intercept the message,' he said. 'I was taken in. My stupidity was responsible for everything that happened thereafter.'

Brave man! Belin thought. *And not so stupid as to attempt excuses or apologies.* 'How long have you held your commission?' he asked.

'Sixty days, majesty.'

'Did it occur to you to ask for extra men to set your trap?'

'Yes, majesty. But I . . .'

'But you're the junior officer in the guard, and you wanted to create an impression.' Belin finished for him, thinking that it was probably a more accurate summary than the young man had in mind, although it was probably far too simple to be the whole explanation of a complicated judgment.

The officer had sense enough not to attempt any correction.

'There *was* trouble at the prison, I suppose?' Belin said.

'Yes, majesty. There was an escape.'

'Which you failed to prevent, in spite of the advance warning.'

The young man's face flushed crimson. 'Yes, majesty. I had been expecting only one man to be released, but the men who went into the jail let everyone out. Then, as soon as the alarm was raised, my men went to the City Gate as fast as they could. Several prisoners escaped in the confusion, including the amber and the brother of the man from whom we obtained the information. It seems that they were part of the conspiracy all along. Their arrests might well have been part of the plan.'

'So they might,' said Belin tiredly. 'It's obvious enough, with the aid of hindsight. But you're not a complete fool, Captain Cerri. No one could have anticipated that this might happen. The citadel of Xandria is one of the wonders of the world, and history tells us that it has been besieged a dozen times in the last thousand years, always unsuccessfully. These walls have been battered by mortar-bombs, and even by freshly forged cannon by those mad enough to take the risk, for tendays on end. They've been bombarded with thousands of gallons of the most powerful stonerots known to man, but they've never been fatally breached. The harbour has been blockaded by the most powerful navies ever assembled, and the city has been sacked by armies a hundred thousand strong, but the citadel itself has always held firm. Who would have imagined that a gang of petty thieves and darkland savages with blowpipes would dare to try to rob it?'

Captain Cerri wisely said nothing.

'I suppose you realise, captain,' Belin went on, 'that these noble gentlemen gathered about me want your blood. They want me to make an example of you – perhaps to have you hanged, or at least condemned to the wall. Not because they think you're any more guilty than they are, of course, but simply because they think you're the most convenient scapegoat. The Chief Steward of the citadel didn't know that half his staff were in league with these villains. The Chief of my Secret Police heard not the slightest whisper that any such robbery was being planned. My beloved son the Prince-Commander of the Armed Forces has such brilliant staff officers that the combined forces of the guard, the constabulary and the militia failed to make a single arrest between them. The Lord High Treasurer failed to take the most elementary precautions regarding the safe storage of the refreshed coin. Between the four of them, they managed to make the unthinkable not merely possible but perfectly straightforward. And they want you to take the blame for them, because nobody who matters a damn cares what becomes of you.'

Belin did not look round to see what expressions his ministers wore, but he took a certain pleasure in the naked astonishment with which the young officer finally condescended briefly to meet his gaze.

'As it happens,' the king went on, warming at last to the task which lay unpleasantly and tediously before him, 'it could have been even worse. No one is dead, so far as we know. That, I think, is something to be grateful for. The thieves caused chaos, but they didn't cut anybody's throat, and they seem to have taken some small trouble to avoid doing so. Their petards were very carefully designed, and just as carefully set. The devices did what they were supposed to do, and no more. The coin they stole is a modest enough fortune, and its redistribution will be a temporary affair – it might even work to the benefit of trade within the kingdom, or between Xandria proper and whichever of its far-flung provinces the thieves select as a refuge. In any case, it's safe to assume that every man in the empire will be keeping a sharp lookout for the coin, whether his intention is to reclaim it for the crown or to steal a portion himself. There are other matters which concern me more.'

He paused, prompting the officer to say 'Majesty?'

'No one is dead, *so far as we know*,' Belin said, 'but several people are missing. One of them is my daughter, Lucrezia. She seems to have run out of the Inner Sanctum immediately after the petard blew the door off its hinges, while the carts were coming out of the stables on their way to pick up the barrels of coin. No one is certain what happened to her after that, but I fear she might have been kidnapped.'

Captain Cerri had the grace to look astonished as well as faintly puzzled.

'I want my daughter back, captain,' Belin said, allowing his voice to become ominous. 'I don't know what the robbers intend to do with her but if they did take her they'll presumably try to hold her to ransom. I want you and the men in your command to find her, and bring her back. If, in the process of carrying out this mission, you encounter the men who robbed the treasury, you should of course kill the lot of them – *but not until the princess is safe*. Until you find her and bring her safely back, neither you nor any of your men will set foot inside the city walls. Do you understand me, captain?'

'Yes, majesty,' the officer replied, although he was not entirely sure what he was agreeing to. The order he had been given was clear enough, but one of the things he had to understand was that unless and until he carried it out he and all his men were banished from the city. It was a milder punishment than the king's ministers wanted, but it was a punishment nevertheless. As for the other thing he had to understand . . . well, no one was going to say out loud that perhaps the princess hadn't been kidnapped at all – that perhaps she, too, had taken the opportunity to escape from her narrow prison.

'Do you have any idea where to start looking?' Belin asked, his voice once again as mild as milk.

'According to rumour, majesty, the person behind the robbery must have been a man named Checuti,' the officer said. 'He's a southerner, from the province of Khalorn . . . but that's not to say he'll go back there. He might be wiser to go to one of the Thousand Isles.'

'My Chief of Secret Police will give you any information he has,' Belin said. He leaned forward, and said: 'What do you know about the amber, captain? The prisoner whose escape you were trying to prevent.'

'Very little, majesty,' the officer replied, with a slight stutter which implied that he might know something he wasn't prepared to admit. 'My men arrested him some days ago, while we were on harbour patrol. I . . . should have realised there was something strange about the planned escape, given that two people had already offered to buy him out.'

'Two people?' For the first time, Belin found himself facing a point of information which had not already been made known to him.

'Yes, majesty. A merchant named Carus Fraxinus and . . . Princess Lucrezia.' The officer blushed, realising that he had placed the names in the wrong order.

Belin looked round at the Chief of his Secret Police, but didn't bother to ask the question that was hovering on his lips. If Fraxinus had been involved in the robbery, he'd hardly have attempted to buy out a man who was required by the plan to be in jail . . . assuming that the attempted jailbreak really was a calculated diversion. He remembered that Lucrezia had mentioned the name of Carus Fraxinus in connection with that of Hyry Keshvara and the expedition to find the source of the seed which she had planned to feed to the amber . . . but he couldn't begin to see what sinister sense there might be in the tangled web of coincidence. Hadn't Lucrezia tried to tell him that there was something important about whatever it was that Fraxinus had planned . . . to the realm, and perhaps to the world? Was that why she had disappeared? Could even she have been part of this amazing plan to steal the Thanksgiving coin? For a fleeting moment, Belin was almost intrigued . . . but then he remembered how terribly tired he was, and imagined the dreadful headache which speculations of that intricate kind might easily bring on.

'Find my daughter, captain,' he said dully. 'Bring her back, alive and well. If you can, bring me this Checuti's head on a pike as well . . . and the amber's, if you want to be sure of the best possible welcome. But don't come back without the princess. Not ever. That goes for your men too. You have two days to make ready.'

'Yes, majesty,' the captain said, bowing low in response to a casual gesture of dismissal. He turned, and made his weary way back to the door through which he had entered, making only the feeblest attempt to simulate a military march.

Another problem solved, Belin thought, as he watched the young man's dejected retreat. *There's not one chance in a thousand of my seeing him again. If only I could be as easily rid of the rest of these chattering apes!*

19

THE SERVANT WHO had shown Jacom into Carus Fraxinus's reception-room bowed and retired. Jacom was surprised to find that the merchant was not alone, and even more surprised at the appearance of the man with whom he was engrossed in conversation. He was old, blind, very ragged and none too clean. It took several seconds for Jacom to realise that this must be the story-teller who had been with the amber in the Wayfaring Tree. Was he too, Jacom wondered, part of the vast conspiracy which had caught him up and ruined his life?

'Jacom!' said the merchant heartily. He leapt to his feet and extended his hand to be shaken. There was a glass decanter on the table before the sofa where his unprepossessing guest sat, and two dark-coloured goblets; now Fraxinus fetched a third cup from a cupboard and filled that too. He seemed to be in a good mood – an excessively good mood, in Jacom's sombre opinion.

'It's good to see you, friend,' the merchant said, guiding him to a chair while resuming his own seat beside the blind man. 'I wish Xury were here, but he's still away – not expected until tomorrow or the day after. Are you well?'

Jacom, perching uneasily on the edge of his seat, could not summon up the energy to lie. 'No,' he said bluntly. 'I'm not. I'm in trouble. I need your help.'

'Ah!' said Fraxinus, not in the least put out by his bluntness. 'I take it that Checuti's mad escapade has numbered you among its many victims. I'm very sorry to hear it. How bad is it?'

'Not as bad as it might be, I'm assured,' Jacom said glumly, 'but quite bad enough, from my point of view. I was on duty last night. I set men to watch the jail, having learned that someone intended to help one of the prisoners escape – a move which must have assisted the robbers in the secret setting of their petards and

147

helped them to prepare their carts unobserved and uninterrupted. My men and I have been exiled from the city, in effect. The price of our return is the safe recovery of Princess Lucrezia.'

Fraxinus seemed suitably amazed, and suitably sympathetic. 'I had not heard that Princess Lucrezia was missing,' he said. 'That's a harsh sentence, Jacom. I can't tell you how sorry I am.'

'The princess is missing, presumed kidnapped,' Jacom said, stressing the word *presumed* very faintly. 'If Checuti took her, I must find him, as quickly as I can.'

'That won't be easy,' Fraxinus observed cautiously. Jacom wondered if the note of caution signified that his careful use of the word *if* had not gone unnoticed, nor its implications unappreciated.

'I'd be very grateful for any help you can offer, Carus,' Jacom said, this time placing a slight emphasis on the word *any*.

Fraxinus took a sip of wine, studying his visitor with a slightly furrowed brow. The blind man was quite still, but he was listening eagerly to every word, well aware of the fact that there would be good money to be earned from the spreading of this tale. Jacom, embarrassed by the tension he had brought into being, sipped from his own cup. 'I believe you're going south very shortly,' he said to Fraxinus. 'To Khalorn.' He wondered why there seemed to be a bitter taste in his mouth when the wine was so silkily sweet.

'That's right,' Fraxinus said neutrally. 'I told you as much when I spoke to you the other day. I also told you then that I know Checuti. What are you getting at?'

'The man whose escape from the jail I tried to prevent,' Jacom said, taking the bull between the horns, 'was the man in whom you expressed a strong interest – the mapmaker. I don't suppose you know his present whereabouts?'

'Jacom!' the merchant protested, maintaining his voice at a gentle level despite the clear note of reproach. 'Surely you don't think that I had anything to do with this business? I've been a respectable man of business since before you were born, and I've never been accused or suspected of any kind of wrongdoing. Why would I try to secure the man's release by stealth when I could have bought him out?'

'The thing is,' Jacom said uneasily, 'that you *couldn't* buy him out – because the princess had already claimed him. If the note which the jailer intercepted wasn't a complete fabrication, it might well have been sent by someone called Zabio. You told me that Myrasol asked you to look for a relative of his – by which he meant one Theo Zabio, according to the jailer. I see that you found the other man he mentioned to you. Did you by any chance find Zabio too?'

Fraxinus had raised his eyebrows, but it was impossible to tell whether he was genuinely offended. 'Andris Myrasol did ask me to enquire after a man named Zabio,' he admitted. 'Alas, I could find no one who knew such a man. I had intended to consult Checuti about that, but I had no chance to do so – he can be a difficult man to find even at the best of times, and I now know that he had other matters on his mind. The story-teller here was far easier to locate, and I wanted to interview *him* for my own reasons. You don't really think that I'm mixed up in this business, do you, Jacom? Surely not!'

Jacom couldn't meet the other man's eyes. 'No, I don't,' he said. 'But the jailer has given this information to the Chief of the Secret Police, and it's his duty as well as his nature to scent conspiracies everywhere. Given that you're about to set out for Khalorn, and that another member of your expedition visited Princess Lucrezia mere hours before the robbery, he's understandably interested. At the very least, you'll be carefully watched for the next few tendays – and I can't promise that you won't be hindered when you reach Khalorn. If you do happen to meet up with the mapmaker . . . well, perhaps you might count yourself more fortunate if you don't, at least until Checuti is caught or the princess found.'

'It all seems a trifle over-complicated,' Fraxinus said in a vexed tone. 'But I do see the logic of it. When you say you want my help, I presume you'd like me to help you locate Andris Myrasol . . . or Checuti. Given that Aulakh Phar and I have extensive contacts in the southland, including darklanders, you think I might be in a position to pick up valuable information.'

'I'd like to travel with you, if I may,' Jacom said, there being no point in beating about the bush. 'I'd be extremely obliged if you could do your utmost, while we're on the road, to catch some whisper regarding Checuti's possible whereabouts.'

'I see,' Fraxinus said. 'Well, you're welcome to come with me, if you wish – you don't really need my permission to follow me along the king's highway. Whatever whispers reach my ears I'll be pleased to pass on to you – but for what it may be worth, perhaps I ought to say that I had no reason whatsoever to try to get Andris Myrasol out of jail. Hyry Keshvara had already persuaded the princess to take steps to provide me with a map as soon as the amber was given into her care. I don't say that Checuti's so-called crime of the century was as much of an inconvenience to me as it has been to you, but I certainly obtained no advantage from it, and would far rather it hadn't happened. Please believe that.'

'I do,' Jacom said unhappily, 'but . . .' He shrugged his shoulders helplessly.

'I'll do what I can to help,' the merchant assured him, 'but I have plans and ambitions of my own – which might turn out in the end to concern matters of far greater moment than the grand gesture of a petty prince of rogues. Would you like to hear the rest of what the story-teller has to reveal?'

Jacom's first impulse was to say no, and protest that he had more important things to do than listen to idle fancies, but the thought of going back to the barracks to face the bitterly reproachful stares of the men who were to share his exile was by no means a pleasant one. 'Why not?' he said, with a careless shrug.

'He has been recalling fragments from the *Apocrypha of Genesys*,' Fraxinus explained, although the title meant nothing to Jacom. 'I believe that he has one more left to relate.' He turned to the blind man, and said: 'I'm sorry for the interruption, my friend.'

'It wasn't the amber who hit the guardsman in the Wayfaring Tree,' the blind man said, with the air of one who had been patiently waiting for a chance to say so. 'It was a man named Burdam. I heard his name quite clearly spoken as he made his escape up the stairway. The amber's an honest man, sir – I have an ear for such things.'

'It hardly matters now whether he was innocent or guilty,' Jacom observed. 'If they catch him again, he's a dead man.'

'It's quite possible that he didn't know anything about the robbery,' Fraxinus pointed out. 'Perhaps Checuti was using him as cynically as he used you.'

'Perhaps,' Jacom admitted. 'But it won't help him if he's caught – and he's not an unobtrusive man. My own situation isn't enviable, but I wouldn't swap places with him.' He suspected from the way Fraxinus looked at him, however, that the merchant would very readily have made the exchange of travelling-companions. 'Go on, then,' he said to the story-teller. 'Let's hear your secret lore.'

The story-teller seemed to be on the point of saying something more, but changed his mind and did as he was told.

'These are the last of the verses I was taught,' he said. 'You will know their substance, I think.' His tone changed very markedly as he slipped into the manner of one reproducing a precious heritage. 'Let it not be thought,' he recited, 'that the ship which sailed the dark between the stars was a place of perfect harmony, and let it not be thought that there was agreement as to the manner in which the people of the world were to be armed for their struggle. The lore which the forefathers made is not the only truth, nor is it even the whole of the truth which Goran desired his sons and daughters to know.

'In addition to the lore and the common wisdom which the forefathers designed Goran drew up the secret commandments, perhaps twelve in number and perhaps thirteen, which he entrusted to a favoured few of the original loremasters, but not to others.

'Goran was wise enough to know that secrets perish easily, and that pretence flourishes wherever secrets are. Secrets perish easily because that which is known to the few cannot be as securely held as that which is known to the many. Pretence flourishes where secrets are because pretenders invent what they do not truly know, for the sake of being thought better people than they are. Goran knew, therefore, that some of the secret commandments would be lost and the remainder polluted by haphazard invention. He could only hope that these processes of corrosion and corruption would not lead, even in the end, to mere chaos. Nevertheless, he gave his secret commandments to the favoured few, and hoped that they might be kept.

'Goran was not the only one among the forefathers to invent such arcana, and others issued secret commandments which contradicted his. They were wise enough to fear that they were sowing the seeds of future wars, but they were brave enough to hope that more good would come of it than evil.

'To all those who believe themselves custodians of secret

commandments, common wisdom has this to say: first, do not fail to keep them; second, do not trust them too far; third, before you do evil at their urging ask what good will come of it.

'What are humans for, if not to fight evil wherever it is found? What are humans worth, if they fear to tread the paths of evil? What will humans become, if they do not aim their endeavours towards the defeat of evil?'

There was a moment's silence when the blind man had finished.

What nonsense! Jacom thought, while Fraxinus offered polite thanks. The story-teller drank his wine, aglow with pleasure. Jacom doubted that he had ever been thanked for news of that particular kind. Everyone had heard of the secret commandments. Everyone knew that they were a joke. Everyone knew – or ought to – that the so-called *Lore of Genesys* was simply a story made up by ignorant men to supply some kind of explanation of their presence in the world.

'You seem unimpressed, Jacom,' Fraxinus said. 'You are a hard-headed realist, no doubt, who has no truck with tales of the beginning of human society?'

'I'm more concerned with practical matters,' Jacom said. 'Now more than ever.'

'So am I,' Fraxinus countered. 'If I'm to go in search of legendary places, is it not practical to be as scrupulous as possible in consulting what legend has to say about them? I admit, though, that this was the least interesting of the three fragments which my friend has taken such care to preserve. The others spoke of the garden of Idun, of Serpents and Salamanders and strange pacts . . . and of the legacy of dreams which connects us, even now, to our remotest ancestors and the world from which they came.'

'We cannot know that they came from another world,' Jacom said stubbornly. 'Perhaps they did and perhaps they didn't – but whatever the truth is, we cannot know it. If there ever was a ship, and forefathers who made the lore, they have rotted down to mere dirt. Whatever our ancestors were, they're gone as completely as if they had never been.'

'Not so,' Faximus said. 'The makers of the lore, whoever they were and whether or not they were truthful in everything they taught, shaped our thoughts, our lives and our nature. We carry the past in our blood and in our minds; it remains incarnate in our flesh and it colours our dreams. The world is the world, though centuries and millennia may elapse; the legacy of its past is everywhere, in every open appearance and every hidden thing. Everything dies and everything rots, but everything gives birth to effects and consequences, however briefly it may endure; life is eternal as well as evanescent.

'The Navel of the World cannot now contain the least trace of the ship that brought our forefathers to the world, if there was indeed a ship, but whatever our forefathers did in the city of Idun and the garden they made when the city crumbled into dust, the consequences of those actions extend even to the present day. I believe that we ought to be interested in those consequences, and they might affect us far more profoundly than we imagine. Perhaps, in the fullness of time, I shall be able to convert you to my way of thinking.'

Jacom understood the implications of that *perhaps* far too well. He had already asked himelf, over and over again, what he might do if – as seemed entirely likely – he never found the fee which would buy his way back into Xandria.

'I hope it won't come to that,' he said unhappily. 'I only want to find the princess, and bring her safely home. I wish you every success in your adventures, but I hope with all my heart that I shall be able to return to Xandria long before you.'

'Then I shall hope so too,' Fraxinus said kindly. 'And for what it may be worth, you shall have my help for as long as you might require it.'

20

ANDRIS WOKE UP not knowing where he was. He lay perfectly still, not daring to move, trying to remember.

He remembered that he had been lost in terrible discomfort for a very long time, but now felt sufficiently detached from the sensation not to be forced to describe it as pain, or even as agony. It had started out as pain, and had more than once veered towards agony, but time had reduced it to a mere framework of his existence, which circumstance inevitably made it fade and become duller. It had been tempered, too, by pride: pride in the fact that he had never given up the ghost, never fallen unconscious, and never fallen off his horse. He had ridden for hours on end, following Merel wherever she led, held firm in the grip of determination to show her that her efforts had not been wasted, and that he was a man worth saving.

He remembered getting down from the horse, and stretching himself out as carefully as he could upon the moist ground. He remembered lying prone and helpless while someone applied something glutinous and cold to his spine. He remembered trying to speak, but being unable to do anything more than twitch and grunt. 'It's all right,' Merel had assured him roughly. 'It's only woundglue. Grandfather always told me never to get into a fight without woundglue in my pouch, and it's a good thing for you I was such a respectful listener. Lie still.'

He remembered making an effort to reply, but failing. How long ago had that been?

His head ached and his whole body felt sore. He had been lying on damp ground for a long time, without so much as a coarse mat to cushion him or keep him dry. He was clothed, but he could remember Merel's intrusive fingers working through an open gap in the back of his shirt, where no gap had been until the guardsman's spear had raked him, and he knew that he was still clad in the same ruined shirt. His trousers had been soaked by mud and such protection as his garments gave him against the unfamiliar cold seemed inconveniently slight.

He knew by the cold that it was still night even before he attempted to open his eyes. When he finally managed to drag his sticky eyelids apart he found that his resting-place was unsheltered by roof or foliage and that the stars were obscured by a great sheet of unbroken cloud. No lamp was lit nearby and he could not see where he was – but he felt intuitively certain that it was going to rain, and that they would be in for a thorough drenching if they could not find shelter.

He tried to get up, but the effort cost him dearly. The movement set his spine and dorsal ribs aflame with agony. He gave up, and decided to lie prone until he felt a lot better. His mouth and throat were very dry, and he felt fearfully thirsty.

But I'm alive! he thought. *And wherever I am, it's not prison.*

'Merel?' he croaked weakly, glad to be able to pronounce the word.

He heard a rustling sound. A match was struck and a candle lighted, but his position was too awkward to allow him to take much advantage of the little flame. He had to tilt his head back to look up into the face of Merel Zabio, who was kneeling nearby, and the effort was too painful to sustain. He laid his forehead down for a second, and then turned his head half-sideways so he could inspect his rescuer from the corner of his eye. She set the candle down, compacting soil around the base to make it stand up. Then she groped in the dark beside her feet, and found a leather bottle, which she uncorked and passed into his hand.

It was good to have something to grip, although his fingers were unbeatably clumsy. He moved the bottle into position and lifted himself long enough to sip a little of the liquid. It was only water, but it was very welcome. He lifted himself again. His second sip was more of a gulp. By the time he had drained the vessel to the dregs he felt almost human again. When he tried to move his limbs he had to fight against the leaden pain, but they all moved freely enough; unfortunately, he could find no position other than prone which did not put strain on his back.

'Lie down and sleep,' his kinswoman had advised, in a soothing tone. 'We can't go on till there's light. The woundglue is long set, and working well. With luck, you'll be well enough to ride by the time we can move on.'

He had not the slightest idea how long he had slept. He had no idea whether the present darkness was the same darkness that had surrounded him when his cousin had first applied the woundglue to his torn back, or whether he had slept through an entire day. Woundglue could do that, especially if it had been mixed strong and laced with some kind of knockout drops.

His back felt a little better, but not much. He made another attempt to get up, but again decided that it was wiser to remain prone.

'Merel?' he said querulously. 'Where are we?' His voice was still hoarse, in spite of the liquid he had drunk. He did his best to look around, but his ignominious position made it difficult for his probing eyes to penetrate the surrounding curtain of darkness. The candle's light was so feeble that the lighted space seemed narrower than the cell he had so recently quit. It was almost as if the world itself had become a prison.

'The middle of nowhere,' Merel told him, adjusting her position to make herself comfortable, 'or as near to it as we could get, given that the walls of Xandria are far too close for comfort. I had to hide us quickly, because I daren't let you bounce around too long on that mare with blood gushing from your back. She's a good horse, though. So's mine – without them, we'd have been lost. Checuti and his men are long gone, but they wouldn't have helped us anyway. You're too easily recognisable. We're on our own, cousin, at least for the time being. We have to make our own way to safety – and it'll be a long journey.'

The ground on which Andris lay was bare, the loose soil having been prepared for planting but not yet sown with seed. He peeped up at his companion's face. She met his gaze frankly, seemingly as interested in his features as he was in hers. They studied one another for a minute and more. He had collected himself now; he felt more like his usual self.

'You'll be fine,' she told him reassuringly.

'Why did you do it?' he said faintly. 'You don't even know me.'

'You're the only family I have,' she told him. 'But I'd be lying if I said it was my idea. I'd never have dared think of such a thing. It was all Checuti's doing. He was the one who told me that I had a kinsman in the jail, and asked me whether I was interested in getting you out. I didn't know what to say . . . I could very easily have told him to forget it. Then he told me what the princess intended to do to you . . . after that, I could hardly say no.'

Andris put his hand up to his forehead, trying unsuccessfully to calm a throbbing ache in his head. 'I'm sorry,' he said, after a brief period of silence. 'I don't understand. What did he tell you the princess intended to do to me?'

'Break your legs, cut off your balls and plant a thorn-bush in your living flesh.'

He looked up at her steadily for a few moments before saying: 'You're serious, aren't you?'

'So was Checuti. He said he felt bad about it, because you hadn't actually done what they put you in jail for. It was one of his men, apparently. Anyhow, he said he'd already planted one of his people in the jail, but that if I was game for it he'd include you in the plan too. The more the merrier, he said – and I think he meant exactly that. I suspect that he has a certain fondness for complication for its own sake, and his scheme was as much a joke – or at least a grand gesture – as a means of getting rich. As I said, I felt obliged to join in. He made it seem as though I'd be turning down the chance of a lifetime if I didn't, even though he didn't offer me a share of the coin. And you are my kinsman, after all – what kind of person would I have been if I'd said no? Checuti said there was a man who might help us if we can only stay ahead of the king's men long enough to get to him.'

'Carus Fraxinus?' said Andris.

'No. He advised me to steer clear of him, at least for now. Too honest, he said. Told me to go to a man named Phar – Aulakh Phar – if we can only get to him. Checuti says he'll pay as much as Fraxinus would for a map, and pay us a wage if we care to join him. The only trouble is that we have to go to Khalorn to find him. It's a long way, and there'll be people looking out for us. Lots of them.'

Andris studied her carefully. 'Are you sure this Checuti wasn't lying to you?' he asked 'About the princess, I mean.'

She shrugged her shoulders. 'Maybe. Would you rather have taken a chance? Have you got any better ideas about what to do now?'

Andris decided, on due reflection, that the answer to both questions was no. He didn't bother saying so out loud. 'How did Checuti know where to find you?' he asked. 'Why was he even looking? I asked Fraxinus to try to find Uncle Theo – I even wrote to the captain of the ship I came in on – but they evidently failed.'

'Actually, they succeeded – but indirectly,' she told him. 'If they hadn't started asking after Theo Zabio, Checuti would never have become interested. He hears everything, you see. He keeps track of everyone else's plans and schemes, just in case there's a chance to cut himself in. That's why I believe him about Phar – he probably knows every detail of this business that Fraxinus, Phar and Keshvara are teaming up for. When he heard people were asking about Theo Zabio he thought he ought to let me know. That is, he thought that it might be worth his while to make me an offer. He knew Grandfather, you see – and me too, though very slightly. Checuti knows everybody.'

'You mean that Uncle Theo was a thief, like this Checuti?'

'No. I'm no more than a thief, I suppose, but Grandfather was a genuine pirate.'

'He was once third in line to the throne of Ferentina,' Andris observed sadly.

'He told me that – but he said it was much safer being a pirate,' Merel observed drily. 'He was a successful man in his way. If only my father had been better able to follow in his footsteps, I might not have fallen on hard times.'

'Was he caught – your father, I mean?'

'He died of a fever. I was only a child. Grandfather supported us after that – until he died too. My mother met another man. I've been getting by as best I can, working ships when I can but mostly working the docks. Not well enough, for the most part. When Checuti told me about you . . . well, I didn't have a lot to lose. They say that when everything you own can be fitted into a belt and the coins in your pouch don't make walking uncomfortable it's probably time to move on. Agreeing to come in on Checuti's plan wasn't quite as brave – or as crazy – as you might think.'

She seemed to mean it, but she also seemed to hope that he might contradict her.

'Yes it was,' he said obligingly. 'It was the bravest and craziest thing I ever heard of. I don't believe that you didn't give anything up or leave anything behind.'

She smiled appreciatively, shaking her head as she did so. She wasn't going to admit to having left anything behind, even if she had. She had a pleasant smile, although her face was a little on the plain side. Andris couldn't see the slightest resemblance to himself or any of his sisters, but that was hardly surprising – she was only a quarter amber, and she obviously favoured her golden forebears.

'You paid me back,' she assured him. 'If you hadn't come between us, that spearman would have spitted me. If the blade of the spear hadn't skimmed your spine . . . well, we're about even, I reckon. It was some show wasn't it? Checuti certainly knows how to celebrate a public holiday.'

If only it didn't hurt so much, Andris thought, *I might be able to agree with that.* 'Is it still the Day of Thanksgiving?' he asked

Merel shook her head. 'It worked to our advantage yesterday,' she told him. 'Everyone takes the holiday no matter what, so there weren't as many people looking for us as there might have been. You slept a full forty hours – it's less than four hours to dawn. Will you be fit to ride by daybreak, d'you think? The horses are well rested, and we ought to make what haste we can. There's just a chance we can stay far enough ahead of the news to keep out of serious trouble. Have to find you some new clothes . . . me too, I suppose. And something to eat. The horses' saddle-bags were empty apart from that one water-bottle. Just my luck – every purse I ever cut was either half-empty or full of rotten coin. I've got a few crowns in my pouch, not to mention half a dozen candles, some matches, a good knife and various other odds and ends, so we're not destitute, and food's cheap out here in the sticks. It's a long way to Khalorn, but if you don't mind riding hard and skimping on the good things of life, we can make it.'

'I can ride hard,' he said determinedly, 'bad back or no bad back – and I've long grown unused to luxury.' He tried flexing his back muscles very gently, by way of experimentation. The result was by no means reassuring, but he knew that there was no alternative. They had no hope of outrunning the king's messengers, given that they could not change horses and dared not use the highway, but there was a good chance that they could avoid the forces rallied in response to the messages, and they ought to be able to stay ahead

159

of any troops that were heading south from the city, provided that they rested regularly and were careful to move on as soon and as fast as the horses were able. More dark nights would help their cause considerably. Everything stopped when the stars were blotted out, even when the contents of the king's treasury were on the wing.

He finally managed to roll over and sit up. Pain flared up along the entire length of his spine, and it was slow to fade to a more bearable level, but he gritted his teeth against the burden. The woundglue had indeed done its work, but it couldn't effect miracles. He would need time to heal.

Merel put out a hand to touch him on the shoulder. 'Sorry,' she said as he winced.

'Don't be,' he said, putting his own hand on top of hers. 'If you're right about the princess . . .'

'They do say some very nasty things about her,' Merel observed. 'But then, they say nasty things about all powerful people, don't they?'

'Some of them are true,' he said gloomily. 'It can be a hard world for folk like us.' He wished his back didn't hurt so much. He had a nasty suspicion that it was going to inconvenience him for a long time, and not just when he tried to ride a horse.

'Weren't you in line for the throne of Ferentina, once?' she said.

'Third in the queue,' he confirmed. 'Just like Uncle Theo. But he was right, you know – it *is* safer being a pirate. We may not have much right now, but things can only get better. We'll just have to huddle together for warmth, until daybreak comes – always provided that I can find a comfortable way to lie down.'

'You lie down,' she said, 'and I'll fit in as best I can.'

He did, and so did she. He had not realised until then how very tired she seemed. While he had slept the whole day, she must have stood watch, worrying all the while.

'It's all right now,' he told her, in the same soothing tone that she had used for his benefit. 'Everything is going to be fine.'

'I know,' she replied dutifully.

He smiled, and carefully mustered all his strength for the long struggle which lay ahead of them. The morning would be a new beginning, a new challenge. Just now, four hours did not seem a particularly long time.

The last thing his cousin said to him, before she drifted off to sleep, was: 'Checuti said you were well worth saving. He was only trying to tempt me, but he was right.'

Andris savoured that judgment, realising that it was the nicest thing anyone had said to him for more than seven years.

Part Two

To the Forest of Absolute Night, uplifted by dreams of adventure

The world of dreams is not so smooth as the world which gave birth to mankind. The world of dreams is flattened at the tilted poles; it dances as it spins, and is ever unquiet. We are children of the world, but we are also children of the world of dreams; the steps and rhythms of its dances reverberate in our hearts, and its inquietude is in our blood.

There is no fire burning beneath the surface of the world, ever eager to erupt, nor any sleeping giant to quake the earth with his restlessness, but our inner eyes have seen mountains vomiting fire and ash, and our nerves thrill to the echoes of tremors which our furry fathers felt a million years ago.

The world of dreams is a place of violent change which has given birth to tyrannous constancy, and the tyrant of that constancy is man. The world in which we live is a quiet and orderly place which has given birth to anarchic inconstancy, whose produce is unbridled corruption. Such is the irony of our twofold existence.

If Serpents and Salamanders dream at all, they may dream of the womb and the tomb, but not of any other world than this. Men may dream of the world where they were tyrants once, and because they may, they must.

Men have ever tried to make prophecies of their dreams, no matter how difficult the task might be. Whether the world be conquerable or not, men will never cease to hunger for its conquest.

Conquest without constancy is possible, with the aid of Serpent's Blood and Salamander's Fire and that which is nurtured in Chimera's Cradle, but there is no destiny and nothing is written in the stars which says that men will conquer each and every world on which they choose to dwell.

The Apocrypha of Genesys

HYRY KESHVARA WAS used to rising long before dawn, and she kept to the habit even though it was obvious when she looked out of the window of her room that there was no possibility of continuing her journey until daybreak. Knowing this, she bathed and dressed unhurriedly.

By the time she came down to breakfast the dining-room was full of men from Xandria – couriers and soldiers – all of them impatient and bitterly inclined to curse the ill wind which had blown dense clouds from the north-west. 'This Checuti is a wizard,' she heard one man complain. 'The elements themselves are partners in his conspiracy. With better weather, we'd have had him by now.' It was a hollow lament.

The unhappy innkeeper had already run out of eggs and beer and his milk-churns were very nearly dry. He could offer Hyry nothing but porridge and black coffee, but she accepted these gladly enough. She took them to a little window-seat where she could sit alone; she had no intention of getting into conversation with the king's men after the way they had treated her the previous evening. They had insisted on searching the packs her donkeys carried, and her saddle-bags too. They had made her count out her money, inspecting every single coin for freshness. She had never before had occasion to offer silent thanks for the fact that nothing in her purse was newly minted.

She had, of course, protested vociferously that she was an honest merchant, very well known in the city, authorised to act as an agent for no less a man than Carus Fraxinus, but the soldiers had been adamant. Soldiers always loved an excuse to be imperious and to handle others roughly, and this was probably the best excuse these particular men would ever have. She knew that for the next tenday – perhaps twice as long again – the king's men would make life hell for everyone who travelled the great highway and everyone who lived near it. She did not suppose for a moment that the fact that she had been thoroughly inspected by these men would excuse her from further harassment by others. Perhaps, she thought, it might be better to leave the highway and travel a more discreet rout – but then, of course, she would run the risk of her behaviour being considered suspicious.

Why did it all have to happen now? she thought. *Why couldn't the crime of the century have waited until New Year's Day, or the King's Birthday . . . or even next Leap Year Day? Fraxinus will suffer exactly the same sort of harassment, even if he delays his departure for a day or two – and it'll be just as bad for Aulakh Phar in Khalorn, as soon as the first messenger gets there.*

While she ate her porridge Hyry marvelled at the way in which the king's men seized every excuse to hurry hither and thither, every one of them anxious to be seen to be *doing something*, even though there was nothing constructive to be done. Their horses were already saddled, although there was no prospect of their actually being mounted and taken out for three hours and more, unless some miraculous wind sprang up to hurry the clouds away. She was careful to take her time about things, being deliberately slow in order to prove that the madness was not contagious and that she was still in full possession of herself and her common sense, but she could not make breakfast last for ever. Her request for a second mug of coffee met with a curt refusal; the innkeeper had introduced an informal rationing system so as to conserve his supplies of hot water. Disgustedly, Hyry went out to the stables to see to her own animals. She had no intention of loading them until it was actually time to depart but they had to be watered and fed.

The stables were crowded to bursting, but relatively quiet. Horses had a sense of proportion in these matters, and her donkeys were masters of the Art of Imperturbability. She chatted to them amiably while she doled out their oats, and then she went to the well to get water. She brought back one pail, having waited patiently in line for the privilege of filling it, and then had to go back for a second.

The queue had cleared temporarily and she found the raised bucket still half-full. She reached for the ladle gratefully, but before her hand could close upon it she was grabbed from behind.

A huge hand was clamped over her mouth, stifling her cry of protest, and she felt herself lifted clear of the ground as easily as if she had been a mere child. She struggled, but her captor had both her arms pinned with one of his, and must have been a very strong man.

The lantern lighting the well was positioned under the angled roof of the well-house; its light was so narrowly confined that she only had to be carried three or four steps before she and her kidnapper were utterly swallowed up by the gloom. He must have had a very good idea of where he was going, because he carried her another thirty or forty mets before someone struck a distant match to guide him further.

When her captor brought her closer to the tiny flame she tried to twist around to see him, but she couldn't do it. She couldn't even see the man who held the match, because he was holding it at arm's length, well away from his face. He at least seemed to be a man of normal proportions.

They had gone a further thirty mets – and had used up three more matches – before the smaller man produced a candle in a tray, and used the last match to light it.

'Now, Keshvara,' a deep voice hissed in her ear, 'will you promise to be quiet if I loose your mouth and set you down?'

Perversity prompted her to try to bite the hand and bring her heel up into the man's groin, but curiosity and common sense suppressed the impulse. She tried to nod her head instead.

The big man lowered her feet to the ground, let her take her own weight, and then removed his hand from her mouth. She immediately turned to look at him. He made no attempt to move away from the light, allowing her to study his features. They were broad and ugly. He was, as she had inferred, a very big man indeed.

'I know you,' she said.

'Very probably,' he replied, in his distinctive bass whisper. 'I dare say I'm famous now – or will be, as the story spreads.'

Although she had spoken the truth when she said she knew him, Hyry hadn't been able to put a name to the man at first. It was the implication of his words which provided the necessary clue.

'Burdam Thrid!' she gasped. 'Are you mad? There are fifty men in that inn whose careers would be made if they could seize you.

Do you know what price has been put on your head? They'd cut your belly and pull your guts out inch by inch, twisting all the while, to make you tell them where Checuti is!'

While saying all this she was very careful to keep her own voice low. The last thing she wanted just now was to be caught – or even glimpsed – in the company of Burdam Thrid, who was known to everyone in Xandria as Checuti's chief lieutenant. A man of his height and breadth was far too easily identifiable.

'I don't like this any better than you do,' Thrid assured her. 'I'd far rather be lying low – but Checuti wants to see you, now.'

'What in corruption's name does Checuti want with me?' she demanded. 'I'm not carrying anything of value – and he's already got a small fortune in fresh coin.'

'Come on!' urged Thrid's companion – a less distinctive man to whom Hyry could not put a name.

'He's right,' the big man told her. 'We're in a hurry.'

He was moving off even as he spoke, and he reached out to take her arm as he did so. She might have been able to dodge and run had she acted quickly enough, but the chance had gone before she gave it serious consideration, and so she submitted meekly to being hustled at a fast walk along a series of winding lanes that were no more than cart-tracks.

More than once they cut across open fields which had been freshly turned by the plough. Hyry was accustomed to using the sun or the stars to take bearings, and soon lost her sense of direction in the darkness. She knew that they were east of the highway, but how far east, and whether they were north or south of the inn, she couldn't tell. Eventually, though, they came to a cottage surrounded by huge barns. Thrid took her in while his companion stayed outside.

Checuti was waiting for them in a room to the left of the narrow hallway, sitting casually on a wooden dining-chair with his booted feet on the tabletop. There was a small monkey squatting on his knees, nibbling a plum. The thiefmaster indicated that Hyry should take a chair set at right-angles to his. When she did so, Thrid took the one opposite his master, drawing it away from the table so that it was near the door.

Hyry had seen Checuti before, but never at close quarters. She studied the man carefully. He was black-haired and black-bearded, his curly tresses being very neatly trimmed. His eyes were steady and sombre. He was conspicuously overweight, but like his lieutenant he seemed more solid than fat. He was well dressed, but wore no colours save for black and white. He reminded Hyry of her father, who had been a fruit factor renowned for his accuracy in judging a green crop. He studied her with just as much care — and, seemingly, with just as much interest.

Checuti suddenly leaned forward, reaching past the monkey to take up a cup from the table. He sipped from it delicately. There was no other cup within reach, and he did not ask Thrid to fetch one. Hyry had let her hands fall into her lap. Now, under cover of the tabletop, she moved to take the hilt of her dagger in her right hand. She had no immediate intention of drawing the weapon, but she let her palm rest upon it anyway. It made her feel better.

While she waited for Checuti to finish his appraisal she glanced around the room. It was drab and sparsely furnished, but the furniture was in very good condition and the crockery arrayed on the shelves was of more than reasonable quality.

'What do you want with me, Checuti?' she asked abruptly. 'Everything I have that's worth stealing is at the inn, with half a hundred guardians at hand.'

Checuti sighed, but the sigh seemed inauthentic. 'Everyone suspects me of wanting to rob them,' he observed sadly. 'I have a terrible reputation, it seems — and reputation always precedes disaster in my line of work. How right I was to think that the time had come for me to bid farewell to Xandria.'

'Your reputation seems to be thoroughly deserved,' Hyry said archly. 'Or do you deny that you were behind the plundering of the royal treasury?'

'Behind it!' Checuti exclaimed, teasing her with an expression of mock horror. 'Indeed I do deny that I was *behind* it. I was in the van, my dear, leading my troops into battle like one of the hero-princes of olden times. I am, after all, supposed to be a prince of thieves. When they began to call me that, I knew my days in Xandria were numbered — fame is to be avoided, if one is to live outside the law — but I felt that I owed it to my admirers to measure up to their claims. So many people in public life let us down, do they not? I decided to retire in style. Mine is, I believe, a crime unprecedented in a hundred generations — although I sometimes suspect that those whose lot in life it is to remember precedents routinely increase the number of generations over which their memories claim dominion.'

Hyry looked at the man with open astonishment. This was not what she had expected.

Checuti smiled, and reached out to pat the monkey lightly on the head as it spat out the plumstone, cleaned of every vestige of flesh. 'Everything went perfectly,' he said, 'or very nearly so. It was glorious. Indeed, one might almost say that it went a little too well. My grandiose gesture became more grandiose than I intended, and I stole even more than I planned.'

'How much more?' Hyry asked in bewilderment.

'My men placed a small firework by the door of the central tower by way of diversion,' he said. 'It was supposed to spread alarm and confusion, and indeed it did – but I had not anticipated that princesses would swarm out of the tower like angry honeybees from a threatened hive, nor that they would leap at my carts like hungry nightcloaks.'

'What in the world are you talking about?' Hyry asked impatiently. It was still dark outside, and would be for a while yet, but she wanted to be on her way by daybreak if it were still possible.

'I'm talking about Princess Lucrezia,' the thiefmaster told her equably. 'She must have seen or heard my men before the firework went off. One of the giants came to investigate, but I had darklanders with blowpipes posted to take care of that possibility. She took her time to fall but when she fell she fell heavily. Unfortunately, the princess followed the giant and tried to climb aboard one of my carts. The driver was in a hurry. He struck out at the invader, without even wondering who she might be, and she fell. He never gave her another thought thereafter, his mind being on the infinitely more urgent matter of loading the coin and getting through the City Gate. Indeed, it wasn't until we came to unload the coin at a secret rendezvous that we discovered her, still lying in the cart.

'She regained consciousness as soon as she was touched – and very soon afterwards told us who she was. We could hardly let her go, as we were very anxious just then that our whereabouts should not be made known. She had seen very little, but there were those present who felt that she had already seen far too much – not all of those involved in our conspiracy intended to leave Xandria, you see, and some of the coin had to stay behind in order that the usual disbursements might be made . . . but I don't want to bore you with details. Suffice it to say that the only practicable alternatives before me were to murder the girl, or to bring her with me. I brought her with me.

'Some of my followers think this was the wrong decision, but I will candidly admit that I am a squeamish man. In any case, I decided from the very start that my grand farewell to Xandria should be marred by as few fatalities as was humanly possible. A prince of thieves can easily be reckoned a hero by common folk, but common murderers tend to be held in much lower esteem. If I'm to pass safely and invisibly through the byways of the empire, and find a resting-place where I might live for ten or twenty more years in relative comfort, I shall need the goodwill of a great many people. I have a reputation for gentleness which I would not like to put at risk.'

Hyry stared at the thiefmaster, almost at a loss for words. 'What do you intend to do with the princess, then?' she asked, when it seemed obvious that Checuti was waiting for some such prompt. 'Will you hold her to ransom?'

'Those of my men who are anxious about what she has already seen wouldn't approve of that,' he said, 'and the risks involved in trying to collect a ransom from her father are far too great to tempt me. I confess that the problem of what to do vexed me considerably – until I explained the difficulty to the princess herself. She was quick to propose a solution which has a certain neat elegance.'

'Oh,' said Hyry, as some suspicion dawned of what might be coming.

'It seems,' Checuti said, 'that Princess Lucrezia has no particular desire to return to the safety of King Belin's Inner Sanctum. Indeed, she says – and I believe her – that she would far rather go south. It seems that her head has been filled with wild dreams of adventure in the fabled lands of the Navel of the World. She has, after all, been educated as a witch, and her imagination has been further stimulated by . . .'

'All right,' said Hyry curtly. 'I get the picture. What do you want me to do?'

'It's not what I want you to do that matters,' said Checuti mildly. He caught the monkey as it leapt nimbly from his lap to his shoulder. 'It's what the princess wants you to do. In this particular matter, however ironic it may seem, I'm simply acting as a loyal subject, obedient to the orders of a daughter of the king. I'm sure that when you've given the matter careful consideration, you'll want to do the same. I ought to warn you, though, that if you were to decide to defy the princess and take her back to Xandria – at considerable inconvenience to your own mission – certain people would probably take steps to prevent your doing so. Personally, I'm going south with all possible speed, but those of my co-conspirators whose intention was to remain in Xandria really are anxious about what the princess saw.'

'But if I take her with me,' Hyry said, 'and the king ever finds out, I'll never be able to set foot in Xandria again myself.'

'It's only because my people understand that,' Checuti said, 'that they can be persuaded to trust my judgment in this matter. Please don't blame me for putting you in this situation – it was the princess who suggested it. She's the one who's now asking you to choose between Belin and her, between your expedition and your home. I'm taking a risk simply by putting it to you – a risk of which poor Burdam doesn't entirely approve.'

Hyry glanced sideways at Thrid, whose glum expression confirmed that his approval was indeed muted. 'This is crazy,' she said. 'Completely crazy.'

'Yes it is,' Checuti agreed. 'Oddly enough, that's one of the things which rather recommends it to me. I don't like things to be too simple and straightforward – it takes all the savour out of life. I can't allow you to go back to the inn, I'm afraid – but I *can* contrive to have all of your goods brought out here, for a relatively small fee. Then I can have you taken to the princess. After that, you'd be free to continue your journey – discreetly, of course. Once you're in so deep that you can't back out without putting yourself in considerable danger, you'll be left alone; I can promise you that much. Now, what do you say?'

Hyry realised that there was no scope whatsoever for polite refusal – or, indeed, any kind of refusal. She had been in too deep from the moment Burdam Thrid had grabbed her at the well. The simple fact that she'd talked to the man who'd hijacked the contents of the royal treasury would be enough to foul up her life for a long time if she were unwise enough to tell anyone. All her own plans were already in ruins . . . unless she could expand them to take the princess aboard.

The royal fool! she thought bitterly. *The rotting little idiot! Why in the world did she have to involve me in her madness?* But she was wise enough to know, even as she silently vented her spleen, that she had brought this on herself. She had fed Lucrezia's appetite for wonders by way of cultivating a good customer, and now she was reaping the full reward of her salesmanship.

'Funny old world, isn't it?' said Checuti, seemingly having read her mind. 'Personally, I like it that way.'

2

As the sun set behind ribbons of thick cloud it stained the air above the western horizon a deep crimson colour which Lucrezia had never seen before. To the south, the dark canopy of the unearthly trees of the Forest of Absolute Night was just visible, giving the lie to the forest's name by shining iridescently purple in the strange light. In the east, a dozen flamestars were already visible. For once, it seemed, they would be able to keep going long into the night.

Lucrezia turned in the saddle to look back the way they had come, scanning the horizon anxiously. There was no obvious sign of anyone following, but there were so many stands of trees that a small group of riders might very easily have been screened from view.

Lucrezia called Hyry Keshvara's attention to the remarkable colour of the sky, but the trader was sourly dismissive. 'The air in these parts is still and humid,' she said grudgingly. 'When the wind blows from the east it picks up dust in the Spangled Desert, but when it blows from the west or the north it brings clouds from the Slithery Sea. When the cloud and dust meet up, as they sometimes do, that red colour stains the sunsets.'

'And the bright purple glow?' the princess persisted, determined not to be silenced by the other's brusque manner.

'The foliage of the trees in the forest ranges in colour from dark green through blue to violet, highness,' Hyry said dully. 'The purples catch the light better. Once we're underneath the canopy it won't seem bright at all – although *absolute night*'s an exaggeration, even when the sky's as dark as it ever gets.' For a moment she seemed to be on the point of elaborating further, but then she decided against it. Her closed mouth set into the familiar grim line.

It seemed to Lucrezia that Hyry had not smiled once since they had come together. Now the trader was trying to urge her horse forward again, so that the princess would not be able to talk while they rode. Lucrezia made her own mount walk a little faster, to keep pace.

'Are you going to keep this up for ever?' Lucrezia demanded.

'I don't know what you mean, highness.'

'For one thing, I asked you to stop calling me *highness*,' Lucrezia said. 'I'm not a highness any more. We're in this together now. If you don't like it, that's too bad – but I thought you were my friend. What else could I have done? Tell me that!'

'Nothing,' Hyry agreed, without enthusiasm. 'Checuti gave neither of us any choice.' She didn't say *highness*, but she didn't look at Lucrezia either, and she didn't make any comment about their being friends.

'*You* might not like what he did,' Lucrezia told her reluctant companion angrily, 'but he did me a big favour, and I'm grateful to him. If you'd rather he'd killed me, perhaps you ought to say so, so that everything's clear between us.'

Hyry condescended to look round then. 'No, highness,' she said, making an evident effort. 'I couldn't wish that. I'd far rather you were alive and here than dead somewhere else. It's just . . .'

'It's just that we've had to stay well away from the road, which has slowed us down. We have to stop more often because we're using both horses, which has slowed us down further. The rain has hardly let up in seven days, which has slowed us down even further. To cap it all, we had Checuti's men trailing us for at least five of those days, which kept us looking anxiously around every time we stopped. I'm sorry, Hyry, but . . .'

'It's not your fault,' Hyry finished for her. 'I know that, high—' She stopped herself halfway through the word – which seemed to Lucrezia to be a minor victory in the unwanted contest.

After a pause, Lucrezia said. 'He didn't have to do it, Hyry. The others wanted to cut my throat. Not that I could have harmed them – I didn't see anything except the inside of a big grain warehouse, and I didn't have the least idea where it was. How could I, when I'd hardly set foot outside the citadel? But they thought that I might have seen faces and heard names. They were scared. Checuti had to bring me with him, and give them his word that I wouldn't be coming back.

'He asked me himself, you know, what I'd do with me if our situations were reversed. For a moment or two I actually thought *he's right; if I were him I'd cut my throat rather than take the slightest risk* – but then I thought again, and I thought *no – no, I really wouldn't* . . . and I told him why. He listened Hyry. He really listened.'

'He has a certain perverse charm,' Hyry conceded. 'Rumour has it that all the thieves in Xandia queued up to be cheated by him.'

'It wasn't like that,' Lucrezia insisted.

'What, exactly, did you say to him?' the trader asked. That, too, seemed like a breakthrough to the princess. Hyry had been too sullen and sulky to ask before.

'I told him the truth,' Lucrezia said proudly. 'I told him that if I were a man like him, I wouldn't bother with such trivialities as robbing the king's treasury, whether the crime had to be compounded by murder or not. If I were him, I said, I wouldn't just ride southwards until I thought I was safe from pursuit or betrayal, I'd keep right on going. If I were a man like him, I said, I'd want to know what lies far beyond the Forest of Absolute Night, and now that there was an opportunity to find out, maybe for the first time in a hundred generations, nothing would stop me trying. If I were him, I said, I'd spend every penny of coin I'd stolen to outfit an expedition like the one you and Fraxinus have put together, and I'd go looking for the garden of Idun and the Pool of Life . . . and I'd find them, or die trying.

'He knew that it was all true. If he hadn't known that, I'm not sure that he'd have passed me on to you. He knew – and he understood what I meant.'

'He's still going to hole up with his stolen money, though,' Hyry pointed out. 'He didn't volunteer to join forces with us, did he?'

'He was tempted,' Lucrezia said determinedly. Then she relented, and put on her most winning smile. 'He's not such a bad man, but he's not like you . . . or me. We're *real* heroes, risking everything.'

'So we are,' Hyry said, not as bitterly as she might have.

'I'm truly sorry that you're risking rather more than you planned,' Lucrezia said, 'but when you think about the dangers we might face in and beyond the forest, surely the risk of being stopped and challenged by my father's men is trivial enough?'

Hyry said nothing to that, but she did manage a half-hearted grin.

It was enough, for the time being.

'I won't be a burden,' Lucrezia said. 'In fact, I'm as useful as any fighting man would be. Checuti gave me back my belt, with everything intact. There's the legacy of five years of training in witchery wrapped up in these packages. If a nightcloak were to swallow me whole it'd die in forty-three different ways. Believe me, Hyry, anyone who thinks we're an easy target because we're so far off the beaten track will get a rude shock.'

Hyry seemed sceptical, but didn't challenge the claim. 'We'd better rest and eat,' she said. 'Now the stars have condescended to light the night for us, we can keep going for at least another eight hours, but the horses need to be fed.'

They both reined in. Lucrezia tethered the horses while Hyry unburdened the donkeys. The trader squatted down beside the packs and took out two small loaves of bread, a few slices of salted pork and some fruit that they had gathered the day before. The bread was already stale and the fruit was beginning to develop an alcoholic edge, but that only encouraged them to eat more, on the grounds that anything they left would spoil. They drank water which Hyry had boiled three days before, the last time she had been able to make a fire.

'Shall we pass close to the city of Khalorn tomorrow?' Lucrezia asked.

'Not very close,' said Hyry. 'I wish I dared send a message to Fraxinus, but it's too dangerous. He might not have arrived yet, and the king's men will be prying into everything. He'll be worried when he finds I'm not there, but he'll proceed as planned. We might be able to meet him in the fringes of the forest, but if we're to be certain that we don't miss him we'll probably have to go deep into the heart of it. There's a river which flows out of the Dragomite Hills away to the east, and then curves to run westwards. It has to be crossed . . . there's a ford we both know about. He's bound to make for that. We'll do the same.'

Lucrezia asked no more for a while, as they made their meal. She was anxious to make further progress in cementing their friendship now that Hyry had finally begun to thaw out, but she knew that there'd be time enough in the days to come. She was

177

glad of the opportunity to lie down and stretch her limbs, although the saddle-soreness which had blighted her every waking hour during the first three days of the journey had eased considerably.

Hyry saw to the horses and the donkeys, then prowled around for a little while. She was ostensibly looking for food, although there was unlikely to be any to be found.

'We'll need fresh supplies very soon,' Lucrezia observed, staring down at the last discarded morsel of her loaf. She had devoured the rest eagerly enough, even though it had definitely not been a meal fit for a princess. 'Perhaps we ought to buy some food from one of the farms, while we still can.'

'They have fresh food in the darklands,' the trader assured her. 'The heartland of the forest's unearthly, but it's almost as easy to live off the land there as it is hereabouts. The pigs and the deer are free to anyone who can catch them – and if we can't, we'll just have to eat what they eat. If we can find friendly darklanders we'll be fine, but even if we can't we won't starve.'

Lucrezia saw Hyry start slightly as she spoke the last few words, and immediately turned to see what it was that the trader had glimpsed.

The region through which they were passing was not under intensive cultivation in spite of the fact that they were less than twenty kims from the city. It was mostly grazing land for woolly sheep, but there were plenty of people about, in scattered smallholdings. They had frequently been seen by others during the last few days, and always closely watched as they passed by, but that normally caused Hyry no concern. This time, she seemed anxious.

Lucrezia followed the direction of her gaze – a little south of east – and caught sight of a small group of men on horseback. They were visible for less than half a minute before disappearing into a small wood. They did not seem to be in a hurry.

'Checuti's men?' Lucrezia said uncertainly. 'Are they still with us?'

'I doubt that they're Checuti's men,' Hyry replied. 'I think *they* turned back some time ago. Not militiamen or farmers, though. I don't think they've had a clear sight of us, although the horses and donkeys were in plain view. With luck, they'll assume that we're as many as our animals.'

'Why *with luck*?' Lucrezia asked.

'Because four mounted men would be more difficult to rob, and rather less rewarding, than two mounted women with two pack-animals. If they're thieves, better they should think us a target too difficult to try. Better still if they fear that we might be thieves too, as likely to seize their possessions as they would be to seize ours. In that case they might go home and bar their doors.'

'Are there thieves everywhere?' Lucrezia asked. 'How is it possible for traders to make profits at all?'

'Yes, there are thieves everywhere,' Hyry told her philosophically. 'But almost all of them are discreet. Trade is the lifeblood of all communities, not just the crowded towns and cities, and no community can afford to deter traders by playing host to robbers. Prudent predators conserve their prey; wise predators do their utmost to make sure that their prey prospers – what's good for the sheep is good for the wolves, as they say hereabouts. Under normal circumstances we'd be fairly safe in this region, but we're a long way from the main road. A passing wolf might judge that we were offering our bare throats to his teeth.'

'We may be two and not four,' Lucrezia said, 'but we have sharp claws.'

'Perhaps we have,' the trader said pensively. 'But it might not seem so to them if they come close enough to count us, all the more especially if they see that we're women. It's always better not to have to test the sharpness of one's claws.'

Hyry had already begun packing away the remains of their meal. Lucrezia went to check that the horses had finished theirs, but didn't make any move to help with the packs until the time came to lift them on to the donkeys' backs. There was a considerable skill in bundling and tying, which she had not yet mastered.

They moved off into the twilight. The western sky had faded now from crimson to purple, and the barely visible forest rim was black even at its western edge. Elsewhere in the great vault of the sky the stars shone brightly – more brightly, it seemed, than they usually did, although Lucrezia knew that must be an illusion.

According to the lore of the Arts Astronomical, Lucrezia knew, the light of the nearest stars took half a year to travel across the intervening void, while the light of the furthest took centuries.

Sometimes, stars exploded and grew temporarily brighter, but for the most part they were perfectly steady, their intensity never varying at all. Only the world's air varied, by virtue of cloud or dust or smoke . . . and the air here was certainly no clearer than the air above Xandria, which was perennially swept by sea-breezes.

Lucrezia was well aware, of course, that there were some in civilised Xandria who said that the Arts Astronomical were even less worthy of the name than the Arts Geographical, claiming knowledge of things which no man could ever have had the means to find out. The stars were too far away, such rigorous sceptics said, for their distances to be calculated by an imaginable method.

Lucrezia had some sympathy with this kind of logic – having found the lore wanting in more than one respect she was no longer given to blind faith – but she was inclined even so to put a certain amount of trust in the astronomers. If men really had come to the world in a ship which sailed the dark between the stars, they must have been in a position to know exactly what the stars were, and how they were distributed about the wilderness of infinity.

Ours is only one of many cradles of life and civilisation, Lucrezia told herself wonderingly. *Although we shall never see our myriad kinsmen, we are not alone. How could it be otherwise, given that the universe is so much vaster than we can imagine? Whatever the sceptics say, such knowledge ought to make a difference. It makes a difference to what we think we are, and what we may aspire to become. I have been a princess, but now I am something else. I have Serpent's blood in my veins as well as human, and whatever that might mean I believe that it makes a real difference to the way I am and the way I think.*

3

ANDRIS SAT WITH his back against the trunk of the gnarlytree and watched the rain falling into the dammer-pool. The rain had slackened now, but had earlier been heavy enough to churn up the shallows into grey, viscous soup. The dammers had taken shelter in their lodge and were nowhere to be seen, but away to Andris's right, below the dam – where the rain had threatened to send the mud-cliffs sliding down into the narrow channel – a dredger was working patiently away, shovelling dirt up the slope with its massive forepaws and compacting it with slaps of its oarlike tail.

It can't be fun being a dredger, Andris thought, as he teased one of his upper incisors with a tentative finger. *Even at the best of times, when every other creature can revel in the sun's warmth, a dredger has to live in the silt, forever hauling it out of the river's bed, knowing full well – if dredgers have brain enough to know anything at all – that the rain will bring the greater part of it tumbling back down. Why do they do it?*

It was obvious that this particular dredger couldn't even expect a reasonable ration of fish as a reward for maintaining the watercourse – the dammers had seen to that. There would be frogs, of course, and insect eggs – dammers, being aristocrats of the animal kingdom, wouldn't soil their shiny teeth with anything humbler than fish and wouldn't bother to compete for lesser prey – but mostly there'd be waterweed, waterweed and more water-weed.

The loose incisor began to move more freely back and forth, but Andris didn't try to tear it away too soon. It would come out in its own good time.

If it weren't for the dredgers, of course, he mused, *there wouldn't be a river here at all, just a swamp. Because there are dredgers to excavate a river there are also dammers, whose lives must seem to the dredgers to be entirely dedicated to screwing things up for dredgers.* Much the same argument, he supposed, could be applied to the farmers, whose drainage ditches must be just as much of an inconvenience – from the dredger point of view – as the dammers' dams. On the other hand, the dammers probably thought they had a rotten time too, because the fur coats that made it possible for them to chase fish in their dammed-up pools were also useful for making waterproof coats for the farmers. Then again, the farmers undoubtedly thought that *they* had a rough deal because they broke their backs raising huge crops which they then had to sell to factors and carters, who knew very well that what wasn't sold instantly would rot, and thus held all the cards when it came to haggling. Except, of course, that the factors and carters had exactly the same problem when they sold the goods on . . .

All in all, Andris decided, as the tooth finally came away, the world was a very complicated place, where everyone and everything faced a desperate struggle to survive: a race against the ravages of corruption in which few could win prizes and most ran themselves into the ground trying unsuccessfully to keep up.

What keeps us all going? Andris wondered. *Why do we keep on running, when there's nowhere to go? Or dredging away, knowing that there'll never be an end to dredging?*

He caught sight of Merel then, making her steady way across the field. The sight seemed to provide an answer of sorts. People kept going until they found their other halves: partners they could settle down with, and form an atom of community. That was what it was all about. That was the be all and end all of human existence. Except, of course, that so many people seemed to find that not long after they'd got what they'd been looking for, it turned out not to be what they'd been looking for at all. Would that happen to him too? For the moment, it seemed inconceivable.

'Here's yours,' said Merel, breaking into his reverie. She'd gone on foot to the nearest farmhouse to buy food. It wasn't really safe for her to go alone, being so slim and lightly armed, but it certainly wasn't safe for her to be seen with an oversized amber or a top-quality horse, given that news of what had happened in Xandria had overtaken them several days ago.

He showed her the tooth. 'It'll take weeks to grow a new one,' he said dolefully. 'It always does. This one isn't even rotted through. Are your new teeth always in such a tearing hurry to get through that they push the old ones out while they're still strong?'

'No such luck,' she said bitterly. 'I always have to get someone to pull the rotten ones out with pliers, and the new ones take *months* to grow. Be grateful.'

The food didn't look very appetising – which was hardly surprising, given that they were almost out of money. For the first couple of days the contents of Merel's purse had easily extended to the purchase of meat, eggs and cheese as well as bread, and they had been able to help themselves to fruit from unguarded orchards, but now they were getting by on bread and pickled vegetables, plus whatever fresh vegetables they could root out in passing. There were very few orchards in this part of the province.

'The horses are eating better than we are,' Andris observed gloomily. The missing tooth made it slightly awkward for him to bite the bread, although it hadn't been a chewing tooth.

'Don't turn your nose up at this,' Merel advised him. 'It could be worse. Khalorn readily soaks up the surplus from these farms even at the best of times. Now, they say, the town's crowded and prices are rising sky-high. Anyway, if the horses weren't eating better than we are, we'd soon be carrying *them*.'

'The king can't have sent that many men south chasing Checuti,' Andris said sourly. 'How can a city the size of Khalorn get overcrowded because of a couple of army units and a few dozen not-so-secret agents?'

'It's not just incomers from the north. There's a considerable drift from the south too. The forest-dwellers are usually self-sufficient but the farmer's wife says there's been a sharp increase in trade lately, with darklanders coming north by the thousand. She probably exaggerated in the interests of driving a harder bargain, but there must be some truth in it. She says there's some sort of trouble in the far south – she doesn't know what. She seemed rather ungrateful, but she's obviously worried about the rain spoiling their chance of getting the maximum advantage out of the higher prices.'

'That's farmers,' Andris observed. 'Complain when the rain doesn't come, complain when it does. How long before we get to Khalorn?'

'Depends whether the rain keeps up. Tomorrow if we're lucky, or the day after. It won't be easy to get to Phar, with all the militiamen in the province looking out for you. Going into the city will be like walking into a dragomites' nest.'

'What exactly *is* a dragomite?' Andris asked.

Merel shrugged. 'I don't really know,' she said. 'According to rumour they're big, nasty and dangerous. Unearthly, of course . . . like giant insects, I think, only not exactly. Nobody I ever met claimed to have actually seen one. I doubt if there's anyone in Xandria who has. A few traders go into the forest, but there's no reason at all to go all the way through and out the other side – or never has been, until now.'

'We ought to find out more about them,' Andris said, 'if we're really going to join up with Fraxinus's expedition. We might be seeing far more dragomites than any sane person could ever wish to.'

'What alternative do we have?' Merel asked flatly. 'There's no place for us in the empire. It's either south through the Forest of Absolute Night, west to the Grey Waste or east to the Spangled Desert – all of which are as bad as one another, if you believe travellers' tales.'

'Perhaps we should have gone north – back across the Slithery Sea.'

'We'd never have got a ship. The harbour's in the citadel's backyard – Checuti couldn't get a sackful of fresh coins out by sea. A huge yellow monster like you wouldn't have stood a chance if we'd tried to hide in Xandria.'

'Maybe not,' said Andris gloomily, 'but *you* could have gone that way, or even stayed in Xandria. No one knew you were involved – no one saw you, except that poor bastard with a broken leg, and he hadn't the faintest idea who you were. There's no need for you to come into any dragomites' nest with me, real or metaphorical.'

'Don't start all that again,' she told him tiredly. 'I decided, right? Not for love, or family loyalty, or good bright coin, but because it suited me. It still does. You don't have to spend the rest of your life worrying about it. We're together now, wherever we go – unless and until you want to be rid of me. Are you tired of me already? Is my skin too dark for your delicate tastes?'

'You know it's nothing like that!' he said – but not angrily. She did know, and he knew she knew.

'If we're lucky,' she told him, 'we'll find out what dragomites look like soon enough – after we've made the acquaintance of nightcloaks and flowerworms and all the other forest nasties. I saw a nightcloak pelt once, made up into an actual cloak. It looked beautiful. The live ones have claws and teeth, of course. Mind you, if we're *not* lucky, we'll never get that far. When I see my first dragomite I'll be delighted, no matter how ugly and vicious it is, simply because it will mean that I've got past the militia and the constabulary, not to mention assorted wild boars, crocolids and whipsnakes . . . nor the darklanders, who are said to have some pretty nasty habits themselves while they're on home ground, although they seem meek enough when they're in the big city. You'll have to do all the dickering once we're in the forest – the savages will probably think that you're a long-lost brother who's finally found his way home.'

Andris finished the last of his bread. 'We could do with a couple of cloaks ourselves,' he observed. 'Dammer-hide, that is, not genuine nightcloak. Just to keep us dry.'

'Dry! Easy to tell that you're a rotting prince, expecting to keep dry when it rains. People like me just get wet and keep going.'

'Just like the dredger,' Andris said, pointing to the beast, which was wholly out of the water at present. It looked like a huge heap of grey mud which had been magically brought to life.

'Not at all like the dredger,' she replied, with a slight hint of asperity. 'Dredgers haven't an enemy in the world, except the occasional protracted drought. Nobody bothers them while they get on with doing what they're supposed to do, day in and day out. I don't have that luxury. I never did and I never will. We'd better get going. It doesn't look as if we'll be able to make any progress once night falls.'

'No,' said Andris. 'Another night, another gnarlytree. Twenty hours of murk and mud.'

'Are you always as miserable as this?' she demanded.

'Of course not,' he told her. 'Sometimes I get depressed.'

She laughed at that, and didn't seem to be forcing the laughter. That helped to lift his own spirits a little, and he resolved to make an effort to be more positive. It was difficult not to reflect the mood of the weather while they couldn't escape its oppression, but it surely wasn't beyond the scope of his intelligence – especially if he made an effort to remember that if Merel had been right, he could have been navel-deep in mud in the garden on top of the Inner Sanctum of the citadel right now, with no balls and a thorn-bush growing in his entrails. He still couldn't believe that Princess Lucrezia had intended to do that to him, but he did know enough about the prevailing moral standards of royal families to be certain that it wasn't beyond the bounds of possibility.

The horses didn't seem any more enthusiastic to be on their way than Andris was, but they weren't in the least mulish about it. They'd been brought up to obey – to them, *every* human being was a prince.

'Good girl,' Andris said to the mare, as she bore up bravely under his excessive weight. 'Look at it this way – at least you're not a dredger. I may be heavy, but I'm grateful, which is more than you can say for mud.'

'Talking to animals,' Merel observed as they moved off, following the lazy river upstream, 'is a sure sign of a deep-seated inability to get along with people.'

'When I was in Belin's jail,' Andris told her, 'I shared my cell with a spider. Best cellmate I ever had – until you came along.'

'That's the nicest thing anyone's said to me for seven years and more,' she said drily. 'In daylight, anyway.'

He was glad that she couldn't possibly mean it. He knew that much for certain – and it seemed, just at the moment, to be a very satisfying thing to know.

4

ALTHOUGH THE HAZY purple edge of the Forest of Absolute Night was now clearly visible along the entire southern horizon Lucrezia and Hyry were crossing country that was rather more open than that through which they had lately come. The terrain was almost flat, although it was frequently interrupted by streams edged with stands of purple-flowered furze. There were ragged clumps of young trees scattered at irregular intervals before them but very few bushes. The streams were a nuisance, for they often ran deep in spite of the fact that they were not broad enough to support dredgers, and Hyry had to pick their crossing-points carefully lest the donkeys' packs got soaked.

The night was clear, and they could have continued riding indefinitely had it not been for the need to conserve the strength of the animals. Like Hyry Keshvara, the horses would have preferred to walk on good roads, spending every noon and midnight in well-roofed stables with straw-covered floors. The animals were not disposed to open rebellion, but they had ways of making their discomfort known. Eventually, Hyry called a halt as they passed close to a long, narrow mound whose shallow ridge was crowned by a young stand of trees.

'What is it?' Lucrezia asked. Although the mound was by no means big enough to be called a hill the ideas of rising ground and dragomites were firmly associated in her mind.

'A farmhouse and barns once stood here,' the trader replied. 'Probably built on a natural rise, which they increased when they rotted down. Maybe the cycle was repeated two or three times. Settlers will move in again soon enough, once the timber's more fully grown, but in sheep country people build where the good wood is, and move on when it's gone.'

It was easy enough to find a clear space within the copse, and there was more than enough leaf litter to cushion the ground on which they spread their mats. They ate again, but it was a meagre meal and they did not let it delay them long. They stretched themselves out to sleep as soon as they could, because they wanted to be on their way again long before dawn, but Lucrezia could see that Hyry was apprehensive. She had taken care to look back the way they had come at regular intervals ever since she had first caught sight of the riders, and she remained anxious about them even though she had seen no clear indication of their continued presence.

There were far too many insects about for Lucrezia's liking, but she had schooled herself to ignore them. The bites she had sustained during her first few nights in the open had caused fierce allergic reactions, but her body had now adapted to the commoner toxins and more recent encounters had caused her much less distress. She felt a certain pride in the fact that she had that kind of capacity, given that she was herself trained in the use of poisons. It would have been an uncomfrotable irony to find that she had an abnormally low tolerance to such tiny stings.

She was very tired, and would have gone to sleep easily enough had it not been for Hyry's obvious unease. Although the older woman was making every effort to control her restlessness the faint sound of her breathing was quite sufficient to communicate a sense that all was not well. Some instinct or intuition was sounding a warning note inside the trader's head, and Lucrezia was disposed to trust its implications. The princess had been in peril before, when she first woke to find herself a prisoner of Checuti's men, but her sense of danger had then been ameliorated by the fact that she could see and speak to her captors. Now, because she had no clear idea of what might be threatening her or when the threat might materialise, her trepidation was far greater.

It was almost a relief when her straining ears finally caught the sounds of approaching animals. As soon as she heard the distant snorting of tired horses she came fully awake and sat up. She would have whispered a warning to her companion, but Hyry had rsponded even more rapidly. The trader moved swiftly to Lucrezia's side, placing a finger over the princess's lips to instruct her to be quiet.

'They might pass by,' Hyry whispered – but Lucrezia knew that she didn't believe it.

Lucrezia felt an electric thrill of fear, but that was preferable in some ways to the aching anxiety of anticipation and she did not allow the terror to take a commanding hold of her. She felt calm and collected in spite of being on edge – and she also felt a certain grim glee at the thought that she was at last in a position to make an authentic field test of the lore which Ereleth had patiently imparted to her. The coming conflict, she told herself, would be far more valuable as trustworthy experience than all her experiments with worn-out slaves. She had already made her plans; now she changed her position to a predatory crouch, and reached into one of the pouches arrayed about her belt. There she found the instrument which best fitted the circumstances. She handled it with all due care.

The clearing in which the two women had camped was broad enough to let a good deal of starlight through, but it wasn't possible to see the approaching men; they had dismounted and were coming forward on foot, as stealthily as they could. Lucrezia tried to judge how many they were from the pattern of the slight sounds they made, and became certain as they spread out that there were at least three.

Lucrezia knew that Hyry had a long, sharp knife in her hand, but she didn't wish that she had one like it. She had more faith in her own resources. She carefully anointed her own weapons: the sharpened and strengthened fingernails of her left hand. The nail of the forefinger had been broken in the course of her recent travails, but she had manicured the remainder with the utmost care in order to maintain their usefulness.

She suddenly became aware that Hyry Keshvara was no longer by her side, although the woman had moved much more quietly than the men who were coming to rob them. She smiled . . . but the smile faded as she realised that the sounds made by the people who were creeping up on them had died almost to nothing. It was as if everyone had paused, waiting for some challenge or signal.

Lucrezia felt an urgent desire to move into the shadow of one of the trees, so that she could feel its trunk against her back, but she didn't dare because she knew that she couldn't do it silently. She tried instead to remain as still as possible, hoping that because she was crouching down she would be unobtrusive.

Suddenly, there was a fizzing sound and a brilliant light burst forth. Lucrezia had not expected it, and had the misfortune to be looking in the direction of the flare. She was dazzled and blinded, and knew immediately what a severe disadvantage she had incurred. She had time to hope that Hyry might have been warned by the fizzing sound, or fortunate enough to have been looking another way, but that was all the time she had – two blurred figures converged upon her from different directions with purposeful haste.

Had the attackers grabbed an arm each and held them hard they might have rendered her incapable, but their first concern was to pin her down, and they had undoubtedly seen in the brilliant flash of light that she held no evident weapon. They thought she was impotent to hurt them, and they weren't afraid.

She lashed out at them, although she had to guess where their faces were because she still could not see them. She made no contact. Then one of them was suddenly on top of her, kneeling on her chest. He was so heavy, and had come down so brutally, that the impact drove the air from her lungs, and one of his hands clenched upon her right wrist – but her left was still free. Once he was still there was no difficulty in finding his cheek, and raking it.

He laughed!

He actually laughed, as if the pain of the scratches was nothing more than a seasoning for the fury of his assault. He was dead, but didn't know it – and he laughed!

Unfortunately, his ignorance had less pleasant consequences too. He struck back at her with his fist, and hit her on the temple above and beside her left eye. The blow was unexpectedly disconcerting, and her vision – which had just begun to clear after the flash – blurred again.

For a moment, remembering that there was a second man still to be dealt with, Lucrezia lost confidence in the immediate practicality of her Art – but then the man who restrained her growled an instruction to his companion to hold her, and when the other grabbed both her arms he raised his weight slightly.

The partial release left her just enough scope to squirm and twist. The one who was adjusting his position – the dead man! – was quick to organise himself, and to bear down on her again, but the other was stupid enough to change his grip as she twisted, and her sharpened fingernails scraped across the palm of his hand. He cursed, but not because he knew what had been done to him. He thought the wound as trivial as a wound could be, probably not having shed a bead of blood.

They thrust her down hard, rolling her on to her back again – and this time they had her securely. Her wrists were pinned and pressed to the soft ground and the first man shifted himelf so that he was sitting on her thighs, groping at her belt.

At first she thought that he had guessed its value, or hoped that there was a well-stuffed purse in one of its pouches, but she realised belatedly that he had another reason for wanting it loosened. He thought – wrongly! – that there was all the time in the world for robbery, and that there was time for amusement first.

Lucrezia had no wish to lose her virginity in such a fashion, but she knew that it was a straightforward race against time, which she might not win. She struggled as hard as she could, in the interests of making their work more difficult, but she had not the weight or the strength to accomplish much. She tried to kick up with her legs, but had so little effect that the man who was inclined to humour laughed again, while his companion grunted something that was half a word and half a cry of derision.

For her own part, Lucrezia said nothing at all. It might have been better to cease struggling, because the man on top of her became impatient with the difficulties she was making, and he lashed out at her again with his fist. This time she took the blow on the cheek. It hurt terribly, but she couldn't feel a broken bone and it didn't knock her unconscious. She felt her trousers being ripped, parted by means of the simple strategy of tearing the seams apart.

Still, it seemed, the dead men had not begun to suspect their fate.

When her tormentor began to loosen his own belt, Lucrezia thought that the race against time was lost – but then, by the light of the stars, she saw him pause, and reach up to his face, to run his fingertips along the scratches she had made. She could see the scratches now, or thought she could – and he was moving oddly, losing control of his limbs.

Slowly – very slowly – he fell.

He fell forwards, but that wasn't such a bad thing. He fell on top of her, and he was so tall that his chest fell on her face. His startled companion took a step back, letting go of her wrists. She clutched the dead man to her, wrapping her arms around him as though to enfold him in a warm and protective embrace. He didn't try to fight her – and his companion didn't try to do anything at all.

Lucrezia turned her head sideways and fought for breath, sucking air into her lungs. The dead man didn't struggle, although his lower limbs were twitching slightly. Her face was throbbing where he had hit her, and she could feel blood and tears mingling on her cheek, but she didn't let go.

It was the other dead man – the man who had still to complete his dying – who finally pulled his companion away . . . but whatever he had intended to do after that was quite irrelevant. He lifted the corpse away from her, and promptly dropped it. When Lucrezia raised her head he was kneeling on the ground, frozen by puzzlement as well as by poison.

Lucrezia stood up. It took some time, because the blows to her head had made her unsteady, but when she was erect he was still kneeling in the same position. She made the fingers of her left hand rigid, and stabbed the middle finger into his wide-open right eye.

He didn't blink, nor did he moan. He simply fell backwards.

Lucrezia turned, all her fingers splayed like the claws of a frightened cat – but the only person she could see was Hyry Keshvara, standing mutely in the shadows, four or five paces away. She had a knife in her hand. Lucrezia couldn't see the blade clearly, but in her mind's eye she saw blood: lots of blood. Hyry looked as if she wanted to race to the princess's side, to help her as best she could – but she also looked as if she didn't dare take the first step, lest she be mistaken for another enemy.

It wasn't easy to make out the expression in the trader's eyes, but the way she stood suggested that she was afraid. She was afraid that the witch-princess wasn't entirely in control of her poisoned claws.

It isn't supposed to be like this, Lucrezia thought. *It isn't . . .*

But then she changed her mind, and what she said aloud, in an exultant whisper, was: 'Oh yes it is. This is exactly what it's supposed to be like.'

Then she sat down with a thump, and took a very deep breath.

'I told you so,' she said to Hyry Keshvara. 'I told you I could be useful. I have poisons enough to kill a whole nestful of dragomites.'

'I dare say you have, highness,' Hyry replied drily. 'But could you kill them before they killed you?'

Lucrezia laughed, and was surprised at the way the laugh took hold of her, and shook her whole body with false merriment. It was only then that she fully understood how awkwardly rigid with fear and determination she had become.

5

JACOM CERRI STOOD with Sergeant Purkin on the steps of the Khalorn Corn Exchange. He studied the crowded market square with a distaste which his father would have found difficult to understand. The midday had barely ended but the whole expanse was a hive of activity from one end to the other. There were horsedrawn carts by the dozen, hand-carts and backpacks and unburdened townsfolk by the hundred, all engaged in a constant war of attrition as they tried to haggle prices up or down. There were countless ragged children in the crowd, dodging this way and that, snapping up anything left as waste and many things not yet relegated to that status by their owners. Everything imaginable was being hawked there: raw and prepared foodstuffs; lighting oil and cooking oil; spices and cosmetics; weak and strong liquor; cloth by the bolt and made-up garments; buttons and needles; jewellery in brass or silver, inlaid with every kind of coloured stone which lapidaries could manufacture; candles and cagebirds; pens and parchment; and – inevitably – a thousand kinds of pastes for a thousand purposes, many of them fake.

'I'm very sorry, sir,' Purkin said, without making the least effort to conceal his insincerity. Jacom had noticed that Purkin never apologised for anything that might conceivably be reckoned his fault. For the sergeant, *sorry* was a token expression of sympathy which, roughly translated, meant *it serves you right you stupid bastard – what the rotting hell did you expect?* The news that had occasioned this particular *sorry* was that two more of the men had vanished, reducing the strength of the company – if it could any longer be dignified by such a name – to ten, including one officer, one sergeant and one man not yet completely recovered from a broken leg.

'Why did they wait until now?' Jacom said wonderingly. 'I

understand well enough why they'd prefer to take their chances living as outlaws in Xandria, where they've got families, but why come all the way to Khalorn before deciding to desert?'

'These two didn't have wives or children,' Purkin told him. 'I guess they just found . . . well, other alternatives.'

'We've only been here three days!'

The sergeant shrugged his broad shoulders. He didn't have to say anything more. Jacom knew only too well that the three days hadn't been at all productive, from his own point of view. He had talked to the governor, the leader of the local militia, the city's chief constable, a couple of local merchants who knew his father, and everyone else who was willing to talk to him. He had waved his royal warrant around as though it were some magical incantation of awesome power. He had waxed lyrical on the subject of the awful dangers threatening an innocent princess and the undoubted munificence of King Belin's gratitude to anyone who assisted in her recovery. He had thrown out dire hints as to the dreadful efficiency and passionate nasty-mindedness of the king's secret agents, and the tortures available for the punishment of anyone caught giving succour to thieves, kidnappers and people in possession of freshly minted coins. The only result of all this activity had been a visit from one of the king's secret agents – or, at any rate, a man who claimed to be one of the king's secret agents – warning him to cease and desist from use of the last-named strategy.

'There's a big amber over there,' Purkin said idly. 'I don't suppose. . . ?'

'There's another,' Jacom pointed out. 'And another. The city's full of big darklanders – not to mention small and medium-sized ones. The local constables seem infinitely more anxious about the number of darklanders in town than the possibility that Checuti and his men have brought several barrel-loads of fresh coin from Xandria. In fact, if I were to try to think of a word to fit their attitude to the second possibility, *anxiety* is not one which would spring readily to mind. Anyway, none of them is quite big *enough*. Andris Myrasol was very big. About the same size as one Burdam Thrid, if I remember rightly.'

'Just about, sir,' Purkin echoed, stiffly unappreciative of Jacom's sarcasm.

'Look, Purkin,' Jacom said tiredly – deliberately neglecting the correct term of address – 'I understand how the men feel. I understand how *you* feel. You all blame me for getting us kicked out of Xandria, and you all blame me for the fact that our so-called mission seems to be a wild goose chase. The princess is probably dead and buried by now, and Checuti has so many friends in this rotting province that the chances of anyone lifting a finger to help us find him are pretty damn slim. I don't blame the men who deserted, and I won't blame you or Herriman or Luca or Kirn or anyone else if you or they did likewise. You don't owe me anything. If you want to go home, go home.'

'No, sir,' said Purkin wearily. 'I wasn't thinkin' of goin', sir. For one thing, my wife's a harridan and my sons are full-grown. For another I've worn the uniform far too long to think of throwin' it away at my time of life. On top o' that, a sergeant's supposed to look after a young officer, an' when the officer falls arse over tit he's supposed to pick him up an' set him right, *sir*, not ship out an' turn bandit. As for the men, sir, the ones we got left are the ones who'll stick it out to the end. You can depend on them, sir. I guarantee it.'

Jacom knew that when Purkin said *stick it out to the end* he didn't necessarily mean that they'd stick to the mission forced upon them by the king until the princess was successfully recovered. He meant that they'd stick to whatever task he – Purkin – decided on. The ten remaining men were loyal, but they were loyal to their sergeant rather than their captain or their king. Even so, Jacom had no alternative but to say 'Thank you', and try his best to sound as if he meant it.

'You're welcome, sir,' the sergeant assured him.

Herriman came hurrying towards them then, from the market-place. His leg was out of plaster now but he was still on light duties, and although he didn't exactly limp there was something curiously tentative about the way he walked.

'Got these in change while buying supplies, sir,' he said, showing Jacom a handful of coins which were obviously no more than fifteen days old. 'Three from the third flour merchant on the right, the rest from the fat pork butcher.'

'Thanks, Herriman,' Jacom said unenthusiastically. 'I'll be sure to report it.'

On the first occasion that his men had found recently minted coins circulating in the marketplace Jacom had reported it – in fact, he'd taken the news all the way to the governor, who had been totally unimpressed by their evidential value.

'Whatever you may think in Xandria,' the governor had said loftily, 'a city does not need a high and phenomenally expensive wall in order to be prosperous and civilised. You may think of us as mere provincials, but we do not trade exclusively in debased and rotten coin. Our money is as sound as anyone's.'

'That's not the point,' Jacom had said. 'These coins are freshly minted and they carry the king's crest. The entire stock of coin reminted for Thanksgiving was stolen – every last one. These *must* have been stolen. Checuti must be somewhere in the province, and the trader who passed these on must be able to set us on a trail that will lead straight back to him.'

'Our cunning men have ways of keeping the king's coinage fresh,' the governor had assured him. 'In profligate and decadent Xandria such arts have probably been forgotten, but we are careful folk. There is no reason whatsoever to assume that these coins were stolen from the citadel of Xandria. I believe, however, that your master's so-called secret agents are busy following half a dozen so-called trails with an assiduousness that does them great credit. You are more than welcome to do likewise.'

It was at this juncture that Jacom had realised he wasn't going to get much help from local officialdom, and that his royal warrant probably wasn't worth the paper it was written on. By now, he had thoroughly learned the grim lesson that a man has precious few true friends even at the best of times, and a man in trouble would be very fortunate to find even one.

'There's your friend Carus Fraxinus,' Purkin said. He emphasised the word *friend* very slightly, almost as if he had read Jacom's thoughts, but he wasn't being ironic. He knew as well as Jacom did that Fraxinus was their only real hope of getting sound information about Checuti's whereabouts, or a reliable rumour about the continued well-being – or otherwise – of Princess Lucrezia. Fraxinus was always busily out and about, very often in the marketplace. He was very well known in the exchanges where the factors struck big deals, and was always gossiping therein, while his associate Aulakh Phar – who seemed to Jacom to be a far shadier character – always seemed to be among the stalls, deep in conversation with the petty dealers in exotica whose coats were full of vials, jars and pouches.

'He don't look too pleased, sir,' Herriman muttered.

Jacom had to agree. Fraxinus looked worried. Although his caravan was now fully kitted out – if two wagons and a dozen donkeys could really be reckoned a full kit for a thousand-kim journey – Fraxinus had been forced to delay his departure because Hyry Keshvara still hadn't put in an appearance, and the confused rumours which were pouring out of the forest along with hordes of apprehensive darklanders obviously did not bode well for the chances of a trouble-free passage to and through the Dragomite Hills.

'Have you had any luck, Captain?' Fraxinus asked, as he reached the little group of guardsmen.

'Not yet, sir,' Jacom told him, employing the same formal mode for the sake of keeping up appearances in front of the men. 'I've no doubt that Checuti and the stolen coin are somewhere in the region, but there's no clue as to the possible whereabouts of the princess. I take it Keshvara has still not arrived?'

'Alas, no. We shall have to set forth without her. I can't delay any further, now that I've arranged delivery of so much food. The caravan must leave tomorrow, come what may – but such a train travels at the pace of the slowest donkey, and Keshvara ought to be able to catch up if she arrives after we've gone. I fear, though, that whatever misfortune has overtaken her has been worse than commonplace, else she'd surely have sent a message to tell us why she's been delayed.'

'Has Phar managed to find a mapmaker in the town?' Jacom asked. 'My noble host the governor is always telling me that the outlying provinces have taken far more care to preserve the ancient Arts than complacent and decadent Xandria.'

'I'm afraid not,' Fraxinus said good-humouredly. 'The governor's fulsome praise of his province is, I fear, wildly exaggerated. He longs to be in Xandria, where true civilisation is, and it's the fact that duty holds him so securely here that causes him to wax lyrical as to the imagined advantages of such a fate.'

'That's the kindest interpretation of his attitude,' Jacom said sourly. 'Sometimes, his stern defence of Khalorn sounds suspiciously close to treason.'

Fraxinus shook his head. 'Mere mention of the word "decadent", however frequent, doesn't signify a rebellious attitude. Khalorn needs Xandria far more than Xandria needs Khalorn; that's why tax revenues flow in one direction rather than the other. The governor knows that and his people know it too.'

'There seems to be a prodigious counterflow of revenues at present,' Jacom pointed out. 'The market place is full of freshly minted coin, as you've doubtless observed.'

'Yes, it does seem that some of Checuti's booty is already in circulation. It's hardly surprising – money rots like everything else, and is better spent quickly than hoarded.'

Fraxinus spoke these words in a perfectly normal tone of voice, nodding his head as though to compliment his own wisdom, but Jacom saw that his slightly narrowed eyes were darting this way and that, as if to see who might be listening to them. Without waiting for any reply to his comments, the merchant reached out to clasp Jacom by the hand.

'But I shall have to say goodbye now, captain,' he said. 'I must see to the packing of my supplies and the gathering of my men. We shall be on our way before tomorrow's dawn – and we shall not have the chance to meet again for a year and more. I wish you the best of luck with your search for the missing princess. Give my best regards to the governor.'

Jacom had sufficient presence of mind to give not the slightest indication that Fraxinus had pressed a small folded square of paper into his palm while they shook hands.

'I've been very grateful for your company on the road, Carus Fraxinus,' he said, raising his voice just a little. 'I wish you all good fortune in your own enterprise, and I hope to see you again some day – if not next year, the year after.'

Fraxinus smiled, and walked away with a farewell flourish of his right arm. If the two soldiers noticed that anything unusual had occurred they too had the sense to keep quiet about it.

Jacom made no attempt to look at the piece of paper immediately, but made what haste he could to retire to the lavatories in the Corn Exchange. As an officer in the king's guard he was entitled to the use of the very best suite, and he took full advantage of his rank. When the door of the cubicle was securely bolted he sat down on the covered pan and carefully unfolded the fragile note, written in soft pencil.

We are both being watched, it said. *Some of the watchers are the king's men, some are not; you would be wise to trust no one. Checuti will be nearby tonight. The princess might be with him, if she still lives. You will need all your cleverness if you are to persuade him to give her up or tell you where she might be found. Gather your men behind the lodge in the Great Park at the thirty-second hour. A man will come to guide you, with the password* dragomite. *I beg you never to tell anyone that I have helped you in this.*

Jacom knew what to do in such a situation; he had heard many stories in which secret messages of exactly this kind turned around the fortunes of heroes whose exploits had brought them to an impasse. He read the words three times, to make certain that he had them memorised; then he crushed the note in his fist and rolled it between his fingers until he had reduced it to pulp. He stood up, lifted the cover on which he had been sitting, and threw the note into the pan. He made full use of the facility before flushing, to be absolutely sure that no one else would ever read the message.

The chain broke as he released it, but such things were ever wont to happen, even in the best-maintained establishments. He gave the broken end to the long-suffering attendant as he left, and tried not to take offence at a muttered reference to 'ham-handed soldiers with shit for brains', even though it was clearly intended for him to overhear.

Reputations are a funny thing, he thought — with Carus Fraxinus in mind rather than soldiers. *What kind of world do we live in, where help in the apprehension of villains has to be rendered underhandedly? What future has the empire, if the most worthy actions of its citizens have to be kept secret for fear of ruining an honest merchant's reputation for dealing fairly with unreliable placemen?*

He did not care to wonder overmuch about the discreet timing of the communication, although he did realise that Fraxinus would almost certainly be gone from Khalorn by the time he returned from his own expedition in search of the elusive Checuti. He preferred to fix his thoughts on the possibility that he might, after all, have a chance of redeeming himself in the eyes of King Belin, the Prince-Commander, his few remaining men and his father – not to mention the lovely Princess Lucrezia. However slim that chance might be, it was as welcome to him as a draught of cool, sweet water to a man dying of thirst in the hot heart of the Spangled Desert.

6

'THESE AREN'T MAPMAKER'S colours,' Andris complained
defensively, after inspecting the array of pigments which
Aulakh Phar had laid out for him. 'This brush isn't the right kind
either – and this lining pen is in a dreadful state.'

'It's the best I could do at such short notice,' said the man who
sat on the opposite side of the table. 'If you can convince me of the
need I'll gladly see what I can do to get better equipment – but
we're supposed to be leaving before dawn and I have a thousand
other things to see to. I took a big risk in coming here, you know –
the king's men are searching everywhere for you, and they're
keeping close watch on Fraxinus in case you should try to contact
him. I'm sorry the tools aren't ideal, but if you can just do enough
with them to convince me that you really are a mapmaker – and I
have reason enough to be sceptical after some of the offers I have
had these last forty days – I'll be glad to make arrangements to
meet you again at some safe place in the forest. Once we're away
from a thousand prying eyes, we can haggle to our hearts' content
over equipment, wages and conditions of employment.'

'I'm only saying that these aren't the instruments I was taught to
use,' Andris protested sullenly. 'Map-drawing is something I
learned to do by rote, the way all children learn their lore. I never
believed my tutors when they told me what a good form of mental
discipline it was, but that's the spirit in which I learned it – as a
series of mechanical actions. If I don't have the right equipment,
the maps won't turn out right. I'll get confused.'

What Andris was really worried about, of course, was that once
Aulakh Phar had seen a map of the Navel of the World he might
become markedly less interested in hiring and hiding a wanted
man. Caution inclined him to make a bargain beforehand, and – if
possible – to collect a down-payment in advance. Aulakh Phar,

alas, was equally cautious and equally determined not to part with a penny. Merel Zabio had easily persuaded him to arrange a meeting but the old man was obviously not convinced that there was any safe ground left in the province. He was almost as nervous as Andris was, although he had selected the inn in whose cramped attic they were now sitting.

'You must have talked to Fraxinus about this,' Merel put in. 'He saw Andris in the jail – he can vouch for his credentials.'

'No he can't,' Phar said contemptuously. 'He never saw you draw a map, did he? Anyway, it's me you're dealing with, not Carus. I don't need every last detail – just draw me the outlines, in any colours you like, and name the major features. If it tallies well enough with what I already know, you're in. If not – frankly, I don't want you within five kims of the caravan. The king's men can make plenty of trouble for us yet, if they've a mind to, and we've trouble enough ahead of us if a tenth of what the darklanders say can be trusted.'

Phar nodded his grizzled head as he spoke, to emphasise the points he was making. The old man's bright eyes and massive but fine-bridged nose made him look oddly bird-like, and the nodding head compounded the impression. His thin-lipped mouth became almost invisible when he pursed his lips but when he spoke, revealing his long front teeth, he also looked more than a little like a rat.

'It's not my fault the king's men are here in such force,' Andris complained. 'It's Checuti they're after. I was caught up in the affair entirely by accident.'

'They don't know that,' said Phar wearily. 'Just stop wasting time and show me what you can do. Then we can decide where we go from here.'

'Draw the map, Andris,' Merel advised. She was standing behind Andris's chair, in the only part of the attic where anyone could comfortably stand, beneath the arch of the room's only window. 'We have to trust him. We don't have any alternative, do we?'

'I know you haven't done this for a long time,' said Phar, softening his tone considerably now that he had won the initial argument. 'But the lore that's pumped into us when we're young is never lost. It's just a matter of getting into the right frame of mind. You can do it, Andris. Once a mapmaker, always a mapmaker.'

Andris was quick to nod his head. 'I know I can do it,' he said, with all the conviction he could muster. 'I can't guarantee that the territory will match the map, but I can draw what I was taught to draw. Even without the right tools, I can make a fair stab at it.'

He lowered his gaze again to the empty parchment. He sat very still, and tried to cast his mind back over the years. He closed his eyes and tried to imagine himself back in his schoolroom – the schoolroom in the palace of Ferentina, which was the finest in all that land. In the dark arena of his consciousness he sketched the high windows, the thick carpet, the book-lined shelves and the ornamented desk. He recalled the faces of his tutors, selecting out the lean and sallow face of the master of the Arts Geographical who had devoted years to the thankless business of engraving his secrets on the ungrateful layers of Andris's maturing mind. He conjured up the precise tone of that dry, cracked voice.

Nothing that is properly stored is ever lost, he heard the imaginary voice say. *What we make a part of you now will be a part of you forever. It is to sustain the lore that the human being has been gifted with such a protracted childhood and such an impressionable mind. Provided that the initial impression is deep enough, forgetfulness is an impossible sin.*

'Stupid windbag,' Andris muttered. Aulakh Phar, realising that the words were not meant for him, did not take offence.

It was as though the voice were a string attached to Andris's hand. The hand reached out, unbidden by any conscious volition of his own, and he had only to imagine the voice saying: *South of the equator, line zero. The Navel of the World. The key to the design is the five-pointed star, crossed by the curved bow, whose arrow has flown into the Nest of the Phoenix. The apex of the star is the Corridors of Power in the Dragomite Hills, and its heart is the Lake of Colourless Blood . . .*

His hand moved back and forth, as if moved by an alien will, making dots and curved lines. His little finger darted hither and yon as it measured and manoeuvred. He opened his eyes by the merest crack to watch the scurrying pen, so that the sight of the emergent pattern might blend in with the imagistic guide-path laid down by his tutor's voice. Andris marvelled at the momentum of it all: the way it flowed within him like a river of darkness, and the way it flowed out of him like a sputtering fountain, scarring the page with ink. It required very little effort on his part to maintain the tempo and the rhythm, and he hardly hesitated at all.

The second point is the Crystal City, the third is Salamander's Fire; the fourth is the lair of Serpents and the fifth the Pillars of Silence. The shaft of the bow is the greatest river in all the world and the string the line of its flood-plain. The arrow's fletchings are the Silver Thorns and its shaft is the Gauntlet of Gladness; the Nest of the Phoenix is the Navel of the World, the arrow's buried head Chimera's Cradle, due east of that the Cities of the Plain . .

Andris paused to look at the marks which he had scratched, and filled his pen again. He added a deft stroke here and a ragged blot there, and tried to ignore his uneasy awareness that it wasn't quite right. He drew a framing line at the top of the parchment, and another to the right. Then, not quite satisfied but fearful of losing his impetus, he laid the pen down and took up the first and coarsest of the three brushes. It was far *too* coarse, and his hand was a bigger and clumsier thing now than it had been when he was half-grown, but he tried with all his mind to think in a delicate way.

The upper frame is the Forest of Absolute Night, said the voice inside his skull, as he swept a purple that was far too blue across the upper part of the parchment. He washed the brush and deftly dried it.

To the right is the Spangled Desert. He applied a yellow that was far too bright, with no silver in it at all, wincing at the garishness of it. *To the left is the Grey Waste.* He used a delicate shade of blue for that, but it was quite wrong.

The Dragomite Hills extend like the curve of a dove's wing in flight, the inner voice went on, as he applied pale green. *The Soursweet Marshes follow the curve of the bow, whose grip is the Lake of Colourless Blood.*

He used pink for the marshes and red for the lake, ignoring the incongruity. He used a deeper green for the area south of the marshes, through which ran the fletched-arrow symbol called the Silver Thorns. He had few colours left to draw the wide-winged phoenix fluttering above her nest, but he blocked the shadowy figure in another shade of purple, and coloured the plain to the east and south of it in green. Then he added in the remaining rivers, in dark blue.

He cleaned the brush for the last time, and set it carefully aside.

Then he took up the pen again and dipped it in the inkpot. He continued for three or four minutes more, dotting and dabbing, adding labels. Finally, he stopped. He looked up at Aulakh Phar, who had been watching him with intense concentration. 'That's enough,' he said. 'It's the best I can do. The colours are all wrong, but it's good enough to show that I know what I'm doing.'

Phar sucked his teeth for a moment or two, then nodded. 'Well,' he said, 'either you really have the lore or you're the best actor I ever saw. But you'll have to interpret these labels for me. Initials won't do.'

Andris cleared the nib of the pen on a piece of rag, and glanced around at Merel, who was smiling in relief. 'I'm not sure the labels mean very much,' he said cautiously. 'They're mostly just vivid names – mnemonic devices, intended to fix things in the memory. PS, for instance, is Pillars of Silence – but what, exactly, the Pillars of Silence might be isn't part of the lore. Not my lore, at any rate.'

'Let's not worry about the meanings for now,' Phar said, pointing to another label. 'This NW is the Navel of the World?'

'That's right.'

'What do the NP and CC close by it refer to? What are these curious symbols here, here and here, which don't seem to be letters at all?'

'I've no idea what the glyphs mean,' Andris admitted, carefully not answering the first part of the question, on the grounds that a wise man ought to keep a little information up his sleeve, 'but I can tell you that out of all the maps committed to my memory, this and the one which describes the country further to the south are the only ones that have them. It's strange, though, that the Navel of the World should be so far south. You'd expect it to be at the equator, wouldn't you?'

'What's the equator?' Merel Zabio asked.

'A line around the middle of the world, like a belt,' Andris told her, pointing it out on the map. 'Here it is, running through the Forest of Absolute Night and into the Spangled Desert. The zero line cuts it here, due north of the Lake of Colourless Blood. That's where the Navel of the World ought to be, not hundreds of kims to the south and way off to the west.'

'Why is there a line around the middle of the world?' Merel asked. 'Who put it there?'

'It's not a real line,' Andris told her. 'It's just a mapmakers' thing – part of the framework which contains the maps. There aren't any . . .'

He never finished the sentence. There was a sudden hammering on the door – which was, of course, barred on the inside – and a stentorian voice shouted: 'Open up in the king's name!'

'Corruption and corrosion!' Phar groaned. 'I thought this place was safe! The innkeeper's a boyhood friend of Checuti's. You can't trust anyone these days.'

If the complaint extended any further than that, Andris didn't hear it. He had begun to move before the challenge was halfway through and was already scrambling past the old man's chair. Merel had opened the window behind her and was clambering up on to the sill. Andris paused only to snatch the map from the table, scattering the paintpots and inkwell far and wide, before he followed her.

The window was rather small, and because Andris was uncommonly large it was by no means easy for him to scramble through it, but fear lent urgency to his attempt. With the aid of Merel Zabio, who grabbed his left wrist and hauled while he was still using his right hand to ram the hastily furled parchment into his shirt, he somehow managed to wriggle out on to the steeply slanted tiles. He glanced back at Phar then, but the grey-haired man was shaking his head, signalling to Andris to close the window while he called out to the men who were clamouring at the door that he was coming. The pace at which he went to let them in was, however, far slower than the waiting men would presumably have liked. Andris made haste to be out of sight before the bolt was drawn.

The opportunity which Andris's imprisonment in Xandria had given him to accustom himself to heights proved, alas, to have done him little or no permanent good. It was one thing to look down from a securely barred window with one's feet solidly planted on a sturdy floor; it was quite another to scramble over a sloping roof, on tiles which seemed everywhere to be crumbling, with nothing but a shallow and thoroughly rotted wooden gutter to interrupt his fall should he slip. Panic nearly froze him, but Merel still had hold of his arm and was pulling him along. He had no alternative but to go.

Andris had no idea of the external shape of the inn, because Merel had hurried him along the lane, through the rear door and up the stairs while his head was voluminously hooded, giving him no opportunity whatsoever to look around. He had to hope that she had paid enough attention to its architecture to know whether there was any plausible way down to the ground.

As soon as his kinswoman let go of his hand he paused to make sure that the map was as secure as it could be. Rolling it up so hurriedly and so untidily and stuffing it inside his shirt was sure to have done a good deal of damage to its colours, but he fully intended to cling on to it as hard and as long as he could, given that it was his only chance of buying the help he needed to get him safely out of Khalorn. By the time he got going again Merel had taken a long lead, but he scurried after her, determined to catch up.

Merel had scrambled up to the ridge of the roof, where she found an adequate handhold with which to steady herself, and began moving along it. She signalled to Andris, instructing him to follow, but it was by no means easy to obey – and when he did try to imitate her he sent three or four broken tiles skidding down the roof. The shards pattered down on the ground, which was enough to make them rattle alarmingly. If any of their pursuers had been stationed below, it would be perfectly obvious where they were – but if anyone heard the falling tiles he did not cry out.

'Don't look down,' Merel advised needlessly, as he continued to follow in her wake in his own far clumsier fashion. He managed to get his left leg over the ridge of the roof, so that he might sit astraddle as he inched himself along; the position was uncomfortable, but it felt secure and no more tiles went sliding away.

'We'll go to the end,' Merel decided, gesturing forwards and whispering theatrically across the three mets which separated them. 'The roof slopes down again from the point, and the roof of the stable's just a short drop below the gutter. If you can refrain from wanton destruction for just five seconds you might get down on it without going clean through. With luck, there'll be something close to the outer wall of the stable to provide a step. If not, we'll just have to jump. I'll go first.'

She moved off, crouching low but actually walking on the vertiginously tilted surface. Andris followed, still using his arms to inch himself along while his legs dangled down to either side. By the time he ran out of ridge Merel was already lowering herself on to the stable roof, supporting herself by clinging to the creaking guttering. It bore her weight, albeit reluctantly, but Andris could tell that it wouldn't be able to support his. He remained in a sitting position as he slid himself down the triangular section of tiling, inflicting less damage on the tiles than he had expected, but the slope was so steep that the further he went the faster he went, and when he reached the guttering there was no way he could halt himself.

The guttering split beneath him, and he was precipitated into empty space, legs extended and arms akimbo.

Had he landed feet first on the stable roof he would undoubtedly have splintered the wood, and might easily have sent splinters deep into his flesh, but he managed somehow to adjust his position so that he landed on his buttocks, spreading the shock of the impact along his legs and his back. Although his back was much better now, the long spear-cut having healed quite well, it was not ready for this kind of maltreatment; the pain was terrible.

The timbers groaned and gave way, but they didn't shatter. Jarred by the impact, and sickened by the agonising wrench of his back muscles, Andris was unable to do anything for a few seconds but lie still, arms and legs outstretched, trying desperately to collect his strength and his wits.

By the time he was able to sit up Merel was out of sight. He squirmed across the slightly slanted beams to the edge of the stable roof. He was now little more than three mets from the ground, but even that seemed like a long drop, and he looked around for something which might allow him to take it in two steps. There was a water-butt placed to catch the spillage from the guttering, and he moved towards it, writhing like a snake.

He had no wish to take a bath, so he knew that he would have to be very careful in placing his feet and balancing himself. He adjusted his position with the utmost care, and lowered himself over the edge of the roof in painstaking fashion, lying face down while he slid his legs over the edge inch by inch.

He groped with his dangling feet for the two sides of the butt, and found it. He tested its solidity as best he could; not until he was fairly certain that all was in order did he transfer his weight, and he did so as briefly as possible. He completed the manoeuvre by executing a jump and turn of which – he was immodest enough to think – a trained acrobat would not have been utterly ashamed.

Unfortunately, the turn part of the manoeuvre brought him face to face with a man very nearly as big as he was, who was holding a very impressive dagger in an unmistakably hostile position. There were two other men behind him. Merel Zabio was nowhere to be seen.

Oddly enough, his first reaction was not fear or despair but blatant outrage.

'I know you!' he exclaimed in astonishment. 'You're that bastard who . . .'

'Be glad that I am,' the big man interrupted, with no more than a slight grimace of annoyance. 'If I were the king's man, you'd be in *real* trouble.'

7

'I CAN SEE the house,' whispered Luca, who had climbed a tree in order to peer over the intervening wall. 'There are lights inside – they're not asleep. I can see one man silhouetted in the window. I think there are others inside, but I can't tell how many.'

'How many men does Checuti have with him?' Jacom asked the man who had met them behind the lodge in the park. He was small and lean, very light on his feet – and very nervous now that he had brought them to their destination.

'How should I know?' the guide complained. 'I'm not one of them – I'm just an honest man who happens to owe money to an honest merchant. Maybe three, maybe thirty. But I can assure you they ain't goin' to lie down an' go to sleep. He only came into town to see someone. He won't hang around once he's finished talking. Don't bank on there bein' coin hid in there, 'cause there probably ain't.'

'It's a big house shaped like an elongated H, with outbuildings in both yards and a big barn off to the right,' Luca reported. 'The house must have at least two doors. The wall doesn't go all the way round but there's a fence – probably rotten in places but I can't see from here. It's a real maze – we don't have nearly enough men to cover the exits.'

'We don't have enough men, period,' said Sergeant Purkin gruffly. 'We should've got help. Plenty of real army about if the militia can't be trusted.' Purkin's original opinion had been that this was a fool's errand, but now that they had actually arrived at the place where Checuti was supposed to be he had changed tack. Now he was making a show of his strong disapproval of Jacom's determination to trust no one but his own men. If the adventure went badly, the sergeant would certainly not be short of arguments to demonstrate that the foul-up had definitely not been his fault.

'We'd have more men if we hadn't lost so many,' Jacom told him, in a faintly accusative tone. 'We'll just have to make do with what we've got left – It's too late now to send for reinforcements. What are our chances of getting right up to the house without being spotted, do you think?'

It was the little man who answered, before Purkin could open his mouth. 'None,' he said flatly. 'There's geese in the sheds to the right of the front yard. Best sentries in the world – you go through that gate an' everyone in the house'll soon know you're around.'

'Peck us to death, I shouldn't wonder,' Purkin muttered contemptuously.

'Naw,' said the little man disgustedly. 'Won't hurt you – but when they hear you comin' they'll start honking loud enough to wake the dead. You'll see.'

'What about human sentries?' Purkin asked, keeping his lips very close to the prisoner's ear so that he could growl instead of whispering. 'Do they have those posted too?'

'How should I know?' the little man replied, a little too loudly for Jacom's liking, although the soft noise made by the wind as it rustled the leaves on the trees was enough to prevent the words being heard more than a few mets away. 'I just know the place. I live round 'ere. Anyway, I gotta go now. You tell Carus Fraxinus we're square, OK?'

Purkin was quick to seize the little man before he could wriggle through the group of guardsmen and race away. 'Oh no you don't,' he said. 'We're not finished yet.'

'Door's opening,' said Luca murmurously. 'Someone coming out. Only one, though.'

'Where is he going?' Jacom asked.

'Can't tell. Too dark in the shadows. Probably taking a leak.'

Suppose we've been spotted already, Jacom wondered. Suppose he's been tipped off that we're coming. He remembered, ruefully, the damage which Checuti's darklanders had done to his patrols on the night of the robbery, with the anaesthetic darts they'd fired from their blowpipes. There had been lamplight as well as starlight to aim by in the citadel, and there was far less light here, but the darklanders' natural habitat was the Forest of Absolute Night, where – if rumour could be credited – there was hardly any once the sun had set. Jacom looked uneasily about, cursing the awkward layout of the farm buildings and the overgrown wall surrounding the junk-laden front yard. The trees growing close to the outside of the wall were hardly dense enough to qualify as a forest but they were old and stout, with very leafy crowns, and they could have hidden a legion of clever savages.

Not for the first time, Jacom wondered whether Purkin was right to argue that he ought to have gone to the governor to raise a company of militiamen. He reminded himself, though, that he had good enough reason to think that any message passed along the governor's chain of command was likely to be broadcast very quickly indeed. It was surely better to be here with too few men than to have come with a small army to find that the bird had flown.

'It's OK,' Luca said eventually. 'He's gone back in. Geese never made a sound.'

'Darklander,' opined the little man. 'Darklanders got a way with birds. Checuti's always been thick with darklanders. Blood brothers or somethin' like. Nasty in a fight – savages, the lot of 'em.'

'You seem very well informed about his habits,' Jacom observed. 'How many men is he *likely* to have with him, do you think?'

'I don't know!' the informer insisted.

'It doesn't really matter, sir,' Purkin said grimly. 'We're too few to rush the place even if there're only half a dozen. Even if we keep watch on all the doors there's any number of escape routes from a place like that. If it comes to a fight . . . well, I don't like charging into a battle without knowing the enemy's strength or the quality of his arms. Far better to set an ambush and lie low. If he comes out when he's finished his business, not knowing we're lying in wait, we'll be able to see whether the princess is with him and we'll have a chance to take him. That's our best bet.'

'We don't want anyone getting killed,' Jacom agreed, knowing that the assembled men would be anxious to know that he wasn't about to do anything foolhardy. 'We're not here to take Checuti, unless we have a clear opportunity to do so. What we want, first and foremost, is to find out whether he still has the princess, and if so, where. If we can get that without a fight, so much the better. Maybe we can talk to him. We may not know how many men he has, but *he* doesn't know how many *we* have. If we can persuade him that he's surrounded, he might be willing to give up the princess in exchange for free passage out of that house.'

'Ambush is best,' Purkin said steadfastly. 'Bluff can always get called. If we pretend we're more than we are, the bastards will either scatter or make a stand – either way, we're not up to it. If we wait, an' concentrate on grabbin' Checuti, the rest might look after themselves an' leave him to us.'

The little man made a small sound of disgust. The last part didn't sound very convincing to Jacom. He suspected, in fact, that it didn't sound convincing to Purkin either. Jacom didn't want to lie in wait, leaving the initiative to the other side. He wanted to act. He wanted, if it was at all possible, to be a hero. Fate surely owed him a chance of that, if there was any fairness in the world at all.

'If we lose him . . .' Jacom began slowly. He didn't continue. There were far to many ifs hanging over the argument . . . and at the end of the day, he and he alone had to sort through them. He was the officer. It would be his fault if they screwed this up, no matter whose advice he took, and Purkin would never let him forget it. Fraxinus had recommended cleverness – but what did cleverness amount to, in a situation like this?

In all the stories he'd been told as a boy, about ever-valiant guardsmen and dastardly enemies of the state, things had gone much more smoothly than his own exploits to date, and no officer had ever made a wrong decision without having a subsequent opportunity to redeem himself spectacularly. It was, however, easy for characters in stories to win through when the appropriate moment arrived: they had dutiful story-tellers to make sure that they'd be all right whatever desperate risks they chose to take. In real life,there were far too many things that could go horribly wrong.

'You're the only one of us who knows exactly what Checuti looks like, sergeant,' Jacom pointed out. 'It won't be easy to pick him out in light like this on the basis of a second-hand description. All things considered, I think we might have to do something a little more enterprising than just lying low and waiting for Checuti to walk into our arms. We *might* be able to persuade him that we're more than we are, if only we pretend hard enough – and he might be prepared to talk, if he's sufficiently uncertain of his situation. He won't have time to plan; he'll have to think fast, and he could easily make mistakes.'

'Don't bet on that,' said their informant.

'Shut up,' Purkin snarled into his ear gruffly. It was painfully clear that he'd rather have said it to Jacom.

'All right,' said Jacom, trying hard to sound like a man in full command of the situation. 'This is what we're going to do. Firstly, we need to post men around the house. It'll have to be threes and twos. Those of you who don't have half-pikes have your swords drawn and ready. Mor, Pavel and Kristoforo, make your way round to the rear. Keep some distance between yourself and the yard – don't start the geese honking if you can possibly help it. Taj, you and Herriman go to the right, Fernel and Aaron to the left. If they do make a run for it, look out for Checuti and look out for the princess. Your first priority is to get the princess, if you can . . . if that's not on, try to grab *somebody*, alive and able to talk. If they don't run, wait for orders. I'll make sure you know if and when it's time to go in.'

'What about *him*, sir,' Purkin asked, meaning the man who had brought them.

'Let him go,' Jacom said. 'He'll only get in the way if he stays. Come down, Luca. You'll be more use on the ground than up a tree if this doesn't work out. Stay with Kirn and Purkin.'

Purkin released the man he was holding, but he let out a sad sigh as he did so. As Luca scrambled down to the ground the little man hurried away along the road.

'We'll wait ten minutes while the others get into position,' Jacom said to the men who had remained by the path leading to the gate. 'I want you three to wait by the gate. Have your swords ready, but don't move unless and until I shout for help.'

'Where were you thinkin' of shoutin' from, sir?' Purkin enquired disapprovingly.

'From the doorway of the house, sergeant,' Jacom said, trying to sound stern as well as brave, 'if I can get that far.'

'You're going to go up there and knock on the door, are you, sir?' the sergeant asked with scrupulous politeness. 'All on your own, like.'

'If our friend knows what he's talking about, I doubt that I'll get to the door before the geese start honking,' Jacom said drily. 'As for being on my own . . . well, let's just remember who it was that got us into this mess. If anything dreadful should happen to me . . . you can all go back to Xandria then, can't you?'

'I'm not sure that we can, sir,' Purkin said, with a noticeable edge to his voice. 'Not as guardsmen, sir — not without the princess.'

It had not quite dawned on Jacom until that moment that if all that had been required for the rehabilitation of his men was that something untoward should happen to him, something untoward might very well have happened already.

It'd be nice to have real friends about me, he thought. *Men that I could trust. Men who'd gladly take a risk on my behalf. But if I have to settle for men who haven't any good reason to stab me in the back, I'll just have to keep reminding myself that things could be even worse.*

'Well,' he said aloud, more than a little sourly, 'in that case, you'll just have to hope that this comes off, won't you?'

'Ambush is safer, sir,' Purkin stubbornly insisted. 'Trust me, sir. Lie low and wait. Always best.'

I tried it once, Jacom thought, *and look where it got me!*

'Bluff is cleverer,' he said firmly. 'And whether we trust one another or not, that's the way we're going to play it, all the way to the last ditch.'

8

THE MAN WHO faced Andris across the low table was over-weight but not flabby; he somehow gave the impression of having earned his size rather than having it thrust upon him by luxury and indolence. His curly hair didn't seem in the least effeminate, and this wasn't because he wore a neat pointed beard of the same ebon sleekness. He was attended by a slender grey monkey which perched on the back of the sofa, tethered to a lamp standard by a thin silver chain.

'The prince of thieves, I presume,' Andris said drily.

'It's not a name I ever sought, nor one I can cherish,' the bearded man answered mournfully. 'I understand they call you *the big darklander*, but I don't expect that you approve of the habit.'

'But I'm not a darklander,' Andris pointed out, 'whereas you certainly do seem to be a thief.'

'That's true,' Checuti admitted with a theatrical sigh, but said nothing more while he studied the map which he had carefully spread out on the table.

'Not that I have anything against you on that count,' Andris said diplomatically. 'Merel speaks very highly of you – and I suppose I owe you my thanks for getting me out of jail, if what you told her about the princess's intentions was true. I'm worried about Merel, by the way – I do think your three bully-boys should have intercepted her too. She'll be anxious and afraid – she probably thinks the king's men have got me.'

The black-haired man didn't seem to be listening. 'This is terrible,' he observed critically. 'If this is an example of the mapmaker's Art it's no wonder the lore fell into such disrepute in Xandria.'

As Andris had anticipated, the premature and rather rough and ready scrolling of the map had done his brushwork no favours at all. The map did indeed look awful. 'I didn't have the right materials to start with,' he retorted resentfully, 'and the work was utterly spoiled when I had to stuff it into my shirt and climb out of the window. Was it really the king's men at the door, or did you arrange that?'

'It was the innkeeper,' Checuti admitted. 'You'll probably recall that he didn't actually say he was the king's man — he just demanded that the door be opened in the king's name. Anyone can do that. What's a king for, after all, but to lend the authority of his name to his loyal subjects — and, of course, to keep the coin of the realm nice and fresh? Burdam didn't want to get into an argument with Phar — he's a touchy fellow, quite unpredictable, and his partner is far too friendly with that young guard-captain. At the very least, Phar would have wanted to come along to keep an eye on you. It's dangerous enough my being here at all, without inviting the whole world. Don't worry about your pretty cousin. She'll figure out soon enough that it wasn't the king's agents who grabbed you. Phar will look after her.'

'If it's so dangerous for you to be here,' Andris said, 'why did you come? Why invite anyone at all?'

'Good question,' said Burdam Thrid, who was hovering by the window looking out into the night. The other men had retired to another room where they had immediately begun to play cards, watched by two silent darklanders. The darklanders had looked Andris over very carefully when he arrived, and he had studied them with equal interest, but Thrid had not bothered to introduce them.

'Burdam's the cautious type,' Checuti said. 'I made him my chief lieutenant so that he might act as a sobering influence, but somehow it hasn't worked out. Every time he tells me not to do something, it increases the temptation to do it. Sheer perversity, I suppose. He says it'll be the death of me. He's probably right.'

Andris couldn't help thinking that the conversation was becoming bizarre. Checuti was not at all what he had expected. He was beginning to comprehend, however, how the idea of robbing the king's treasury might have proved irresistible to such a man.

'I'm right about this business being sheer madness,' Thrid said. 'I should have slit the bitch's throat myself, the instant we found her.'

'What bitch?' Andris wanted to know.

'Princess Lucrezia,' Checuti told him. 'It's partly because of what she told me that I wanted to see you – and the map.' He smiled faintly, presumably in response to Andris's blank stare. 'My master plan was perfect,' he explained, 'in every respect but one – or perhaps two. At the citadel, it succeeded just a little too well. We escaped with all the coin, but we also carried away an unconscious princess who was surplus to our requirements. She hadn't seen anything very damaging, but my cautious associates were all for killing her regardless. I let her talk me out of it. In the course of doing so, she told me some interesting things about what might or might not be happening south of the forest. She told me about Keshvara's seeds, thus confirming what I'd already heard rumoured about the exceedingly unpleasant death she'd marked you down for, and she told me everything Keshvara had told her about Fraxinus's plan to cross the Dragomite Hills and the unique opportunity presented by the blight which seems to have wiped out so many nests.'

'All horseshit,' opined Burdam Thrid.

Checuti ignored him. 'This information was intriguing in itself,' he went on, 'but I probably wouldn't have paid any more attention to it if my plans hadn't started to go slightly awry at this end too. You see, I'd rather reckoned on living a quiet and orderly life from now on. I thought that rural Khalorn – which is, after all, my homeland – would be the perfect setting for an idyllic retirement. Unfortunately, things seem to have changed while I've been away. Darklanders are flooding out of the forest in considerable numbers, bringing tales of invasion by dragomites with human riders – demon women descended from children stolen in the distant past to be nest-slaves.

'I've had darklander friends since I was a child. I spent time in the fringes of the forest in my younger days – I've known those two men you met just now for fifteen years. I'm one of the few goldens to be inducted into the Uluru.'

'What's the Uluru?' Andris asked.

'It's a secret society – all darklanders belong to some such society. All the societies naturally claim to be the biggest and most secret of all, but the Uluru's definitely the one to be in around these parts. I always thought of it as a kind of game – a game that could be turned to my advantage. That's how I contrived to involve darklanders in the robbery, of course. Normally, darklanders live in small family groups which don't co-operate with one another, let alone anyone else, but the societies bind together much larger kin-groups. It's said that the women have one of their own, but I wouldn't know about that.

'Anyhow, to cut a long story short, the kind of obligation which I exploited to get the darklander help in Xandria works both ways, and now the society to which I belong is trying to make claims on *me*. The game has somehow become serious. The darklands are in turmoil, it seems, and the darklanders are trying to form an army – an actual army, though nothing could be more foreign to their usual way of life – to drive out these mysterious invaders. I can't tell how bad the problem really is because of the superstitious fears that have become confused with it. The darklanders are muttering about the end of the world and Serpents reclaiming their heritage and all kinds of nonsense – and the Uluru want my help to fight the good and glorious fight. They expect to get that help, in whatever form I can best deliver it.

'In some way – I don't yet know exactly how – all this must be connected with what the princess told me, and this exploration team that Fraxinus and Phar are putting together. Burdam thinks that I don't owe the darklanders anything, and ought to let the thing alone, but the men in the back room disagree, and I have a nasty feeling that the thing might not let *me* alone – or any of us, come to that – if I try to stay out of it. I need to find out more about what's happening, Andris. I was rather hoping that this might help me.'

He waved his palm over the ruined map as he said *this*.

'I can draw another one,' Andris said, 'if I can only get hold of the right equipment.' He was about to add *But I don't see what good it will do* when his mind's eye conjured up an image of Merel Zabio's face, wearing a despairingly censorious expression. He quickly changed his mind, and said instead: 'For a price, of course.'

Checuti didn't react to that. 'It's odd, isn't it,' he said ruminatively, 'that your fate and mine have become entangled? All because you happened to be sitting at a particular table in the Wayfaring Tree at an unfortunate hour, listening to that blind beggar recite his fake lore. Did Phar tell you, by any chance, what he and Fraxinus are really after?'

'He didn't tell me anything,' Andris said. 'Why? Do you think he's after some specific treasure?'

'I wish it were as simple as that,' Checuti said with a sigh. 'That would make things so much easier to understand, wouldn't it? Phar and Keshvara might be in it for simple profit, but Fraxinus has higher motives in mind. The darklanders are very big on signs and omens, you know . . . one of the things that holds their secret societies together is the notion that they're a chosen people, having sole custody of certain secret commandments passed down from the days of the forefathers. The darklanders think that this business with the dragomites coming out of the hills and into the forest isn't just an inconvenience – they think it's a sign of something much more ominous. Burdam, of course, thinks it's all just mumbo-jumbo . . .'

'Horseshit,' Thrid corrected him dourly. 'Demon women, Serpent magicians and secret commandments . . . all horseshit.'

'. . . but it might just be,' Checuti continued, as if he had never been interrupted, 'that there are more things in the world than his narrow mind is willing to accommodate. I'm not a superstitious man, Andris, but I am an initiate of a society whose rules require me to . . . well, to take an interest, at least. Tell me, how do you feel about entering my employ?'

'In what capacity?' Andris wanted to know, still having Merel's stern face fixed in his mind's eye.

'Fighting man . . . mapmaker . . . imitation darklander.'

'What about Merel?'

'She's already one of my secret legion, by courtesy of bargains struck in Xandria. So are you, in the eyes of the law. While you're on the run anyway . . . it's far better to be part of a team, don't you think?'

Andris hesitated. There was an echo in this situation of the one which he had faced in Belin's jail. Once again, it seemed, he was being offered a choice without being told what he might be letting himself in for. He was opening his mouth to prevaricate when he was rudely interrupted by a sudden raucous clamour coming from the yard beyond the window at which Burdam Thrid was standing. Thrid started, but not as violently as the little monkey which began to look wildly about, chattering its teeth.

Thrid muttered yet another curse as a human voice shouted above the din: 'Checuti! This is Captain Jacom Cerri of the king's guard. My men have surrounded the house. You're outnumbered and you can't escape. Send Princess Lucrezia out. Provided she's unharmed, I give you my word that no harm will come to you or any of your men.'

'In a pig's eye,' Thrid muttered, as the door burst open and the card-players tumbled into the room, looking urgently to their leader for guidance. 'It's a trick!'

'If it's a trick,' said Checuti dubiously, 'it's a peculiar one. If the geese gave them away while they were sneaking up on us, why didn't they simply charge in? Do they really think the princess is here – and if not, what do they have to gain by playing for time?'

'There isn't time for this,' Thrid said, drawing a huge dagger from his belt. 'Let's go.'

'No!' said Checuti. 'There's no knowing what we'd be running into. A little cleverness might get us all out alive and uninjured.'

The two darklanders were in the doorway now, waiting expectantly – but they seemed perfectly calm and patient. It was to them, not to the card-players, that Checuti looked now. 'They'll have someone watching the back door,' he said. 'Don't let them see you. No matter what you find, don't start a fight. Let's figure out exactly what we're up against before we turn the place into a battlefield – OK?'

The darklanders nodded, and immediately turned away. It was Thrid who said: 'It's not OK. Somebody's turned us in!'

'I'll handle it, Burdam,' Checuti said quietly. His face seemed to Andris to reflect the same firm imperturbability that he had seen in the faces of the two darklanders, recalling all that he had said earlier about being party to their secrets. 'Just be patient, will you? If we do have to run, look after Andris – he and I still have some talking to do. Take him to the meeting-house; I'll come when I can. Tell me, Andris – are you a gambling man?'

'Only for money,' Andris replied acidly, as an all too familiar sinking feeling asserted its grip once again within his lower abdomen. 'I don't like to risk my life, if I can possibly help it.'

'Very sensible,' said Checuti, reaching out to pat the anxious monkey reassuringly on the head. 'Neither do I.'

9

AFTER SHOUTING OUT his invitation Jacom stepped back ten or fifteen mets. The geese didn't stop honking but they became gradually less strident. Jacom could feel the beating of his heart as time leaked away. At least three minutes went by before the door opened and a lone figure appeared, silhouetted by a lantern which had been set on the floor of the corridor behind him. The figure was stout but solid. His arms were spread wide and his fingers were splayed, to make it obvious that he held no weapon. He didn't seem to be wearing a swordbelt.

'Captain Cerri?' The man's voice was level, with more curiosity in it than fear.

'Here!' Jacom said. He stepped forward again, but the other held up his hand.

'That's near enough. I can see you.' The noise of the geese was so murmurous by now that it wasn't necessary for him to shout.

'Send out the princess,' Jacom said again. 'Then tell your men to lay down their arms and come out quietly.' He felt a little more relaxed now that he had actually seen Checuti and heard him speak. The man didn't look so very fearsome, and he sounded perfectly civilised.

'I don't think that's necessary,' Checuti replied. 'If you'd mustered enough men to storm the house, or even to surround it, I'd surely have been warned of your coming before my feathery friends sounded the alert. Who told you we were here?'

'My first priority is to make sure the princess is safe,' Jacom said, sticking doggedly to his own agenda. 'I've been commanded by the king to bring her safely back to Xandria at all costs.'

'I'm almost tempted to pretend that she's here,' Checuti said calmly, 'but there really isn't much point in our both becoming lost in a maze of bluff and counter-bluff. I'm sorry, but I don't have the princess in my charge any more.'

'Is she dead?'

'No.'

'Can you prove that?'

The silhouetted figure laughed briefly. 'Of course I can't prove it, captain – but if she were dead, would you dare to carry the news to Belin? I wouldn't, if I were in your shoes. Wouldn't it be a relief, in a way, if she were dead? Then you could simply stop worrying about your commission and become a soldier of fortune. I hear that Phar is having difficulty hiring men because the darklanders he was relying on have other commitments. As it happens, though, I have no reason to doubt that the princess is alive and well. I handed her over to Hyry Keshvara two days after leaving Xandria. Keshvara agreed to bring her south.'

Jacom carefully considered this surprising news. 'I don't believe you,' he said, after a brief pause. 'Keshvara should have arrived three days ago, ahead of Fraxinus, to join Aulakh Phar. She hasn't shown up.'

'Of course she hasn't,' Checuti said equably. 'She isn't going to show her face within twenty kims of the city while she has the princess in tow. She's probably gone into the forest already – she'll link up with Fraxinus there. If you want her, you'll have to go with Fraxinus yourself. Did *he* help you find us? You must have had help from someone, and he's the only man I know who might have sufficient pull in these parts to turn one of my men around.'

'Why did you give the princess to Keshvara?' Jacom asked, ignoring Checuti's questions. 'Why should Keshvara take her south instead of returning her to Xandria? It doesn't make sense – it has to be a lie.'

Jacom felt less than confident in saying this. Checuti was quite wrong – and probably knew it – to suggest that it might come as a relief to Jacom to know that the princess was dead and that his own fate was sealed so far as Xandria was concerned. On the contrary, Jacom wanted desperately to be assured that the princess was alive, that she was safe in the custody of Hyry Keshvara, and that she might well ride into Khalorn tomorrow morning, deeply grateful to be delivered into the protective arms of her would-be rescuer. Unfortunately, he couldn't think of any possible way that Checuti could convince him of this.

'The princess knew Keshvara,' Checuti said blandly. 'She asked to be delivered into her custody. It suited my friends, too – they were afraid that the princess might be able to tell the king's agents something that would prejudice their safety – so I obliged. When I explained to Keshvara that they might both end up dead if she tried to take the princess back to Xandria, she hadn't much choice but to bring her south. If you can find Keshvara, I expect she'll be only too glad to hand over the princess – your real problem will be persuading the princess to go with you. She's seen enough of the Inner Sanctum to last a lifetime, and she seemed distinctly averse to the prospect of being married off to that island princeling Belin had marked out for her. If I were you, captain, I'd hurry back to Khalorn. Catch up with Fraxinus and Phar and stick with them. Keshvara will bring the princess to you when she can, and you can negotiate your future prospects with the girl herself. There's nothing for you here but a chance to die. Neither of us wants to take chances like that, do we?'

Jacom considered this proposition dubiously. It was, he decided, far too easy. If he walked away now, and found out later that this was all lies, he'd look a perfect fool. Even if it were all true, how could he let a chance to capture Checuti slip through his fingers? On the other hand, Checuti was right about it being a chance to die. How many men, he wondered, did Checuti have in the house? Did the fact that the thief was prepared to come to the door and talk imply that he hadn't enough to come out fighting, or so many that he felt confident of mounting a successful defence if he were attacked?

'I need proof,' he said, knowing even as he said it that it was a ridiculous thing to say. What proof could Checuti possibly offer?

'I think you should go now, captain,' the man in the doorway said. 'You've been very sensible so far. I don't want bloodshed any more than you do, and I've told you what you want to know, so it would suit us both very well if you simply went away.'

'I'm afraid I can't do that,' Jacom replied reluctantly. He was uneasily aware of the weakness of his position, but he felt that he had no choice. 'It's a matter of duty. If the princess isn't here, I must ask for your unconditional surrender. If I don't get it, my men will slaughter your entire band of brigands.'

'That's no way for a reasonable man to conduct his affairs,

captain,' Checuti said, in a voice that was gently derisive without being openly insulting. 'It might be brave, and it might even qualify as dutiful, but it's not sensible. People could get killed – including you. How would Belin get his daughter back then? Carus Fraxinus won't turn back once he's in the forest no matter what problems might drop into his lap. Your first priority is to find Lucrezia – isn't that what you said? Go find her, then. Don't waste time with stupid heroics. It isn't worth the risk.'

'It's a matter of duty,' Jacom informed him again, wishing that his voice didn't sound quite so doleful. 'And a matter of personal pride, too. It was my men your darklanders felled, my men you lured away using the amber as a diversion. Did you arrange for him to be captured in the first place? He was working with you all along, wasn't he?'

'No,' the thiefmaster said. 'He was just an innocent man *you* arrested, and you didn't let out even when you discovered that he didn't cripple your guardsman. His release was just an extra twist I added to my little plot, for purely aesthetic reasons. You laid the groundwork yourself for the trap which you fell into, captain – you and you alone.'

That accusation stung, by virtue of its accuracy. Jacom had been the officer in command; he had jailed the amber and then laid an ambush to stop him getting out of jail. If he had only been in the courtyard outside the Inner Sanctum and not high on the wall, perhaps the princess would never have been captured. He could have run to intercept her, to save her from a fate worse than . . . but this was no time for flights of idle fancy.

'If you don't come out peacefully,' Jacom said stubbornly, 'we'll have to come in after you.' He heard Purkin's words echoing in his mind: *Ambush is safer, sir . . . Lie low and wait . . . Always best.* Why did the patronising swine always have to be right?

'The world would be a far better place if all would-be heroes were strangled at birth,' the thiefmaster opined with a heavy sigh – but he was quick to add, in a more confidential tone: 'If you're playing this scene for the benefit of your men, forget it. They don't want to risk their lives any more than you want to risk yours. I've told you how to find the princess – that's reward enough for a night's work.'

The trouble was, Jacom thought, as he examined his options,

that Checuti was very probably right. He began to wish — perversely, he knew — that he had not initiated this conversation. Checuti was right to argue that no reasonable man would start a fight in which half his company could end up dead unless he had no choice — but on the other hand, wouldn't it make a mockery of everything he was supposed to stand for as an officer in the king's guard if he simply walked away from the man who'd stolen the contents of the king's treasury on the day before Thanksgiving? In a romance, of course, he would have challenged Checuti to single combat, but he knew full well that if he were to suggest anything along those lines the only response he could sensibly expect would be loud and mocking laughter.

'I have to take you with me,' Jacom said, desperately casting about for a face-saving move. 'If you come out now, the rest of your men can go free. I promise that you won't be harmed.'

'My men wouldn't like that,' Checuti said. 'They'd lose faith in me if they thought I was the sort of fool who'd hand himself over on the strength of a promise like that. To tell you the truth, captain, they're a lot more enthusiastic to fight than I am. My darklanders are very edgy — trouble at home, you see — and the others are prepared to fight to the death rather than lose all the lovely bright coin they worked so hard to earn. What I *can* do, though — as it happens — is give you the big amber. You could take him back to Khalorn with you, and hand him over to the governor.'

Jacom was startled by this offer. 'You just said he wasn't one of your men,' he pointed out.

'He isn't,' Checuti said. 'I've just been having a chat with him, about matters of mutual interest. But he is here, and if you're determined to take someone away with you, I'd rather it was him than me.'

'I don't want him,' Jacom said. 'I should have turned him loose myself instead of trying to stop you getting him out and I'm not going to make the same mistake again. If you can't hand over the princess, then it has to be you, Checuti, alone or with everyone else. I can't settle for anything less — not without a fight.'

Jacom stiffened as a second figure appeared in the hallway behind Checuti. It was a very big man, and for a moment he assumed that it must be the amber — but then he saw that the man was too dark, and guessed that it must be Burdam Thrid. Thrid whispered something in Checuti's ear.

Checuti suddenly burst out laughing. '*Ten men!*' he called out to Jacom. 'You're running this bluff with *ten men*! You're a man after my own heart, captain – but with only ten men you can't even catch us, let alone fight us. Next time, bring an army.'

As he stepped back, leaving the door open, Checuti casually flicked his right foot sideways. The lantern fell over, the tall glass shattering as it hit the wall. Oil spilled out of the reservoir, igniting as it flowed. The hallway filled up with blazing liquid and smoke billowed out of the doorway. Checuti and Thrid had moved back along the corridor; they were no longer in view.

Purkin was already coming forward at a run, with the other two men close behind, but Jacom knew that Checuti was right. Ten men had little or no chance of intercepting and capturing the people running out of the farmhouse – especially if their exact disposition was known, as it had to be if they had been so accurately counted.

A mad cacophony of sound burst forth as the geese, startled by the fire and smoke, gave voice again.

'Get Checuti!' Jacom shouted as he ran forward. 'Never mind the rest of them – just get Checuti.'

He had no doubt that his men would do their very best to obey the order, but no confidence that they would be able to do it. While he was drawing his sword Purkin raced past him, and made as if to jump the moat of blazing oil that was now sealing the doorway, but changed his mind. Jacom didn't blame him for falling back – it would have been a stupid thing to do.

Purkin bawled at the men with him to go left and right, to cover the windows as well as the doors. When the sergeant chose to go to the left Jacom immediately went to the right, but he was already possessed by the cold certainty that it would all be for nothing. Cleverness had indeed been needed to win the day, and he had not found enough of it. Yet again he had proved himself inadequate.

As he ran, he held his sword high, ready and eager to cut at anyone he met. He was, however, able to curb the impulse when he finally did run into someone – which was perhaps as well, given that it was only poor Herriman, limping painfully because some callous brute had kicked him very hard on his bad leg.

Fortunately, that was the only significant injury Jacom's party sustained. Unfortunately, it was the only significant injury *anyone* sustained – although it took a long time to ascertain the fact because it was not until several hours had elapsed that the last of the men trudged back to the governor's manse in Khalorn to report that their miscellaneous pursuits had all ended in ignominious failure.

10

LUCREZIA SOON DECIDED that the Forest of Absolute Night was even more beautiful by night than it was by day. By day, the sunlit canopy was like a huge ornamental ceiling in which greys, greens, blues and purples extended infinitely in a mad but fairly consistent pattern, while the amazingly intricate peripheral flora which each of the vastly thick boles supported presented the appearance of a vast shock of wiry hair which had gone almost completely grey. By night, however, the canopy became a vast mysterious vault of not-quite-darkness, in which there were millions of tiny moving lights – fireflies, glow-worms, and the light-lures deployed by angler-anemones – while the parasitic communities dressing each tree-trunk came strangely alive, each one revealed by its luminous webwork as a miniature forest in its own right.

The princess realised for the first time that 'Absolute Night' had never been intended to signify 'Absolute Darkness', but rather to imply shades of meaning too delicate for ordinary patterns of expectation. It was easy to think that this was, indeed, true night: night lit entirely by courtesy of living things both earthly and unearthly and not by virtue of distant suns.

All these night-time illuminations were very pale indeed, far less bright than the starlight of an open and cloudless sky, but such was the architecture of the forest – with extensive 'highways' of flat bare ground between the root-discs which extended for three or four mets from every bole – that travel was by no means impossible. Nor, according to Hyry Keshvara, was it overly dangerous. Hyry had taken great care to prepare Lucrezia for this part of their journey even before they reached the forest proper.

'There aren't so very many dangers, if you're careful,' Hyry had explained. 'Even at night, when the forest fauna is at its most active, it's reasonably safe if we can carry lanterns as we go. The lanterns won't light enough of the forest floor to let us see our way, but their yellow glow is unusual enough to make most of the night hunters steer well clear.

'The monkeys are mostly harmless, although they can give you a nasty bite if they're frightened. They live way up in the canopy, but they're curious as well as omnivorous, and every bit as active by day as by night. They occasionally come down to the forest floor to forage, and they sometimes come into a camp when people are sleeping. If you don't panic, they won't.

"The smaller panthers are much more discreet, being stealth hunters with more sense than to stalk humans, but the big ones can be nasty. The biggest ones of all are the nightcloaks; they're the ones whose favourite trick is to lie on the lower boughs and drop down on passing prey. They're usually after chevrotain and pigs, but they take the darklanders' goats whenever they get the chance, and a horse or a donkey looks to them like a feast and a half. If ever one should drop on you when you're riding don't waste time wrestling, just do whatever you can to get clear — the nightcloak will always stay with the horse.

'Not all flowerworms are dangerous, but only darklanders can tell the poisonous ones from the harmless ones. I dare say you've got three or four kinds of flowerworm venom in that belt of yours, and the relevant antidotes too, but don't think that makes you an expert on the live creatures. Play safe and avoid the lot. The same applies to whipsnakes, but if you do get bitten, don't get hysterical. People usually recover, even without treatment.

'If you run across wild pigs, don't annoy the males — they can be very bad-tempered. The same applies to tame pigs — don't think that they'll be as docile with you as they are with the darklanders who own them. Come to think of it, the same applies to the darklanders themselves — the males can be very touchy when they're on home ground, and it's annoyingly easy to offend against their multitudinous taboos quite by accident.

'In general, if you see anything you don't recognise as safe, steer clear. You'll accumulate the usual motley of bites and stings, but you've already had your ration on those, and some of those healing salves you have are at least as good as anything Aulakh Phar uses. I know — I'm the one who's been selling them to Ereleth for years years and more.'

The last item in this catalogue of advice had been imparted less than politely, but Lucrezia was glad of every admission that the instruments of her Art really were of some value. Privately, Lucrezia thought that the manner in which she'd coped with the attack three nights before had demonstrated that fact beyond a shadow of doubt, but Hyry had not been impressed, even when she had seen the bodies and measured the exact extent of their accelerated corruption.

'It's too slow,' Hyry had said. 'Look at you – all bruises. If they'd been fighting men instead of country bumpkins they'd have killed and butchered you long before they keeled over. Anyhow, poison is too indiscriminate, even if you put it on a knife instead of your fingernails – it poses too much of a danger to its user. Having the antidote on your person is no guarantee that you'll have time to use it.'

The princess had contented herself with replying that what she'd done had been necessary. That was true, and Hyry knew it was true. 'I'm no knife fighter,' Lucrezia had pointed out, 'and had I not done my part, you certainly couldn't have killed all four of them, even though they *were* mere farmhands.'

After that initial exchange, whose sharpness had been accentuated by a keen awareness of how lucky they had been to avoid death or serious injury, they had both avoided the subject – but Lucrezia still felt a fierce desire to prove to Hyry that she was, in fact, a useful companion to have. Now, as they stopped for what was scheduled to be a longer than usual midnight rest, Lucrezia thought that it might be both safe and sensible to advertise her wares a little.

'I know more than you might think about the forest and its produce,' she told Hyry. 'Witch-lore inevitably touches on the unearthly, and the forest is the best-known haunt of unearthly life-forms around the empire's borders. The lore handed down to me contains a good deal of information about flowerworms and the like.'

'I know that,' Hyry said. 'It was because I trade in this region, with the darklanders, that Ereleth became a valuable customer. I may not be an initiate into all of Ereleth's mysteries, but I know more than you might suppose about your potions and pastes – more, perhaps, than Aulakh Phar. Not being a woman, he's at a disadvantage. Among the darklanders it's the women who are the healers and herbalists, and they won't discuss such matters with their own men, let alone golden men. That's probably why kings of Xandria traditionally wed witch-wives instead of appointing male ministers of witchery. The eccentricities of darklander folkways have effects which extend as far as the citadel of Xandria – you might remember that when we run into the darklanders.'

'I'm surprised we haven't seen any of them yet,' Lucrezia said, while she pondered the implications of these comments.

'It's a very big forest,' Hyry said. 'The darklanders are nomadic herdsmen, moving with their pigs and goats in small family groups. They have big festivals occasionally, at which times they come together in large numbers, but they have to disperse again fairly quickly or their animals would graze all the way to the bark of the neighbouring trees. Although ninety per cent of that white fuzz is purely parasitic its presence actually protects the trees against various nasty blights which would otherwise never allow them to grow so big. The darklanders have to be careful to limit the damage their animals do – I suppose that's the sensible basis of their system of taboos, although random additions have elaborated it into a mad riot of mostly arbitrary commandments.'

'Ereleth's actually been here,' Lucrezia said. 'A long time ago – when she was an apprentice herself. None of her royal apprentices ever came south, but there's a lot I could learn hereabouts, if I had Ereleth or some other witch to teach me.'

'I'd like to help, highness,' Hyry said insincerely, 'but I'm no custodian of that kind of lore. I just happen to have picked up a little useful knowledge here and there while doing business. I don't have an armoury like yours. How did you come to be wearing it when you fell into Checuti's cart?'

'I'm a practitioner of the Art,' Lucrezia said, rather stiffly. 'A true Artist is never without her resources. I never went to bed naked, even in the privacy of the Inner Sanctum.'

'No wonder they said . . .' Hyry stopped abruptly, and opened her mouth again as if to say something else instead.

Lucrezia was quick to intervene. 'What did they say – whoever they might be?'

'Nothing,' the trader said.

'The one thing that was never said within the walls of the tower was *nothing*,' Lucrezia observed contemptuously. 'Everyone had an opinion about everything, and the gossip doubtless spread to every corner of the citadel before spilling out into the streets and harbours of the city. Did they say that even my father was afraid of me, and couldn't wait to export me to some godforsaken isle three-quarters of the way across the Slithery Sea? Did they say that Lucrezia the pupil had outstripped her teacher Ereleth, in zeal if not in expertise? That much was true, I believe – but if they said that I'm mad, or dangerously foolish, they were wrong. I'm a witch, but witchery is just one more aspect of the lore, like mathematics or mapmaking but more useful.'

'Neither mathematics nor mapmaking requires that you kill people for practice, highness,' Hyry said, in a low tone. 'You can't blame people for talking about things like that.'

'People are killed every day,' Lucrezia said dismissively, 'for far less reason than testing the accuracy of lore which has been corrupted by falsehood and mystification. My father condemns men to death in hundreds of different ways, of which the scaffold is merely the quickest. Nor is murder a royal prerogative in a city like Xandria, where the struggle for survival is – so I'm told – more than usually intense. Do you think the men I took from the wall-gangs weren't as good as dead already?'

Hyry Keshvara did not reply.

'Witchery generates dread by virtue of superstitious awe, not by virtue of killing people,' Lucrezia said, quoting Ereleth word for word. 'That's part of the Art, part of the mystique – but you of all people should have a better understanding. You may be too delicate to use weapons like mine, but you're entirely happy to supply them, aren't you? You brought me the murderous seeds from the Navel of the World, and told me what to do with them – are you any less responsible for the consequences than I am? This forest is only half-unearthly, but the land to the south has far less of the earthly in it, hasn't it? It's a land full of witchery – and you can hardly wait to get there, to pass through territories which have long been closed to humankind, in search of the place where man-eating thorn bushes grow wild. Do you have the temerity to disapprove of me because of *palace gossip*? I thought you were my friend, Hyry. Or were you only cultivating a *good customer*?'

'I am your friend, highness,' Hyry said firmly, 'and I've killed my share of men, not always under threat of my own death.' Her tone was sincere, but Lucrezia couldn't help wishing that she hadn't appended the *highness* to the first claim.

Lucrezia would have said more, but at that point she was interrupted by a strange noise in the crowns of the nearby trees. The canopy was never silent, even by night, but the voices of the birds which sang and the frogs which croaked were faint and unobtrusive; the new sound was not loud but it was strangely insistent and ominously ever present. It was an oddly throaty sound . . . as if the entire forest were on the point of choking.

'What in the world is that?' Lucrezia asked.

'It's rain, highness,' Hyry said, seemingly glad of the opportunity to speak lightly. 'Only rain.'

Lucrezia looked up and around, squinting to make the most of the yellow lamplight and the white auras surrounding the tree-trunks. 'But none of it is reaching the ground!' she said.

'The trees are greedy for all the rain that falls,' the trader said. 'Even if it falls in torrents, the canopy catches almost every drop. These unearthly trees have webs, rather like those on a duck's feet, extended between their lower boughs — as you can see by day if you look very carefully into the confusing riot of colour. Some rainwater trickles down through channels in the bark, hidden by the surrounding growth, but most is directed through veins deep in the boles. Every full-grown tree is hollow at the heart. The surplus is leaked into the soil, where the roots reclaim it later.

'There are streams in the forest, and one great river, but far the greater proportion of the water they carry flows from the Dragomite Hills. The forest is always breathing, you see — moisture evaporates constantly from every leaf, and the interval before its return to earth can be a time of trial if it's too long extended. There's no need for you and I to fear thirst — the sap of the trees can always be tapped, if you know how — but we might have to let the two extra horses go if we can't get to the river quickly enough.'

They had four horses now. Two of the mounts ridden by the men who had attacked them had run off before Hyry could secure them, but they had kept the others in order to relieve the pressure on their own. Lucrezia knew that 'letting the two extra horses go' meant trading them to darklanders in exchange for supplies of food and other easily perishable goods. The darklanders would use the horses as meat – they weren't enthusiastic riders.

'How long will it take us to reach the river?' Lucrezia asked.

'Hard to tell,' Hyry said evasively. 'It's not so easy to navigate when the stars are never visible and you can hardly tell which part of the sky the sun's in except for the few hours near dawn and dusk. We might find darklanders willing to guide us, but even they don't have a perfect sense of direction. We'll certainly hit the river bank eventually, but I can't guarantee that we'll arrive within an easy walk of the ford, and following the watercourse would take us by a winding route. Might be five days, might be eight. Could be ten if things go badly.'

'Things haven't gone badly so far,' Lucrezia said, 'except for those men who tried to . . .'

She trailed off, realising that Hyry might well think that things had gone exceptionally badly, simply because she had been forced to bring the princess – but all Hyry said in reply was: 'There shouldn't be any difficulty, provided that the nightcloaks leave us alone and neither of us sticks her hand into a flowerworm's tentacles. Once we meet up with Fraxinus and Phar, everything will be fine . . . until we reach the Dragomite Hills, that is.'

'That will be the beginning,' Lucrezia said softly. 'All this is just the prelude to the real adventure.'

'We'd better get some sleep, highness,' Hyry advised, hauling blankets and protective netting out of the pack against which she had been leaning. 'Prelude or not, tomorrow will be a long and arduous day.'

11

ANDRIS HAD LITTLE option but to follow Burdam Thrid when the big man said 'Let's go!' The idea of surrendering to the king's guard didn't hold the least appeal, and although the prospect of a fight was little more attractive it seemed that sticking close to Thrid was the most likely way to effect an escape. Checuti's other men left clandestinely *via* dark windows, but Thrid went through the rear door and charged into the darkness like an angry bull, wielding his big knife in one hand and a heavy cudgel in the other. The news that there were only two men covering the back of the house had dispelled any anxiety he might have had as to the possibility of being captured.

It was dark among the outbuildings, but Thrid moved with perfect confidence. Thanks to the darklanders' careful scouting he knew exactly where the guardsmen were stationed, and where he would have to make his stand if they moved to intercept him.

As things turned out, Andris caught only the merest glimpse of the two men, who took only one step forward before hesitating. He couldn't blame them. Thrid was an intimidating sight in his own right, and once the guardsmen had glimpsed an even taller man behind they must immediately have come to the conclusion that the contest was too unequal to be worth a serious attempt.

They didn't stop running when they were clear of the farmyard and the guardsmen. Thrid didn't know whether the guardsmen had horses, and didn't care to hazard a guess as to whether discretion would continue to dictate their actions if reinforcements arrived. Considering his huge girth Checuti's henchman was a good runner, the awesome length of his stride making up for a slight awkwardness of gait. Andris was easily his equal, though – and when stamina eventually came into play, his superior.

When Thrid's breathing grew terribly laboured and his pace

faded to a drunken walk, Andris still had strength in reserve. He could have slipped away then, but he didn't have the slightest idea where he was or where he might start to look for Merel, so he continued to keep company with Thrid. For his own part, Thrid didn't seem to care overmuch whether Andris stayed with him or not.

They had been going for more than an hour by the time their journey came to an end, at a nondescript building set beside a well-used cart-track. Thrid opened the door and staggered in, then collapsed on one of a series of wooden benches, panting hard. Andris judged that it would be several minutes before his companion recovered his breath sufficiently to engage in conversation, so he closed the door and waited behind it in the near-darkness, listening for sounds of pursuit.

Eventually, Thrid came to his feet and lurched forward, bumping into several of the benches before reaching the far end of the room, where – after some groping around – he struck a match and lighted several candles set in brackets on the wall.

The starlight streaming through the high windows had already informed Andris that he was in an unusually large room with little or no furniture save for the crude benches, but the candlelight showed him far more. The ceiling was supported by a strangely complicated web of wooden beams which filled the overhead space like some kind of crazed spider-web. There was not a chair or table to be seen, although there was a waist-high wooden partition separating out a rectangular space at the far end of the room. The floor between the rows of benches was strewn with padded mats in a very poor state of repair, each one far too small for anyone but a dwarf to sleep on.

Inscribed on the far wall was an enormous plus sign, and below it the recently repainted words:

CHANGE AND DECAY IN ALL AROUND I SEE
O THOU WHO CHANGEST NOT, ABIDE WITH ME

'What is this place?' Andris asked.

'It's a meeting-house,' the big man told him. 'Some call it a church. Don't you have deists in the frozen north?'

'The climate's temperate in Ferentina,' Andris informed him. 'It's a pleasanter and more civilised nation than Xandria – which might account for the fact that we have no deists there, whatever deists are.'

'It's got nothing to do with civilisation,' Thrid told him. 'There're more deists in cities than out in the wilds. You never heard of them? God and all that?'

Andris had heard of God, although the notion was by no means fashionable in Ferentina. 'Oh, *God*,' he said, as the significance of the plus sign and the words inscribed beneath it became clear to him. 'You mean this place is used by people who believe the world was created by some awesomely powerful being, who lives in a parallel world immune from all decay?'

'That's right – *deists*. They think life is a kind of rehearsal for some better existence, but that you have to be a believer in order to get the extra stretch. That's why they have the plus sign up there. They have a set of secret commandments – just like the darklanders Checuti used to hang out with, only it's probably a different set. Anyone who thinks you can still be alive after you die is crazy, but they're harmless. I got nothing against 'em.'

Andris remembered that such believers were reputed to be given to a strange occult practice called 'prayer', and concluded that the meeting-house was where such rites were carried out.

'One can see the attractions of the idea,' Andris said. 'A second life, lived in world immune from the ravages of decay, would be a wonderful thing. Just think how easy life would be if everything didn't rot so rapidly and so resolutely. It's like the legendary incorruptible stone writ large . . . if you're going to believe in incorruptibility, why stick at a stone? Why not a whole world . . . or a whole universe? They say the stars are incorruptible, don't they?'

'Except for the ones that explode,' Thrid agreed. 'But it makes no sense to me. Life is a constant battle against corruption and corrosion – I mean, that's what it *is*, that and nothing more. A world which has life *after* life, without death and decay, is just . . . horseshit.' He smiled at his own joke.

Andris echoed the smile. For the first time, Burdam Thrid began to seem like a human being instead of some kind of monster.

'Why come here?' he asked. 'Is Checuti . . . ?'

' 'Course not,' Thrid was quick to reply. 'It's just a good place to hide out a while. No one else ever comes here . . . except, of course, the deists. They wouldn't hurt us or turn us in.'

'Are there many deists in these parts?' Andris asked, figuring

239

that he might as well keep the conversation going now that Thrid had thawed out a little.

'A fair number,' the big man replied. 'Checuti says it's just like the darklanders' secret societies. We don't live in such small groups, but even in towns most people stick pretty close by their families, following their own trades and conserving their own lore. Something like deism binds all kinds of different people, from all parts of the empire, into a network of mutual aid. According to Checuti, it doesn't really matter that the things they do and believe are silly – the fantasies are just the glue that holds the whole thing together.'

'I see what he means,' Andris said. 'When I came south to the Slithery Sea the only way I could try to make useful contacts was to look for Uncle Theo – who turned out to be long dead, though mercifully not without issue. If I'd been a deist, I could have looked for whole communities which might have made me welcome and found me a place.'

'Right,' said Thrid. 'Like people from the so-called provinces going to Xandria. The rich move into the circles of the rich, the undeserving poor have people like Checuti to help look after them, and the deists have other deists.'

'And the ideas at the heart of it aren't *that* silly,' Andris said, warming to the discussion. 'It's certainly no sillier than taking the *Lore of Genesys* seriously. Who can really believe that there used to be another world circling another star, from which the forefathers came in a huge ship? I mean, how did the people get to *that* world? What sort of ship could sail the void between the stars? The ship would have to be just as incorruptible as this imaginary world the deists believe in.'

'It's not something I worry about,' Thrid told him. 'Checuti seems to be getting over-anxious about such matters, but that's because the darklanders are on at him about dragomites and Serpents in the forest, and everything coming to an end. I told him we didn't need those darkland hunters to rob the citadel, but he just had to be clever about it. I told him that if he wanted to be squeamish about killing people a sharp tap on the head was as good a way of knocking them out as any, but . . .'

The big man stopped as the door opened and Checuti stepped through. He was alone, save for the grey monkey which once again sat quietly on his shoulder, and he didn't even seem to be out of breath. He had the map clutched in his left hand, rolled up rather more neatly than Andris had been able to roll it when he had earlier taken to his heels.

'Everything went well,' Checuti assured them, as he pushed the door to behind him. 'Not a life lost on either side, not a drop of blood spilled. I only hope the good captain believed me when I told him the truth. Fool though he is, he might turn out to be an inconvenient fool if he's found reinforcements and decided to chase us. The governor might well think that he could get a much bigger cut if he could lock us up for a while in one of his prisons – you can never trust these petty officials who have a greedy finger in every pie. Shall we go?'

He had stepped towards them while speaking, but not quite far enough. When the door behind him was thrust violently inwards it crashed into his back and precipitated him forwards in a very ungainly manner. He tripped before reaching the nearest of the benches and stumbled heavily. The monkey leapt from his shoulder as he fell, chattering in panic.

An enormous shadow filled the open doorway, but the candles were too far away to reveal to Andris and Thrid exactly what manner of being it was. Andris, awed by the sheer size of the shadow, stood as if rooted to the spot, but Burdam Thrid was made of sterner and more reckless stuff. Snatching his knife and cudgel from his belt the bandit went forward full tilt, hurdling the benches with surprising agility and co-ordination.

As Thrid ran past the fallen body of his master the shadow in the doorway moved. The light was so poor that Andris thought for a moment that it was moving away, but it was not. It was coming forward to meet Thrid's assault – and it did so with contemptuous ease, in spite of the fact that it had no weapon in either of its enormous hands. As Thrid danced towards it with his cudgel raised and his blade extended he was met by a force sufficiently powerful, and so skilfully deployed, that he was hurled backwards far more abruptly than he had hurled himself forwards. For all his bulk – which was very unusual by ordinary human standards – he was thrust back by a single dismissive slap. He fell supine upon the ground, with a sickening thud – and he showed not the slightest sign of getting up again.

Checuti sat up, rubbing his head where it had come into bruising contact with one of the benches. He looked down at the body of his stricken lieutenant, then up at the vast form looming over him, as if he couldn't quite believe in either of them. His pet monkey jumped up and down on another bench, spitting defiantly and baring its teeth, but made no move to approach the giant.

It really was a giant, Andris realised. Her skin was dark, more bronze than golden, but her hair was unnaturally fair and astonishingly long. It caught both the candlelight and the starlight uncommonly well.

Andris came forward, very slowly, with arms outstretched to display his open palms.

The giant reached out a helping hand. Checuti took it mechanically, and she hauled him to his feet. A second figure had entered the building behind her – a figure of very different proportions.

The newcomer closed the door again, very gently. 'Now,' she said, 'we can talk. I too would like to conclude our business with no life lost and no blood spilled, but I shall stand no nonsense. I want to know where the princess is.'

Checuti groaned. He had evidently had enough of that particular question tonight. 'Who the rotting filth are you?' he asked wearily. 'And how in the name of chaos did you find me?'

The woman took no obvious offence at Checuti's bad language. She reached out to stay her companion's arm as the giant lifted him up, threatening to suspend him in mid-air. 'Don't hurt him, Dhalla,' she said. 'Not yet.' To Checuti, she said: 'My name is Ereleth. You've heard of me, I have no doubt.'

Andris knew the name. *King Belin's witch-wife!* he pronounced silently.

Checuti must have known what danger he was in. 'What I told your guard-captain is true!' he protested. 'I swear it!'

'I sent no captain,' Ereleth said contemptuously. 'I've an army of my own, and I'm not here on Belin's business. You, of all people, should understand what I mean.'

'I didn't kidnap the princess, majesty,' Checuti was quick to say, astounding Andris with his sudden humility. 'Lucrezia fell into my temporary custody by accident, and I made not the slightest attempt to keep her. I refused to kill her, in spite of the urgings of my colleagues. I released her as soon as I possibly could – to Hyry Keshvara. You, of all people, should understand why.'

Ereleth did not seem amused or flattered by his imitation of her phraseology.

'You're the guard who saw what happened, aren't you?' Checuti said to the giant who held him, although Andris thought he could not know for certain and must be guessing. 'You were there. You must have seen it, even if the dart's effects stopped you going to her aid. She came out to help you, and fell into the cart by chance. *I didn't mean to take her!* I really did hand her over to Keshvara. Tell them, Andris!'

'He's telling the truth,' Andris said – although he was uncomfortably aware of the fact that he couldn't know it for certain. 'Keshvara and the princess will join Carus Fraxinus in the forest as soon as they can.'

The woman turned to look at him for the first time. Andris had the uncomfortable feeling that she was smiling, although the light was too dim to display her expression. 'You're the amber, aren't you?' she said. 'The one who offered his services to the princess.'

'I didn't know what service she had in mind,' Andris retorted. 'Nor did she take the trouble to explain.'

'No matter,' the witch-queen said. 'Fortune has been kind enough to set matters to rights. You may now make good your promise, on somewhat kinder terms. The princess has need of you. As for *you*, friend of the darklanders . . . you owe the princess rather more than you have so far granted her. Perhaps you, also, will offer your services, until the princess is safely recovered.'

'You don't need me,' Checuti said defensively. 'If you have darklander friends of your own – and I assume that's how you found me, if you didn't send the eager young captain – they're far better placed to help you than I am.'

'It's not as simple as that,' Ereleth said stonily. 'As *your* friends must have told you, the forest is a very dangerous place just now. If the princess and Keshvara have gone into it, not knowing what hazards they face, anything might happen to them. If Carus Fraxinus sets out at all he's an utter fool . . . but I have little choice in the matter, and neither have you.'

'All right,' Checuti said swiftly. 'I'll help you . . . I'll do whatever I can.'

'What about you?' Ereleth asked Andris.

Andris glanced at Burdam Thrid, who was still quite motionless and very possibly dead. Although he and Checuti were two against two the giant was obviously stronger than both of them put together. 'Yes,' he said glumly. 'I'll help you to find the princess.'

'Will you give me your word?' the old woman asked.

Andris assured her that he would, and Checuti did likewise. Andris took it for granted that they were both lying. So, it seemed, did Ereleth.

'Hold him, Dhalla,' the old woman ordered, reaching inside her dark cloak to her belt. Dhalla already had hold of one of Checuti's arms, and now she swung him round so that she was behind him. With her spare hand she took a handful of hair and tilted his head slightly backwards.

Ereleth lifted something out of her belt. Andris couldn't see what it was, but she held it gingerly.

'Open wide,' she said to Checuti.

The thiefmaster gritted his teeth, setting them firm against any attempt that might be made to put anything into his mouth. Dhalla let go of his arm and used her fingers to pry his teeth apart. She lifted the hand which clutched his curly hair so that he was up on tiptoe, and he must have known that he was helpless, even though his arms were now free. Ereleth stepped forward, and slipped whatever she held into Checuti's mouth. Dhalla closed his jaws upon it.

'Swallow!' she said.

Checuti had no choice. Andris, knowing that this was his one and only chance, broke into a run, heading for the door. Without releasing her grip on Checuti or slackening it in any way the giant moved swiftly sideways and kicked out. Her huge boot crashed into Andris's midriff, knocking all the air out of his lungs. He went down, doubled up and trying desperately to draw breath. He thought for one awful moment that several of his internal organs must have been ruptured, but as he writhed and squirmed the air suddenly came back into his lungs and his guts ceased to churn.

Thirty or forty seconds must have gone by while he wrestled with his agony, but the giant waited for him to recover a measure of composure before she picked him up. When she opened his mouth Ereleth deftly inserted what felt like a small wriggling worm.

'Swallow!' the old woman commanded him.

The giant's fingers gave him no chance to spit it out. She held his mouth firmly shut and pinched his nose. He had no option but to swallow, and did. The thing slid down his gullet, wriggling as it went.

Checuti was gagging slightly, but it was obvious that he was not able to bring his own worm back up again. Not that it would have done him any good if he had been able to – Andris didn't doubt that Ereleth had more in reserve.

'What is it?' Checuti asked, in the voice of one facing unpleasant death.

'Just a worm,' Ereleth replied, with perfect equanimity. 'Harmless, in itself . . . provided that it doesn't multiply. Should she lay eggs, though, she will spawn hundreds more – and they, in their turn, hundreds more. One worm will only take a tiny fraction of the food you eat, but hundreds . . . well, I've seen fatter men than you fade away to become mere skeletons in a matter of days.'

'Then I pray she won't find a mate,' Checuti said, not optimistically.

'She already has a mate,' Ereleth told him, with a certain relish. 'She carries him inside her, a parasite in her own gut. An intriguing arrangement, don't you think? But there's a certain fruit – more of a fungus than a fruit, if I might be forgiven the pedantry – which has the effect of sterilising any eggs she may lay, although it won't harm the worm herself. Provided that you take a little of the fungus regularly – once in every tenday, or thereabouts – no eggs will hatch . . . but if you should go without too long, your decline into starvation will be inexorable and horribly swift. You might live thirty more days, if you ate with obsessive heartiness . . . but no more.'

'You have a good supply of this contraceptive, of course,' Checuti said, while Andris contemplated the horror of their predicament.

'I have,' said Ereleth, 'and I know how to find more. But I know of only one other person who has it, or knows how to locate it.'

'Your apprentice, Princess Lucrezia.'

'Precisely. The worm won't live for ever, of course – nothing does. If it's kept from reproducing, it will be dead in a year . . . six hundred days at the most. After that, you will need me no more, and may go your own way with impunity. If you serve the princess well, of course, I know another fungus which will poison the worm overnight . . . but you'll have to perform with exceptional heroism to earn such a dose as that.' Her voice trembled on the brink of laughter.

'How do we know that you're telling the truth?' Checuti demanded – although it seemed to Andris to be a pointless question. How could they ever be sure that she wasn't, unless they cared to gamble with their lives?

'I give you my word,' said the witch, 'as you gave me yours. We can trust one another now, I think. We're a team, committed to the same goal. We start for the darklands at first light.'

The feeling in the pit of Andris's stomach now was worse than any mere sinking or bruising.

'You didn't have to do this,' Checuti said sullenly. 'I've told you the truth, and nothing but the truth. It wasn't necessary.'

'From now on, my friends,' said Ereleth ominously, 'I'll be the judge of necessity.'

12

On their second day in the forest Hyry and Lucrezia met a party of eight darklanders, consisting of five full-grown women and three girl-children. Both parties were on the move when they met, travelling in diametrically opposite directions, but the darklanders were ready enough to stop and talk and Hyry Keshvara was still enthusiastic to find guides willing to escort the princess and herself to the ford where she hoped to meet Carus Fraxinus and his party. They set up a common camp for the midday.

Lucrezia was grateful for that; all her life she had been used to sleeping twice a day, according to the customary pattern of city life, and her internal rhythms had not yet adapted to Hyry's preferred regime of taking short stops during daylight hours and sleeping for ten or twelve hours while it was dark.

While Hyry went into a huddle with the older darklanders Lucrezia unloaded the donkeys and saw to the horses; then spread the mats on the ground and made a cooking-fire. Two of the children watched her all the while, but from a safe distance; they would not reply when she talked to them. One of the adults made similar preparations for temporary accommodation, laying out mats of an identical design, tethering the goats and throwing up a makeshift enclosure for their other livestock. In the meantime, others of her party went out foraging for food.

Lucrezia studied the remaining darklanders almost as carefully as they were studying her. Their pale skins seemed strangely luminous in the uncertain daylight; and the pupils of their eyes, though not dilated to the fullest extent, seemed unnaturally penetrating. Their clothing was light, consisting of loose shirts and trousers which barely came down below the knee, but it was surprisingly neat. They evidently had access to Xandrian cloth and

Xandrian needles, which they plied with considerable skill – but they went barefoot, and they carried their goods in satchels rather than in pouches gathered at the belt.

Lucrezia finished her work long before Hyry concluded her haggling. The old women seemed to be more interested in trading goods than in gossip, and were anxious to obtain something in exchange for anything Hyry might require, including information. In the end, though, it seemed that Hyry found out what she needed to know – and that the news was definitely not to her liking. By this time the children were at play, although they continually interrupted their games to steal covert glances at the goldens and their animals. When the conference finally broke up the two parties didn't merge into one; the darklanders made no move to take advantage of Lucrezia's fire, in spite of Hyry's invitation.

'I'm still trying to persuade one of the old women to come with us, but they're very reluctant,' Hyry reported in a low voice. 'They'd usually be much friendlier – all the more so in the absence of the men – but they're scared and suspicious.'

'Of what?' Lucrezia asked.

'Their men have gone off to some big tribal get-together. It seems that the territory south of the river has been invaded. I can't get a clear and coherent account of what's involved – there's talk of dragomites and Serpents, but it's all based in rumour which might well be nine-tenths fantasy. There are darklander legends about human girl-children being stolen away, and others about Serpents having the power to command dragomites, and it seems that these talents have been invoked as a kind of explanation for what's happening beyond the river. There are wild tales abroad of human dragomite riders attacking darkland families at the behest of malevolent Serpents – and the darklanders are bent on going to war in consequence.'

'Could it be true? About the dragomite-riders?'

'I can't believe it. I think what's happening is that dragomite workers have been driven by hunger to forage for food in the forest, and that in the meantime more explorers from the far south have crossed the hills. The darklanders might have added those two facts together and come up with the notion that there's some kind of unholy alliance in force, threatening their entire territory with an apocalyptic invasion. I certainly never heard of humans riding dragomites before, nor of warlike Serpents. The men from the south who supplied the things I bought on my last trip certainly weren't warriors and clearly wanted to make friends with the darklanders, but it seems that the darklanders have fallen out among themselves over such matters as that. Some traditionalist elders are arguing that all the present troubles started because their younger and less wise brethren began trading in tainted goods. Some diehards among the elders have always been against *any* commerce with goldens, and it may be that they're using the confused rumours from the south to whip up a storm for their own reasons. Anyhow, things have changed since I was last here, and for the worse. It's not going to be easy . . .'

She left the sentence dangling, and contented herself with a shake of the head while she put a kettle of water on to boil.

'I'll make a big pot of coffee,' Hyry said, still speaking in a low tone so that the darklanders couldn't overhear. 'That'll help get things moving. If they don't drift this way I'll take it over to them. They certainly won't refuse a gift like that. The oldest woman, Elema, is a senior member of the Apu – that's a kind of semi-secret society which the women have. I've never been initiated into it, although I've tried to get in for the sake of making deals, and there *are* precedents – some goldens even come into the forest from time to time, to be apprenticed to the old women in order to learn their healing arts.'

'And their killing arts,' Lucrezia put in. 'That's what Ereleth did. She always says that witchery transcends all tribal boundaries . . . but then, all lore's supposed to do that, isn't it?'

'If Ereleth was actually apprenticed to some darkland witch-wife,' said Hyry contemplatively, 'she was almost certainly accepted into the Apu. Now, if you're *her* apprentice . . . no, it's too tenuous. Elema would never go for it.'

'Do the men have a secret society too?' Lucrezia asked.

'Oh yes. Several of them, I think. They'd never talk about them to someone like me, but that old rogue Phar has useful contacts. That's how he gets a lot of his playthings. He told me once that he even has an anti-dragomite salve, although he didn't seem to believe in its virtue. We might have to try it out sooner than we anticipated, if a substantial number of dragomites really have been driven into the forest by the effects of the blight. The blight must have started in the south and worked its way northwards – that's why the bronzes from the far south knew what was happening long before we did – and it's possible that dispossessed dragomites drifting northwards in search of food have been driven right out of the hills. According to Phar, the workers aren't usually aggressive, but there are other kinds, including warriors, which are very nasty indeed. He says they're like honey-bees, each nest having only a single queen with hundreds of sterile females to serve her, but I don't know how he can be sure of that. It's all rumour – nobody really knows very much about dragomites.'

'Except for the people who ride them,' Lucrezia suggested. 'Maybe the people from the far south have all kinds of tricks we know nothing about. Maybe they've domesticated dragomites the way we've domesticated pigs and sheep.'

'Pigs and sheep are earthly,' Hyry pointed out. 'Dragomites aren't. That's why the darklanders think that Serpents have magical ways of controlling them. They make use of a lot of unearthly species, including foodstuffs, but they're still very superstitious about the ones they haven't accepted into their way of life.' She stopped suddenly, and signed to Lucrezia that she would say more later. While Hyry had been telling Lucrezia what she had learned the darklanders had been having a similar discussion of their own, and now that it was over they were beckoning to her.

Hyry smiled as she poured boiling water on to the ground-up beans in the coffee-pot. 'This should get things going,' she muttered, as the aroma filled the air. 'Sharing a cup of coffee is just the sort of thing to remind them that all women are sisters under the skin, whether they've ever been initiated into the Apu or not.'

Lucrezia helped Hyry to carry the pot over to the place where the darklanders were waiting, then waited her turn as the trader made a big show of pouring it into the wooden cups which the darkland women held out.

As Hyry had anticipated, the coffee helped considerably to overcome the barriers of suspicion. The conversation which followed was guarded and calculatedly trivial, but Lucrezia was able to take part in it. By the time the meal was finished, it had clearly been established that they were now all friends. Again, though, Lucrezia was left to do the greater part of the work which remained to be done, while Hyry entered into intense discussion with the woman called Elema. That discussion was still going on when the other darklanders laid themselves down to sleep, and Lucrezia followed their example, feeling more like a serving-maid than a princess.

She would have slept soundly for a long time, but she was not allowed that luxury. Something touched her arm and she woke up abruptly, thinking of nightcloaks and wild pigs. To her surprise, she found that Hyry was still asleep and that all the darklanders except the old woman to whom Hyry had been talking were gone.

Elema had brought her own sleeping-mat to where Lucrezia and Hyry had bedded down, and had set it next to Lucrezia's. She was sitting on it cross-legged with her eyes wide open, staring into empty space, but Lucrezia knew that it must have been the old woman who had touched her. The princess sat up, yawning, and Elema condescended to look at her in a curiously conspiratorial fashion.

'I am Elema,' the old woman said formally. 'You are Lucrezia. You are daughter to a queen, Keshvara says . . . near-daughter to a queen named Ereleth.'

'Ereleth taught me the witch-lore,' Lucrezia confirmed, 'some of which she learned here in the great forest. Do you know her?'

'We know of Ereleth,' the old woman said, although Lucrezia wasn't quite sure whom she meant by *we*, or what she meant by *know of*. 'Have you Serpent's blood, child?'

Lucrezia glanced around at Hyry, but the trader was still sleeping, and could give her no guidance. In the end, she said: 'So I was told when I was small, but I don't know what it's supposed to mean. I've never seen a Serpent.' She knew that she was taking a risk, given what Hyry had told her about darklander superstitions, and what she had said about reports of malevolent Serpents being in the forest south of the river, but she didn't want to tell a lie.

The old woman nodded, but it was impossible to judge whether the nod signified approval. 'I'll take you to the river,' she said, 'and I'll stay with you while you wait. If we see the dragomite-riders, you mustn't cross. Perhaps the men will drive them from the forest, but if not then you must wait, Serpent's blood or not. Do you understand me, child? Whatever stirs in your blood, you must have patience. The wise know how to wait — always remember that.'

It was Lucrezia's turn to nod ambiguously – but Elema seemed satisifed that she meant yes, and that she did understand.

'One more thing,' the old woman said. 'Keep clear of darkland men. To them, Serpent's blood is bad. Some things they don't understand. Trust the Apu, but no one else.'

Hyry began to stir then, and turned over. Some moments passed before she opened her eyes, and when she did she gave no sign of having heard what had passed between Elema and Lucrezia – but Lucrezia knew better than to take that for granted. Hyry looked up at the daylit canopy, and seemed to be annoyed that she had gone to sleep.

'We must pack up now,' the trader said, coming slowly to her feet. 'We'll have to walk – Elema has never been on a horse. I don't think we'll miss Fraxinus – we should still be ahead of him, and he'll surely take his time coming through the forest when he hears the rumours. He won't want to take his people into a war-zone. With luck, he'll decide to wait at or near the ford until the darkland men return with news of their campaign.'

The trader's tone of voice was optimistic, and it seemed to Lucrezia that all the tension which had been between them was now relaxed. Elema's presence made them seem more of a pair, two civilised goldens in a world of primitive ambers and mysterious invaders.

They walked for a long time – fourteen hours by Lucrezia's reckoning, although her time-keeping was not renowned for its accuracy. They rested at regular intervals but never for long.

Lucrezia found the walking less trying than the riding had initially been, but her feet were unused to such hard usage and soon made their complaint felt. The shoes she had been wearing when she fell into Checuti's wagon were totally unsuitable, and Hyry had quickly replaced them with a pair of good boots from her luggage. Unfortunately, Hyry's feet were considerably bigger than Lucrezia's, so the princess had been forced to use several extra pairs of stockings to pad them out. That had not been so bad while she was riding, but it quickly became very inconvenient now she was asked to go on foot.

'It's probably all to the good,' Hyry observed. 'The extra layers will make your feet sweat, but that's better than a crop of punctured blisters and bloody sores.'

The stockings did feel hot, especially while the daylight lasted, and Lucrezia very quickly began to envy Elema her bare feet, which were so hardened by a lifetime's experience that she was able to walk all day and all night barefoot with blistering. It didn't take long for the princess to decide that whatever Hyry chose to do, she had to ride, if only at a walking pace. Elema didn't seem to mind this is the least.

Lucrezia had grown used to the forest by now, and the changes its ever-dim light underwent as it passed from day to night no longer startled or amazed her, although she was still able to derive a good deal of aesthetic pleasure from its subtle metamorphoses. As the exhaustion and discomfort of the unusually long day took root in her sensations it began to seem that she was walking through a strange and magical underworld, which had been shrouded by day in deep blues and glossy purples but which faded now to a patchwork of pitch black and pale white. She and Hyry both carried lanterns, while Elema carried a 'torch' of silver-white glowmoss, which lit their way adequately, but it seemed to Lucrezia that the shadows simply stepped back a single pace out of courtesy, while remaining essentially inviolate.

The pace at which they now went was more conducive to conversation than the one they had maintained before meeting the darklanders, but now that Elema and Hyry had completed their exchange of information they had little more to say, either to one another or to Lucrezia. Darkness seemed to suppress any inclination to communication they might have had, and they walked in silence, seemingly concentrating their minds on the dogged process of putting one foot before the other while the princess began to feel guilty about her own privileged station. Lucrezia reflected that no one who had not experienced it could ever have imagined that a life of adventure could be so utterly tedious, so empty of any stimulation save for discomfort and unease. When they finally stopped again to sleep Lucrezia found it perversely difficult to close her eyes, and spent some time lying flat on her back with her eyes open, watching the tiny flickering lights moving within the interstices of the lowest stratum of the forest canopy and wondering whether every pit of shadow might be a nightcloak moving stealthily to a position from which it could leap down to choke and smother her.

Once the sun had risen on the following day Elema found the impetus to involve Hyry in a long discussion, but seemed deliberately to be excluding Lucrezia, who gathered that she was one of the topics of the conversation. Because she was riding while the older women walked, Hyry gave the leading-reins of all the animals into her sole charge – a commission which proved surprisingly awkward because the animals seemed stubbornly determined to take different paths to either side of every tree to which they came close.

Three times on that day and twice on the next they met other darklanders – all of them women and children – and stopped to barter food and water with them. There were no new rumours abroad, but all the old ones were repeated in lurid terms. As they passed further into the forest depths their diet changed as much as the pattern of their days. Wheaten bread and cakes became things of the past, as did cows' milk and all its products, and most familiar root vegetables. The darklanders did have a kind of bread substitute baked from a mixture of crushed nuts and the pith of a certain kind of tree-branch – whose collection required climbing to extraordinary heights – but they relied more heavily on fruit than their golden neighbours and were more tolerant as to the kinds of meat they used.

Hyry explained that in normal circumstances they would have been able to obtain meat in abundance because the darklander men were expert hunters of birds, frogs and monkeys, with bows and blowpipes alike, but the women had no such skills. Lucrezia was not particularly distressed by this once she had sampled such delicacies as pickled frogs' legs and smoked monkey on a stick; the scarcity of such items seemed to her to be easy enough to bear.

On the second night following their meeting with Elema they crossed paths with a female elder who was travelling south-eastwards with two young girls. She had news of Fraxinus which Elema was quick to pass on to Hyry, and which Hyry immediately brought to Lucrezia.

'The caravan is in the forest,' she said. 'Fraxinus didn't wait in Khalorn, but he's taking his time, as I thought he probably would. We should certainly be able to meet him at the ford, although we will arrive at least a day ahead of him.'

'That's good,' Lucrezia said.

'There's other news which isn't so good. The elder has talked to some darklander men who were hurrying south in the hope of catching up with the men who have gone to fight. They mentioned you, saying that there are people in Khalorn who are searching for you, offering to pay a good price for your safe return – I presume they were talking about the king's men. If we meet other darklanders travelling south, it's not inconceivable that they'd be prepared to change their minds about taking arms against the dragomites.'

'I thought we'd be far beyond the reach of my father's agents by now,' Lucrezia said crossly. 'We're outside the bounds of the empire.'

'We're well within the scope of the temptations posed by the empire's wealth,' Hyry observed.

'Would you be tempted to sell me to any such darkland adventurers?' Lucrezia asked.

'No, highness,' Hyry replied, perhaps a little too promptly. 'Not now. Nor would Elema – she likes you. I can't quite figure out why. She says you have Serpent's blood, which would normally be an insult, or an excuse for refusing to have anything to do with you, but seems not to be in this particular instance. She's heard of Ereleth, or says she has.'

'I know,' Lucrezia said. 'She told me.'

'Don't take what she tells you too seriously,' Hyry advised her. 'I know these people – sometimes, they can be a little crazy.'

'I dare say they think the same of us,' Lucrezia said lightly.

'I dare say they're right – about some of us, at least,' Hyry countered, obviously determined to have the last word in this particular exchange.

13

A T FIRST, ANDRIS found the Forest of Absolute Night quite
fascinating, but the novelty soon began to pall. He and his new
companions had to make frequent stops, having only five horses
between the four of them, one of which they used as a pack-
animal. The food which they had in the pack was soon consumed,
and the new supplies which Ereleth bought from the motley
groups of darklanders they encountered seemed to Andris to be
distinctly unappetising. After the second day he began to feel
hungry all the time, but he could not tell whether the effect was
increased by the depredations of the worm which Ereleth had
forced him to swallow. When they slept – which they did at very
irregular intervals – he had to lie on the bare ground, but the
discomfort never became intolerable. It was always dry, even after
rain, and never very cold.

The horses were a poor lot, except perhaps for the one which the
giant rode, which might have been an excellent example of its own
kind, although it had certainly not been bred to be ridden. It was as
large in proportion to ordinary members of its species as Dhalla
was to the goldens of Xandria. It was the kind of horse used by
farmers to pull a heavy plough or a hay-wain, and had no pace
faster than a plodding walk. What it lacked in speed, however, it
made up for in tirelessness.

The darklanders they met were all in awe of the beast and its
rider. None of them had ever seen a giant before, and they
regarded Dhalla more as a supernatural being than a human. In
her company Andris's own height seemed to take on a more
sinister significance, and his amber colouring did not in the least
encourage them to treat him as one of their own kind, as they
might have been inclined to do in other circumstances. Andris
could not help but wonder whether Ereleth's authority over the

darklanders would have been as easy to establish had she not had such a remarkable companion, but there was no doubting her power of command. The darkland women, in particular, treated her as if she were a queen of their people as well as her own.

'There's something very strange about all of this,' Checuti confided to Andris while they were resting in the middle of their third night in the forest. 'Almost all the darklanders we meet are females and children. Given that Ereleth is so reluctant to share the news she receives from them I would be very pleased to encounter Uluru, but it seems that there are none to be found.'

'What I want to know,' Andris said, 'is why Ereleth couldn't – or didn't choose to – intercept Fraxinus's caravan south of the city? Surely we should have caught up with him in a couple of days – his company can't be going any faster than we are if they've got wagons and a whole train of pack-donkeys. I'm worried about Merel – I want to be certain that she got safely back to Phar.'

'I suspect that Ereleth left the citadel in secret,' Checuti said. 'She might be almost as keen to avoid the king's men as we are, and I presume that Captain Cerri took my advice to ride after Fraxinus. I doubt that Keshvara's joined the caravan yet, and one of these damned darkland witches has probably told Ereleth where Keshvara's most likely to make the rendezvous. Ereleth wants to get to Keshvara and the princess before Fraxinus, if it's humanly possible, so I assume we're trying to overtake the caravan without their knowing it. Then again, perhaps she doesn't want us to talk to Phar, in case he knows how to get rid of these damn worms she fed to us.'

'If that isn't just a bluff,' Andris said gloomily. 'As you pointed out at the meeting-house, she could have given us anything to eat, and lied about its effects.'

'A lifetime of gambling has taught me that you shouldn't ever call a bluff unless you're prepared to lose,' Checuti said. 'We agreed, didn't we, that while gambling with money is not unpleasurable, gambling with life and death is a fool's game?'

'What does she want with us anyway, given that the giant's worth at least three men and she seems to be in a position to give orders to the darklanders?' Andris wanted to know.

'She probably wants me to deal with the Uluru,' Checuti guessed. 'Her influence is confined to the women. She probably wants you as a bargaining chip to use against Fraxinus. He still wants a map and a mapmaker, and she now has both – and we do constitute useful reinforcements, even though she has the giant. She can't have known until she arrived in Khalorn how bad things are in the forest, and the darklanders must have been feeding her the same lurid stuff they fed me. Maybe they've convinced her that the end of the world really is imminent – she'd never admit it, but I think she's scared.'

'She shows no inclination to run away,' Andris observed mournfully.

'No, she doesn't, does she?' Checuti agreed reflectively. 'She knows that she's going into a region where darklanders and dragomites are fighting for possession of the forest, with who knows what other human forces involved. She must have a very powerful reason for doing that – a crazy reason, maybe, but far more powerful than mother-love for the princess. I think it might have something to do with the secret commandments. That could be what binds Ereleth and the darklander women together. They're all witches – parties to the same secret lore.'

'That's superstitious rubbish,' Andris said.

'Perhaps it is,' said the thief-master, 'but crazy situations bring out the craziness in people. I need to know what's going on if I'm to figure out a way to get us out of this.'

'We wouldn't have got into it in the first place,' Andris pointed out, 'if you hadn't played that idiotic trick on me back at the inn. If you'd just stayed at home counting your coin and left me to make a deal with Phar, neither of us would need saving from the witch-queen and her over-sized lackey.'

'That's true,' Checuti admitted ruefully.

'Personally,' Andris said, 'I think you're as crazy as she is. If I'd just brought off the crime of a lifetime I wouldn't have allowed myself to be distracted by the nonsensical claims of your blood-brotherhood with a bunch of savages. Surely you could have found a way around it?'

Checuti didn't answer for a minute or so, and Andris wondered whether he might be turning the question over in his mind, seeking for a clue as to the cause of his own folly. Finally, he said: 'I suppose I could. To tell you the truth, it wasn't just the Uluru – I'd become curious on my own account about what the princess told me and what Fraxinus planned to do. You may think me all kinds of a fool, but it was the adventure in it that got me hooked. I've always been a sucker for that kind of thing. That's why I made my exit from Xandria with such a flourish – believe it or not, the business of stealing the coin in such spectacular fashion meant far more to me than actually *having* it. It was the crime of a lifetime – far more was involved than mere greed. I never had so much pleasure out of anything as I had from its planning, and from the execution of the plan. Afterwards – as soon as it was done, without any interval at all – I began to feel empty, hungry for further intrigue, desperate for something else in which I could immerse myself. I was wide open to infection by new dreams, and the princess just happened to be on hand to provide a few. Does any of that make sense?'

'If it does,' Andris told him drily, 'you certainly got your wish. We're immersed in this up to our necks, and we're infected with something very nasty indeed.'

'As I told the witch,' the thief-master said, with a wry smile, 'she might have won our co-operation far less brutally. I was looking for an adventure, not a tooth-and-nail fight for survival.'

'What chance do we actually have of finding the princess, do you think?' Andris asked.

'If she's still with Keshvara, very good,' Checuti answered. 'Keshvara knows her way around, and she's a force to be reckoned with no matter what she and Lucrezia have to face in the heart of the forest. The real question is, if we *do* find the princess, what then? Somehow, I don't think Ereleth will simply let us go. I think she has further plans. I wish I knew what they . . .'

He stopped abruptly as Ereleth walked over to where they were sitting. 'We need food for tomorrow,' she said. 'One of you will have to come with me, to help me gather what we can.'

'It's the middle of the night,' Checuti said unenthusiastically. 'All kinds of nasty things are abroad. The thickets around the tree-trunks will be alive with flowerworms.'

'That's why it's a good time,' Ereleth retorted. 'Provided that you know what's edible and what's not.'

'If I had a darklander's blowpipe and a darklander's knowledge I might be able to agree,' Checuti countered. 'As it is . . .'

'You!' said Ereleth, pointing at Andris. 'You can come. Don't be afraid – I won't ask you to stick your precious hands into any place where they might get stung. You'll just have to hope that I don't get stung either – or that if I do, I can get the antidote out quickly enough.'

Andris got up slowly. There didn't seem to be much point in complaining. Ereleth gave him a lantern and two sacks to hold, then led him away from the makeshift camp. She went from thicket to thicket, studying each one intently for several minutes. All she picked out of the first few were vegetable growths that could have been taken at any time, but eventually – somewhat to Andris's horror – she found a cluster of squirming slug-like creatures busy within one of the palely lit miniature forests and plucked them one by one.

'Don't worry,' she said to Andris. 'The ones that sting are bigger and flatter, with bunches of tentacles on their backs. There's one of the bad ones, see – higher up.'

Andris followed the direction of her pointing finger. The thing she was pointing at was nearly thirty sims long and eighteen broad, with a big hump in the centre of its dorsal surface, from which protruded eight or ten tentacles, each about four sims long. Its body was dappled with various shades of grey, but the tentacles were milky white. He stepped back – but they were already moving on to the next tree.

'These won't even make you sick,' Ereleth said, dropping another into the sack while Andris held the neck open to receive it. 'If only we could find a climber or two to go up into the canopy for us we'd be able to stock up with fruit and birds, but that's not women's work.'

'You'd find it much easier if you only had two mouths to feed,' Andris pointed out. 'We're no real use to you here.'

'You will be if we run into dragomite workers,' Ereleth said tersely. 'A man your size might even be able to tackle a warrior. The fat man can deal with darklander men far more easily than I can . . . and it might be as well to have something to trade if Keshvara's inclined to be difficult. I have your map now . . . and the unswerving loyalty of its maker. Don't underrate your usefulness.'

'You're not going to let us go when you find the princess, are you?' Andris said dully. 'You've no intention of going back to Xandria.'

'We'll go back one day,' the old woman said calmly, 'but not immediately. We have other business first.'

'In the Dragomite Hills?'

Ereleth laughed sharply. 'No,' she said, with altogether unnecessary contempt. 'In the Grey Waste.' She was moving on yet again, having picked nothing but bulbous fungal growths from the last thicket. For a moment, Andris thought she was joking – but he couldn't believe that Ereleth was the kind of person who indulged in banter.

'I thought nothing earthly can live in the Grey Waste,' he said. It was a place he had only heard spoken of in curses and legends.

'Not much that's earthly does live there,' she agreed, 'but *can* is a different matter. You'll eat a lot of unearthly food while we're in the forest and be none the worse for it. We'll survive.'

'But what possible reason . . . ?'

'Serpents live there,' she added, almost as if it were an afterthought.

'There are said to be Serpents in the forest as well as dragomites,' Andris said guardedly. 'Serpents *controlling* dragomites, in fact – or so Checuti says.'

'Perhaps it's true,' Ereleth said, teasingly giving nothing away. 'Perhaps we'll meet them, if it is true. There are no Serpents in the far north, I suppose?'

'None that I know of,' Andris told her.

'Too cool. Serpents like heat almost as much as Salamanders. Earthly things thrive in temperate climes, but they have a harder time of it in the tropics. Hereabouts there was a kind of balance . . . but it was always more delicate than it seemed. Nothing lasts for ever, you know, and when balance fails, chaos is quick to come.'

'Is that what's happening?' Andris asked curiously. 'Is chaos coming – first to the hills and the forest, then to Khalorn . . . and ultimately to Xandria itself? Is that what your precious secret commandments are all about? Do they tell you what to do when chaos comes?'

She rounded on him then, and he saw, somewhat to his surprise, that she was genuinely alarmed.

'What do you know about the secret commandments?' she asked, with some asperity.

He opened his mouth to tell her that they were just myths and idle fancies, and that he knew no more about them than anyone else, but immediately changed his mind. There might, he thought, be some advantage to be gained from humouring this kind of craziness.

'Ferentina is a civilised nation,' he told her. 'Like you, I have royal blood in my veins, and I learned royal traditions in the schoolroom. I was taught to beware of false commandments but always to respect the true.' He cast about desperately for something clever which might be used to back up these hazy implications, and remembered the legend which the blind story-teller had told him in the Wayfaring Tree. 'There are no Serpents in Ferentina,' he said, 'but that doesn't mean that we don't know what gift it was that the Serpent brought to the forefathers in Idun, or what promise it was that the forefathers made and failed to fulfil.'

Andris was warming to his task now, and had begun accompanying his inventions with dramatic gestures. Unfortunately, one of these expansive flourishes swung the lantern so violently that the flame – which had grown feeble – suddenly guttered out.

They weren't left in total darkness, but the removal of the bright light left their eyes in dire need of adaptation to the fainter radiance of the thicket next to which they stood. Andris cursed his luck, and took two brisk steps away from the tree, lest there be flowerworms of the kind Ereleth had pointed out lurking amid the parasitic halo.

It was a wise move – or would have been, had he not been under such a powerful obligation to his undesired companion.

Ereleth, less anxious about the darkness than he, began to ask a question which she obviously considered urgent, but she only got as far as 'Tell me . . .' when she was abruptly cut off. The next word stuck in her throat, restricted to a faint gurgle which was a most unsatisfactory symbol of alarm and astonishment.

It was Andris who screamed, as the dull sound of impact told him that something – it was quite impossible to see or guess what – had dropped out of the branches of the tree to fall over Ereleth's shoulders like a great black blanket.

The old woman fell to the floor beneath the creature's weight, but Andris knew that she hadn't been knocked unconscious. She was wrestling the thing as best she could, thrashing madly with her arms against the shadow-shape, which was as black as black could be.

Andris dropped the useless lantern and the two partly loaded sacks. He had no weapon but he dared not hesitate. He stepped forward, reached down, grabbed two great handfuls of coarse fur, and hauled the thing away from its victim.

It was unexpectedly light – and unexpectedly agile. Suddenly, it was all teeth and claws, which seemed to be ripping at him from every direction, scoring his flesh in a dozen different places.

Absurdly, the one thought which echoed in his mind was *when balance fails, chaos is quick to come* . . .

Andris realised that the creature with which he was locked in mortal combat must be at least two mets from snout to toe, with long lithe limbs. While he held it up as he was doing now it was free to maul him, and he knew that his only chance was to stifle its movements. He turned on his heel so that he was facing away from the spot where Ereleth had fallen, and deliberately fell over, coming down as hard as he could.

Just as the creature had dropped from above to force its victim to the ground, Andris now forced it down in its turn – and Andris was a much bigger, much heavier creature than the forest predator. As his weight came crashing down upon it the monster let out the most astonishing wail of anguish.

The idea Andris now had in his mind was that he must grab the creature's forelegs in a kind of hammerlock, forcing its claws wide while his knees pressed down on its body from behind. Unfortunately, there was far more optimism than realism in this intention, and although his big hands pulled the thick fur this way and that he had not the slightest idea whereabouts he had taken hold of the beast. He had certainly not managed to render its claws harmless, for it still seemed to be lashing out in every possible direction – thankfully without making much substantial contact.

He bore down more powerfully, trying to flatten the creature out upon the bare ground, but it was wriggling free now. He felt a set of talons raking the top of his head, and was glad that his hair was lately grown into a thick, untidy mat. Even so, blood began to pour down his forehead and into the corners of his eyes.

Screaming with rage, Andris clenched his fists as hard as he could within the shaggy hide, and changed tack. He hauled backwards with his arms while using his massive legs to anchor as much of the beast as he could, stretching its spine in the hope of snapping it like a twig. Something gave, but it wasn't the creature's spine. The beast screamed again, but it didn't stop lashing out. Desperately, Andris hurled himself down again, crushing his adversary against the hard soil.

He heard Checuti shouting something, but if it was an instruction he could not get the sense of it for the blood roaring in his ears.

He felt hot breath upon his brow, and knew that the beast must have twisted in his grip to face him. Its breath carried a foetid carrion smell which made him feel strangely faint, and he found to his amazement and alarm that the creature had wriggled out from underneath his body and was now on top of him, where it was far more accustomed to be in respect of its usual prey. It was scrabbling with its claws in a further attempt to rake and rend him.

Andris now had the idea in his mind that at any moment one of his companions might leap to the rescue, thrusting a spear into his attacker's heart, or lopping off its head with a single stroke of a sword – but his mind's eye bathed in the glow of his fevered imagination, while the real world around him was so dark as fully to justify the forest's ironic name.

He was flat against the ground now, but he rebelled reflexively against the threat of being rendered helpless and torn apart by trying to roll over, taking his adversary with him as though it were some other man with whom he was engaged in a game of wrestling.

The creature would not consent to being rolled, let alone to being rolled *on*. It writhed within his grip, and struck out with its vicious forepaws, catching him about the head not once but twice, knocking him dizzy – but he was fighting man enough to know when to cling tightly, and cling he did, trying with all his might to force his face forward into the thick black fur, so that his poor battered head would be out of the demon's reach. Dimly, he was aware that Checuti was still shouting, yelling his heart out as though to destroy the beast of prey with lethal echoes. The weight pressing down upon him grew more oppressive still, and suddenly his face was far too full of choking fur, his open mouth blocked with coarse hair that was alive with lice or some other kind of vermin.

His unclawed hands dug into the flesh they held with all the fervour he could muster, and now he was utterly desperate to roll, if only to free himself long enough to take a breath – but he felt that all the breath had been squeezed out of him, and that there was an enormous pressure in his chest, and a terrible tension in his throat. His lungs were doing everything they could to draw air, but impotently . . . all there was to be drawn was rank fur and vermin, and all there was to be felt was horror and dread . . .

The only heroic thing left for him to do was to think: *Better this than slow starvation!* But he did, at least, manage to think it, and think it almost as if it were a defiant shout, before his mind's eye and his mind's ear were lost in dizziness, and it seemed that death was rushing to meet him at a truly awesome velocity . . .

14

Aᴄᴛᴇʀ ᴀ ʜᴀʀᴅ day's ride to catch up with Fraxinus's expedition in the fringes of the Forest of Absolute Night, when time
seemed to fly past, Jacom Cerri found the next three days
exceedingly boring. The caravan moved at an unhurried pace
along a well-worn trail without encountering trouble of any kind.

Carus Fraxinus had made no objection when Jacom told him of
his intention to tag along until they met up with Hyry Keshvara —
indeed, he had confessed himself pleased to have his numbers
augmented by ten good fighting men. Jacom gathered that he and
Phar had expected to recruit a dozen darklanders to serve as an
escort, but that circumstances had forced him to make do with half
that number, two of whom were hardly more than boys.

'To tell you the truth, Jacom,' the merchant said, in a rare
confidential moment, 'we don't really know what we're heading
into. The rumours about dragomites invading the forest with
human riders are probably exaggerated — everything Aulakh
knows about their habits suggests that they rarely leave their nests
for very long, and don't associate with human beings — but
whatever blight has opened a way through their own territory has
obviously disturbed them. Aulakh has a salve which is supposed to
stop them attacking its wearers. They use odours for communication and this particular stuff is supposedly construed by the
workers and warriors alike as a command to let well alone, but I'm
a little doubtful as to its efficacy. I'm sorry that your encounter
with Checuti didn't work out as you hoped, but I have to confess
that a company of men bearing swords and half-pikes might be a
handy thing to have in reserve if we do encounter dragomites.'

'I'm only interested in the princess,' Jacom told him, to make his
intentions perfectly clear. 'If Keshvara still has her when she
arrives to join you, I'll be taking her home immediately.'

Fraxinus had made no answer to that, but it was plain to see that he was anxious about Keshvara, and not at all certain that she would contrive to join the expedition – and that rumour had reached his ears about Checuti's allegation that the princess was unwilling to return to her father's care. Jacom had as yet no firm plans as to what he would do if Keshvara and the princess failed to appear by the time the caravan reached the far side of the forest, nor what he might do if the latter refused to return with him to Xandria. For the moment he was hoping – rather forlornly – that everything would go smoothly.

In addition to the six darklanders Fraxinus and Phar had four goldens with them to help tend the horses and the donkeys and to drive the two narrow but heavily laden carts which accommodated the greater part of their supplies and trade goods. One of the four goldens was a young woman named Merel Zabio. It didn't take Jacom long to figure out that she was Andris Myrasol's cousin, and that she was expecting the big amber to catch up with the expedition as soon as he was able to do so. She was most definitely not glad to have Jacom and the guardsmen along, and she repulsed all his attempts to question her. Jacom considered the possibility of placing her under arrest, but Aulakh Phar went to some trouble to persuade him to promise that he wouldn't take any action against her or the amber.

'We're a long way from Xandria now,' Phar pointed out, 'and he really wasn't the person who injured your guardsman. Anyway, if he turns up, we still need him. I'd rather have his map on hand than rely on my vague memory of it. To tell you the truth, I'm anxious about his failure to show – Merel caught up with us easily enough, and he ought to have been able to do likewise, given that he seems to have escaped from your men without injury. I don't know what Checuti's playing at, but it's a complication we could well do without.'

Jacom agreed to reassure the girl that he meant no harm to her or her cousin, and that he accepted what he had been told about Myrasol not being involved in the robbery. He ordered Purkin and Herriman to do likewise, but she continued to steer well clear of them.

As the trail they were following gradually dwindled away the carts made slower progress, but the gigantic trees were so widely spaced that there was rarely any serious impediment to their passage. Fraxinus's team worked with practised efficiency, its members ceaselessly occupied whenever the caravan paused. Only the young darklanders seemed to have much time on their hands, and they also seemed to be the only ones interested in the soldiers. Before the end of their third day in the forest Jacom had befriended a darkland boy six or seven years of age, whose name was Koraismi.

Koraismi seemed to be fascinated by Jacom: by his colouring, by his uniform, by his manner, perhaps even by the frustration which continually seethed beneath the surface of his words and actions. Jacom gave the boy a few coins, and small metal implements of the kind that were always in demand in the forest, where such things had even shorter lives than in Xandria. In return, Koraismi proudly brought birds which he had shot down with poison-tipped darts from his blowpipe. Herriman plucked these and cooked them very carefully to make sure the poison was denatured. The boy kept the soldiers supplied with various other comestibles too, some more appetising than others.

In addition to these gifts of food Jacom got a ceaseless stream of information from Koraismi, mostly based on gossip picked up from the other darklanders they met. Jacom assumed that no more than half of these rumours were likely to be true, but it was difficult to tell which half it might be. Sometimes Jacom got the same information, later, from Carus Fraxinus – but when he received contradictory accounts he had not the slightest idea which to favour.

Koraismi told him that many evil things were now abroad in the forest, and that the darklanders disagreed among themselves as to exactly what needed to be done. One group, the Uluru – to which Koraismi apparently belonged – favoured direct action to drive all invaders from the forest, but other groups – including a secret organisation of witches called the Apu – had different and altogether wrong views. Koraismi thought that all the trouble in the forest and the Dragomite Hills had been caused by Serpents, who had been secretly planning a war of extermination against men since time immemorial. Koraismi assured Jacom that some human beings had Serpent's blood in them, which would cause them to turn traitor against their own kind when the final war for possession of the world was to be fought, and that the Apu too were likely to turn traitor if their menfolk couldn't keep them under control.

Jacom thought it impolitic to mention to his new friend that Princess Lucrezia was reputed in Xandria to have Serpent's blood. He wasn't superstitious himself, but he couldn't help beginning to wonder why it was that the princess was allegedly determined not to go back to Xandria, and whether her removal from the citadel might not have been an accident after all.

Fraxinus confirmed, when Jacom asked him, that Serpents had been sighted in the forest, and that their presence was as unusual in its way as that of the dragomites and their alleged riders. 'But there's nothing to fear,' he added. 'Serpents keep themselves to themselves and aren't in the least aggressive, no matter what darklander superstition might say. These legends about dragomites kidnapping human children at the behest of Serpents which secretly control everything that goes on in the so-called Corridors of Power deep within the Dragomite Hills have no basis in fact, so far as Aulakh and I can tell.'

Jacom accepted this as the verdict of a wise man, although he couldn't help noticing the scrupulous qualification with which the judgment was concluded. Exactly how much, he wondered, did Carus Fraxinus and Aulakh Phar really know about the nature and inclinations of dragomites?

Koraismi also told Jacom that the darklander army which had gone south was the biggest ever raised, and that every steel blade in the forest had gone with them, because blowpipe darts were no good at all against the armoured hides of dragomites. 'Those rider-women better watch out, though,' he said, with pride. 'We'll shoot every last one of them off their monster-mounts' backs and bring them back as prizes. We'll trade them to Khalorn as field-workers or whores.'

Jacom wasn't at all sure that Koraismi knew what a whore was, but didn't press him on that point. Again he was careful to cross-check the information with Fraxinus.

'The darklanders fight wars like anyone else,' Fraxinus told him, 'but their wars are usually petty affairs of clan against clan – ambushes and skirmishes rather than battles and sieges, involving a couple of hundred men at most. This *is* different, although the men who've gone south are probably split up into warbands of sixty or eighty rather than gathered into a single army. Dragomite workers have always scavenged the southern borderlands of the forest, but the darker regions are too far from the hills to offer a profitable return and there's long been a tacit boundary between dragomite territory and darklander territory. The darklanders have never had to organise themselves against the dragomites before, and I don't think the men who've gone south have the faintest idea what to expect. The one thing I'm certain of is that they won't want to fight a long and bloody battle if they can possibly help it. If I had to bet I'd wager that they'll all come home in ten or twenty days, boasting about the way the dragomites and their supposed riders turned tail rather than face them, and beat a hasty retreat to the hills.

'I suspect that the dragomite workers in the forest are confused and desperate, but if they have warriors with them they might well be dangerous; perhaps the best thing would be to let them alone unless and until they start trying to build new mounds. What the likelihood of that is I can't tell – so far as I know, no human has ever been inside a dragomite mound and returned to tell the tale. No one's ever seen a dragomite queen, or even knows for certain that they really do have a social organisation identical to that of a beehive.

'I also suspect that the humans who've come into the forest from the south aren't connected in any significant way with the dragomites. I think they'll turn out to be Hyry's bronzes – traders like us, hoping to forge profitable links with the north. I'm hoping that we can meet them before they get into a serious conflict with the darklanders, but we might well be too late for that. If we *can* link up with them, they'd be invaluable as guides to the territory beyond the hills.'

With this last point Koraismi fervently disagreed. His greatest hope was that the expedition would *not* encounter any humans in the distant reaches of the forest, because he was utterly convinced by the stories of humans and dragomites working together to evil ends. He was openly derisive of the merchant's scepticism.

'This Fraxinus thinks he is a very great man,' Koraismi said, 'and his ancient companion thinks he is supremely wise. They come into the forest bringing iron and silver, cloth and spices. *We are city folk*, they say, as they swagger through out little villages. *We know how to make things; our artisans know all the lore of the world before the world; we are rich.* They think we are simple, stupid folk, easily cheated in the game of trade. They hire our men to be killers and carriers – but when those men return from the cities of the north they speak of a great wilderness of stone, burned and bleached by the naked sun, where the rich walk among hordes of the very poor: labourers condemned by law forever to rebuild the mighty walls, or to work in mines, or to ply oars in huge slow ships. Your precious cities are full of beggars and thieves, but we have no beggars here, and no thieves. Men like Fraxinus and Phar cannot know what is happening here in the forest. Men are men, they say, and all men are traders – but I tell you, friend Jacom, that what is coming from beyond the forest is evil and tainted, and that those who try to trade in tainted goods may themselves become tainted. The Serpents and their kin are avid to reclaim the world that once was theirs from the men who came from the world before the world, and they have been waiting for thousands of generations for the children of men to forget the ancient knowledge which allowed their forefathers to win the world. That is why there are Serpents in the forest now, and humans serving dragomites.'

'Have we forgotten the ancient knowledge?' Jacom asked. 'Are you talking about city folk, or have the darklanders forgotten it too?'

'We darklanders have forgotten too much,' Koraismi admitted dolefully. 'But not as much as your people. You think that your people have forgotten less than we have, because you have your loremasters and your guilds, but it is not so. Your golden women come to learn the arts of poisoning from the Apu, and Phar is always prying into the secrets of the Uluru. We know secrets which golden arrogance lost long ago.'

All of this might have been more believable, Jacom thought, had Koraismi been some ancient wise man who had actually seen such things as dragomites and Serpents with his own eyes, but because it came from a boy it sounded exactly like the kind of tale that all boys loved, redolent with mystery and melodrama. Aulakh Phar, by contrast, must have been thirty if he was a day, and he did lay claim to having seen dragomites and Serpents – though never a

Salamander – with his own eyes. He was more than willing to talk about them when Jacom and Sergeant Purkin found an opportunity one midday.

'Dragomites are frightening,' he confirmed. 'It's not that they're so very powerful, nor that they're as enthusiastic for the taste of human flesh as vulgar horror stories claim, but they're ugly and they're unearthly, and you know when you look at them that those big jaws could cut a man in two – and that's just the workers, never mind the warriors. Like all insects, you see, they wear their skeletons on the outside instead of the inside, and like honey-bees the great majority of their kind are sexless instruments with no proper self-interest. We mustn't forget, though, that they're not really insects. They're unearthly, and it doesn't do to make too many assumptions about the parallel evolution of earthly and unearthly species. Whatever honey the dragomites may make surely can't be sweet to human tongues.

'Serpents are ugly and unearthly too, but not nearly so fearful. They're slender and scaly but if the brains inside their bulbous heads are as big as they seem they're certainly not stupid. It's easy to get paranoid about what might or might not be going on behind those beady black eyes, and I can see how they got their reputation for being patient plotters, but I never heard of one offering violence to a human being and the ones I've talked to have been unfailingly polite.'

'Do you believe that the world was theirs before men came?' Jacom asked curiously. 'Did our forefathers really arrive in a ship, as invaders?'

'Perhaps – and perhaps not,' was Phar's cautious answer. 'Some say that we're all products of evolution, that all our ancestries can be traced to the first stirrings of life in the primeval mud, and that the separation of life-forms into earthly and unearthly is a distinction without a difference. Maybe there are just two different lines of descent which diverged very early in the history of life, with honey-bees, horses and humans being the ultimate products of one and dragomites, Serpents and Salamanders the ultimate products of the other. Whatever the truth of the matter, you musn't take darklander anxieties too seriously. The kind of people who choose to live in a Forest of Absolute Night are bound to be a little strange.'

Jacom didn't repeat Phar's opinion of the darklanders to Koraismi, but Koraismi knew it well enough. Koraismi informed him that the darklanders had a saying about people living under the sun being touched by the sun, and lots of proverbs about the tendency of direct sunlight to dazzle and burn. Darklanders, he affirmed – not without some justice – had the keenest vision of which men were capable, by virtue of living in such quiet light, and they alone could see clearly what was happening to the forest . . . and what, in the fullness of time, would happen to the world.

'Mark my words,' Koraismi said, 'the world is not a safe place. There are too many things in it which do not like mankind. Their enmity must be recognised, no matter how polite they seem. Your Xandrian traders might think that we darklanders are dull of mind because we have no rich merchants, but we have a saying: *A man who lives by barter alone will one day give his fortune for a poisoned pig*. I tell you this because you have told me that your father is a grower of fruits and a keeper of herds, friend Jacom, and because I think you will understand. It is good to be a fighting man for a while, and a wanderer – else I would not be here now – but it is also good to know when to come home.'

Jacom thought that such advice would sound infinitely better coming from a much older man, but he also felt a certain affinity for the sentiments expressed. Was it possible, he wondered, that even a half-naked darklander boy had more true wisdom than a physician-adventurer like Aulakh Phar? And if it were, what in the world was he doing marching his remaining men over the edge of an abyss, in search of a rebel princess with Serpent's blood?

15

WHILE HYRY KESHVARA wrung the water out of a motley collection of clothes, then draped them over the earthly bushes which formed a ragged rampart along the river bank, Lucrezia sat on a tussock of grass staring out across the dark watercourse at the solid-seeming wall which ran along the opposite shore. It was black now, but in the morning – when the ribbon-like tract of starlight exposed by the width of the river turned to true day-blue – it would be purple and green, brighter and gaudier than anything she had seen for a long time.

The river was broad and sluggish here – they were no more than fifty mets below the ford – but it narrowed again downstream where the dredgers only had soft silt to deal with.

'This is a good place to wait,' the trader said, when she had finished. 'There's a ready coign of vantage in that sagging gnarlytree which leans out over the water – from there we can have a clear but discreet view of the crossing-place. Elema says there isn't another for thirty kims and that Fraxinus will certainly head for this one. The caravan can't pass us by without our knowing – nor can anyone else.'

'What if Fraxinus and Phar never arrive at all?' Lucrezia asked. 'What do we do then?'

Hyry made no attempt to deny the possibility. 'If things go wrong to that extent,' she said dourly, 'your appetite for adventure might be more fully met than you had hoped. Don't drink the river water unboiled, by the way – it's mother to a hundred kinds of infection, some of them very nasty indeed.'

As she stretched herself out on the ground, relaxing her weary limbs, Lucrezia reflected that her appetite for adventure had so far been so meanly fed that it was hard to imagine a surfeit.

'Be careful, child,' Elema said to her, returning to the camp from a brief exploratory foray. 'It's not safe to lie too close to the shore when there are crocolids about.'

Lucrezia immediately sat up again. She had not yet seen a crocolid, but Hyry had warned her that they were to be found here, and having had ample opportunity to study Hyry's scar she knew that they were creatures it was better not to come upon unexpectedly.

The banks of the river were an earthly enclave in the heart of the unearthly forest, but their resident fauna was by no means identical to that of the rivers which flowed through Xandria's farmlands. There were dredgers, of course, but their neighbours included amphibious reptiles never seen in the empire – not just crocolids but constrictor snakes too. Such creatures were intimidated by the scent of human artifacts and the smoke of cooking-fires, but Elema was adamant that the three of them ought to take turns keeping watch, for safety's sake. No one was inclined to disagree.

During Lucrezia's first watch a crocolid did indeed appear, creeping uncomfortably close to the horses. Their whinnying raised the alarm, though, and the princess chased it away by waving a smoking brand from the cooking-fire at it. She couldn't see it clearly in the undergrowth, but she caught sight of its teeth as it snapped back at her while sliding into the water.

The next day she saw one much more clearly – and saw Hyry kill it by driving a knife through its skull, with an altogether natural vengeful glee. The trader then spent hours skinning the beast and butchering its carcase, assisted by Elema.

'The leather of its skin is by no means worthless,' Hyry explained, 'and the best of the meat is worth eating in spite of its toughness.' Lucrezia suspected, however, that the work she and the darklander were putting in was more a matter of whiling away the time than laying in valuable supplies. When they had taken all they wanted they threw the rest of the corpse into the water a little way downstream.

'That'll take the edge off the appetite of its kinfolk,' Hyry said.

Later in the day Elema found fourteen crocolid eggs buried in the sandy soil of the bank and gave them to her companions while she went out on a more serious foraging expedition. Hyry boiled the eggs along with some thin strips of the creature's meat, but Lucrezia found the ensemble less palatable than she had hoped.

'You must learn to forget that eating was ever a pleasure,' Hyry advised her. 'Think of it simply as a dour necessity. If you can do that you won't be distracted by tastes you've yet to acquire – and when you find yourself once again in a place where the cuisine is to your liking, you'll relish it all the more.'

'I shall never return to Xandria,' Lucrezia said. 'I must learn to savour different things. Are there fish in the river?'

'A great many, and not so difficult to catch in the shallows,' Hyry told her, 'else there would not be so many crocolids. Alas, I have neither fish-hooks nor spears with which to go after them. Whatever you might have heard about the virtues of bent pins, they're no substitute for the real thing – and there's lustrust even here, where you would never think to find any iron, so my pins are staying safe in their sterile jars.'

'I could harvest many poisons hereabouts,' Lucrezia said, with a trace of mischief. 'I ought to make what effort I can to test my skills and advance my Art while we wait.'

'By all means, highness,' Hyry agreed. 'Elema will doubtless give you very good advice on that score, since she likes you so much and counts herself a witch of sorts. Unfortunately, there is little enough scope here for the exercise and improvement of my own Art, notwithstanding the ready availability of crocolid skins.'

'Trading isn't an Art,' Lucrezia said, for the sake of argument. 'I don't mean to demean it by saying so, but it simply isn't. It has no lore.'

'It's because it has no lore that it's the only *true* Art,' Hyry retorted, with all apparent seriousness. 'In spite of all your lamentations as to its unreliability, much of *your* Art is nothing more than plain rote learning, done by method and mental trickery. It's not so easy to keep track of the values of a thousand kinds of goods as they fluctuate without ever settling down, let alone to guess the value of things that no one has ever bought or sold before. Order is ready to be mastered, chaos is not – and sometimes, even the best of bargains can twist in your hand like a scorpion and sting you where it hurts.'

'What you mean by that, I suppose,' said Lucrezia lightly, 'is that she who trades with poisoners always risks a bellyache.'

'As a manufacturer of aphorisms, highness,' the trader riposted, 'you still have far to go.' But there was so little bitterness in the way she said it that she almost smiled.

Elema returned then, although the sack she had taken with her was no more than half-full. She kicked dirt over the remains of the cooking-fire to douse it, and gathered in the last of the clothes that had been hung out to dry.

'What is it?' Hyry asked.

Elema flipped her right ear with the forefinger of her right hand, then pointed across the river. 'Better you both stay hidden,' she said. 'Leave this to me.'

Lucrezia listened hard, and was just able to detect the distant sound of singing. There were many voices. Someone was marching along the far bank, behind the rampart of bushes.

'Stay here,' Hyry said to Lucrezia, pulling herself up into the branches of the gnarlytree and vanishing into its leafy crown.

Elema didn't bother to repeat her own warning before moving off towards the ford, where she could meet the newcomers when they crossed. Lucrezia glanced briefly at the sheltered spot where the animals were tethered before moving into the bushes, trying to find a position from which she could see a long way upstream without herself being clearly visible.

Although she had no idea what to expect, what she actually saw seemed disappointing. The singers were male darklanders, apparently in good heart. As they crossed the ford in single file she counted them; there were thirty-three. Most carried steel-tipped spears, although a substantial minority had bows and arrows.

Lucrezia half-expected Elema to bring some or all the darklanders to the camp, but when she came back she was alone. Hyry jumped down to meet her.

'They say there has been a great battle and a great victory,' she reported. 'They say that the dragomites have been driven from the forest – but they have not been in a real fight. They have seen dragomites, but not many, and those they saw did not attack them. They think they are heroes for having chased the creatures away . . . but I think they have returned too soon, having little stomach for a bigger effort against unknown foes. We have better men in the darklands than that, Keshvara . . . best to hide the little witch from *that* kind.'

'The little witch has little to fear from men with no stomach for effort,' Lucrezia boasted.

'You once killed two fools, and took a beating for it,' Hyry told her sternly. 'Don't think you can turn back the wind on that account.'

'Those in search of easy victories are more dangerous to womenfolk than real fighting men,' Elema observed, 'but the news, such as it is, is good. If the dragomites which have come into the forest are not disposed to fight, so much the better.'

'What of their riders?' Hyry asked.

Elema shook her head. 'According to the men, the riders fled too – but if they had really seen humans with the dragomites they'd have given a much fuller account of the wonder. Those men met no demons – although they were afraid that they might, else they'd not have come back so quickly.'

'Boys' games,' Lucrezia murmured, remembering Dhalla. 'Lots of noise, but mostly pretence.'

There was no sign of the caravan that day, and when the middle of the night came again they settled to the same routine of watching and sleeping by turns. The visibility of the stars seemed to Lucrezia to be a comforting thing, and no crocolids came to disturb her.

By the time Elema's turn came to sit up the princess felt more at peace with herself than she had since the explosion had blasted open the door of the Inner Sanctum and put a spectacular end to her childhood. She went to sleep very easily, and her dreams were pleasant ... but her subsequent awakening was rough and urgent.

'Get up!' the old woman's voice hissed in her ear. 'Not my people this time, nor yours – strangers!'

For once, Lucrezia's reaction had more fear in it than excitement. If the usually imperturbable Elema was alarmed, there must surely be more than adequate cause for alarm. *Dragomites at last*, she thought, *and perhaps their riders too!*

That judgment was premature. 'People at the crossing,' Hyry whispered to her, as she came to her feet, 'hesitating on the far bank. Goldens, I think, with horses. They must have come downstream for quite a distance – they can't decide whether or not to cross. Be very quiet.' With that she turned away, and went to the gnarlytree, swinging herself up into the dark foliage with practised ease.

Elema took up a position in the bushes very near to the spot where Lucrezia had stood to watch the darklanders. Lucrezia, forced to stand a little further back, could not see half as well.

'These men are very scared,' Elema whispered, after a minute of careful listening.

'Are they definitely goldens?' Lucrezia asked.

'Not ambers,' was all that Elema would concede. The starlight evidently wasn't bright enough to distinguish goldens from bronzes in her untutored eyes.

Lucrezia heard rustling in the boughs of the gnarlytree as Hyry tried to get into a better position, creeping like a lizard along a branch which overhung the river. She too was having difficulty seeing in the poor light, and she too thought it important to figure out who these newcomers might be.

Lucrezia moved closer to Elema and craned her own neck. She could see horses as well as men, which implied that these were not the legendary dragomite-riders. Might they be the people who had started this whole affair by bringing into the darklands the goods which Hyry Keshvara had bought? If so, they ought to be bronze, not golden.

'They're coming across!' she suddenly said to Elema, although the darklander could hardly be unaware of the fact.

'Not all of them,' the old woman replied anxiously. 'Only scouts, to see how the land lies.'

'They'll never find us in the dark,' Lucrezia whispered, but she knew that she couldn't be certain of that. She wondered whether she ought to prepare her armoury again.

Four men were clearly visible, making their way very gingerly across the ford. They knew shallows when they saw them, but they were testing the crossing with the utmost care. It was impossible to tell how many more men were skulking in the trees, or how many horses they had, but Lucrezia had the impression that the whole party was less than twenty strong, perhaps no more than a dozen. Their skins seemed dark, but she couldn't be sure that they were bronzes rather than goldens. Their clothes were dark too, cut to hug their bodies rather more closely than Xandrian clothing. The men in the water carried neither spears nor swords in their hands, although they might well have had knives in their belts. One of them – the second in line – was dragging a thin cord; Lucrezia presumed that he intended to use it to draw a thicker rope across should the crossing prove difficult, for use as an extra support.

'If they knew how many crocolids there are hereabouts they'd move a lot faster,' Lucrezia muttered.

Again the princess heard the boughs of the gnarlytree rustle as Hyry moved higher in search of a better vantage-point . . . and then she heard a gasp. It was an awkward and awful sound, and she was convinced that it would have been much louder – perhaps as loud as a scream – had Hyry not been making such an effort to be silent.

Elema looked up in sudden alarm, and Lucrezia knew that the same thought must have crossed both their minds. Flowerworms preferred the unearthly giants to gnarlytrees, but they were not exclusive in their habits, and anyone who went climbing in the dark was at some risk.

The branches of the tree rustled yet again, and now their rustling seemed horribly ominous. A bad sting would have paralysed Hyry's arm, and the paralysis might easily spread to the rest of her body. If she were not solidly wedged . . .

Don't fall! Lucrezia thought fervently. She repeated the invocation, as if the urgency of the silent command might somehow lend it force. *Please, Hyry, don't fall!*

Hyry's body shifted again, moving even further out, and then became still. The rustling ceased, and Lucrezia almost breathed a sigh of relief. For a moment or two she was certain that Hyry was clinging tight, and that all was well – but then the unfolding disaster took a different turn. The trunk of the gnarlytree began to creak and groan, and there was a horrible glutinous sound as the roots shifted within the bank – which suddenly seemed far softer than it had before.

Lucrezia realised that the roots of the ancient tree must be rotten, and that they no longer had sufficient purchase in the muddy soil. The weight of the crown, augmented and unbalanced by Hyry Keshvara's body, was dragging them free – and Hyry, hurt by whatever injury had made her cry out, could make no adequate response.

The tree toppled, and its crown met the shallow water with a gigantic splash, which must have frightened the men at the crossing half to death.

For a few seconds Lucrezia thought the matter might be over and done with, but the water was not quite shallow enough.

As the roots broke free the slow current dragged the crown downstream ... and the whole tree began to float away, with Hyry Keshvara trapped in the branches that were underwater.

16

JACOM SAT ON the backboard of the smaller wagon while Aulakh Phar knelt to examine his left leg. The calf was badly swollen and he could hardly walk.

'I see what's happened,' Phar said. 'You've had a run-in with a tacktick. They're not fliers, so the netting which keeps most of the bloodsuckers at bay while you sleep isn't so effective against them – they can just crawl under it. If you don't mind me saying so, that red skirt that comes with your uniform is a liability – bare legs are an open invitation to tackticks.'

'Have you got something to put on the bite?' Jacom asked curtly. He was not in the mood for lectures about his mode of dress.

'It's not a bite, as such,' Phar told him. 'The problem is that the tick sinks her whole head into your flesh to get at a deep-lying blood vessel. Left to herself she'll take it out again when she's full, but you must have felt a slight itch and scratched, severing the body from the head and leaving the mouth-parts embedded in your leg. They've rotted and caused an infection. I can give you something to knock out the bacteria, but it needs to be properly lanced to make sure the remaining bits of tacktick are all cleaned out.'

Jacom didn't like the sound of that. *Properly lanced* sounded like medic-talk for *This is going to hurt*. 'I don't believe in all that mumbo-jumbo about bacteria,' he said sourly.

'Bacteria don't care whether you believe in them or not,' Phar retorted. 'They just keep right on multiplying and your blood keeps right on turning to pus in the attempt to keep them under control. If you want it fixed, it'll have to be cleaned up. If you're too squeamish to have it done with a local anaesthetic I can get one of the darklanders to knock you out, but it'll smart just as badly when it wears off.'

Jacom knew that the soldierly thing to do was to opt for the local anaesthetic and watch Phar carve and cauterise with a stout heart and an unflinching eye, and he certainly didn't want anyone thinking that he'd taken a less courageous option. 'Go ahead,' he said, with a sigh. 'Get it over with.'

Phar climbed up and rooted around in the back of the wagon until he found a corroded bottle containing a turbid liquid. Jacom hauled himself into a clear space and lay down on his stomach while the physician carefully dripped the liquid on to the back of his leg. A comforting lack of feeling soon possessed the leg from the knee downwards. Phar unfurled the canvas strip in which he kept his instruments, and picked out a suspiciously rusty knife. He rubbed it with a cloth soaked in alcohol, then passed it lightly through the flame of an unshielded lantern.

'Hold still,' he said.

Jacom held still, gritting his teeth – not against the pain, of which there was none, but against the power of his imagination, which told him all too clearly what Phar was doing.

'Surely you don't really believe all that stuff about invisible bacteria and viruses causing decay and disease?' he said, feeling a dire need to distract himself from contemplation of what was happening to his leg. 'I mean, how could anyone know even if there were such things? It's just empty jargon, to convince people that doctors are authentic magicians instead of people who've learned a set of useful treatments refined by the trials and errors of past generations.'

'As it happens,' Phar replied drily, 'I do believe it. I believe in bacteria and viruses, cells and organelles, chlorophyll and haemoglobin, genes and chromosomes, molecules and atoms . . . the whole set. Call me a romantic fool if you will, but I'm pretty damn sure that the people who put together the lore which has been handed down to us were a lot smarter than we are. I don't know how they got to be that smart, or how they knew all the things they claimed to know about things we couldn't possibly find out, but I'm prepared to believe that they really did have microscopes and telescopes and lots of other kinds of scopes and that they really did try their damnedest to pass on as much of their wisdom as they possibly could to our ancestors. Maybe forgetfulness isn't the only sin, but every time I ask myself where I'd be –

where any of us would be – if it weren't for the lore, I understand well enough why it's the worst sin of all.'

'I'm not disparaging the lore,' Jacom complained. 'I'm just saying that it isn't what it pretends to be. I think it was discovered by ordinary people not much different from you and me, who dressed it up to make it seem far more awesome than it really is. When you get right down to it, it's just a set of recipes for making things. The fancy words don't actually add anything, do they?'

'They add a theoretical framework,' Phar said flatly, while he whittled away with the point of his knife. 'They add a way of thinking about the world, a way of understanding it as a set of interlocking systems. They add an account of the things which underlie mere appearances. I think that's worth something. If I didn't, I wouldn't be risking my life trying to find out what the mysteries of Genesys are all about.'

'If there was anything to understand,' Jacom told him stubbornly, 'the people who made up the lore would have said what they had to say in plain language. There wouldn't be any mystery – and there certainly wouldn't be any vague warnings and prophecies or any so-called secret commandments. Don't you find all that stuff just plain silly?'

'No, I don't,' Phar told him agreeably. 'If I were a loremaster of old who had to transmit a message over hundreds or thousands of generations, without knowing how long it would take for the circumstances to arise in which it would become relevant, I might be tempted to use sneaky tactics like passing secret commandments to a supposedly favoured few and instructing them to guard them from others at all costs, or framing enigmas calculated to tease and tantalise. It's one thing, you see, to ask people to remember things which they have to use year in and year out, but quite another asking them to remember things which won't have any practical value for thousands of years. No matter how sinful forgetfulness is, people are only too ready to indulge themselves when what they're remembering seems to have no immediate pay-off . . . as illustrated by our unfortunate failure to recruit a mapmaker to this expedition. There! All done. I'll just slap some woundglue on. In five or six days it'll be as good as new. You'll probably find it more comfortable meanwhile to ride than walk, though.'

Jacom breathed a massive sigh of relief. He shuddered at the thought that more filthy bloodsucking insects might creep under his protective netting and malevolently leave their heads embedded in his flesh when he brushed them off. Nothing like that had ever happened on his father's estate, where a man could sleep naked under the stars – though not, of course, under the fierce midday sun – and suffer no serious harm.

What am I doing here? he thought. *What am I doing in a bizarre half-world full of vile things, in the company of madmen who are prepared to risk everything on the strength of a handful of garbled myths?* He was only too well aware, though, that the price of returning home – or to any safe haven within the empire's borders – was the recovery of Princess Lucrezia.

As he lowered himself gingerly from the back of the wagon, careful not to trust his weight to his numb leg, Koraismi raced towards him in a state of high excitement, shouting something to the effect that golden women were coming.

Jacom instantly leapt to the conclusion that he must mean Hyry Keshvara and Princess Lucrezia – but his sudden elation was short-lived. By the time he had hobbled to a position from which he could look back along the trail which the expedition had been following the newcomers were clearly in view, and he saw immediately that this was a very different, and much more surprising, company.

In the lead came a giant, striding along purposefully on foot and leading an enormous horse, over whose back lay an unconscious figure which was only just recognisable as an old woman. This huge animal was followed by a much smaller horse bearing a much bigger rider – a rider who was neither a woman nor a golden, although the copious bloodstains about his head made it very difficult to tell exactly what he might be. It was the fact that he was nearly as large as the giant rather than his colouring which told Jacom who he was.

Behind the second horse came a third, bearing a stout male rider, and behind that one another, on a leading-rein, with two darkland women walking beside it.

To his astonishment, Jacom recognised the stout rider as Checuti, Xandria's one-time prince of thieves. He was by no means disconsolate to observe that the thief-master was looking very gaunt and haggard about the face, with a haunted expression in his eyes. It was not until the party had come to a halt and the bloody figure of Andris Myrasol had stumbled from his mount, that he recognised the person who lay unconscious over the saddle of the giant's horse. It was Princess Lucrezia's mentor and fellow-gardener, Queen Ereleth.

The giant made straight for Aulakh Phar, who had come up behind Jacom very swiftly. It was obvious that his healing talents were urgently required. Myrasol remained where he was, rocking back and forth as though he might fall at any minute, while Merel Zabio ran anxiously to meet him. Checuti, by contrast, turned his sorely tired horse in Jacom's direction and did not dismount until he had walked it to within a mere couple of mets. He had an oddly twisted smile upon his full lips.

'Captain Cerri!' he said. 'I never thought I'd have to say so, but I'm glad to see you.'

'It's a giant!' Koraismi said excitedly, as he bobbed up and down by Jacom's side. 'A true giant! Did I not tell you that strange things are in the forest? Did I not tell you that the world is changing, and will never be the same again?'

To the boy, the giant was every bit as exotic as a Serpent or a Salamander, more so than a dragomite; Jacom did not bother to explain to him that this prodigy, at least, was not from the mythical lands beyond the Dragomite Hills, and was not in the least to be feared by folk such as he. Instead, he looked up at Checuti and said: 'What brings you here?'

'Dreams of adventure,' Checuti said sardonically. 'What else?'

Aulakh Phar set to work as soon as he had taken a closer look at Ereleth's unconscious body. He instructed one of the other darklander boys to set water to boil in a cauldron while he went back into the wagon to delve for woundglue and bandages, salves and potions. Merel Zabio began to complain that her kinsman ought to be treated first, but the big amber restrained her. Jacom was impressed in spite of himself by the awesome speed and certainty of Phar's actions as the old man rushed back and forth, checking the wounds which scored the flesh of the amber while the witch-queen was laid out on a sleeping-mat.

'What happened?' he asked Checuti, placing his hand on Koraismi's supportive shoulder so that he did not have to hop on his one good leg. The thief did not seem in the least surprised or embarrassed to find him here, and stepped towards him for all the world as if the two of them had always been fast friends.

'You too have suffered an injury, I see!' he remarked, gushing forth false sympathy. 'What a terrible place this forest is – and we have not yet caught sight or sound of one of those hideous dragomite invaders! The unfortunate Ereleth was attacked by a nightcloak. Andris and I were obliged to go to her aid. We fought like heroes, but poor Andris was badly mauled about the head and body, while the witch-queen was knocked unconscious and proved so difficult to rouse that we feared for her life. We were fortunate enough to meet these darkland women, but their witchery was inadequate to revive the queen and we did not know how we might use the medicines in Ereleth's belt to soothe or dress poor Andris's wounds. They were good enough, however, to guide us here with all due speed. Dhalla, of course, has been a veritable tower of strength.'

Jacom felt that this explanation left out rather much in the preliminary stages. 'What in the world were you doing in the company of the queen and the giant?' he asked, wishing that he were not too lame and too bewildered to strike the kind of interrogative pose which would have been more fitting for an officer in the king's guard.

'We were helping her to find the princess,' Checuti replied, as if it ought to have been obvious.

'You didn't seem in the least inclined to help me do the same,' Jacom reminded him.

'The queen has greater powers of persuasion,' Checuti remarked, twisting his odd smile into an even more ironic configuration. 'Is the princess not here, then? Have I brought my companions on a wild goose chase after all?'

Jacom was uncomfortably aware of the fact that Checuti was teasing him. 'Not yet,' he said brusquely. 'I hope that she and Keshvara may arrive soon – before we have to face hordes of marauding dragomites, and who knows what other monsters.'

'I'm relieved that we shall have the cream of the king's guard to defend us from such dangers,' Checuti said mockingly. 'I know we shall be safe with such a man as you to protect us.'

'I can't imagine how you come to be here,' said Jacom, tiring of a game which he seemed to be losing, 'but you're under arrest. When we take the princess back, we'll take you along with her, dead or alive. Although I still have no more than nine men with me, you're certainly not going to get away this time.'

Checuti sighed. 'What a tiresome young man you are, captain,' he said amiably, 'and how little you understand about the ways of the world. I only hope and pray that Ereleth makes a full recovery, so that she may teach you the sad error of your ways. Will you put me in irons right away, or may I be allowed to help my friend Andris and make what efforts I can to comfort his pretty cousin? I promise I won't try to escape.'

Jacom looked across at Merel Zabio, who was now kneeling with Phar beside the supine body of the big amber. Myrasol was still conscious but seemed to have lost a lot of blood. Jacom couldn't help hoping that the wounds weren't as bad as they looked.

Oh well, he thought. *At least Phar has his mapmaker now, for a little while – much good may it do him.*

Somehow, Jacom felt in his bones that it was going to be very difficult indeed to make good his latest threat against Checuti. When the stout thief-master turned away, he made no move to stop him – but he remembered King Belin's words, which seemed to echo now inside his skull: *If you can, bring me this Checuti's head on a pike . . . and the amber's, if you want to be sure of the best possible welcome.*

'I will, majesty,' he murmured. 'At least, I'll certainly try.'

17

WHEN THE TREE in which Hyry Keshvara was trapped began to drift downstream Lucrezia leapt forward, and would have jumped into the water had Elema not caught her and held her fast. Her grip was remarkably strong for such a frail and ancient creature. Lucrezia fought against the constraining hand but the old woman would not be denied, and the fact that they were wedged into the bushy rampart was not to Lucrezia's advantage.

Lucrezia watched helplessly as the tree rolled in the water, so that the part of the crown which had been underwater slowly began to emerge. She hoped that this process might lift Hyry's imprisoned body clear of the water, but the crown was too thick for her to see. The rolling continued, but it was slow and irresolute and there was no way to know what effect it might be having on the trader's chances of survival. The tree drifted further out into the river, to the channel which the dredgers had cleared, and began to move more rapidly downstream.

The princess wanted to shout Hyry's name at the top of her voice, as if by doing so she might summon her back or cause her to rise up out of the dark swirling waters . . . but the order to be quiet still held sway over her tongue, even though the splash of the tree as it hit the water had been loud enough to be heard four hundred mets away.

The water was now so murky with mud where the tree had fallen that it seemed as black as ink and as thick as blood. Lucrezia thought she could imagine how it might feel to be trapped in that kind of cold soup, desperate for air. She wondered if it might be better to hope that Hyry had been stupefied by the sting, and now had not the slightest idea what was happening to her . . . but she could not hope any such thing. Instead, she hoped – desperately, for she knew how frail a hope it was – that the tree had turned sufficiently to bring Hyry's head above the surface, and would continue to hold it there, so that she could not possibly drown.

The princess tried again to escape from Elema's grip, but the attempt was less than half-hearted. She had learned to swim in the baths which one of Belin's remote ancestors had caused to be hollowed out beneath the seaward side of the citadel, but she knew how utterly foolish it would be to dive into the river after her friend. She kept her eyes on the tree's course lest Hyry's head might yet bob up in its wake as it floated serenely downstream, but there was nothing to be seen.

Then the strangers arrived.

Lucrezia was unconscious of the near presence of other people until Elema suddenly released her and shoved her away from the bank, saying: 'Run! Hide!'

The order came too late. Someone laid a hand on her shoulder almost immediately, and although she bounded away she could not quite evade its clutch. The man followed her, and as she stumbled he caught her again. She struggled to draw a knife from her belt but he knocked her arms away. She fell to the ground, sprawling untidily, and knew that if he had intended to hurt her he could have done it then – but he hesitated.

At such close quarters the starlight was sufficiently bright to inform her attacker that she was a woman, not a warrior, and a golden too. This was enough to make him refrain from hitting her while she was down.

Elema had not even tried to fight. The old darklander was standing still, with her empty hands raised aloft, shrieking: 'Friends! Friends!' It seemed, though, that the man who was attacking Lucrezia was unimpressed by this gesture; indeed, he reacted fiercely against it, actually turning away from Lucrezia to round on the old woman. He grabbed Elema's arm and pulled her clear of the bush, handing her back to another man following close behind. 'Hold her!' he commanded.

His accent was strange, but there was something faintly reassuring about the familiarity of the words. He was golden, after all – a distant kinsman, no doubt, but a kinsman nevertheless.

Lucrezia tried to get up again, but paused in a kneeling position to look back in the direction of the floating tree. There was still no sign of anything in the water except the tree. The further the tree went the quieter the water became, but nothing popped up from the depths.

Lucrezia stabbed an urgent finger in the direction of the tree. 'My friend!' she shouted at the goldens. 'Go after her, I beg of you! Save her, if you can!'

They didn't move. She looked up, helplessly, at the man who had cast her down. He was poised to do it again if she made any threatening gesture, so she remained exactly where she was. He seemed uncertain as to what to do next, but he obviously had no intention of diving into the river. Even if he had, she told herself bitterly, the crocolids would probably have got him before he was halfway to the tree – and if Hyry couldn't swim away from the tree, she was almost certainly dead.

A fourth man joined the other three. They stood in a ragged arc, studying Lucrezia carefully – rather more carefully than Elema, who was still hard held by one of them. They must have learned far more about her in three minutes than she learned about them; she could not stop thinking about the enormity of Hyry's tragedy.

Lucrezia knew that she had to concentrate on the new situation now, and forced herself to do so. The men who had come to seize them were goldens – darker than she was, but unmistakably goldens; that must be why the one who had knocked her down was uncertain as to whether she was friend or foe, although he plainly had no love for darklanders. If they had met darklanders south of the river they had probably been attacked as invaders; if so, they might now be desperate to find allies. They were probably a long way from home; perhaps they had not intended to come so far, and were dismayed to find the forest so vast.

'It's all right,' she said firmly. 'We're not your enemies. You're quite safe.'

'Where do you come from?' asked the man who stood over her – the one who had knocked her down.

'From Xandria,' Lucrezia answered, automatically adding: 'The greatest city in the world.'

There was no flicker of recognition in his wary expression. He had never heard of Xandria, it seemed.

'Where are you from?' she countered.

'Ebla,' he answered brusquely.

One of his companions had gone to look at the tethered animals.

291

He was inspecting them carefully. 'Good horses,' he observed eventually, 'except for these two.'

'They're donkeys,' Lucrezia informed him, wondering if it might be a joke.

'Is that what women ride in your land?' asked the man who had spoken first, in a tone that seemed more contemptuous than bemused.

'Xandrian women ride horses,' the princess said stonily, and could not resist adding: 'What do your women ride – dragomites?'

That wiped the smiles off their faces. The man who stood over her pulled her roughly to her feet. He let go once she was upright, but his manner was unmistakably threatening. She knew that she had said entirely the wrong thing.

'Are the mound-women your friends?' he demanded. The question was obviously not trivial.

'No,' Lucrezia said, raising her arms in a placatory gesture. 'I've never even seen a dragomite, and I never heard of *mound-women* until you spoke the word. There have been rumours of dragomite-riders abroad in the forest, but I thought they must be false.'

The man had already turned his attention to Elema. 'And you?' he said harshly. 'Do you know the mound-women?'

'No,' the old woman replied. 'My people have taken up arms to fight the dragomites and their human nest-slaves. Have you not seen them about their work?'

The Eblan shook his head. 'Ambers attacked *us*,' he said vehemently. 'First the mound-women attacked, then the ambers, then the mound-women again. Your people should have greeted us warmly, if what you say is true. We have always been enemies of the dragomites, and of any humans who ally themselves with such monsters.'

'The darklanders couldn't have known that,' Lucrezia said, without getting up. She felt that she ought to do her utmost to soothe their captor's frayed nerves. 'They found you on their land, and assumed that you were allied with all the other invaders. You'll be safe on this side of the river. There are no dragomites here. We can talk at our leisure – as friends.'

It seemed that he accepted this – and there was no reason why he should not – but after turning away to exchange glances with his companions he suddenly rounded on Lucrezia and grabbed her again. She fought against his grip as fiercely as she could, but he was too strong. He forced her down on the ground, and held her there while one of his companions produced a length of cord with which to bind her wrists. Elema tried to escape while this was happening, but the man beside her was quick to seize her again, and she made no further resistance while they bound her hands too.

'We are friends,' the old woman said reproachfully. 'We do not treat friends this way.' Lucrezia noticed, however, that she did not seem particularly surprised by the treatment she had received.

'We won't hurt you,' the spokesman assured them, 'but this is a dangerous place. We have too many enemies nearby, and they're far too close for comfort. We can't take chances. We must rest here, where we can watch the crossing-place.'

The Eblans sat Elema down with her back to a bush, and placed Lucrezia beside her. One of them stood guard over them while another went to report back to their fellows on the far bank. The spokesman had removed the knife from Lucrezia's belt and was studying it carefully, although it was a very ordinary knife, much less impressive than Hyry Keshvara's dagger. She noticed that none of them had a knife of his own, and wondered whether iron was in short supply in Ebla, wherever it might be. If so, that was an important thing to know. Xandria's mines supplied the greater part of the empire with most useful metals; had the Thousand Isles been better resourced the empire could not be nearly so large. Lucrezia had been told by one of her stepmothers – not Ereleth! – that the best measure of Xandria's supremacy over all other nations was the cunning of its smiths in defying the ravages of lustrust and all its corrupting kin.

The Eblans showed considerable interest in the packs which the donkeys had carried, but after some whispered debate they decided not to investigate further for the moment. More men were arriving now, bringing scrawny horses with them.

By the time the company was fully assembled, Lucrezia counted fifteen of them. They seemed very weary. The one who had taken her prisoner explained the action he had taken to the man who was presumably in charge of the entire expedition. He evidently approved.

'Your men didn't need to do this,' Lucrezia told the leader, when he had heard everything. 'We're not your enemies.'

'I'd like to believe that,' the leader replied, in a low voice, 'but we're in too much trouble already to risk finding more. Can you be quiet, or shall I have to gag you? Some few of our enemies are close behind us, and I'd prefer it if they continued downstream along the far bank rather than crossing the river to search for us on this side. When they've gone by, we can talk – until then . . .'

He left the sentence hanging.

'We can be quiet,' Elema said calmly. 'But we have friends close behind us, and if they find us like this they will not like it.'

'Then I must hope they won't find us,' the Eblan said, 'at least until our pursuers have gone by.'

Well, said Lucrezia to herself, *here's adventure and no mistake – but how I wish that Hyry were here to share it! How shall I ever survive it without her?*

Thought of Hyry reminded her that she had not yet had the time to mourn. Now that she was still, with her hands tied, she was suddenly overcome by a black tide of grief.

Silently, helplessly, she began to weep.

She kept her head stubbornly bowed, lest her rude captors mistake the reason for her emotion. She did not want them to think that she could be easily reduced to tears; she was, after all, a princess, and must behave like one even though these savages had not bothered to discover her rank or her name. But she made no attempt to hold back the tears, partly because she didn't think that she would be able to, and partly because she thought that Hyry Keshvara was fully entitled to have them shed on her behalf.

If it is within my power, dear Hyry, she thought miserably, *I'll finish what you started. I'll carry through your mission, or die trying – that I swear.*

18

THE SEATED GIANT looked up as Jacom Cerri and Koraismi approached. She seemed oddly forlorn and faded to Jacom; she was clearly exhausted and deeply disturbed by the fact that Ereleth still lay unconscious in Phar's wagon.

To Koraismi, however, the giant must still have seemed terrible. Jacom could see that he regarded her with naked awe and trepidation. The boy probably would not have dared go near her in normal circumstances, but he had come to think of his golden friend as a secure protector against all things uncanny. Jacom liked to think that this was a sound judgment – or, at any rate, not an entirely foolish overestimation.

Dhalla looked up at Jacom from her good eye. The other had been injured – according to Checuti's testimony – when she pulled the nightcloak off Andris Myrasol, after he had pulled it off Ereleth. It was by no means ruined, and she would be able to see out of it soon enough, but for the time being it had been firmly closed by a swelling that was oozing yellow pus from the places where Aulakh Phar had stitched a four-sim gash. *Bacteria again, Jacom thought. What busy creatures they are, toiling away in their invisible world so that they might export a due measure of pain and ugliness into ours.*

'Captain Cerri,' she said unenthusiastically. 'What can I do for you?'

'How are you?' he asked awkwardly.

'Well enough,' she grunted, in typically terse fashion. She had a few claw-scratches on her bare arms as well as a bad eye, but they were healing cleanly. Her one-eyed stare was strangely disturbing; the eye was so big, and the pupil so large in the dim purple light that Jacom felt as though he were peering into a black pit of infinite depth. *If there is any Absolute Night to be encountered in this forest,* he thought, *it is in the eyes of persons who are accustomed to live in brighter light.* He was uncomfortably aware of Koraismi, who was half-behind him, grasping the tail of his jacket in one hand while peering around his waist.

'You did a good job,' Jacom said carefully. 'In catching Checuti and the amber, I mean. If we can find the princess we'll have a clean sweep. We'll both be fêted in Xandria when we return. I'll make sure that you get your full share of the credit.'

Dhalla stared up at him, with an irritatingly enigmatic smile about her lips. She was finishing off the vestiges of a meal, and she used her tongue to pluck out some morsel between her enormous molars, then proceeded to swallow it.

'You will help me bring Checuti back, won't you?' Jacom said, this being the matter which he had come to investigate, not altogether confidently. 'Dead or alive – it doesn't much matter. Your duty and mine are exactly similar, are they not? We both owe allegiance to King Belin.'

'We have to find the princess first,' she said dismissively.

'Of course – but you have an interest in bringing the thief to justice too. He stole your wages as well as mine.'

'If we don't find the princess,' the giant said laconically, 'he's a dead man. Maybe he's a dead man anyway. He won't be spending any more of the coin he stole – rest assured of that.'

Jacom didn't know how to read the coldness of her tone or the stoniness of her temporarily cyclopean gaze. He couldn't take it for granted that she was just like any other human being but larger. After all, she belonged to a distinct species that was in some respects quite alien. He had no idea how far one could trust the dirty jokes people told about the ways giants might become pregnant, but he trusted the common knowledge which assured him that it couldn't involve male giants because there were none. Giants were in demand in Xandria and in those of the Thousand Islands which preserved similar kinds of kingly privilege, but they were native to some mysterious land in the far east, beyond the Spangled Desert. They spoke the same language as everyone else, but – as an old adage warned – people who used the same language didn't necessarily mean the same things by the same words.

'He seems peculiarly cheerful for a dead man,' Jacom observed uneasily. 'He seems to think that he knows something I don't. Is that mere bluff, do you think?'

'Probably,' said Dhalla dully. 'He has no reason to be cheerful that I can see.'

She came to her feet. Her body seemed to take an unnaturally long time to unfold. When she had raised herself to her full height she was looking down at him at much the same angle as he had been looking down at her.

'Fraxinus and Phar don't want my men to go back to Xandria at all,' he said. 'They're careful about what they say, but they really want us to join the expedition. They've both dropped hints about there being a greater service I could do the empire than returning a princess to the Inner Sanctum – or even a prince of thieves to just punishment. They'll want to keep the amber, of course, even after he's re-drawn that precious map which you seem to be holding tight to your chest. I'm prepared to compromise on that, if he really wasn't involved in Checuti's robbery – but I'm not prepared to compromise in the matter of Checuti, or in the matter of the princess. Can I rely on your help, if necessary, to bring them both safely back to Xandria?'

The way the giant stared steadily down at him, without answering, seemed to Jacom to be confirmation of his worst suspicions. She wasn't here on the king's business at all – she was here on Ereleth's business, whatever that might be. Why did things have to be so complicated? 'I'm your superior officer,' he said, wishing he didn't sound so querulously tentative. 'From now on, you're under my orders. I want to make that perfectly clear.'

The dark abyss that was her eye seemed darker still now that it loomed above him, and even her blonde hair seemed night-dark, silhouetted as it was against the purple canopy.

Jacom wilted under the oppressive gaze. His voice faltered as he forced himself to recognise defeat. 'You don't intend to go back, do you?' he said. 'You're not in this as an agent of the king – you're in it out of personal loyalty to the princess. Checuti was telling the truth when he said that she was desperate to run away. Neither you nor Ereleth has the slightest intention of trying to persuade her to go home. Do you realise what will happen to me if she won't go back? Do you have any idea what a mess I'll be in?'

Dhalla's jaw moved again as she rescued yet another stranded morsel, but she eventually said: 'Not my problem.'

Jacom sighed. *I'm a captain in the king's guard,* he said to himself silently. *That's supposed to mean something. It's a position of trust and responsibility, which ought to command the respect of every citizen of the empire. Am I really so unconvincing in the role that no one except a darklander boy will take a blind bit of notice of what I think or what I want?*

'Earlier today, Koraismi spoke to some men who came across the river yesterday after helping to drive the dragomites out of the forest,' he said. 'They talked to an old woman at the ford, but they didn't see Keshvara or the princess. Koraismi says Keshvara wouldn't have crossed over if she had any sense – he says that she must still be behind us. It looks to me as if we're going to have to go north again if we want to find the princess.'

For the first time, Dhalla's stare showed a flicker of interest – not concern, just interest. She shifted her gaze to look contemplatively at Koraismi, as if she were carefully weighing his minuteness and insignificance.

'We'll see,' she said finally. 'The queen will decide.' She addressed the boy directly and he was quick to move further behind Jacom, as though shielding himself from the baleful gaze.

'Ereleth may not be able to decide,' Jacom said sourly, 'even though she's sleeping normally now. She's an old woman, after all. Myrasol might not have pulled the nightcloak off her in time – though why he did it at all I can't imagine. Fraxinus isn't going to hang on here waiting for her to make a full recovery. He'll go on, now that he's heard that the dragomites are on the run. You might have to choose which way to go, and who should go with you. Personally, I'd rather head north than head into a war-zone. I'm not so sure the dragomites are on the run – and even if they are, that might make them all the more dangerous. Koraismi says that Serpents have been seen in the forest too. Have you ever seen a dragomite, Dhalla?'

'No,' she admitted.

'Or a Serpent?'

'My people know Salamanders,' she countered. She obviously didn't like to be at too much of a disadvantage in a contest of implied insults.

'That's not the same thing at all,' Jacom insisted, taking care to sound as dismissive as he could – although he himself had never seen a Serpent or a Salamander, and knew next to nothing about either species.

'The princess has Serpent's blood,' Dhalla retorted.

Jacom felt Koraismi stiffen, and the clutch of the little hand upon the jacket of his uniform tightened. He knew that the statement meant nothing in literal terms, of course – one of the few things he did know about Serpents was that they couldn't possibly interbreed with humans – but he also knew that in terms of darklander superstition it might mean a good deal.

I'm losing control of this argument, he thought furiously.

'That's not true, Dhalla,' he said firmly. 'It's just something they made up in the citadel – malicious gossip, probably invented because she seemed overly assiduous in listening to Ereleth. Anyway, the point is that we don't know what we'll be heading into if we cross the river, and given that we have reason to believe that the princess is still in the north . . .'

'It's not gossip,' Dhalla contradicted him belatedly. 'It's true. The princess inherited Serpent's blood from her mother.' The giant was still watching Koraismi, and had observed his adverse reaction to her claim. Taciturn and ponderous of manner she might be but she was by no means slow-witted.

'It doesn't mean anything,' Jacom said wearily. 'People can't and don't have Serpent's blood.'

'Nor Salamander's fire?' said Dhalla. 'In my country, they say giants have Salamander's fire in their hearts. Sometimes, I feel it here – *burning.*'

She tapped her ribs, beneath her left breast.

'It's just a metaphor,' Jacom said, uneasily aware of the fact that she must know that as well as he did. Either she was teasing him, or she was trying to suggest, delicately, that the allegation that the princess had Serpent's blood in her veins must mean *something*, even if it were not entirely clear *what*.

'Serpent's blood is bad witchery,' Koraismi whispered to Jacom. 'You should let this princess alone.'

If only I could! Jacom thought. 'It's all right,' he said to the boy, patting him on the head. 'Aulakh Phar has charms against bad witchery, just as he has charms against all other ills.'

Dhalla recognised the irony in this, and smiled.

'We're supposed to be on the same side, Dhalla,' Jacom said, trying to take some encouragement from the smile. 'We both want the princess to be safe. Remember that, when you have to decide which way you're going to go, and who you're going to trust.'

'I will,' she promised. There was no hint of mockery in her tone. As he turned to go, however, she added: 'Checuti is ours now – he belongs to Ereleth, and to the princess. Leave him to us. The amber too. Don't try to interfere, if you value your life.'

The naked threat unleashed a tide of angry resentment within him, but he fought hard to keep it hidden. He knew there was no point in arguing. He'd played his cards, and they weren't good enough to make any impression on her. In spite of the livery she wore she was yet another adversary, determined to thwart his one chance of reclaiming his careeer. It seemed that he had far too many adversaries, and not a single true friend on whom he could depend. In the circumstances, neither Fraxinus nor Purkin could be counted as a true friend – and if Dhalla was his enemy too, he was on his own against the whole world, with only a darklander boy to help him.

'She's bad,' Koraismi said, once they were at a safe distance. 'Tainted. Best stay away from her, and all things like her.'

'That might well be good advice,' Jacom admitted glumly, 'but those who live under the sun must share its light with all creatures. There's no safety from the taints which stain the world, not even in the Forest of Absolute Night.'

19

THE LEADER OF the Eblans, who had told Lucrezia that his name was Djemil Eyub, studied his two prisoners pensively. Elema studiously looked away, as if the man were beneath contempt, but Lucrezia stared back at him defiantly, challenging him with her eyes.

The princess had assured Eyub that there was no need for him to keep their hands tied, but he would not relent, although he did seem slightly ashamed of his refusal. The Eblans were clearly exhausted by whatever ordeals they had undergone. Once they had all assembled, the greater number had laid out sleeping-mats and thrown themselves down. There was an element of despair in their fear.

One man had been sent back to the ford to keep watch, while another had been stationed in the bushes where Lucrezia and Elema had stood. Apart from these two, only Eyub now remained awake, and only he was free to take an interest in the two women. He seemed harmless enough – he had touched Lucrezia only once, and that for the sole purpose of examining the texture of her clothing. He seemed far more ambivalent about her than Elema, whom he clearly regarded as an enemy by virtue of her pale skin. His men had not relished their encounter with the darklanders. Lucrezia grudgingly admitted to herself that his present attitude was understandable.

Lucrezia was able by now to meet Eyub's troubled gaze sternly. She had contrived to hide the signs of her grief over the loss of Hyry Keshvara. Although he was standing and she was sitting, and his hands were free while hers were not, she did not feel that the advantage was entirely his. She had watched the Eblans carefully while they made ready for sleep, and was confident that they were primitive by comparison with her own people. They had very little metal with them; almost all their cooking apparatus seemed to be made of stone and glass, even their knives, forks and spoons. Their clothes were well tailored, which suggested that they had good needles, but the saddles and harnesses their horses wore were crude.

Eyub came to a sudden decision and sat down in front of the princess, leaning forward so that he could speak to her in a low voice. 'You are not a native of the forest,' he said cautiously. 'You come from a city, as we do – a great city, so you say. How many people has it?'

'Two hundred thousand live within the city walls,' she informed him matter-of-factly. 'A further half-million live in the surrounding lands of Xandria itself. The western and southern provinces contain two million more. I don't know how many people live in the Thousand Isles, but there must be at least a million and a half, probably two. Say five million in the empire as a whole. What population has Ebla?'

'Not nearly as many,' he conceded. He spoke guardedly, trying to imply that Ebla might have been comparable with Xandria but happened to be a little smaller, but it was obvious that the figures Lucrezia had quoted were of an order of magnitude higher than he could have imagined.

'Where is Ebla, exactly?' Lucrezia asked, while his mind was still distracted by contemplation of the figures.

'It's the biggest of the river towns,' he said vaguely. 'It's rumoured that the Cities of the Plain in the far south have more people, but no one from that region has come to Ebla in my lifetime.'

'Do you mean this river?' she asked sharply.

'No. There's another river, much bigger and deeper than this one, which flows south from the Dragomite Hills. It passes through Ebla and several smaller towns before veering westwards into the Soursweet Marshes. You're a person of rank, I presume?'

Lucrezia had told him her given name but not her title; it was, however, obvious from her clothes – although they were rather dirty and ragged by now – and her unspoiled hands that she was a leisured person, unlike Elema. She contented herself with saying: 'I'm high-born, within the greatest empire in the whole world.' She was quick to add: 'I can speak for the empire; any treaties which I make will be honoured by my people.'

He was sceptical about that, as he had every right to be. 'There are some in Ebla who boast of their knowledge of the world,' he observed obliquely, 'but the loremasters claim that the globe's circumference is not less than sixty thousand kims. If so, it would take half a lifetime to ride around it, even if the road did not run through all kinds of unearthly wilderness. Who can possibly say that any city is the greatest in the whole world?'

'In Xandria we know more of the world than most,' she told him, unwilling to surrender the point even though his judgment seemed perfectly fair. 'We command the waters of the Slithery Sea, which may not be the largest ocean in the world but has the advantage of not being too shallow. Although it has very many islands the greater number have harbours usable by deep-keeled and fully laden ships. Our merchants trade with two thousand other cities, none as great as Xandria.'

'Ebla is a great city too,' Eyub told her, with equally stubborn pride. 'It has more water-mills than all the river towns put together, and better canals to irrigate the surrounding fields. We are by necessity a warrior race but we live in peace with our nearer neighbours. The dragomites have long been reckoned our enemies, but they never bothered us unduly until the plague came. When we realised that the nearer hills had been depopulated we set forth to explore the extent of the disaster. We did not expect to encounter the mound-women, although we have legends about girl-children being stolen by dragomites to serve as nest-slaves. Are the mound-women your allies? Do your merchants trade with them?'

'Dragomites are unknown in the lands north of the forest,' Lucrezia told him. 'Few men of Xandria have ever seen one, although our merchant-adventurers are prodigious travellers. The darklanders are our friends, but they too had only legends concerning humans associated with dragomites, until the forest was invaded. If darklanders attacked you, they must have mistaken you for the dragomite-people.'

'How could they do that?' Eyub wanted to know. 'Are we not men? Have we not horses to ride?'

'They regard the forest as their own territory,' Lucrezia said defensively. 'This is a time of crisis for them, and they are apprehensive. Some among them are talking of the end of the world. The warriors who attacked you made a mistake, which needs to be repaired. You have nothing to fear from Elema, and would be wise to befriend her before more darklanders pass this way, lest another mistake should be made.'

Eyub spared Elema a passing glance. She continued to ignore him; she refused to speak to him while her hands were tied. Lucrezia wondered whether she ought to have been similarly proud.

'Are you, then, a merchant-adventurer?' Eyub asked of Lucrezia.

'My erstwhile companion is – or was,' she countered. 'The falling tree which brought your men here carried her away in its crown. She must have been stung by a flowerworm while trying to obtain a clearer sight of your men.'

Eyub arched a sceptical eyebrow at this, although he must have deduced from the horses and the outlay of their camp that Lucrezia had had another companion.

'We were waiting here to join a much larger company,' Lucrezia added cautiously. 'They should be here any day. They are more than a dozen strong, and very well armed, but they will do you no harm if you meet them peaceably. Elema and I can both be useful to you as intermediaries, but if you insist on keeping us prisoner you will surely invite the enmity of our friends.'

So this is the game of diplomacy, she thought proudly. *I believe I have a talent for it.* She knew, however, that the proper time for self-congratulation would not arrive until her hands were freed.

'Where is this *larger company* going?' Eyub asked quietly. 'And why?'

There seemed to be no reason to withhold that information, so she answered promptly and accurately. 'Rumour had reached Xandria that it might now be possible, for the first time in many generations, to cross the Dragomite Hills. My friend had earlier bought goods in the forest which were said to have come from the Navel of the World.'

She was about to add that these goods had been supplied by bronze men, but thought better of it. The Eblans seemed to be at odds with so many people that mention of another group might complicate matters further. Instead, she said: 'Perhaps it was your people who sold these things to my friend?'

Eyub shook his head pensively. 'The Navel of the World and the so-called Chimera's Cradle are mere myths,' he told her firmly. 'They're said to lie in the far south-west, beyond Salamander's Fire and the Silver Thorns, but no one who values his life has gone into those regions for centuries. Whoever sold the things you mention must have been lying about their origins, perhaps to boost the price. They might have been from one of the downriver towns, whose people are somewhat given to lying – but they might not.' His tone implied that the latter possibility was the more ominous.

'Wherever they came from,' Lucrezia said, 'the fact that they came at all was enough to excite interest in Xandria. My companion and others were anxious to discover whether there was indeed a road through the Dragomite Hills.'

'I can assure you that there is no road,' said Eyub, with a short, barking laugh. 'But there is a way of sorts, littered with dead dragomites and the putrefying produce of their unearthly fields. The world is changing, it seems. There has been a great shift in the fortunes of the dragomites – and also, it is said, of the Serpents in the west. I cannot believe that the world is ending, but I could believe that it is the beginning of the end for everything unearthly – which I would reckon a good thing, although the mound-women might not agree.'

'The darklanders certainly wouldn't,' Lucrezia observed. 'The trees which make up this forest are themselves unearthly. Perhaps that's why they're so anxious. Perhaps they fear – and justifiably so – that the blight might spread from the hills to the forest. There is little that is unearthly in the lands around Ebla, I take it?'

'Ebla and its neighbours occupy the best and purest land to be found between the Soursweet Marshes and the Spangled Desert,' he said proudly. 'our ancestors often had to hold it against invaders, and we remain as zealous as they to root out any and all unearthly things which threaten to become established there.'

That was not the philosophy of the bronze men who sold Hyry Keshvara the seeds which drew me into this affair, Lucrezia thought. *These are simple-minded folk – more simple-minded, in their way, than the darklanders, who make more complicated calculations as to what might be reckoned tainted.*

'You've been forced to stray further from your homeland than you would have liked, I believe,' she said carefully. 'You didn't cross the ford hoping to make friends on this side of the river, I think – you've been *driven* north by angry pursuers.'

Eyub did not confirm this guess, but the manner of his silence led her to conclude that she was right. Perhaps the Eblans had never intended to enter the forest, nor would have had it not been for their unexpected encounter with the dragomites' human allies.

'My friends are peaceful men,' Lucrezia said. 'They're interested in exploration and the possibility of opening new trade-routes. The darklanders are not barbarians, even though they live simply, and they aren't inclined to wage war against their neighbours unless they're threatened, as they were by the recent incursion of dragomites. They attacked you because of a misunderstanding, but they aren't your enemies, and will become your friends – as they are ours – if you let them. Many of them know what it is to fight dragomites, and will pay you the respect you deserve if you are dragomite-fighters too. Is it not so, Elema?'

Elema was perfectly prepared to talk to Lucrezia, if not to Eyub. 'It is true,' she said calmly. 'I could take these men to a meeting of the Uluru, so that they could explain who and what they are. The Uluru could teach them signs which would announce them to all darklander warriors as friends.'

'And I could speak on your behalf to my friends,' Lucrezia added, speaking directly to the Eblan leader. 'Perhaps we can combine forces, to make sure that we can cross the southern reaches of the forest and the Dragomite Hills in safety. You might sell your services as guides if you already know a safe way through the hills, and you would certainly benefit from being allied with a heavily armed company like ours.'

Eyub was unprepared to take all this on trust, although he must have desired very ardently to believe it. 'When can you make good these fine promises?' he asked suspiciously.

'As soon as you will permit it,' Lucrezia said, hoping that it might be true – although she was uncomfortably aware of the fact that she could not be certain of a warm welcome from Carus Fraxinus and Aulakh Phar now that Hyry was not with her.

'I must think carefully about what you have told me,' he said, with uneasy formality. 'I fear that I'm very tired. When dawn comes and my men have rested we will speak again . . . until then, I fear, I must keep you tied. I'm truly sorry.'

The princess opened her mouth to protest, but then thought better of it. Eyub was a long way from home, and things had obviously gone badly for him. The prospect of doubling the strength of his company for the return journey southwards – and increasing its steel a hundredfold – would in the end prove irresistible, but he dared not take everything she had said on trust, and he must be aware of the grave risks involved in greeting a superior force of total strangers with open arms. Lucrezia understood that.

She also understood, of course, that his natural anxieties were not entirely unjustified. Knowing her father and his ministers as she did, Lucrezia did not doubt that they would delight in the notion of adding yet another city to the empire's list of subject states, even though Ebla was so far away that it could never be anything but a client of Xandrian mercantile endeavours. A nation as iron-poor as Ebla seemed to be might be very vulnerable to that kind of trade even though it had nothing to fear from Xandria's armies.

Eyub had already risen to go to his bed, but he paused. 'These things that were brought across the hills from the southern side and sold to your friend,' he said, speculatively. 'What were they?'

Lucrezia hesitated, but she didn't want to seem overly evasive or be caught out in a downright lie. 'I encountered only one of them,' she confessed. 'It was said to be a marvel – a kind of thorn-bush which grows from seeds planted in human flesh – but I never saw it brought to full maturity.'

'That is a vile thing,' said Eyub uneasily. It was not entirely clear whether he had ever heard of such a plant before or not. 'We take great pains to banish such unearthly horrors from our lands. It sounds to me like Serpent witchcraft. Do your people trade with Serpents?'

'Serpents are sometimes seen in the cities of the far west, I believe,' she admitted, 'but they keep themselves to themselves. They're said to be quite harmless.'

He snorted expressively. It was obvious that Serpents were not said to be harmless in Ebla.

'The darklanders never trade with Serpents,' she added, thinking that she ought not to give Eyub's men any more reasons to be wary of the forest people. 'The goods in question were brought into the forest by men.'

'Mound-women?' Eyub countered.

Lucrezia was not certain whether or not it was a rhetorical question. 'No,' she said, to be on the safe side. 'Ordinary men, much like you or me.'

He looked down at her darkly. There was a great deal for him to think about, and to worry about. It wouldn't be easy for him to go to sleep, no matter how exhausted he might be.

He turned and walked away.

Lucrezia breathed a sigh of relief, realising for the first time how tense she had been. She felt that she had acquitted herself well, and that she might yet succeed in becoming a great peacemaker, a true mover in the fortunes of cities and empires.

Hyry would have been proud of me, she thought – but the thought brought tears to her eyes again.

'Don't be afraid,' Elema whispered. 'All will be well in the morning. You cast your spell cleverly, little witch. You have him in the palm of your hand.'

It was a sincere compliment, and Lucrezia accepted it as such – although the metaphor was not a happy one, given that the palms of her hands were uncomfortably jammed together by the cord that was cutting into her wrists.

'Try to sleep,' the old woman advised. 'Tomorrow might be a long day.'

Tomorrow, Lucrezia thought, *Fraxinus and Phar will surely arrive. If they had only got here one day sooner, Hyry would be alive and I would be free, and . . . why is the world such a stubborn place, where loose ends never quite meet? But this is not the end; it is the beginning. Tomorrow, I shall be an ambassador, a healer, a player in the game. This is what I wanted, and what I wanted to be . . .*

She realised then that Djemil Eyub was not the only one who was going to have great difficulty in going to sleep.

20

ANDRIS RAISED HIS head and looked down dazedly at the bandages which were wrapped around his right wrist and hand. He could feel another bandage wrapped tightly about his skull, and cool ribbons of woundglue winding about the contours of his face in grotesque confusion. His head was swimming, and he quickly lowered it to the pillow again, fighting to keep hold of consciousness.

He felt far worse now than he had after being injured by the guardsman's spear during his escape from Xandria. The night-cloak had mauled him badly, and the ride through the forest had been far longer than the ride through the byways outside the city wall.

'My head hurts,' he complained.

'I'm not surprised,' said a tender voice, whose solicitousness was extremely welcome.

'Merel?' he said, trying to focus his eyes. He realised that the grey blur above his head was in fact an awning of some kind, lit by a single candle. He also realised that the strange feeling of movement which he had was not so strange after all, given that he was lying in a wagon which was indeed on the move. He found Merel's face at last, and looked her in the eyes. She smiled, evidently happy that he was back in the land of the living. He recovered a vague memory of dismounting from a horse while Merel ran to greet him.

'It's all right,' she said reassuringly. 'We're in Aulakh Phar's cart, heading south. Your wrist isn't broken, and the other wounds will heal. The scars will make you look fierce, but not much uglier than you already are. We're perfectly safe – until we run into the dragomites. Even then, Phar has some aromatic potion which will supposedly make them leave us alone.'

Andris remembered how he had come to hurt himself. 'Is Ereleth alive?' he asked sharply.

'Yes. Don't worry – she's in the other cart. She's awake now, and her injuries are no more serious than yours, although they laid her low for a little while. Checuti told me what she did. I can understand why you were so desperate to rescue her that you nearly got killed. He gave the young darklanders a rousing account of how you tackled a nightcloak with your bare hands, and they think you're a great hero – unlike Captain Cerri, of course. He doesn't like you, even though I've explained that you're not to blame for his misfortunes.'

'Cerri? Is he here? Why?' Andris recovered another vague memory. Yes, there had indeed been guardsmen looking when he had tumbled from his horse. Those silly red skirts . . .

'The same thing as everyone else,' Merel informed him. 'He's looking for Keshvara and the missing princess. If they ever do manage to catch us up, there'll be quite a competition to decide what happens to the prize. She, apparently, wants to join the expedition, but the handsome young captain's career will be ruined if he can't take her back to Xandria. I still want to wring her neck because of what she intended to do to you – and Ereleth seems to have secret plans of her own which she's disinclined to share with anyone.'

'The Grey Waste,' said Andris off-handedly.

'What about the Grey Waste?'

'I think that's where Ereleth wants to take the princess. I don't know why – something to do with Serpents and secret commandments. She's not here, then – the princess, I mean.'

'There's been no sign of her since we left Khalorn. Fraxinus is afraid that something might have happened to Keshvara. She'd have been safe enough on the road, he says, but if she had to go across country because the princess was with her they'd have made a tempting target for bandits. Tomorrow, apparently, we should reach a river crossing. Fraxinus says that if Keshvara's not there, waiting for us, she must have got into trouble, but we've met darklanders who crossed there very recently, and they didn't see any sign of her. What Ereleth and the guardsmen will do if she isn't there, I wouldn't like to guess. Checuti's asked Ereleth, of course, but she won't say.'

'Perhaps she'll be so grateful to me for saving her life,' Andris said, without much conviction, 'that she'll give me something to kill that filthy worm she made me swallow, and let me go my own way.'

'Perhaps,' said Merel, reaching out to touch his cheek gently. She mustered a little more conviction than he had, but Andris knew that she'd had a lot more practice in the art of dissimulation.

The wagon rocked as someone else scrambled aboard at the rear. Andris didn't bother trying to raise his head again; he waited for the newcomer to sit down beside Merel. It was Checuti.

'I thought I heard voices,' the thief-master said. 'I'm glad Phar didn't over-estimate his healing gifts – it seems that you're the only friend I have hereabouts. Even the boy who belongs to the Uluru seems to be fast friends with the surly guard-captain, and I still haven't forgiven Fraxinus for telling the guard-captain where to find me that night we fell into Ereleth's untender clutches.'

'It it weren't for you,' Merel pointed out, 'Andris wouldn't be in this mess. If you'd only left us alone instead of playing that stupid trick at the inn, everything would be fine.'

'You see – even your delightful cousin is annoyed with me,' Checuti said to Andris, in a hurt tone. 'Remind her, if you will, that if I hadn't made a last-minute adjustment to include you in my grand plan, you'd be working for the stonemasons on the Great Wall by now, with nothing to look forward to but a lifetime of back-breaking labour.'

'The world of ifs is an infinite wilderness of lost opportunity,' Andris quoted drily.

'What bores the forefathers must have been,' Checuti remarked, with a contrived sigh. 'Do you think they spoke in solemn aphorisms all the time, or did they sometimes curse and lie like common folk? But you're right, of course – let's not lose ourselves in a desert of regrets. The real question is, what do we do next?'

'Who's this *we*?' Andris complained. 'The only *we* I have in mind right now is myself and Merel. Any plans I make are highly unlikely to include you.'

'I understand how you feel,' Checuti assured him, with a sigh that was almost as contrived as the previous one, 'but our fates have been bound together by that damned witch and her pet giant. She has something we both want – something we direly need, if her word can be trusted – and we'll stand a better chance of getting it if we pool our resources. I was hoping that Phar might be able to help, but he says that this worm isn't something he's encountered, and he has no idea how to stop it breeding. He seems sceptical about its supposed capabilities, but it's easy for him to dismiss it as a bluff when he doesn't have anything to lose. We'll have to make the most of what few advantages we have – including your injured arm.'

'How is that an advantage?' Merel wanted to know. 'Do you think Ereleth might be persuaded to release Andris because he hurt himself defending her?'

'Only if pigs can fly,' Checuti said bitterly. 'Queens don't recognise moral debts the way we thieves and pirates do. What I mean is that while your drawing hand is useless, the smudged and smeared map which presently exists – which Ereleth's pet giant still has in her possession, hoarded for the witch-queen's vile advantage – can't be replaced. Now, if anyone should happen to bring that map to you and ask you to explain it, or ask you to draw another, the sensible thing to do is to procrastinate. While you're still of some use to them, Fraxinus and Phar won't want Ereleth to take you back up north to search for the princess in Khalorn.'

'But surely you want to go north again,' Merel objected. 'That's where all your loot is.'

'Not if Captain Cerri and his men are along for the ride,' Checuti said. 'Neither of us wants to be given into his care – and I have a nasty feeling that Ereleth might try to make a deal with the captain and his men if and when she decides to part company with Fraxinus. He's just about desperate enough to trust her if she says she'll intercede for him with Belin, even though that stupid giant's as good as told him that Ereleth has no intention of going back to Xandria.'

'It's all too complicated for me,' Andris complained, weakly. 'My head hurts worse than ever now. I think I need another day's sleep. I've taken more punishment in the last twelve days than in all the previous twelve years.'

'You're as tough as they come,' Checuti assured him. 'Twice as tough as poor Burdam, who's probably still lying on the floor of that meeting-house. From now on, I want you as my right-hand man – and if you've any sense you'll take the job. Just let me do the thinking, and I'll get us all out of this in one piece. Believe me, we three will make a great team.'

Merel expressed her scepticism with a wordless grunt, but she took care to look away from Checuti while she did so. She wasn't brave enough to meet his ironic eye. She seemed glad when the awning to her right was pulled back, giving her a slightly belated excuse for looking in that direction.

Aulakh Phar clambered over the back of the driver's bench, having presumably handed the reins over to someone else. He must have heard every word that had been spoken, but Checuti didn't seem in the least put out by that thought.

The look which the two men exchanged wasn't exactly hostile, but it couldn't have been described as warm. Phar's expression implied that he considered Checuti's existence in the same world to be a nuisance he could well do without, but Checuti's answering smile was slyly tolerant.

'Anyway, I'm delighted that you're feeling better, my friend,' Checuti said to Andris, in his most amiable tone. 'I'll leave you in Phar's capable hands – do let me know if there's anything you need.'

Phar watched the thief-master make his way to the rear of the wagon, and waited until he had vaulted down before greeting Andris.

'You'll feel better soon,' the physician assured him. 'The cuts were bad, but you've got a very solid skull. You certainly saved Ereleth's life, but Dhalla just as certainly saved yours, so the old witch probably doesn't think she owes you any favours. If you really have got a worm in your gut that could eat you alive, she's not going to kill it for you just yet.'

'Thanks for the prognosis,' Andris said unenthusiastically.

'I'm just the doctor,' Phar reminded. 'I only bring the bad news – I don't make it. I'm on your side, and not just because Fraxinus and I would still like a decent map. I'd like things to be a little less complicated too – an under-strength expedition heading into dangerous territory needs all the extra members it can recruit, but it's no good if they're all at one another's throats. If I can persuade Ereleth to lift this stupid curse she's put on you I will. We need your sword-arm as well as your drawing-hand – and you need better friends than Checuti.'

'I dare say you're right,' Andris admitted.

'Let's hope that we find the princess tomorrow,' Phar said. 'If she and Keshvara are at the ford we might be able to sort everything out. I don't say it'll be easy, but until we find the princess we'll all be constantly at one another's throats. Once she's got what she wants, we'll have a good chance of persuading Queen Ereleth to see reason . . . and Captain Cerri too.'

'You ought to persuade Ereleth to tell you what she already knows – or thinks she knows,' Andris told him sombrely. 'I'm not sure what significance you and Fraxinus have read into this business of the blighted hills, but she thinks it means something too. Did you hear what I said about her wanting to take the princess to the Grey Waste?'

Phar nodded his ancient and bird-like head. 'The princess is said to have Serpent's blood,' he observed. 'That means something to Ereleth . . . perhaps she expects it to mean something to the Serpents too. She's not exactly keen to talk things over with Fraxinus at present – he and she seem to rub one another up the wrong way – but things might change if Hyry and the princess do meet us at the ford.'

'Something very strange is happening, isn't it?' Merel said. 'Something that's never happened before, in all the time that humans have been in the world.'

'Perhaps,' Aulakh Phar replied cautiously. 'On the other hand, if it's never happened before, why does Ereleth think she knows how to respond? Fraxinus has got a bee in his bonnet about the so-called *Apocrypha of Genesys*, after hearing what that blind man had to say, but it's all so vague it's too easy to read things into it. It would be truly amazing if there were any hidden meaning in such ancient lore. How could the forefathers possibly have known that something of this sort would one day happen – thousands or tens of thousands of years in their future? If all this stuff about Serpent's blood and the secret commandments makes sense, it must be a very peculiar kind of sense.'

Andris wished that he could laugh dismissively, but Phar's manner was too earnest. 'Is there any other kind?' he asked. 'The more I see of it, the more I think that the world's an exceedingly peculiar place, which wasn't made for simple folk like me.'

'It's a very big place,' said Merel, in a faintly aggrieved tone.

'There's probably room in it for all of us, if only people would let us alone.'

'All worlds are small,' Phar told her, with a smile that seemed to have no humour in it at all. 'They only seem to be so big – and so peculiar – because we're so small and so limited in what we can carry in our heads. If there's any truth at all in the lore, we've only been here for a short period of time, in terms of the age of the world. Our forefathers' invasion seems to have been a success, but if Fraxinus is right, from the very first day that our remotest ancestors landed their marvellous ship we've been fighting a long war of attrition against the things that were already here. So far, earthly order has held out against unearthly decay, just as the walls of Xandria have held out against invasion . . . but it seems to me that it's a war which, by its nature, can never be finally won. Fraxinus thinks that we might have been losing it for thousands of years without being fully aware of the fact. For him, that's what this expedition is all about.'

'But you don't agree?' Merel said, that seeming to be the implication of his tone of voice.

'I'm only in it for the profit,' Phar said – but he didn't say it as if he expected to be believed.

'So am I,' Andris said. 'Unfortunately, you have to break even before you can start making a profit . . . and you have to survive before you can break even.'

'Don't worry,' Phar told him. 'We've a way to go yet before things get desperate. I'll do what I can to ensure your survival. Fraxinus and I need a right-hand man just as badly as Checuti does, and ours is the nobler purpose. In addition to which, we're presently in a position to pay more. Bear that in mind if you have to decide where your loyalties lie.'

'I will,' Andris assured him. Privately, however, he reminded himself that when it came to deciding where his loyalties might lie, Ereleth had the whip hand, and the most vital currency of all safely tucked away in her pouch.

When Phar had gone, Merel said: 'You're right; you do need more sleep. Things will look better tomorrow. And whatever happens – *whatever* happens – I'll be here. No matter whose right-hand man you are, I'm yours. Believe me, that leaves you better off than you've ever been before – and don't laugh, or I'll twist your wrist till you beg for mercy.'

'Oh no,' he said, rejoicing in the fact that his horrible predicament was not entirely devoid of gladness. 'You're absolutely right. Just as long as you're there when I wake up, tomorrow will be a better day than all my yesterdays put together. Come worms, come dragomites, come man-eating bushes and all the darkland demons that were ever glimpsed in the most hideously nightmarish of dreams . . . I can face them all.'

'The only problem is,' she said softly, 'that you might have to.'

Part Three

Into the Dragomite Hills, Hurried on by the Tide of Happenstance

We may not raise mountains or hollow out the ocean depths, nor may we set a moon within the sky. We may devise seasons in calendars and mine salt from the soil, but we may not set the world atilt nor make the seas as salty as our blood. We must live in the world as we find it, not as we dream it, but we cannot help dreaming the dreams which rise from the depths of our being, and we cannot entirely resist the temptations of prophecy.

Here, then, is prophecy born of dreams to suckle at the breast of hope: though change be eternal, corruption can be checked; though death comes to every living thing, life may be the victor in the war against decay; though the world be at odds with our blood and our hearts, it is ours to rule if only we can contrive to steady our governing hand.

The Apocrypha of Genesys

I

LUCREZIA WOKE UP with a sudden start, but didn't know what it was that had startled her until she opened her eyes.

Elema's ancient face was very close to hers. The darklander wore an expression of deep concern, which seemed to Lucrezia to be cause for considerable anxiety. The princess knew that the old woman must have touched her gently in order to bring her back from sleep. She had sense enough not to make a sound.

It was still dark, but the sky was brightening upriver; a new dawn was on the point of breaking.

Elema reached out to touch Lucrezia's cheek, and Lucrezia realised, somewhat belatedly, that the darklander had managed to free her hands. The princess immediately made as if to roll over so that Elema could start work on the cords knotted about her own wrists, but the old woman shook her head. 'No time,' she mouthed silently. 'Lie still.'

The darklander's eyes were darting back and forth, her gaze never settling. Lucrezia realised that the ancient was very frightened, and that her warnings had to do with something far more serious than the possibility of waking the Eblans.

Disregarding Elema's advice, Lucrezia tried to raise herself into a sitting position. The camp was quiet, but not silent; the horses were astir. There was no sign of anything amiss except for Elema's attitude, but that was indication enough for Lucrezia. She looked wildly about, trying to figure out what the danger was, and from which direction it was coming.

Elema suddenly came to her feet, sparing the princess a single apologetic glance, and ran.

No shout of alarm followed the darklander, and Lucrezia deduced that the Eblans were wide open to attack, their sentries having gone to sleep or – even worse – been quietly eliminated.

The old woman ran downriver, and that was clue enough to tell Lucrezia which way to look for whatever was coming. She looked upriver, and had not long to wait.

There was no warning – the sentry who had been posted at the ford was presumably dead. By the time one of the recumbent men reacted, it was far too late. The enemy came swiftly, with weapons at the ready, and it was obvious to Lucrezia that their intention was to cut down as many of the Eblans as they could before a hand could be raised against them.

The first warning that was shouted out turned into a scream before it was fully formed, but it was a lusty scream and it must have cut through the most languorous dream like a rusty sawblade.

Once alerted to their peril the Eblans wasted no time in puzzlement; they had been living under threat for so long that they were on the very edge of panic even while they slept. They leapt up and reached for their weapons – but their weapons were a sorry lot, including more quarter-staffs and clubs than spears. Such blades as they had were short, and their bows and arrows were of little use in the kind of conflict which had been thrust upon them.

Some of the Eblans tried to run for their tethered horses without pausing to pluck their scattered belongings from the ground, but while they tried to free their mounts their enemies were already on top of them, hacking this way and that with their own clubs and stone-headed axes. One of the Eblans had his bow in his hands, with an arrow ready notched, and he managed to loose off a close-range shot at the marauders. The arrow flew straight, but struck a broad breastplate of some material Lucrezia had never seen before. The breastplate was evidently strong enough to ward off a direct hit even at that range, and did not break even though its wearer stumbled backwards under the force of the impact.

The attackers were wearing helmets as well as breastplates, which masked their faces and gave them the look of nightmarish beasts, but their leather-clad arms and legs were plainly human. As if their superior armour and the advantage of surprise were not enough, they outnumbered the Eblans at least three to two.

Lucrezia saw the sense in Elema's warning now. This would be a massacre rather than a battle, and her best hope of survival might be to play dead. With her hands tied behind her back her own breast presented a wide-open target, and she might easily be slain by a single blow – but she did not lie down. She stayed where she was, half-sitting, so she could watch the unfolding scene and savour all its horror. She shrank backwards, pressing herself against the resistant branches of one of the bushes which lined the river bank, but she made no real effort to wriggle into the body of the bush.

The attackers' hands and the flesh that was visible at their necks told Lucrezia that they were pale goldens, almost but not quite ambers. They were certainly not kin to the Eblans. The cut of the clothes they wore beneath their armour was markedly different, as was the style of their weaponry. They carried as little metal as the men they had come to kill, and had tried to make good the deficit with glass and ceramics, but they favoured axes and maces over spears and quarter-staffs. Any disadvantage they suffered in terms of reach seemed more than compensated by their speed and agility. The Eblans were obviously used to fighting from horseback, but the newcomers had no horses, and they had evidently devoted all their training to the skills of fighting on foot.

The horny material of which the attackers' armour was made was also to be seen in the heads of their short stabbing-spears, but it was their helmets which showed it off most gaudily. Most were black or red-brown, but a few were iridescent green. All of them were very oddly decorated, with dangling filaments not unlike plaits of coarse hair and strange wing-like projections at the front. These fearsome apparitions hurled themselves upon the unready Eblans as if they were fighting dogs avid for blood.

Djemil Eyub had not tried to run to the horses; he had remained where he was when he came upright from his sleeping-mat. He tried to rally his men with a cry, but only one ran to stand beside him. Eyub had snatched up a weapon which was essentially a quarter-staff, although its two ends had been carefully weighted with twin rounded stones to give it a little extra power when twirled or jabbed; at first he used it to stab at the attackers' bodies, hoping to knock them backwards, aiming for the axe-wielding arms and the helmeted heads. He struck out at elbows and forearms, with accuracy and noticeable effect. He forced at least three weapons to be dropped as his blows brought howls of pain from the assailants thus disarmed – but the warriors in question could not be put out of the battle by such tricks, and there were too many of them.

Had Eyub's men been as clever as he was they might have grouped and mounted sufficient defence to stave off defeat for ten or twelve minutes, but they were not. Two men standing together could put up a better show than one alone, but there were a dozen axe-wielding dancers capering around them, taking turns to dart forward and strike. Eyub was agile enough to dodge two such rushes, but the third feinted with an ornamental club to send him the wrong way, then changed the manner of the thrust. Eyub adjusted his defence but was tripped by a trailing root. He used his staff to help himself back to his feet, but he would not have been allowed to do it had it not been for the protection provided by his companion, who hurled his spear like a javelin at the attacker who came to make sure that the fallen man stayed down. Then it was Eyub's turn to defend his rescuer, lashing out yet again with the staff as more axe-wielders came to take the place of their bruised comrades.

The ferocity of the onslaught was awesome. Within a minute half the Eblans were down and dead, while not one attacker had sustained a mortal wound. Within another minute most of the men who had run to the horses had been cut down, and still the marauders had not suffered a single serious casualty.

It was obvious to Lucrezia that the Eblans had neither the heart nor the stomach for a fight of this kind – they wanted to run, and would have if they could, but they were given neither time nor space to flee. Now none remained standing except for Djemil Eyub, his close companion and one other, and they were doomed. Lucrezia saw that they had the advantage of height over their tormentors – although they were by no means tall by Xandrian standards – and probably had greater reserves of brute strength, but they could hardly land a telling blow on their opponents.

The lone Eblan was dodging back and forth between riderless horses, trying to use them as living shields. The tactic served him reasonably well, but he had no chance to find a real avenue of escape. Lucrezia saw his enemies corner him twice, but on each occasion it was his blow rather than theirs which told, and for a moment she thought he might win the time to mount up and make use of the horse's strength and aggression – but when his adversaries closed upon him for a third time he was caught by two opponents at once, and could not move his own weapon cleverly enough to counter both of theirs. After a flurry of desperate thrusts he went down, and stayed down.

For almost a minute Eyub and his friend had forced their own opponents to draw back cautiously. They had established a clear space around their station, but this was not really a victory. They had slain no one, and they were trapped – their only achievement was to force their adversaries to pause and make a plan. They had the relatively bare bole of a gnarlytree behind them, and were thus able to stand angled back to back, like two points of a triangle. Their weapons had sufficient reach to intimidate any attackers who might come one by one, and none did – but as the field of battle was finally cleared, more and more armoured warriors became available to keep Eyub and his companion hemmed in.

There was a brief pause as the attackers gathered and grouped – a moment when it must have been in Eyub's mind to surrender, had any such opportunity been offered – but his enemies were in no mood to stop short of their objective.

When Lucrezia saw that the Eblans' pursuers had no objective in mind save for the annihilation of their foe she felt a sharp pang of terror – but no one had as yet come forward to smash or stab her; she could not even be certain that any of the marauders had deigned to notice her. She wished that Elema had had time to untie her hands, and that she had a good metal blade with which to defend herself – preferably something carefully anointed with deadly venom on tip and blade alike – but she knew how futile such wishes were. She knew, too, that there was nothing in her armoury of poisons that could be relied upon to bring her safely through such a situation as this.

If the helmeted figures were determined to take no prisoners, she would be dead before she ever got the chance to see their faces.

Eyub was still lashing out with his quarter-staff, trying desperately to use each end in quick succession. He disarmed one more adversary and hurt another, but then the end of his weapon was caught and held. While he tried to wrench it free another armoured figure leapt forward to grapple with him.

Within a few seconds it was all over. Eyub's brave defender went down too, caught out by the impossibility of trying to ward off three weapons at once.

The attackers were jostling one another now for the opportunity to get in a blow at the last of their victims. Lucrezia could not tell how badly Eyub and his companion were being hacked about because she could not see through the crowd.

The few seconds which passed before the armoured figures turned away from their gruesome work seemed unnaturally extended to Lucrezia, who was anticipating the moment when they would direct their attention to her with much trepidation. When that eventually happened, she felt that she had already lived through the moment, and that their slow approach was something she had already experienced, perhaps a thousand times. It seemed unreal.

They came to stand in a semicircle, looking down at her from the eye-slits in their horrid masks. For the princess, time came almost to a standstill, and did not resume its normal pace until one of them – perhaps the leader – reached up with oddly delicate hands to remove a glossy black helmet which looked as if it had been forged from the carapace of a huge beetle.

The face which emerged from behind the mask seemed unnaturally devoid of expression, but that was a trivial matter. What astonished Lucrezia was that the face was obviously female, and rather beautiful in its peculiar fashion. She guessed even before the others copied the first and removed their own helmets that they were all female. She felt a sudden flood of intuitive relief as she made a further guess that she – unlike the Eblans – was in no immediate danger, simply by virtue of her sex.

She found her voice, and said: 'My name is Lucrezia. I am from Xandria, which is a city far to the north of the Forest of Absolute Night. I am not your enemy.'

There was no reply to this. The ring of faces presented no changes of expression; the women continued to study her minutely. Her own skin was considered delicately pale in the Inner Sanctum, but it wasn't as pale as the complexions which now confronted her. There was nothing of the darklander about these faces, however. Lucrezia had no doubts as to the origin of their peculiar armour. These, she knew, were the mysterious companions of the dragomites: Djemil Eyub's 'mound-women'. The rumour of a great and conclusive victory won by the darklanders over the dragomites and their demonic companions was evidently

324

exaggerated. A darkland warband would undoubtedly have presented more vigorous resistance to the kind of attack she had just witnessed than the exhausted Eblans had contrived to muster, but they could not have been sure of a significantly better outcome.

'The Eblans took me prisoner,' Lucrezia said, when she tired of waiting to be asked a question. 'I would be very grateful if you would be kind enough to untie my hands.'

Still there was no answer to her overtures, and no one made any move to comply with her request. The one who had been first to remove her helmet raised a hand to make a curt sign, but it was not directed at the sitting princess. Most of her companions turned away, scattering as they did so. Some went to look at the fallen Eblans, others to collect the untethered horses, others to gather together the various goods strewn about the battlefield.

In the meantime, their leader continued to look down in her stony-faced fashion, paying close attention to the details of Lucrezia's clothing.

Lucrezia had begun to wonder whether the women knew human language at all when she finally spoke. 'Xandria,' she said, in a remarkably flat tone. 'You come from Xandria.'

'That's right,' Lucrezia confirmed. 'I have friends nearby – traders. They have all manner of goods to offer, including metal implements. They are far better equipped to fight than the men you just slaughtered or the darklanders you might have encountered south of the river, but they are not your enemies. They would be pleased to befriend you.'

'We have not forgotten Xandria,' the armoured woman remarked impassively. 'It has a high wall, has it not?'

'Very high,' Lucrezia informed her, concealing her surprise, 'and very solid.'

'We have higher walls by far,' the other assured her. 'Walls impenetrable to anyone who does not serve the dragomite queen.'

'The Dragomite Hills,' Lucrezia said evenly. 'We have heard that a great catastrophe has come to the hills – have you come into the forest in search of help? We will gladly give it, if we can.'

All the woman would condescend to say in the face of such generosity was: 'You need not fear that we will harm you.' Delivered in a markedly unenthusiastic tone, it was not a reassuring statement. Having heard it, Lucrezia wasn't overly

325

surprised when the woman turned away without showing the least inclination to free her hands.

Djemil Eyub left me tied because he was afraid, Lucrezia thought, *and he was not so contemptuous as to refuse to tell me who he was. This one is afraid of nothing, but she will not set me free. And she will not deign to tell me her name. A pox on politeness, then.*

'Why did you kill the Eblans?' she called after the retreating figure. 'They could not have harmed you.'

The armoured woman turned to look back at her, pausing in her stride. 'They attacked us,' she said flatly. 'This is how we deal with those who attack us. We are warriors, after all.' She did not continue on her way, though – for the first time she seemed curious to see how Lucrezia would respond.

Did you come all this way because you were attacked in the hills? Lucrezia wondered. *I can't believe that. If you didn't come in search of help, you must have come in search of land. Do you intend to found new Dragomite Hills in Khalorn – and eventually in Xandria itself? If so, you have surprises in store. Wait until you see real cavalry, instead of these ragged mounted bandits. Wait until you have Xandria's finest to face, on an open plain without trees or bushes, with their steel-headed lances and their sabres. Then you might see an authentic battle . . . and might easily be on the receiving end of a massacre.*

The princess struggled to her feet. 'The four best horses and the two donkeys are mine,' she stated firmly. 'Their packs contain goods which I intend to trade. Your people might be very interested in what they contain. Have you a queen of your own, or are you merely slaves of the dragomites?'

'The horses *were* yours,' the woman replied. 'Now they – and you – belong to us.'

'That is not the way of civilised folk,' Lucrezia said, as boldly as she could. 'In Xandria, we abide by the law, and we expect others to respect our property.'

'In the Corridors of Power,' her new captor said contemptuously, 'there is no law but the word of the mound-queen, who is the human voice of the dragomite queen. We are her warriors, not her slaves. Her will is our will, her life is ours.'

Perhaps, Lucrezia thought, *the game of diplomacy is not quite as easy as I thought. It seems that my talent for it is to be subjected to a severe test. But I'm ready. Whatever you are and whatever you intend, I'm ready.* These were, however, merely the words that she brought to the forefront of her mental arena; behind and beneath them was a deeper, more honest layer of thought, whose echoes were decidedly querulous. *If only Hyry Keshvara were here!* wailed this tiny and tremulous voice. *If only Carus Fraxinus and Aulakh Phar can get here in time . . .*

2

WHEN THE NEWS of the massacre which had taken place ahead of them first reached the caravan – and flew from head to tail with astonishing alacrity – Jacom Cerri's first thought was to ride forward with instructions that everyone in the long column must stay in tight formation, with their weapons ready. He quelled the impulse, reminding himself he was not in a position to give orders here, and that he ought not to annoy Carus Fraxinus by overstepping his allotted mark. He contented himself by speaking to his own men, although they were hardly in need of warnings to be careful. His next thought was to get the best information possible as to what had happened, and for this purpose he naturally went directly to Koraismi, even though he had to dismount in order to talk to the boy, thus renewing the pain in his bad leg.

'Elema won't tell everything to the men,' the boy informed him glumly. 'She's gone to hatch witchy plots with the old woman in the big wagon now. She was taken prisoner by men from the far south who were running from the dragomite-riders – but they couldn't run fast enough or far enough. She watched the demon-women cross the river again. They took your princess with them.'

Jacom's heart sank as he received this last piece of news. 'Are you sure about that?' he demanded.

'That's what she said,' Koraismi confirmed, with an aggrieved shrug of the shoulders. 'How can I know whether she's telling the truth?'

'I've got to talk to her,' Jacom said. 'Will you tell her that?'

Koraismi shrugged again. 'She is Apu,' he said, as though that were the end of the matter. 'She's talking to the witch.'

Jacom felt that the whole world was against him, determined to frustrate his every purpose and ambition, no matter how trivial.

'How heavily are these dragomite-people armed? How many are there? Are they really mounted on dragomites?'

Koraismi didn't know how many there were in the party which had captured the princess or how heavily they were armed, but he admitted, reluctantly, that they hadn't had any dragomites with them when they came across the river. 'Maybe dragomites don't like water,' he suggested. 'Maybe the dragomites are waiting on the far side of the river. Maybe the demon-women stayed behind when the dragomites were put to flight by the Uluru.'

'What about Keshvara?' Jacom demanded, with rather more asperity than was warranted.

'Dead,' the boy reported laconically. 'Fell into the river and drowned after being stung by a flowerworm.'

'I have to find out more,' Jacom told Purkin, who had come to hover nearby. 'I've got to see the queen.'

'Rather you than me, sir,' Purkin said sourly. He had not received the news gladly. Like everyone else, the sergeant had been hoping that the princess might be waiting at the ford even though he thought it unlikely. To find out now that she really had been there, but that she had been snatched away mere hours before, was doubly frustrating and disappointing.

Jacom mounted up again and rode forward to the larger of the two wagons. It was still rolling onwards at its customary steady pace, and he was forced to dismount, and then to hobble along while he tethered his horse to the backboard. By the time he had done that his leg felt as if it were on fire, but he contrived to clamber up into the wagon.

Ereleth and the old darklander were deep in conversation, and didn't seem at all pleased to be interrupted. The giant was there too, and the three of them seemed as thick as thieves. Carus Fraxinus was nowhere to be seen. The conspirators were doing their best to speak in tones too low for the wagon-driver to overhear.

'I heard the news, majesty,' Jacom said resolutely. 'It seems that the princess is in great danger, but that if we can only act quickly enough we might be able to save her. I need to know the enemy's strength before my men ride after her, if you'll allow me to question the old woman.'

'If I need you, Captain Cerri,' the witch-queen said coldly, 'I'll send for you.'

'Yes, majesty,' Jacom said, trying to make his calculated misinterpretation sound sincere. 'I merely anticipated your command. Here I am, ready to hurry my men forward at a moment's notice. Please tell me everything you know.'

Ereleth sighed theatrically. 'They're at least two dozen strong,' she said. 'They've just captured twenty horses, although it's not clear whether they'll be willing or able to ride them. They're not well armed but they're skilful fighters. Even if that were all, and even if Fraxinus's darklanders were willing to ride with you, you'd have a hard fight on your hands. Unfortunately, that might not be all. There might be more of them across the river – and if these women really are allied with dragomites, they might have powerful protectors waiting for them. Even if they don't, they'd probably use the princess as a hostage if they were attacked. This isn't a time for brute force and reckless heroism, captain; it's a time for careful planning and cleverness. Wiser heads than yours will decide what to do, how and when – as I said, I'll summon you again if I have need of you.'

Jacom actually opened his mouth to say *I can't do that*, but he caught himself in time. A queen was a queen, after all. It occurred to him that it might be better, if he did go after the princess, not to involve Ereleth or Dhalla, whose ultimate aims obviously didn't coincide with his own. 'Yes, majesty,' he said aloud. 'Sorry, majesty.'

He lowered himself to the ground again, having first untied his horse. He was about to mount up when his elbow was taken by Carus Fraxinus, who held him there until a respectable distance had opened up between their position and the women. Jacom guessed that he must have jumped down from the front of the wagon.

'Don't do anything foolish, Jacom, I beg of you,' Fraxinus said. 'I heard what you said in there and I know what you meant – so did Ereleth. She's right, Jacom – this is no time to rush in. We have no idea what we're up against.' As he finished the final sentence he began to walk, and Jacom walked along with him, steeling himself against the pain.

'If we don't move quickly, Carus,' Jacom said tautly, 'we'll lose whatever chance we've got of getting the princess back. Ereleth's right about one thing – if the people who took her link up with a larger force, we'll be heavily outnumbered. If . . .'

'*We don't want a fight, Jacom!*' Fraxinus was quick to say. 'If it's at all possible, we want to make friends with these people. They could see us safely across the Dragomite Hills, if they were so disposed. They're probably anxious – with good reason, if they've met darklanders who think they're demons – but Lucrezia's no fool, and by now she must be just as desperate to find us as you are to find her. She'll do what she can to persuade them to wait.'

'*Your* main objective may be making friends who can help you cross the hills,' Jacom said, 'but it's not mine. At the end of the day, you don't really care what happens to the princess. Perhaps it would suit your purposes very well if I didn't manage to get her back – but I have priorities of my own.'

'You have no cause to say that,' Fraxinus said, in an aggrieved tone. 'I'm not your enemy, Jacom, and I never have been. If you decide to stay with the expedition I'd be delighted – but I have no intention of trying to trick you or force you. If you and your men gallop off now, though, you'll be splitting our arms and armour in two. If you fight and don't win, you'll ruin your own chances, you'll leave us in an impossible situation, and you might very well get the princess killed. Please, Jacom! It seems that I've already lost one good friend – I don't want to lose any more.'

Jacom took this for cunning flattery, but he knew that the assumption was ungracious, and perhaps unfair. 'I'm sorry about Keshvara,' he said, 'but . . .'

'No buts, Jacom. Believe me, your best chance of recovering the princess is to remain with us. If anyone's to ride ahead, let it be Dhalla. She might succeed in talking to Lucrezia's captors, where you'd almost certainly fail. Did Ereleth or Koraismi tell you that the warriors who have her now are all women, and that they seem hostile to men in general? If their social organisation mimics that of a dragomite hive, however loosely, a warrior woman might have a fair chance of opening negotiations with them. Don't go, Jacom – even if you aren't riding into an impossible situation and delivering your men to the slaughter, you might do irreparable damage to your own cause.'

Jacom saw that Sergeant Purkin's horse had drawn level with them now, and that the sergeant had stopped to listen. Jacom was horribly conscious of the fact that the few men he had left in his command might abruptly cease to be in his command if he gave

them an order they didn't like. Purkin clearly had a lot of respect
for Fraxinus, and might be glad of a good excuse to switch his
formal allegiance, and that of all the remaining men. He was
suddenly sure that if he wanted to hang on to the ghost of his
commission, he had to do what Fraxinus wanted. 'I'll wait, then,'
he said miserably. 'Let's see if Dhalla can find out exactly what
we're up against before we do anything reckless.'

Carus Fraxinus smiled as he stepped back, finally releasing
Jacom's arm so that the captain could mount up again. While
Jacom got up, gently spurring his horse so that it could move into
step with Purkin's, the merchant hurried to the smaller wagon,
and vaulted up on to the driving-seat to join Aulakh Phar.

Jacom sank into a depression which Purkin's relative cheerful-
ness proved utterly incapable of lifting. They hardly exchanged a
dozen words before the sergeant ostentatiously dropped back to
leave his superior officer to his own bitter devices.

They arrived at the scene of the massacre within two hours.
Jacom's men helped the darklanders to chase away the nightcloaks, crocolids and carrion birds which had gathered about the
ripening cadavers, while Jacom sat astride his horse and watched
in sombre silence.

The corpses had been stripped of everything of value; such
clothing as had been left to them had been ruined by rents and
bloodstains. The darklander boys made a rapid check to make
absolutely sure that none was still alive, moving with a clinical
efficiency that Jacom found strangely disturbing. Although his
own men were trained soldiers it was obvious that they were
nauseated by the carnage. Jacom was appalled by the sight of so
many men crudely hacked and bludgeoned to death, and he found
it very difficult to restrain the urge to vomit. Fraxinus and Phar
contrived to be business-like, but he judged that they too were
deeply disturbed by what they had found. Fraxinus asked Elema to
show him exactly where Hyry Keshvara had met with her
accident, but there was not the slightest sign to offer hope that she
might have survived.

While Jacom stood helplessly by, looking across at the far bank,
Checuti came to stand beside his stirrup.

'A horribly bad business, captain,' the thief-master said.

'You, at least, should find some cause for satisfaction in it,'

Jacom growled angrily. 'If we'd found the princess here you'd be on your way homewards, and not to spend your ill-gotten gains either.'

'Truce, captain!' said Checuti, not at all mockingly. 'I've come to make peace, not to pour further acrimony into our troubled relationship – and I can take no pleasure at all in such sights as this. Once we cross this river, it'll be odds against any of us returning to the land and life we love, and this is a ghastly reminder of the dangers which face us. It's time to put aside old differences. I'm as anxious for the princess as you are – it's in her best interests if we work together.'

'I know about *your* anxiety for the princess,' Jacom said sourly. 'What Ereleth did to you and Andris Myrasol is common knowledge by now.'

Checuti did not seem particularly disconcerted by the news that his shameful secret had been broadcast. 'Bearing grudges can eat a man up inside as surely as any cunning worm,' he said calmly. 'You have no reason to love me, captain, but that shouldn't make it impossible for us to deal courteously with one another. A truce would work to everyone's advantage. You have no real enemies here – not even the witch-queen, who's more dangerous to your ultimate ambition than I could ever be. Why must you be so surly?'

'You're Ereleth's creature now,' Jacom pointed out vindictively. 'You can have no friends unless she commands it.'

'That's not true,' Checuti told him. 'Her creature may be nestling in my guts, but that doesn't make me her slave. I'm my own man, not hers, and I always will be. I'll admit, though, that I'm now a member of this expedition at least until Ereleth decides to quit – just as you are. There's no profit for either of us in continued enmity. I wish you could admit that.'

'I'd sooner trust one of those,' Jacom said, pointing to a crocolid drifting in the shallows, waiting patiently for the time to come when it would be allowed to return to its meal.

'That's not the choice before you,' Checuti pointed out dourly. 'It's dragomites that we might have to deal with, not crocolids. Dragomites and warlike dragomite-lovers. Not to mention witch-queens and secretive darklanders and princesses with Serpent's blood and starry-eyed merchants hankering after the garden of Idun and the Pool of Life. You might think the purple forest's unearthly, but it's nothing compared to what we'll find in the far south, if that's where we're fated to go. Crocolids are earthly, at least . . . there are creatures in the world far stranger and far less friendly, and we're about to stroll into their back yard. Aren't we, sergeant?'

The last remark was occasioned by Purkin's arrival, in the company of Guardsman Kirn. 'Never seen killin' like it, sir,' Purkin announced mournfully. 'Crude but quick. Not a single one of *them* dead, unless they took the body with 'em.'

'We're a long way from home, sir,' added Kirn. 'A long way from home.'

Do you think I don't know it? Jacom thought bitterly. *At least I had a home – a true home, on my father's land, not just a rented hovel in some city back street. I'm the biggest loser here, by a very wide margin. If you had one hundredth of what I had you'd have deserted long before we set foot upon the road.*

Aloud, he said only: 'We have a way to go yet, I fear – and we don't have much choice about the company we'll keep while we're getting there.'

'You little realise how badly you need a friend or two, captain,' said Checuti, in a sadly sympathetic fashion. 'I only hope that you learn better before it's too late.'

As the thief-master walked away, Purkin spat on the ground. 'I could cut the bastard's throat, sir,' he said speculatively. 'Surreptitious, like.'

'No, sergeant,' Jacom said with a sigh. 'Don't do that – not yet, at any rate. It pains me to admit it, but we might yet need him.'

'Not thinkin' of turnin' back, then?' said the sergeant, with a sidelong glance at Kirn.

'No,' said Jacom. 'There's no question of that. However difficult this business becomes, I'm in it to the end. I'm a captain in the king's guard, after all. People like us don't give up easily, do we, Purkin? In fact, people like us never give up, while we have breath in our bodies.'

'No sir,' Purkin said, with a careful respectfulness which might or might not have been feigned. 'I suppose we don't.'

3

LUCREZIA SOON FOUND cause to regret the fact that the men from Ebla had been so rapidly overtaken by their enemies. Djemil Eyub had not had the opportunity to tell her much about what to expect in the southern part of the forest and the lands beyond, and her new captors were not in the least inclined to answer, even when she volunteered to trade information on a point for point basis.

The leader of the mound-women, who eventually confided that her name was Jume Metra, seemed to possess considerable intelligence – she was, at least, highly efficient in the business of organising the efforts of her taciturn companions – but she was remarkably incurious. She was not at all averse to making arrogant little speeches, but she was extremely parsimonious with information and explanations and she seemed utterly dismissive of the possibility that she might learn anything important from Lucrezia. Either the old maxim that knowledge was power had never penetrated the depths of the so-called Corridors of Power, or its meaning was construed differently there.

Although the warrior women would not untie her hands except when she was given food and water the princess was not treated badly. They did not take her belt away, and seemed indifferent to the possible purposes of the various potions which it contained. Had they questioned her about it she would have laid claim – half-truthfully – to esoteric medical expertise, but the fact that they didn't even bother to ask made her battery of poisons seem almost contemptible.

When they crossed the river again the mound-women allowed her to ride on one of Hyry's horses, but they remained on foot. Although the horse was on a leading rein it might have been possible for her to force it to a gallop and leave her captors behind, but while her hands were tied she would have no way of steering the animal and she knew that would probably end up lost, alone and vulnerable to any passing predator.

It was obvious that the warrior women did not feel at home in the forest. They were always watchful, ready to react to the slightest noise or movement, and their caution seemed to Lucrezia – who was used to Elema's ease and confidence – to be out of all proportion to the actual dangers posed by nightcloaks and constrictors. The company's archers persistently and indiscriminately fired arrows at any creatures they glimpsed in the treetops, but they very rarely hit their targets and frequently lost their arrows. Lucrezia understood that in spite of their superficial impassivity they were every bit as frightened as the Eblans. They too were far from home, and they too found the strange foliage and the dense thickets which grew about the boles of the trees profoundly unsettling.

On the far side of the river they collected some luggage which they had set aside during the attack, but Lucrezia had little opportunity to examine the contents of the various bundles. It appeared that the only sizeable objects they habitually carried with them, apart from arms and armour, were lanterns. They were the strangest lanterns Lucrezia had ever seen. They used neither flames nor captive fireflies, relying instead on some kind of fungus or lichen which emitted a soft white light that was hardly discernible in the purple daylight. Lucrezia inferred that the so-called Corridors of Power – which she supposed to be tunnels excavated by dragomites in their huge artificial hills – must be lined and lit by the same fungus.

Although the women who took turns leading her horse remained stubbornly uninformative Lucrezia refused to give up her attempts to question them. Indeed, the more obvious it became that the women were firmly committed to silence, or at least to evasion, the more determined she became in her attempts to elicit more informative responses. She repeated certain questions over and over in the hope that sheer nuisance might shake angry answers loose, and she also tried to think up new questions by the hundred, in the faint hope that she might eventually hit on a magical key which would unlock the secrets dammed up in her captors' steadfast minds. It quickly became a kind of game – and although she was forced to consider the possibility that it might also be a game to the women, she couldn't quite believe it. Their reticence didn't seem to be born of fear, but it seemed nevertheless to be deep-seated and natural to them. Her own stubborn pride wouldn't let her give away any information which might be of value without adequate recompense, but there seemed to be no reason why she shouldn't speculate aloud about *them*, and so she began to propose hypothetical answers to her own questions, in the hope of provoking some kind of confirmation or denial.

'You're clearly primitives,' she told a tired Jume Metra while they ate a very frugal and unsatisfying meal after a long morning's trek through the unchanging forest. 'You're little more advanced than the darklanders, although you obviously have a very different social organisation; as hunter-gatherers you're dismally incompetent. You don't feel at home in the forest, although you don't show the least trace of that fear of the dark which is inclined to affect people who live under the sun, like the Eblans. That's obviously because you live mostly underground, in harmony with the dragomites. The darklanders think you're the descendants of children stolen by dragomites to serve as slaves. I think they're probably right, although I'm keeping an open mind. Perhaps you're only half-human, bred for a modicum of cunning but not for real imagination or initiative, conditioned from birth to be obedient to the voice of this mound-queen of yours – who is, by your own admission, nothing more than a mouthpiece for the dragomite queen.'

'You can't begin to understand,' Metra countered unemotionally. 'You are the half-human, not I. Ours is the true way, the true being.'

'There's a good reason for my inability to understand,' the princess pointed out. 'But I do know some things about you, don't I? I know that you're fond of fighting, that you're unimpressed by the idea of Xandria's walls, that you have hardly any metal, and that you have at least some respect for Goran the Forefather's dictum that the worst sin of all is forgetfulness. On the other hand, you don't give much evidence of being masters of the ancient lore.'

'True humans do not need to babble ceaselessly to show what they know and remember,' Metra told her, with the air of one quoting a familiar saying. 'That which humans know and do not say is no less secure than that which is shouted into the empty dark.'

'That's a saying we don't have in Xandria,' Lucrezia admitted, making a note of the fact that the woman preferred to speak in plurals. She decided to try yet another strategy. 'We're not so very different, you and I. You seem to regard me as an alien – some fabulous beast that you've captured as a prize for the greater glory of your beloved mound-queen – but we're both goldens, both fully human in spite of the insults we've traded. We can be friends, you know. You and I; your people and mine.'

'We are warriors,' Metra replied, as if that precluded the very notion of friendship.

Lucrezia remembered what Hyry had told her about the dragomites' beehive-like social organisation, which had surely been confirmed by Metra's references to the dragomite queen. Could it be that the society of the mound-women was organised in a mirror-image of their associates, and that Metra's company really were warriors and *nothing but warriors*? If so, perhaps they really were incapable of friendship, incapable of anything resembling normal social intercourse. But how, Lucrezia wondered, could a single human individual take on the sole burden of reproduction for a whole tribe? And how could the dragomites – which were, after all, unintelligent creatures – have imposed this alien pattern on their human commensals?

'Yes,' Lucrezia said pensively, 'you certainly are warriors. I thought the Eblans' fear of their pursuers might be based in an exaggerated notion of how far away from home they were, but they really did have good cause to be terrified. Why were you so enthusiastic to slaughter them? Not because they posed a threat to you, that's for sure. Did you come into the forest purely and simply to chase and murder the Eblans? You say they attacked you – but they told me that *you* attacked *them*. Either way, a long pursuit is a ludicrous waste of resources. You must have had some other objective – but what? Perhaps you can't tell me because you don't actually know? Are there other mound-women nearby – not warriors but some other kind? Is your mound-queen waiting nearby?'

Metra laughed derisively at that.

'No,' Lucrezia said promptly. 'Of course she isn't. She's safe in the nest, with the dragomite queen whose voice she is . . . in the *blighted* nest. Perhaps she's *not* safe at all. You've been away a long time. Perhaps she's already dead. Perhaps the Corridors of Power have become a single vast mausoleum.'

That struck a nerve, as it had been intended to. Metra scowled, her eerily beautiful features becoming ugly – but she said nothing.

'Who's really in command of your expedition?' Lucrezia asked, feeling that she was now playing the game of diplomacy as ruthlessly as it could be played. 'It's obviously not you. Will your commander be satisfied, do you think, when you bring back a single captive woman? Wouldn't you have been wiser to wait, as I suggested you should, for my friends? Or is warrior nature so deeply ingrained in you that you can't respond to any substantial company in any other way than all-out attack? I can't believe that – it's too absurd.'

'Be quiet,' Metra said. 'What needs to be said will be said, in time.'

Lucrezia took this to mean that she would get the explanations she desired, but not from Metra. It was a reassurance of sorts, but it left the important question dangling. If these warriors were only warriors, and the mound-queen was a thousand kims away in her mound, who – or what – was really in command of this raiding party?

'You're running away now, aren't you?' Lucrezia said, changing tack again. 'Having completed your allotted task in wiping out the Eblans, you're in full retreat – because you know that the darklanders have gathered their forces together. The warband we met may have been a little premature in claiming a glorious victory, but their ragged army really has put your dragomite friends to flight, hasn't it? The invasion is all over. Am I just some scrap you can throw to the mound-queen, in the faint hope of persuading her that the whole thing wasn't just a waste of time?'

'Time is never wasted,' Metra said flatly, almost as though she were correcting some elementary mistake in the discourse of a child. She stood up, turned away, and signalled to her followers to tell them that it was time to move on. It was one of the others who helped Lucrezia back into the saddle and led her away.

They moved on very quickly, and Lucrezia knew that they must be travelling at least as fast as Fraxinus and Phar. If Elema had

339

succeeded in fetching help, any would-be rescuers would need fast horses and some expertise in tracking as well as a considerable advantage of numbers to have any chance of catching up with her. She knew that the probability of any such rescue was small, but she was careful to conserve the hope.

Soon after they had got under way again, however, that hope dwindled almost to nothing. Lucrezia caught her first glimpse of something huge and alien moving through the trees on a parallel course, and her heart immediately sank. She knew full well what the glance must signify: her captors had caught up with a company of the unearthly monsters whose allies or servants they were, and the two parties were fusing into one.

She noticed the change in the attitude and bearing of her guards before she was able to get a clear view of one of the monsters. They had earlier been walking as if they were half-entranced by anxiety, but now they relaxed and their gait became easier. Her horse, by contrast, raised its head to sniff the air, and clearly did not like the scent it caught. The animal began to look around warily, and the woman leading it had to shorten the leading-rein.

On the basis of the information given to her by Hyry Keshvara Lucrezia had imagined that dragomites must resemble beetles or hairy wolf-spiders writ extremely large — an image which had by no means been contradicted by the realisation that the helmets and breastplates which the mound-women wore were probably parts of dragomite exoskeletons. She saw now, though, that the difference between dragomites and the insects she knew was no mere matter of magnification. As the mound-women and the dragomites came closer together she was able to study the unearthly creatures in all their horrific detail.

She saw that the decorations of the warrior women's helmets were impressionistic imitations of structures which the dragomites bore on their own heads: the huge antennae mounted on top of each glossy and dark-hued skull, and the serrated jaws and manipulative palps which were arrayed about each wide mouth. The dragomites' eyes were not, however, the compound eyes typical of insects. They were forward-mounted, with great vertical lids which closed like curtains upon huge jet-black orbs. Their necks were thick, more like a bull's than an ant's, armoured by a series of overlapping plates. The last and broadest of these neck-plates extended into an ornate frill as it curved over each creature's shoulders.

Each dragomite had six legs, mounted and jointed like an insect's, extending horizontally from the body to the first and biggest joint and then descending vertically to complex and very hairy feet. These legs seemed to Lucrezia to be very slender considering the bulk of a dragomite – even the smallest must have weighed at least three times as much as a man – but they were versatile. After a few minutes' observation she understood that the feet could be clenched into supportive pads or 'opened' into complex webs of finger-like palps; she saw dragomites which had paused at the thickets surrounding the tree-trunks, supporting themselves on four legs while the two front legs became 'arms' and 'feet' unfolded into 'hands'. The movement of the creatures was fundamentally insectile, in that they tended to keep three 'feet' on the ground in tripod formation, but she observed that they could change gait relatively easily, to walk on their four hind legs much like any earthly quadruped.

The dragomites' bodies were lean, slightly flattened in the vertical dimension. Each one had a dorsal ridge of backward-slanting spines and a smoother ventral shelf, rather like a keel. Their scaly sides were decorated with elaborate patterns and each one had a second set of hairy palps at the hind end.

It might be possible, Lucrezia judged, for a woman to ride such a beast, provided that she were thin enough to slot herself in between the two largest spines – but the warrior women made no move to mount their companions, or to use them as beasts of burden. The dragomites, for their part, showed no conspicuous interest in the horses and donkeys which the women had in train.

It was not long before Lucrezia glimpsed dragomites of a second type, with much larger heads and more fearsome jaws, stouter in the legs and more compact in the body. These, she knew, must be warriors, ranged on either side of the column of workers with whom the company of human warriors had merged.

The stab of alarm which Lucrezia had felt when she first caught sight of the dragomites was slow to fade away, even though she had every reason to believe that they shared a common purpose with her captors. When they looked in her direction with their huge eyes, though, they displayed no evident interest at all, and it was easy enough to think that the disinterested attitude of the warrior women was a simple reflection of the calm impassivity of their unearthly allies.

As the combined force walked on through the forest, hour after hour, Lucrezia became more used to the proximity of the monsters. The horses – including the one she rode – became quieter, accepting the nearness of the dragomites. She continued to study the creatures, eager to find evidence of their authority over the mound-women and perhaps to identify the true leader of the combined force, but there was no sign of any tyranny of the unhuman or of any commands being communicated between species. She began to wonder whether the awe and fear with which people habitually spoke of dragomites might simply be an unthinking response to their ugliness and their unearthliness, exaggerated by the effect of unfamiliarity. Perhaps, she thought, they were as meek and mild as sheep. Perhaps it was the humans who were masters here after all, the dragomites serving as their hunting dogs.

When they stopped again to eat and rest, in the early afternoon, some of the dragomites actually brought food to the women – which they accepted gladly – and then they discreetly withdrew, until they were hardly visible between the trees, which were more densely packed hereabouts than on the north side of the river.

Lucrezia was hungry and thirsty, and her wrists had been badly chafed by the cords which bound them, so the luxury of having her hands free to convey food and water to her mouth absorbed all her attention for several minutes. Although Jume Metra was with her she made no attempt to resume her insistent questioning, and thus did not immediately notice the change in her captors' attitude which signified that something new was about to happen.

When she finally did look up, Lucrezia was facing the wrong direction – northwards – and had to turn around. More drago- mites were approaching, coming towards the place where they sat as if to meet them. Two were warriors, and this unusually close approach gave her a better chance to appreciate their menacing qualities – but for some reason she could not quite fathom, it was the third which instantly claimed her full attention.

This one was much more slightly built than the workers, with a smaller head. Its mouth-parts were gathered together into a bundle which tapered almost to a point. It walked on its four hind legs, with its forelegs lifted and folded, the 'hands' pressed together like those of some unctuous human orator. Its black eyes, peeping out from beneath half-closed lids, looked directly at her. Dragomite faces, carved as they were in rigid unearthly chitin, were not capable of expression, but Lucrezia felt as she met the stare of those infinitely deep black eyes that this one was curious, and contemplative, and *dangerous*, in a way that none of the others were.

Could this, she wondered, be the commander-in-chief of the dragomite expedition?

Jume Metra stood up to welcome the newcomers. The two giants halted ten mets away, but continued to watch; the one that was small by the standards of its kind came to stand before the armoured warrior, eventually turning its head away from Lucrezia to look at her. While standing on its hind legs it seemed very tall in spite of its relative slightness of build – taller even than Dhalla. It peered down at Metra from a height of three mets, and parted its hands to offer a cursory half-salute with the left. Its antennae were already moving rapidly, and the palps around its mouth now began to unfurl.

Every movement semed pregnant with meaning.

It's mostly illusion, Lucrezia told herself. *It's just that the antennae are reminiscent of waving arms. There's no true intelligence in this pantomime – not much, at any rate. This may be the director of operations, but it's not a monstrous master mind.* She did not know, however, whether she ought to accept her own advice on this matter.

Jume Metra reached up as if to touch the slender dragomite's face, but could not quite reach it. Lucrezia could not judge from such a simple gesture whether she approached the creature as a man might approach a faithful pet or as a slave might approach his master – and the fact that she could not tell for sure disturbed her almost as much as the eerie appearance of the monster itself.

The dragomite ducked its head, and lowered its antennae, almost as though it were a king reaching down from his throne to a kneeling supplicant. Neither antenna actually touched Metra's outstretched fingers, any more than a king would actually condescend to touch the hand of an imploring subject – but they did briefly curl under to touch the palps about the monster's own mouth. There was nothing in this that Lucrezia could conclusively identify as *language*, but she didn't doubt that there was some kind of understanding between the warrior woman and the slender dragomite.

Unthinkingly, Lucrezia took half a step backwards. It was a mechanical move, certainly not part of any planned retreat, but Metra instantly turned to grab her left arm, and one of the other women hovering nearby was quick to seize her right. Lucrezia had no idea what they intended to do, but she struggled reflexively. It was useless – they were strong and they twisted her arms back to minimise the force of her resistance. They actually lifted her feet from the ground as they thrust her forward again.

She knew that they were not merely bringing her into confrontation with the slender dragomite but making an offering of her.

'What are you?' she said, more fearfully than she would have liked, as she met that horrid stare, looking into the infinite depths of its black pupils. 'What do you want with me?'

For the briefest of moments, as its peculiar mouth-parts moved, she thought that it was actually going to reply in human language – but then something lashed out from the tangle of palps like a striking snake, and struck her on the neck, just beneath her left ear.

It was as if she had been stabbed; she felt something penetrate her flesh like a stiletto. *Was I brought here just to be killed?* she thought, near to weeping because of the absurdity of it, because she had expected so much more, of the situation and of life.

Several seconds went by when she was simply numb with shock, unable to feel anything. If there was blood coursing from her wounded neck she could not sense its wetness. Then her head began to spin, so dizzily that she tried with all her might to close her eyes.

She failed. She could not avoid that terrible stare, which filled the field of her vision with hypnotic intensity.

She wanted desperately for consciousness to fail and darkness to fall, but the world would not let her go, even though she knew that she had lost all power of command over her limbs and her inner being.

It was as if the moment of the unexpected assault had somehow become infinite, imprisoning her thought and her desire more securely than the tomb.

4

HYRY KESHVARA WAS accustomed to dream while she slept, but she somehow knew as she struggled back to wakefulness that she hadn't dreamed for a long time. She resented the fact, for she felt entitled to her dreams. It wasn't that they were invariably pleasant, nor even that they made such a deep impression on her mind as to remain unforgotten, but simply that she thought of herself as the kind of person who wouldn't easily settle for cold oblivion even on a temporary basis. Her mother, whom she resembled closely in many ways, had once comforted her after a childhood nightmare, saying: 'It's far better to dream than not to dream, little one, for we are what we are by virtue of the continuity of our thoughts. If we were truly to sleep, to become nothing inside ourselves, how could we ever know when we awoke that we had not become someone else while we slept? Don't be afraid of nightmares, Hyry. Never be afraid to *be afraid*, because fear is one of the things which makes us what we are.'

It was with this fond memory in her mind – which she had reconstructed only slightly with the passing of the years, for the sake of tidiness – that she opened her gluey eyes and looked into the face of the Serpent.

She knew immediately what the Serpent was, although she had never seen one before. It was far too sleek and slender to be a Salamander, and there was nothing else it could possibly be. Its lustrous patterned skin was not as scaly as she had imagined, and its dark, uniformly coloured eyes were not as gemlike. The hood which connected its temples to its shoulders was relaxed at present, so she couldn't tell whether it would be as broad and smoothly curved as it was in pictures drawn by Xandrian artists. But its tongue *was* forked; she could see that when it opened its thin-lipped mouth in what might have been a smile.

'Hello,' it said softly. Its throat pulsed as it formed the word.

Hyry knew that Serpents could make almost all the sounds which human language contained, but they had to master awkward tricks of pronunciation which their own tongue never demanded of them. Some Serpents, it was said, refused to learn the human language because it made demands upon them which they deemed to be contrary to their essential nature. With the aid of similar trickery, according to common belief, humans were able to make all but a few of the sounds commonly employed in Serpent language, but few ever took the trouble to learn – not because it would have been unnatural, but because Serpents were rare, shy and possessed of very little which humans might want to beg, buy or steal.

Hyry tried to say 'Hello' as she sat up, but her dry throat couldn't cope with the soft syllables, and the word came out as a meaningless grunt.

The Serpent handed her a cup. She used the tip of her tongue to taste the liquid within it before drinking. It was a syrupy kind of sap which could be squeezed from certain kinds of forest fruit if one knew how. The Serpents evidently knew how.

Hyry looked around as she sipped the liquor. She was still in the dense heart of the Forest of Absolute Night, which was presently illumined by the purple half-gloom of daylight. There was no sign of the river, nor of her horses and donkeys, nor of Princess Lucrezia and Elema. There were two other Serpents reclining on the ground some ten or twelve mets away, but they were ostentatiously not looking in her direction.

Her thirst slaked, Hyry flexed her limbs experimentally, and tried to clear the fog from her brain. She looked down at her left hand, which was swollen, discoloured and slightly numb. The Serpent waited patiently while she composed herself.

She decided, after methodical investigation, that she was not in bad shape, physically. She was not as weak as she might have been – or, indeed, ought to have been if her system were still full of flowerworm venom. She raised her left hand to look more carefully at the place where the flowerworm had stung her. The scars were impressive in their complexity – no less than six sting-cells had discharged their burden of poison into her – but she could see that the yellowing puncture-marks were almost completely healed. She wondered how bad the swelling had been at its worst.

'Five days,' she guessed thoughtfully. 'Maybe six.'

'Ssix,' said the Serpent, extending the *s* in a most peculiar fashion. Did that imply that there was no s-sound in the Serpent's language, she wondered, or that there *was* an s-sound, and this was it?

'Did the tree really fall?' she asked, trying to remember. 'Or was that just dizziness? Did I actually tumble into the river, or do I only think I did?'

'Were in river,' the Serpent told her. 'Lucky not to drown. Head jusst out of water when tree floated. Lucky we found you. Could have sstarved. Bad ssting.'

'You pulled me out? Fed me, even while I was unconscious?'

'Yess. Ssifuss wanted throw you back. I ssaid no. SSumssarum said OK. Not hard to do. My name Mossassor. You?'

'Hyry Keshvara,' Hyry replied, resisting the temptation to extend the *s* in Keshvara into a hiss. 'Why did your friend want to thow me back?' She suspected that many humans who found an injured Serpent floating in the river might throw it back, but she wasn't one of them.

'Ssinkss you disseasse.'

'He thinks I have a disease? What disease?'

'No. Ssinkss humanss *are* disseasse . . . exssept oness wiss Sserpent'ss blood. Ssifuss not *he* – not sshe eisser. Nor me.'

Hyry frowned. Three more or less distinct trains of thought had been stirred into motion by this answer, and needed disentangling. In other circumstances she might have followed up the first line of enquiry, but having just spent a troubled tenday in the company of Princess Lucrezia she concentrated instead on the second.

'You believe that there are humans with Serpent's blood?' she said uncertainly.

'Not you,' Mossassor replied. It was not the most helpful answer imaginable.

Hyry blinked as her efforts to concentrate filled her head with jagged pain. It was a strong disincentive to further pursuit of that particular argument, so she decided to shelve it in favour of something less problematic.

'Where are we?' she asked, although she quickly realised that even something as simple as that couldn't qualify as a question which readily lent itself to a satisfactory answer. She amended it to: 'Are we still near the river?'

'Long way ssouss,' the Serpent said, with what might have been a hint of apology in its tone. 'Pale men chassed uss. No choisse.'

'I was with a friend,' Hyry said uneasily. She would have said 'friends' but thought it might be undiplomatic to mention Elema if the Serpents had been forced to run from a darklander warband. 'We were camped near a river-crossing. Armed men were coming – dark men, not pale ones. They . . .' She broke off because Mossassor had come suddenly to its feet. The other two Serpents were already standing.

'Musst go,' Mossassor said. 'Can walk?'

Hyry realised that for six days, at least some of which had been spent running away from other humans, the Serpent – with or without help from its companions – must have carried her. Mossassor was no taller than she was, and no more heavily built. Save for a belt with pouches much like her own it seemed to have no luggage of its own, but even so she could not imagine how – or why – the creature had done such a thing. Even if she were not to be reckoned a disease, would it not have been far simpler to abandon her for the darklanders to find, leaving them to decide whether or not to care for her?

'I can walk,' she said, although she wasn't certain that she could walk far or fast enough.

'Good,' the Serpent said. 'Need help, lean on me.'

The other two Serpents did have packs of a sort – half-full sacks without drawstrings or shoulder-straps – and these two brought up the rear while Mossassor led the way. At first, Hyry found it difficult to move at all, and her head began to ache continuously as soon as she was on her feet, but the first few steps were the worst. After that, she simply gritted her teeth, stubbornly determined to resist the pain at all costs.

She tried to reduce herself to the status of an automaton, which could move with mechanical regularity no matter what internal storms might beset its fugitive consciousness. It was a trick she had tried before, and she knew that she was capable of it. She soon slipped into a kind of limbo which was not quite sleep and contained no dreams. How long she walked like that she could not tell.

Once or twice she found the Serpent's arm about her, lending her support, but whenever she became conscious of it she roused

348

herself to independence. She was, after all, a human being, and human beings were supposed to be the true lords of the world.

It was not until nightfall that they stopped again, at which point Hyry was quick to lapse into authentic unconsciousness. She slept fitfully because of all her aches and pains, but she did dream, of runaway princesses and battle-hungry darklanders, of poisonous flowerworms and merciful Serpents.

When she awoke again Mossassor brought her food, and more liquor. When she had eaten, the Serpent became enthusiastic to talk to her again. She realised then that its efforts on her behalf might not be entirely altruistic. The Serpents hadn't come into the forest on a whim; something had stirred up a special kind of curiosity, and whatever its companions thought Mossassor was evidently of the opinion that Hyry might be able to tell it things it wanted to know.

As soon as she understood this, Hyry became wary, and she began to think like a trader again. When Mossassor began to quiz her on her reasons for being in the forest, and the destination she had been trying to attain, she was careful not to give away too much and to match question for question whenever she could.

'I was supposed to join a party of Xandrian merchants,' she said. 'We hoped to cross the Dragomite Hills to the lands beyond, having heard that a way across had been opened by a blight that had depopulated many of the mounds. What brought you here?'

'Alsso heard of dissasster in the dragomite landss,' Mossassor admitted. 'Became anxssiouss, in casse it iss warning. Sserpentss have sstoriess, ass humanss do.'

'Stories?'

'Yess. Humanss have sstoriess about coming of chaoss. Sso have we. Ssome of uss ssink ssey are ssings for sshildren, but ssome not sso ssure. I curiouss, like you. You ssearssh for garden?'

'We do have stories about the lands to the south,' Hyry agreed, trying to conceal her surprise at the turn which the conversation had taken. 'Many men think of them as mere inventions, but we're careful to preserve them nevertheless. We have a saying which tells us that the only sin is forgetfulness. Maybe you have something similar.'

'Not uss,' Mossassor said. It was difficult to judge whether it was being deliberately enigmatic. 'We good forgetters. Have to be. Ssometimess too good. You ssearssh for garden? Garden of sstoriess?'

349

'Do you mean the garden of Idun? In the *Lore of Genesys*? Is that where you're going?'

'Not know namess. Iss very possible you remember ssingss we forget. Musst put all togesser, like pussle. Tell me sstoriess, pleasse.'

'Will you tell me your stories in return?' Hyry countered guardedly – not because she had any particular desire to be initiated into the secrets of Serpent mythology, but because she thought it was important to preserve the principle of fair exchange even in a situation where she was at a disadvantage and clearly owed her rescuer a debt of gratitude.

'Yess. Tell me about garden.'

Hyry racked her brains, knowing that she ought to be able to remember the beginning of the *Lore of Genesys* word for word, but in the end she had to settle for a paraphrase.

'According to the lore,' she said slowly, 'humans first came to the world in a ship, which had sailed the dark between the stars for thousands of years. According to the story, the people who lived aboard the ship had no need of legs, because nothing there weighed very much, and their lower limbs were extra arms – but when they sent their sons and daughters into the world something called *Genesys* gave them legs. Genesys wasn't a person, more like a set of tools and a plan to guide their use, although no such tools exist today.

'The story says that the people of the ship were anxious for the sons and daughters they sent into the world, because the world was under the dominion of the three evils: corrosion, corruption and chaos. Aboard the ship the three evils had long been contained and kept in check, because that was easy to do in the dark between the stars. People lived for hundreds of years aboard the ship without ever falling ill, and there was no forgetfulness aboard the ship at all.

'There were some people aboard the ship who didn't want to send their sons and daughters into the world, because the world was such an evil place, but there were others who said, if I remember it right: *What are humans for, if not to fight evil wherever it is found? What are humans worth, if they fear to tread the paths of evil? What are humans to become, if they hide in the dark between the stars for ever?* It was for these reasons, the story says, that the people of the ship used Genesys to reshape their sons and daughters, and sent them into the world.

'The people of the ship knew that the people of the world would lose much in coming under the dominion of the three evils. The people of the world had to submit, to a degree, to the forces of corrosion, corruption and chaos. *We cannot give you all that we have,* the people of the ship said to their sons and daughters, *and much that we give you will undoubtedly be lost, but we will shape for you a manifold lore and a common wisdom, which you might preserve in full even though you must rely almost entirely on word of mouth for its preservation. You must hold the lore and the wisdom as a sacred trust, and preserve it even though you cease to see the sense in it, for it is the most precious thing in all the world.* Or words to that effect.

'People with legs were by no means the only things that Genesys made, according to the story. It made animals and plants for the people of the world to use, for every purpose imaginable. The world had lots of kinds of animals and plants already, but Genesys made many more – thousands, at least. Many of the creatures made by Genesys were too small to be seen; some of these were instruments whose use was defined and described in the lore given to different guilds, but some were released into the world to do their work without any supervision by the men of the world.

'*The war against the three evils will be long and hard,* the people of the ship told the people of the world, *but you will have many unseen allies. The war might never be won, or might take a hundred thousand years in the winning, but you are humans and must never cease to fight or despair of victory.* That's the essence of the lore, more or less. It goes on and on, but only trained loremasters can recite it word for word.'

Mossassor had listened to all of this very attentively, and Hyry observed that its companions were also listening in, even though they were still sitting some way apart, careful to place themselves beyond a tacit boundary, as though she were in quarantine.

'Iss ass I ssought,' Mossassor said. 'Ssiss iss what we ssought humanss ssink. Iss ssere nossing consserning uss in ssesse sstoriess?'

'Yes there is,' Hyry was quick to say, realising that she ought perhaps to have given that part of the lore more prominence in this particular telling. 'I'll try to remember exactly how the story puts it. Among the animals which were in the world before humans came, the lore says, there were two kinds of almost-people, which the people of the ship called Serpents – that's you, of course – and Salamanders. *Neither fear nor hate these almost-people*, the people of the ship said to the people of the world, *for they are not your enemies. In time, if you are fortunate, they will become your steadfast allies in the war against the three evils, and the war will be easier to win if you and they can fight side by side*. That's almost word for word, but not quite.

'According to the tale, when the people of the ship had made the lore and the common wisdom, and had given it to their sons and daughters, the ship went on into the dark between the stars, in search of other worlds. *We must leave now*, the people of the ship said to the people of the world, *and we shall never be able to return, for the universe is infinite and we must go for ever on, because our purpose is to be equal and more than equal to all the challenges of existence. The world is your challenge, and we have every confidence in your ability to meet it – but challenges are better met if they are not met alone. Whatever enemies you make, among your own and other kinds, always remember that all enemies may become friends when they stand against the greatest of the evils, whose name is chaos*.'

'I told you sso,' said Mossassor, not to Hyry but to its two companions – although it spoke in the human tongue so that she might understand it. 'Sshe iss ssearsshing for garden. Sshe not on sside of dissasster. Sshe doess not want Sserpentss wiped out. Sshe iss not disseasse.'

Hyry wished that she could read Serpent expressions. The two whose names were presumably Ssifuss and Ssumssarum made no reply, either in human language or their own, and their sombre eyes were quite inscrutable. Somehow, though, she felt that they were still sceptical – as she might have been herself had anyone tried to win an argument by citing the evidence of ancient mythology.

'What disaster do you mean?' she said. 'What is it, exactly, that you're searching for?'

'Great changess coming,' Mossassor said succinctly. 'Great dangerss. Chaoss, exsstincssion. Ssearssh for garden. Iss debt, you ssee. Iss debt, musst be paid. You wiss uss, undersstand? We ssearssh for garden togesser, whesser Sserpent'ss blood or not.'

Hyry dared not lay claim to any real understanding of what the Serpent was saying, and she didn't feel that the time was ripe to tell it that she knew where a human might be found who did have Serpent's blood – whatever that might mean – but she knew, no matter how inscrutable its eyes might be, that Mossassor was appealing to her for help and support – and she did owe it a debt.

'Yes, I understand,' she said, rather grandly. 'We're all on the same side: humans, Serpents, Salamanders. We all want to live our lives peacefully and securely. Chaos is the enemy of us all. We'll search for the garden together, if that is what you think needs to be done. Believe me, I'll do everything I can to help. I owe you that.'

'Ssee,' it said to its friends. 'Iss ssettled.'

This time, one of them did reply, but not in human language. Within seconds a fierce argument was raging, of which Hyry could not understand a single syllable. She had already noticed that the Serpents had no weapons with them save for knives of human manufacture, and she was glad of it now as their voices became faster and faster – but they showed no inclination to physical violence, and in the end she simply lay down on the ground and closed her eyes, wondering what in the world she had got herself into.

Oddly enough, it was with a certain perverse fondness that she thought: *Lucrezia, my troublesome love, you should be with me now! This is a stranger adventure by far than the one I promised you before, and I truly wish that you were here to share it.*

5

THE DRAGOMITE HILLS were the most remarkable sight that Andris had ever encountered in all his years of wandering. He had never seen a landscape which looked more profoundly unnatural, and this was by no means because it had lately undergone a kind of devastation. He had never seen slopes so precipitous and so irregular, nor peaks so raggedly sharp, and these would have been just as strange – perhaps even stranger – had they been decked according to their usual fashion.

The kind of 'forest' which had grown everywhere upon the hillsides until the blight had come to obliterate the greater part of it could still be seen in scattered patches. These fertile enclaves were composed of dense masses in which huge fungoid growths mingled with gargantuan moss-like plants, the mossy greens competing for visual attention with a riot of creamy whites and ochreous yellows, dappled with occasional bursts of pale blue and dark red. The most extensive reaches of this kind were situated on the highest ridges; in the narrow winding valleys through which the expedition's course ran, all but a few of the unearthly plants had been rendered down into shapeless sticky masses whose colours had darkened into ugly browns and funereal blacks.

In their healthy state the plants provided food for the dragomites which had raised the hills – and were, according to Aulakh Phar, very carefully cultivated by these instinctive agri-culturalists –but the plague must have brought starvation to all the mounds.

Andris judged that the battles which must have been fought between rival nests for the dwindling resources had all but run their course by now, but Fraxinus steered the expedition well away from the ridges where the vegetation remained rich, and with good reason. Once Andris had caught a glimpse of the massively armoured warriors which guarded these fields – far more intimidating than the common workers which were more frequently to be seen – he had not the slightest inclination to take a closer look.

If the blight were as bad throughout the hills as it was in the region they had so far crossed, Andris reasoned, then the expedition would have little or no difficulty winning through to more hospitable lands. Fraxinus had placed both food and water on strict ration as soon as the wagons left the Forest of Absolute Night behind, but it had rained on each of the last three days, so the chance of their running out of water seemed thin, and the food they had was relatively well preserved. Unfortunately, he had no confidence that he would be allowed to remain with the expedition. Queen Ereleth would not condescend to discuss her plans with anyone but she had clearly become very anxious about Dhalla's failure to return from her mission to track and intercept the princess's captors.

Although she had not yet abandoned all hope of recovering the princess, Ereleth was obviously in two minds as to what to do for the best and there seemed to be every chance of her deciding to return to the forest and to the darkland witches over whom she had some authoritarian hold. She had, of course, made it perfectly clear to Andris that the effort he had exerted in saving her life from the nightcloak did not qualify him for an early release from his enforced servitude. He had meekly eaten the contraceptive fungus which she had given to him on the appointed day, wincing at the foul taste – and even more resentful of the gleam in her eye as she watched him, which might or might not have signified that she was playing him for a fool.

The reek of the decaying vegetation had been exceedingly unpleasant at first, but Andris had grown used to it quickly enough. By now it was simply an everpresent reminder of the fact that corruption was the greatest tyrant in the world, whose invisible armies had the measure of any petty empire, whether it be human or alien, earthly or unearthly. If anything, the desolation was worse here than in the fringes of the range, but the decay had so nearly run its full course that the worst of the stink had passed, and the rain had helped to wash it from the air. It was possible to see hereabouts that the mounds themselves were disintegrating along with their external embellishments: a stark reminder of the fact that they were products of artifice, like the walls of Xandria, in need of constant maintenance if they were to endure. A great deal of rain would have to fall before the region was evened to a plain, but the beginning of such a process was already evident.

In the natural course of events, Andris thought – presuming for the moment that the darklanders' whisperings about the threatened end of the world were mere alarmism – future generations of dragomites would reclaim their heritage long before the forces of erosion could complete their work, and start a new cycle of growth. He could not help wondering, though, as the expedition trudged over hundreds of kims of devastated land and saw no hint of an end to it, whether this catastrophe really could be considered part of the *natural course of events*.

Decay or no decay, Andris had to admit that the Dragomite Hills were a true marvel. The hills and valleys of Ferentina, such as they were, curved as gently and as sweetly as a woman's hips – or so Andris was pleased to remember them now, bathed as they no doubt were by a gentle aura of nostalgia. Even in Ferentina, the processes of erosion which tended to even out all such landmarks were valiantly opposed by the grasses and bushes which resolutely heaped them up, generation by generation. In Ferentina, however, as in Khalorn, these processes were in such close balance that watchers on the highest towers looked out on a land as gently rippled as a weed-choked pond. The forces shaping the land around the Slithery Sea were slightly more violent, but even the most powerful waves, in alliance with the most stubborn grasses, could not build dunes a tenth the height of the mounds which the patient dragomites erected. Even the walls of the mighty citadel of Xandria – which was certainly among the tallest constructions ever raised by the hand of man, even if one were prepared to doubt its inhabitants' claims as to its uniqueness – had nowhere near the height of perfectly commonplace drops engineered by dragomites. Nor was the 'empire' boasted by Xandria, despite its vastness in human terms, of any significant size by comparison with the extent of the recently fallen empire of the dragomites.

Perhaps Fraxinus was wrong to see this happening as an opportunity, Andris thought, as he guided his stolen but ever-faithful mare around a sticky pit of black corruption. *If Phar is right about the internal organisation of the dragomites' nests, this must certainly have seemed like a visitation of doomsday to those hypothetical queens which have so long been monarchs of all they surveyed. Can we be sure that it will stop here? Perhaps the superstitious darklanders really do know better than civilised folk. Perhaps the blight will move on to claim the Forest of Absolute Night . . . and then, in turn, the fields of Khalorn and Xandria itself — for who can say that earthly species will resist what so many unearthly species could not? What use could Xandrian steel and Xandrian cavalry be against such an enemy as this?*

He looked up abruptly as he caught sight of a lone dragomite on the slope above him, but it was only a worker and it was already ducking back into one of the myriad tunnels which honeycombed the hills. He had seen more than a hundred of the creatures since the caravan had first moved into the region, but never one which showed the slightest inclination to attack. He had begun to wonder whether Aulakh Phar's salve, with which he anointed his forehead at regular intervals, was really necessary. He had no way of knowing how many more of the monsters might be lurking close at hand, invisible within their nests, but the overwhelming impression he had was that most of the dragomite workers he had seen were dispirited, desolate and lonely, altogether disinclined to aggression.

Although Fraxinus had been careful to direct the expedition in such a way as to avoid any companies of warriors the sentries espied, Andris had formed the impression that even they were entirely devoted to their own internecine squabbles. Sometimes, to be sure, they formed menacing ranks on the ridges, silhouetted against the sky, but they never attacked or pursued the humans or their animals. What their reaction would have been had the humans not been so careful to steer clear of them Andris could not tell, but he had begun to stop worrying about the possibility of a sneak attack in the midday or the midnight, and was sleeping more easily now than he had for a long time. None of his injuries pained him much nowadays, although he still felt an uncomfortable stirring in his gut from time to time which might or might not have been Ereleth's worm.

While he was still reined in, looking at the place where the dragomite worker had disappeared, Merel Zabio caught him up.

She had only recently mounted again, having taken a turn to rest in one of the wagons – both of which they still had with them, in spite of the difficulties posed by the terrain.

'Fraxinus wants to ask you something,' she said. 'He's poring over your new map again. He thinks that he's established our exact position with the aid of the stars whose position he was plotting last night, although he has no training in the Arts Astronomical. He's worried about something.'

'He usually knows what he's talking about – more or less,' Andris conceded, leaning over to caress her cheek by way of farewell before he turned the mare and trotted back to the wagon.

Fraxinus greeted him warmly, but Ereleth – who had burrowed out a home-from-home in the overcrowded spaces of the larger wagon in spite of the merchant's objections, and was always lurking there like a nightcloak in the lower branches of a tree – was as coldly contemptuous as ever.

'Our latitude is easy enough to determine,' Carus Fraxinus told him, as he settled himself into an uncomfortably narrow niche. 'The only difficulty lies in determining how far to the east or west we are. I believe, on the basis of careful observations of the stars, that we're just about *here*, very nearly at the place which you've marked CP. That stands, I think, for *Corridors of Power*.'

'That's right,' Andris said, 'but I don't know what the name's supposed to mean. If that's where we are, there's no sign of it out there. All the dragomite mounds look pretty much like another to me. Mind you, if any one of them were sufficiently different to require a label, the difference would probably be inside. Maybe the Corridors of Power is where the empress of all dragomite queens lives.'

'Perhaps,' Fraxinus echoed, although that was obviously not what was exercising his mind. 'If I'm right, we seem to have made our way here with remarkable accuracy.'

'It's on a direct route across the narrowest reach of the hills,' Andris pointed out. 'We had to pass by it sooner or later.'

'Not quite direct,' Fraxinus pointed out. 'Anyway, we haven't followed a straight course. We've changed direction several times to avoid approaching dragomite warriors.'

Andris met Fraxinus's eyes steadily, not quite able to take aboard the inference which the merchant seemed to be inviting him to draw. 'You're not suggesting that the warriors have been *steering* us towards this spot, are you?' he asked.

'I don't know,' Fraxinus said. 'It sounds ridiculous, doesn't it?'

Ereleth made a noise that might have been a laugh or a snort of disgust.

'If you're right about our position,' Andris said, determinedly ignoring the old woman, 'it looks to me like good news. We can't be certain that the range of the hills is exactly the same now as it was when the map was determined, but if it's broadly similar, and this inlet of marshland still exists, we're less than two hundred kims from the edge of the marsh – provided only that we maintain a course as close to due south as possible. We'll be out of here pretty soon.' He carefully didn't add: *Provided that we can stay out of trouble.*

Fraxinus nodded, accepting the change of tone readily enough. 'We'd then be able to swing south-west towards the river,' he said. 'Its banks boast several sizeable towns if what the Eblans told Elema is true.'

'We might bear slightly east of south instead, to the Lake of Colourless Blood,' Andris pointed out. 'It might be interesting to find out what such a name signified – and if your ultimate destination is the Navel of the World, that would be a straighter route.'

'That region's in the heart of the marshes,' Fraxinus said dubiously. 'It might well be unpopulated and the territory's certain to be difficult, perhaps impossible for the carts. We've brought them so far that I'm reluctant to abandon them now. If there are towns along the river there'll be roads between them, and merchants who might pay a high price for metal goods. If we follow the river until it bends sharply to the west, a direct route from there to the Navel of the World would take us close to this place you've marked as Salamander's Fire. Do you have any idea what that might mean?'

Andris had no idea what any of the names inscribed on his map might mean, but this was a phrase he had recently heard spoken, and recognised. 'You might ask Dhalla, if she ever returns,' he said uncertainly. 'That darklander boy who's always hanging around with Jacom Cerri told Merel that Dhalla claimed to have Salamander's fire burning in her heart.'

Fraxinus turned to Ereleth, who was watching them impassively. 'She will return,' the witch-queen said, for all the world as if there could not be an atom of doubt about it.

'Do you know what the phrase might mean, majesty?' Fraxinus asked, with scrupulous politeness. Andris had not been witness to many conversations between Fraxinus and Ereleth but it was common knowledge in the camp that their inevitable differences of opinion regarding the future of the expedition and its members had ripened into a profound mutual dislike.

'It's a metaphor,' Ereleth said, in a patronising and faintly insulting manner. 'It refers to courage and strength of will, in much the same way that one might say that a person with an inborn talent for witchcraft had Serpent's blood.'

'In this particular context,' Fraxinus observed, 'it must refer to something concrete.'

'Your map is full of metaphors,' Ereleth pointed out in her turn. 'Who knows what secrets and mysteries they might conceal? Perhaps the whole thing is the prank of some ancient loremaster, or a pretty folly.' The way she said it implied that if anyone knew the truth it would be a witch-queen, but that she had no intention whatsoever of sharing her secrets with lesser mortals – although she had allowed Andris to draw a new map for Fraxinus once they had crossed the river in the forest. Andris doubted that she was serious in suggesting that the lore of the forefathers might be corrupted to the extent that it entertained pranks and follies, but he still had cause to regret the low esteem in which most Xandrians held his art and the jibe stung.

'Does the map's reference to the Corridors of Power imply that people had explored the Dragomite Hills before the map was designed?' Andris asked, in the hope of reducing the tension by raising the discussion to a safely theoretical level. 'Why else should a single location within such a vast swathe of territory be marked for special attention? Perhaps there were people living in association with the dragomites even then, and the Corridors of Power are the nests which humans and dragomites share.'

'Perhaps that's so,' admitted Fraxinus. 'Although the dark-landers didn't know for certain that there were humans in the hills until very recently, their legends told them it was true.'

'I don't understand how or why people should ever have entered into such an association,' Andris said. '*Were* they captured as nest-slaves, do you think, or did they set out with the intention of domesticating the dragomites?'

'One way or another, people seem to get everywhere,' Fraxinus said. 'Those fungus-forests which grow on the slopes of the dragomite mounds are unearthly, but as you saw in the Forest of Absolute Night, humans can live quite adequately on a diet of unearthly food, and much that's unearthly is useful in other ways. Aulakh could probably list half a hundred unearthly items of medicinal value — and half a hundred poisons too. Perhaps dragomites *can* be tamed. Perhaps the secret of taming them was known to the forefathers, even though we have forgotten it.'

'If you've calculated our position accurately,' Andris said, looking down at the map uneasily, drawn back to dangerous speculative ground in spite of his earlier intentions, 'we're as close now to the Corridors of Power as we ever will be. Practically on their doorstep, in fact. If the people who captured Princess Lucrezia were allied with dragomites, they might be bringing her here. She might be here already — though I can't imagine how we could begin to look for her.' He didn't look at Ereleth while he said this, although he was well aware that his words were likely to be of more interest to her than to the merchant.

'That's pure speculation,' Fraxinus said dismissively. 'I'm sure, on reflection, that our position is mere coincidence. Tomorrow . . .'

'Tomorrow will come soon enough, Carus Fraxinus,' Ereleth said, in her irritatingly knowing fashion. 'So will trouble, if it has the inclination. There is a destiny which overhangs us all, whether or not you have the wit to see it. You think that you are master here, but the hand of fate has made a pawn of you.'

It was obvious to Andris that Fraxinus thought this speech a fine farrago of nonsense, designed to irritate him, but the merchant only sighed, with a slight smile about his face. 'I dare say that you're right, majesty,' he said. 'We common men are not party to your witch-lore, let alone to the secret commandments which guide you. We can only stumble blindly towards our own destinations, guided by delusive dreams and half-remembered myths. You must find us very amusing when we pore over our enigmatic maps and try to fit their seductive labels to the little lore we know, and to the few fragments of the *Apocrypha of Genesys* we have gleaned along the way.'

The queen's eyes darkened at the mention of secret commandments, but she knew that she was being teased. 'A merchant's eyes are never blind,' she said calmly. 'It's merely that they find it difficult to focus on anything but wine, coin and finery.'

Fraxinus laughed. Andris didn't.

Fraxinus was quick to make a better reply, saying: 'We are all traders here, except yourself, majesty. Even Checuti understands the value of information and the price of loyalty, and knows that there comes a time when bargaining has to cease so that trust and friendship may begin. Perhaps it's true that I look at the map with a trader's eyes, whereas a queen of witches might find it easier to decipher – but I'm no less anxious to know the truth behind its every detail, and I must make what efforts I can to divine that truth. I'd be grateful for any help you cared to give me, whether your motive were to aid my efforts on Xandria's behalf, or merely to mock my ignorance.'

'I would be glad to help you,' Ereleth said, making it sound more like a threat than an offer, 'if I could be certain of your loyalty.'

We are all traders here, Andris echoed in the privacy of his thoughts, *and your majesty is clearly no exception – but Fraxinus won't rise to that kind of bait. He won't place his expedition under your command, nor divert it to your whim by so much as a sim.* When he spoke, however, it was to make yet another attempt to steer the conversation away from conflict. 'I fear that the lore in which this map is based is very old,' he said to Fraxinus. 'Perhaps the meaning of the labels was clear enough in those days, although we have lost the sense of them. On the other hand, it may be that the things to which the labels refer no longer exist, and it would be no help to us to know what they once meant.'

'Perhaps,' said Fraxinus. 'But not all the labels are unhelpful or unknown. I've never heard of the Pillars of Silence or the Silver Thorns, but people still speak of the Crystal City as an actual site in the south of the Spangled Desert. It's not an actual city, but it *is* a place. Serpents' Lair is probably straightforwardly descriptive, and it may be significant that Serpents were rumoured to be in the forest as well as dragomite-riders. Perhaps they too have found a route across where none existed before. Similarly, Salamander's

Fire may mean no more than a region where Salamanders live.' He paused to glance at Ereleth, but she made no comment. 'Chimera's Cradle and the Navel of the World are known to us from the *Lore of Genesys*,' he went on, 'in connection with the Pool of Life and the garden of Idun. Although these are not among the labels on the map we might expect to find them – or the place where they once were – in this same region. The phrase *Nest of the Phoenix* is suggestive of some kind of regeneration, and I am tempted to link it with the Pool of Life, from which the *Lore of Genesys* promises that the incorruptible stone might one day be born . . .'

'. . . nourished by milk and blood,' Andris quoted, remembering, 'but not *colourless* blood, I presume. How does the next passage go?'

'When that day comes you must seize and use the stone, and turn the evil of corrosion to the good of inscription,' Fraxinus said promptly.

Had Ereleth not been there Andris might have asked him whether that was the ultimate aim of the expedition, but he was wary of embarking on such a flight of fancy while the old woman's acid tongue threatened corrosions of its own.

Fraxinus must have sensed his reluctance, because he went on in a different tone. 'Perhaps I'm a fool to interest myself in such things,' he said lightly. 'The kind of fool who thinks that there are things in the world more valuable than newly minted coin. The kind of fool who seeks for treasure in dreams, and takes Goran the Forefather too seriously by far when he tells his remotest descendants that there is no sin but forgetfulness. In Xandria, I fear, we have committed that sin a thousand times over. We *know* that we lost the art of making maps because the Slithery Sea defied the maps we made – but how much more must we have lost along with the memory that we once had it? Such things as this were not invented and shaped without reason. Although the vast chain of tellings and re-tellings might have altered them and distorted them to some degree, they still retain shadows of their original meanings. I'm the kind of fool who believes that we must respect the reasons our forefathers had for asking us to remember these things.'

Still Ereleth said nothing, although she must have been tempted. Andris wanted to reply, to say that if a man like that might be reckoned a fool, then he would be one too, but he was distracted by an uncomfortable sensation in his guts, which was probably the ordinary legacy of a slightly spoiled meal.

All this is futile, he thought, though he was ashamed to say so in front of Carus Fraxinus. *In the end, it will come to nothing. I am a pawn in the hand of fate, as Ereleth says, and I have no choice but to go to the destiny which she appoints. I can't afford to care about badly coloured maps and merchants' dreams, no matter how sincerely I might wish that I could.*

The flap of cloth which screened them from the driver of the cart was pulled aside then, and the driver poked his head through the gap. It was one of Jacom Cerri's men, Kristoforo.

'Rider comin' up to the column from the right-hand side, sir,' he reported laconically. 'All alone – looks like the giant.'

Andris could not help meeting Ereleth's triumphant gaze.

'Now,' she said, 'we shall know what there is to know. Then we must do what there is to do – merchants, soldiers, thieves and princes all alike.'

Andris discovered, somewhat to his distress, that he felt suddenly and horribly certain that the caravan *had* been steered to where it now was, and that the Corridors of Power – whatever they might be – had not as yet been utterly destroyed by the blight which had cut such a swathe of desolation through the enigmatic hills.

6

MOSSASSOR AND ITS fellows had been running for some time before they found Hyry Keshvara, and their pursuers had almost caught up with them while she was a burden to them. Once she could walk they began to draw ahead again, but the darklanders who were following them did not give up. Hyry supposed that they thought – correctly – that a party of three Serpents in the company of a single injured golden might be far the easiest prey on offer in the southern reaches of the forest, while still constituting a conquest of which they could boast to their dragomite-chasing fellows.

Three times Hyry suggested to Mossassor that she should go to meet the darklanders and do what she could to persuade them to abandon the chase, but Mossassor would not hear of it. She got the impression that its two companions – especially the one named Ssifuss – would have been glad to see her put to some practical use, but Mossassor evidently believed that she was a valuable addition to their party.

'Musst not try to sspeak to ssem,' it told her sternly. 'Ssey have dartss, put you to ssleep. Sshoot firsst, assk quesstionss mussh later. Too late for uss. Reassh hillss ssoon. Ssey give up ssen. Sscared.'

Until they reached the hills, however, the Serpents maintained a relentless pace, rarely sleeping. She got the impression that they might not have stopped to sleep at all had she not been with them, although they certainly were not free of the need to sleep. She realised after a while that the seemingly hostile and disdainful attitude of the two Serpents who rarely spoke to her was due at least in part to their weariness. Much of the time they seemed to be in an almost trance-like state, semiconscious at best.

Hyry didn't find it easy to get Mossassor to redeem its promise to tell her stories by way of recompense for the one she had told it, and didn't like to press the matter too closely while it was in a distressed state, but she did gather that its own people had myths which referred to the ship which had supposedly brought humans to the world, and to the things that the forefathers had built when they first disembarked from their marvellous craft.

'Firsst humanss did not undersstand, you ssee,' Mossassor said, on one of the occasions when it strove to make good its word. 'Did not know sstealthy wayss of chaoss. Did not know sslyness of prossessess of *sshange*. Sso wisse, sso *young*. My anssesstorss knew ssat only life sstandss againsst dissolution, only permanensse iss *reproducssion*, ssecretss musst be hidden in *flessh*. Your forefathers made *ssity*, mine sshowed them how to make *garden*. Iss debt for ssat, you undersstand. Iss debt you owe. Iss not your fault you hardly remember . . . you have no ssecretss hidden in flessh, Kesshvara. Only humanss wiss Sserpent'ss blood have ssecretss. Too few . . . always too few. Sserpent'ss blood and Ssalamander'ss fire iss ssere, but not enough. When all iss well, no ssecretss. When catasstrophe comess, ssecretss ssurfasse. Ssee?'

Hyryr didn't see, although she felt that she had caught a fleeting glimpse of the beginnings of an explanation, but her attempts to elicit more exact information only served to reveal that Mossassor didn't quite see either. The source of the Serpent's supposed wisdom really was some story that had been handed down across the generations like the *Lore of Genesys*, undoubtedly corrupted by errors and perhaps irredeemably garbled. Given that Serpents were – according to Mossassor's account – good at forgetting things, this was not entirely surprising.

The main difference between human lore and Serpent lore, so far as Hyry could judge, was that Serpent lore spoke of something new happening in times of strife – the surfacing of some secret 'hidden in the flesh' of Serpents and of those humans who had the mysterious thing called 'Serpent's blood'. Mossassor thought that some such secret was already awakening in its own flesh, and would become clearer with time and appropriate stimulation. Its companions evidently felt no such stirrings – and Sssifuss at least was sceptical about Mossassor's – but they appeared to owe some kind of debt to Mossassor, which they were discharging by accompanying it on its quest.

Hyry pressed the Serpent as hard as she could for a more detailed account of what it imagined to be happening to the world as a result of the strange blight that was consuming the Dragomite Hills, but it had told her as much as it could. When it had reached the limits of its limited understanding it had only one more thing to say, which was: 'Iss human word for ssurfassing of ssecretss in flessh, I ssink. You will know what it meanss if I ssay. I ssink iss pronounssed *pee-doh-gen-ess-iss*. Iss right? You underssstand now?'

Unfortunately, Hyry Keshvara had never heard of any such word. It sounded like the kind of word that Aulakh Phar might know, or Carus Fraxinus, but to Hyry it meant nothing at all. Its etymological relationship to *Genesys* seemed obvious enough, but what the prefix might signify she had no idea.

Hyry's spirits were by no means uplifted when she saw the Dragomite Hills, and it was quickly apparent to her that Mossassor's companions were deeply disturbed by the devastation which the mounds had suffered. Ssifuss condescended for once to express an opinion in human language, so that she might appreciate the extent of its anxiety. 'Iss bad,' it said. 'Iss ferry, ferry bad.' She didn't attempt to contradict or reassure it.

They continued into the hills for some six or eight kims before Mossassor decided that they were finally secure from the possibility of a darklander attack.

'Ssafe now,' it said, to Hyry as well as its companions. 'Ssleep.'

'This isn't going to be easy,' Hyry told it. 'We didn't have any chance to stockpile food and water while we were moving so quickly through the forest. We'll starve or die of thirst long before we get to the other side – and we're surrounded by desperate dragomites.'

'Not be afraid,' it replied. 'Ssome dragomitess have Sserpent'ss blood. Dissasster makess ssem sshow it.'

Hyry wasn't at all sure that this judgment was entirely reliable – and neither, it seemed, were Ssifuss and Ssumssarum. They did, however, lay themselves down to sleep, giving every indication that any and all other questions could wait until they had fully recovered their strength and composure.

Perhaps because Hyry had lain so long unconscious after the flowerworm stung her, or perhaps because she had slept in brief snatches whenever the Serpents had stopped in the forest, she found it annoyingly difficult to sleep now, beneath the iridescent brilliance of the myriad stars. She dozed off several times only to wake again; although she lost all track of time she never quite lost touch with the world. The stink of the hills was always in her nostrils, and the silence seemed oppressive after the ceaseless rustlings of the forest.

So deep was the silence, in fact, that every slight and momentary sound struck her ears like an alarm. Twice she sat up and looked wildly about, only to see a worker dragomite on a surprisingly distant ridge. She had seen such creatures half a dozen times in the forest, but always in retreat, and the Serpents showed not the slightest fear of them. She wondered whether the rumours about Serpents having the ability to control dragomites might be true. Perhaps, she thought, they had the power to secrete aromatic compounds like the one Aulakh Phar had, which acted as an olfactory instruction to dragomites to return to their nests.

The third time Hyry sat up, however, she was certain that the sound was different, and close by, and threatening. She was right. Had the night been cloudy she might not have been able to pick out the men who were skulking in the shadows, but the flamestars were wonderfully bright, and her eyes were sharp. It was not a good night for a sneak attack.

Without a moment's hesitation she rolled over and began to shake Mossassor. It awoke almost immediately.

'Darklanders,' she said. 'They came over yonder ridge not a minute ago. Five hundred mets away, at the most. I couldn't count them, but it looks like a full warband. Thirty, maybe forty.'

'Sshouldn't do ssat,' Mossassor said, in a peevish tone.

Hyry sympathised with its annoyance. She too would have laid odds against the darklanders coming out of the forest. Their normal fear of dragomites had obviously been eroded by their 'victories' in the forest and the sorry state of the mounds.

Ssifuss and the others were awake now, gathering up their meagre luggage.

'I'm certain that I can talk them into going back now,' Hyry said urgently. 'They won't hurt me – I'm sure of that.'

'*No!*' said Mossassor determinedly. '*Musst* come.'

Had it been human, she might have been pig-headed about the

matter and insisted on exercising her own judgment, but the fact that it was not human somehow made it easier to defer to its command. Unfortunately, the way forward in the direction opposite to that from which the darklanders were coming was uphill, and they had to toil up a very awkward slope. Before they reached the ridge that would hide them their pursuers came over the rim of the shallow hill immediately behind them, and caught sight of them – perhaps for the first time in several days. They responded to the sighting with an ebullient chorus of war-cries.

They can't stop me shouting, Hyry thought, and half turned to call out: 'Go back! You have no business here!' Their only response, alas, was an increase in the fervour of the shouts with which they urged one another forward.

'Run!' Mossassor urged, and Hyry knew that there was no alternative but to obey. The darklanders might be even more inclined now to loose off their various weapons at the earliest possible opportunity, going for a quick kill and yet another easy 'victory'.

The Serpents were strong and long-legged, good runners even at the worst of times, but they were not so speedy on uneven ground as they were on level terrain. The weight of their tails, which kept them nicely balanced while they ran on flat ground, seemed to be an inconvenience here, whether they were heading up or down. They were awkward and ungainly, and they tended to skid and slip on the oily patches which spotted and streaked the hills like some leprous infection. In the forest, Hyry had often found it hard to keep up with the Serpents in their faster paces, but her booted feet found better purchase here than their naked ones and her tailless body was far more adaptable to the task of scrambling up or half-sliding down precipitous slopes. Before they had travelled a thousand mets – nearer six hundred as a bird might have flown – it was obvious that the agile darklanders were gaining.

A couple of arrows bounced at their heels. Hyry knew that it would need a very lucky shot to prick one of them, but the darklanders must have known that even the slightest injury would deliver up a victim ready for the slaughter.

'We're not your enemies!' she shouted back. 'You have no reason to do this.' She still felt stubbornly sure that if she could only get them to listen she could make them understand that they were making a mistake, but they would not reply to her.

If only they would pause for just a moment, she thought breathlessly. *Savages they might be but they're human, thinking beings who have no real reason for engaging in this mad hunt.*

It was all true. The violation of the darklanders' territory had not been a real invasion; they had nothing at all to fear either from dragomites or from Serpents ... but none of that seemed to matter. The darklanders, like the Serpents they were chasing, had been overtaken by an acute sense of crisis and by the awareness of what they took to be omens of the world's end. They, like Mossassor, wanted to feel that they were *doing something*, even though they had only the vaguest notion of what it was that they ought to do. If only they could be persuaded that the appropriate thing was not to kill strangers on sight, but rather to join with them in a quest for a mysterious and long-lost garden ...

What am I doing here? Hyry thought. *If only Checuti had missed me on the road, and I had joined forces with Fraxinus in Khalorn, as we had planned ... where is he now, I wonder? Somewhere in the hills, making his patient way across them, with everything around him under his wise and careful control ...*

Then, while she was still taking some satisfaction from her superior agility and the efficiency of her boots, she leapt on to a patch of decaying fungus that was slicker and more liquid than the rest, and skidded horribly. She windmilled her arms, trying to stay on her feet, but it was no good. Had she had a tail she might have reached out with it to make a tripod, and thus steadied herself, but she was only human.

She fell, as heavily and as awkwardly as mere humans were ever wont to do, and found herself rolling down a slope, her head spinning literally and figuratively. When she came to rest she was supine, and felt that every bone and sinew in her body had been wrenched and jolted.

Mossassor was suddenly with her, reaching out to her. She knew that it was alone, that its companions were far too wise to stop for her sake, but she had no breath to scream at it to be gone, and she could only thrash about, ungraciously and ungratefully, with her bruised arms. She was trying with all her might to command the creature to go, and go with all possible haste, but it didn't understand.

They won't hurt me! she thought defiantly, as the airway into her lungs opened with a horrid, agonising abruptness and let her breathe again. *I can handle them!* No audible words came out of her gagging throat.

The starlit space above her seemed to fill up with blurred shadows, looming from every possible direction, and it seemed that her tear-filled eyes were telling her that it was all over: that Mossassor was doomed and so was she. But then she realised that no amount of blurring could turn those nightmare shapes into angry darklanders, and that what she was seeing was a host of dragomites, which was welling up out of the ground to either side of the place where she lay. The huge creatures were scampering past her on both sides, the noise of their multitudinous feet becoming thunderous, as they headed off Mossassor's pursuers.

The darklanders were shouting at one another again, but these shouts weren't war-cries or exultant encouragements – these were screams of fear and howls of anguish.

By the time Hyry was able to sit up the dragomites had formed a protective phalanx before and to either side of the place where she and Mossassor were. One glance was all it required to show her that there was nothing at all accidental about their array. This was no mere coincidental confusion of three independent groups. The dragomites had come forth from their devastated nest purely and simply for the purpose of screening a Serpent and a human woman from their foolish enemies.

The dragomites were mostly workers, with only a handful of warriors among them, but the darklanders were in no mood to make nice distinctions. They turned tail and fled, pausing only to launch a brace of badly flighted javelins – and that, Hyry felt sure, was only because the men carrying them had been direly anxious to disemburden themselves in order that they might run faster.

Something very strange is happening here, Hyry thought, as Mossassor rested a reassuring hand on her shoulder. *The whole world and the order of things within it has been turned upside-down. I am a part of it, but I can't understand what's going on. Can anyone, I wonder? Is there someone, somewhere – or perhaps something – which is in control of all these miracles, laying them out one by one like a logical train of thought, carrying us all towards our magical destiny?*

She wished that it might be so – that there might be someone *in charge* of this mad adventure – who could and would see to it that the adventure came in the end to a satisfactory conclusion . . . but she knew, in her heart, that it was not so, and that whatever weird destiny had taken her in its unkind grip was every bit as blind and helpless as she was.

There was a human word for what was happening, apparently – but she had no idea what it meant.

When she had breath enough, she laughed.

Then the dragomite workers turned around, to direct their huge and fully open eyes at her – or, to be strictly accurate, at Mossassor.

'Not be afraid,' Mossassor advised her, with an insistence that did not seem entirely sincere. 'Iss good, thiss. Iss very, very good.'

She wondered if Ssifuss and Ssumssarum would agree, if and when they found out what had happened in their wake.

7

J ACOM KNEW THAT he should have been glad to be able to see the stars. He should have been able to rejoice in the fact that the clear skies had given the expedition a chance to make better headway than it had during the previous two nights. Unfortunately, he couldn't quite persuade himself to see things that way. He couldn't shake off a dolorous awareness that every kim that passed underfoot took him further away from the land of his birth, further reducing his chances of ever seeing that land again.

The Forest of Absolute Night had been bad enough, with its perpetually eerie light and its sly unearthliness, but the Dragomite Hills seemed infinitely worse. The landscape seemed to him to be the very essence of corruption: the plain crumpled into a nightmarish ragbag of ups and downs, lavishly dressed with putrefying slime. He felt that he had been riding into the maw of death for days on end, and had almost reached his destination.

Purkin, who was patrolling while Jacom and Herriman stood watch to the left and right of the rear end of the column, stopped beside him, eyeing him uncertainly. Jacom, fearing that his state of mind might be embarrassingly obvious, tried to pull himself together.

'No sign of any movement, sergeant,' he said. 'The good weather doesn't seem to have brought the dragomites out of their burrows.'

'No sir,' said Purkin dutifully. He remained where he was, as if he were waiting for something.

'I still don't know any more than I did at nightfall,' Jacom said petulantly. 'If anyone bothers to tell me what's going on, I'll pass the message on.'

So far as he knew, Dhalla had concluded her secret conference with Ereleth several hours ago, but if Ereleth had formed any plans she certainly hadn't taken anyone else into her confidence. Nor could he imagine any kind of plan which Ereleth might make.

'Thought that boy of yours might've heard somethin' more, sir,' the sergeant wondered aloud.

'He's asleep,' Jacom said. 'It's been a long day.'

'Some of the men think she might go into the mounds,' Purkin reported hesitantly. 'They figure she might think that 'cause the dragomite-tamers were all women, and 'cause they killed all the men but not the princess, she and the giant might find a welcome of sorts.'

'She's no coward,' Jacom observed, 'but she'd want a better argument than that before walking into the dragomites' den. Anyone would.'

'The men were wondering if . . . well, maybe the giant didn't just track the women. Maybe she caught up with them. Talked to them.'

'I don't think so,' Jacom said wearily. 'Nobody's said anything to me about it. All I know is that the women who took the princess met up with dragomites, and the princess has been taken into one of the mounds. What could there possibly be to add?'

'Well, sir,' said Purkin tactfully, 'that's pretty much what we were thinkin'. As far as the men can see, sir, the princess is either dead or as good as. They think – and I'm inclined to agree, sir – that our last chance of ever gettin' the princess back vanished when she went into that mound.'

'I see,' Jacom said, and waited for the sergeant to go on.

Purkin nodded his head, as though Jacom had agreed with him. 'It's like this, sir,' he went on, still trying – not altogether successfully – to employ maximum tact. 'This Carus Fraxinus seems to us to be a decent sort. Good employer, adventurous without bein' reckless, determined without bein' stubborn. The men feel, sir – meanin' no disrespect – that as the princess is beyond our reach now . . . in any case, sir, they wouldn't feel right if they were to leave Fraxinus in the lurch, with him bein' under strength an' all.'

'Or to put it another way,' Jacom said dully, 'they reckon the time has come for the final phase of the mass desertion. What you're trying to tell me is that you're no longer members of the king's guard, and no longer under my orders. From now on, you answer to Carus Fraxinus. I'm on my own.'

'Not on your own, exactly,' Purkin hastened to reassure him. 'Just . . . well, sir, I'm not sayin' anyone else is *takin' charge*, but . . .'

'That's OK,' Jacom said, feeling that there was not the least need for any further beating about the bush. 'Message understood. No problem. As of now, I resign my commission. As of now, you can stop calling me sir. From this day forward, I'm just a common or garden merchant-adventurer in exile, just like everybody else. One of the boys.'

He had not anticipated the relief he would feel when he said all that. Nor had he anticipated the look of sheer amazement which possessed Purkin's face.

'Sir . . . ?' Purkin said. He had nothing to add; he was at a loss for words. He had expected a flaming row, a fierce argument or – at the very least – an animated discussion. He had not expected meek surrender.

I've made a mess of it again! Jacom thought. *Whatever I do, it's wrong. If I'd tried to shout and bluster he'd have despised me for not being able to see what's what. Because I didn't, he thinks I'm a coward. What in the world am I supposed to say?*

'You can call me Jacom now,' he said aloud, determined that he must at least maintain a civilised front. He didn't bother to ask whether Purkin had a first name. Captain or not, he was still the son of a landed gentleman. He didn't suppose that Fraxinus would pay him a higher wage than anyone else – the merchant had been scrupulously even-handed with his generosity to date – but that didn't mean that he had to address his new fellows as if they were old friends. Xandrian propriety still meant something, even in the rotten heart of the Dragomite Hills.

'I'll tell the men it's sorted,' Purkin said, refraining from the use of any name or title. As an afterthought he added: 'Thanks.' Then he marched off, in properly military fashion, along a trail that was already well worn although it took him wide of the area they had cleared while making camp. The fungi which grew on the mounds were soft and flimsy at the best of times, easily trampled and crushed. The diseased mulch to which almost everything had now been reduced was easily flattened out. The marks of Purkin's previous circuits stood out very clearly in the sparkling starlight.

Jacom relaxed again. Once the bitterness occasioned by Purkin's reaction to his capitulation had eased he was left with no particular sense of loss or defeat. He had, after all, simply acknowledged a truth which had been manifest for some time.

He looked up as he caught a slight sound from the slope which veered sharply upwards some ten or twelve mets in front of him, but he couldn't see anything moving there. He turned his head slightly to concentrate all his attention into his sense of hearing, but the constant murmur emanating from the camp and from the place where the horses and donkeys were tethered made it impossible to separate out the sound of anything which might be moving beyond the brow of the nearest ridge.

There was a good deal of restlessness in the camp in spite of the lateness of the hour. No one should have been unready for sleep, given that they had been on the move for nearly twenty hours, with only a brief rest in the midday, but the ex-guardsmen must have been waiting for Purkin to bring a response to their cautious ultimatum, and they were presumably rejoicing in the good news.

Jacom walked forward a few mets, crossing the ragged line marked by Purkin's footfalls. There was ample light to display the slopes which were in his direct line of vision, but the undulations of the mounds were so sharp that a hidden army could have been massing within half a kim. He told himself that he was being oversensitive, but he felt the hairs on the back of his neck prickling with growing alarm. He felt certain that something was out there.

He touched his forehead reflexively, where he had anointed it with Phar's magic salve – to whose odour the dragomites were supposed to react by turning tail. So far, he had no cause for complaint against it, but how could he be sure that it was really the salve that was keeping the monsters at bay?

A few thin clouds had drifted up from the western horizon to streak the starscape with shadows, and the light suddenly seemed far less than perfect. He took another step forward, peering anxiously into the darkness. He drew his sword, weighing it carefully in his hand, but he made no move to raise the alarm, because he had no clear sensory evidence that anything was wrong.

Then he saw the shadows moving over the ridge: the shadows with eyes.

Their bodies hardly reflected the starlight at all, but their eyes were moist enough to gleam, and the faint hint of light seemed quite uncanny. For a moment he had the illusion that the eyes were human eyes, no more than half a dozen paces away, but he knew that they were much larger and much further away. Unfortunately, they were coming closer all the time.

There was nothing remotely human about the shadow behind the eyes – and he could now make out the insectile pattern of their movement. He could even see the huge jaws – huger by far than those of the ordinary dragomites he had grown well used to seeing on the slopes. These were not workers, but the rarer creatures Koraismi had pointed out to him and called 'warriors'.

He opened his mouth, but as he was formulating his alarm call it was overtaken by another voice. Herriman, who was posted on the far side of the encampment, yelled out a split second before him, and quite took his breath away.

Corruption and corrosion! he thought. *The bastards are all around us!*

The camp had come to life with a vengeance now as everyone reacted to the alarm, running this way and that to grab weapons and take up defensive stations around the wagons and the rope enclosure where the anxious horses were. Jacom, with his sword in his hand, began to walk slowly backwards. He dared not turn to run because that would have meant taking his eyes off the shapes silhouetted against the stars, which were still increasing in number. It somehow seemed that while he moved slowly and purposefully *they* moved slowly, with equal care.

He realised that the warrior dragomites weren't charging. This was no attack: they were simply massing on the slope, making their presence felt but keeping their distance.

It's Phar's magic salve! he thought. *It really works. They're not attacking us.*

He had backed up far enough by now to bump into another man, who reached out a hand to steady him. 'Careful, captain,' a voice murmured in his ear. 'Look where you're going.' It was Andris Myrasol.

Jacom shook off the steadying hand. He was seized by a sudden perverse conviction that all this was the fault of the big amber. If he hadn't been in the Wayfaring Tree that night when Herriman got hurt, none of this would have happened. No sooner had he thought this than Jacom felt ashamed of the injustice of it, but he couldn't keep a certain churlishness out of his tone as he said: 'Not *captain* any more, Prince Myrasol. Had they only come yesterday, I could have died an officer and a gentleman, but not now. That's life, isn't it? First you lose everything, then you die. The rot sets in before you're even born.'

'We're not dead yet,' the amber muttered, his voice hardly above a whisper. 'They haven't come to kill us. They've come to move us on. They haven't quite got us where they want us – yet.'

Jacom turned to look up at the big man's pale face. 'What the filth are you talking about?' he demanded, bitterly angry at the thought that this mere vagabond might understand what was happening far better than he did.

'I'm not sure about the ones we saw further north,' Myrasol said, 'but these warriors have a guiding mind behind them – a mind with plans and projects of its own. We're close to the Corridors of Power, where something lives ... *still* lives, I presume, in spite of the thing that's laid waste to all of this ... which is more than a mere mob of unearthly insects. We have something it wants, I think. I only wish I knew what, and what it will cost us to deliver it.'

'You're mad,' Jacom opined, wondering why he had such an ingrained habit of saying things he didn't mean.

'Maybe,' Myrasol conceded. 'But it seems to me that they're sane enough, and they seem to think we need an escort, to make sure that we go exactly where they intend us to go. You might as well sheath that sword, captain – it's about as much use against that lot as a sewing-needle.'

How can he take it all so calmly? Jacom wondered. *Maybe he thinks he's as good as dead already, with Ereleth's worm eating him away inside – but he's no worse off than the rest of us. We're all as good as dead. I've been as good as dead since . . .* He let go of the unhelpful train of thought, and concentrated on the huge moist eyes of the dragomite warriors, which were glimmering faintly in the light of the sea of stars.

'According to Aulakh Phar,' he said, keeping his voice absolutely level and calm, as the loreless code of heroism somehow seemed to require, 'they're all female. Did you know that? All female, all sterile. He thinks each mound has its own gigantic queen, buried deep beneath the surface, but no one's ever seen one and returned to tell the tale. No one knows for sure.'

'Maybe this is our chance to find out,' Myrasol said drily, reaching out with one of his absurdly long arms to take his scrawny cousin by the shoulders, and draw her into his protective clasp.

'Rather you than me,' Jacom riposted, confident that he could maintain the tone for as long as appearances demanded it. 'If it's all the same to you, Prince Mapmaker, I'll just help to mind the horses. After all, I'm not an officer any more. From now on, I can skulk in the rear with everybody else, as safe as safe can be.'

Unfortunately, he knew only too well that, in the present circumstances, *as safe as safe can be*, wasn't very safe at all.

8

LUCREZIA WAS CERTAIN, afterwards, that she had never truly lost consciousness, but that thought and sensation had somehow been suspended for a while in a timeless void, never allowed to lapse or even to relax. The image of the dragomite's eyes remained with and within her throughout that phase of her existence, as if some vast supernatural being were holding her beneath its external gaze, forbidding any kind of escape.

She thought at first, when time began again, that she would soon recover herself completely, but that was an illusion. The balance of her mind remained horribly awkward for a further and much longer interval, while paralysis still held limited sway over her limbs. She was not incapable of movement, but her body felt so heavy that the greatest force she could exert was hardly able to twitch a finger or a toe. This second phase of her captivity was worse than the first.

She was aware of a long journey through the Forest of Absolute Night, and the green fringe-forest, and a further trek across the nightmarish slopes of the Dragomite Hills, but her perception of these surroundings was oddly distorted. In the peculiar existential state in which she found herself it seemed that one impression did not have to be tidied out of the way into the storeroom of memory before another could take its place; the images overlapped and overlaid one another, becoming facets of some monstrously complicated and ever-growing crystal, building into a vast confusion in which daylight and starlight, darkness and purple radiance, leaf-mould and green grass, greasy mud and clear water, gnarled twigs and bulbous deathcaps, the slitted eyes of dragomites and the tiny eyes of mound-men, the stink of horse-sweat and the staleness of spore-laden air, up and down, inside and out, everything and nothing were all woven together into a horrid chaotic vortex.

While this accumulation occurred she could neither speak nor move nor weep, but she was capable of a kind of self-sensation and a kind of emotion, whose produce likewise built in a sort of mad crescendo, in which terror and horror, mortal dread and panic formed a great web of sublime anxiety.

Her awakening from this phase of the experience was more ordinary, because it brought her back to what she thought of as a normal state of being. It was no surprise, though, to find that she felt desperately and overwhelmingly tired. Returned though she was to the possibility of commonplace thought and speech, the only desire of which she was immediately capable was the desire to leave it again, in order to enjoy a more natural kind of absence: to sleep, and thus, authentically, to rest. For this reason alone she had to face a third and final awakening, which was almost a rebirth.

After this third awakening she remembered that she had spoken, briefly, and had heard words spoken to her, but that it had been too dark to see where she was or who had been with her. She had taken food and water, too, but the taste of them was quite gone. If she had dreamed while she was asleep she had forgotten her dreams utterly – but she had not forgotten that awesome never-ending moment in which she had been trapped when the dragomite stung her, nor that frightful crescendo which had followed her partial recovery from the effects of the sting, when she must have been drugged repeatedly to keep her docile. Her memory of all this was peculiar in the extreme, for she had no sensible way to accommodate it within the familiar narrative that she had so far made of her life, but it was all there.

That, she thought wonderingly, when she had the leisure to do so, *was the true gateway to adventure, the threshold decisively separating my old life from the new. I am free at last to go beyond the horizons of ordinary experience, to venture into unimagined realms, to discover the unexpected. This is what I have always sought, under the spur of my Serpent's blood; this is what I have always longed for without knowing what it was I needed. This is the prize, the treasure, the sacred gift which was required to make me complete. What now? How does it begin?*

She opened her eyes and looked around.

She was in a dimly lit chamber whose ceiling, floor and walls were all smoothly curved. The light, though wan, was very white and it shone, albeit unevenly, from every visible surface. The mottled walls were covered in the fungus which the warrior women had carried in their lamps; this was its natural habitat. The air was very warm and humid; it was almost as if the walls were sweating and the corridors breathing.

The three human figures which loomed over her, peering down at her curled up and recumbent form, appeared at first to be less than solid. It was as if they were shadows detached from the fleshy forms which once had cast them – but that was merely an optical illusion. As her eyes adjusted to the strange light she was able to make out their features, and realised that they did indeed have real substance. They were very real, very ordinary people.

One of them was Jume Metra; the other two were differently dressed, smaller in build and less stiff in their posture. Lucrezia guessed that these were humans of a different caste: workers, not warriors.

As she became accustomed to the glowing walls she saw that the chamber she was in had not a single corner anywhere; all its angles were rounded. Three passages led away from it, but none of them was in the same plane as the hollowed-out 'floor' on which she lay. The floor was not entirely bare, but such patchy light as it emitted was mostly obscured by numerous untidy heaps of armour and piles of indeterminate debris. There was no furniture of any kind.

If these were the legendary Corridors of Power, Lucrezia thought, they hardly warranted such a dignified name. She was determined that she must not be afraid, even though she knew that she was in the secret depths of a dragomite nest.

'Can you speak?' asked Metra, not ungently.

'I can,' she answered. Metra helped her stand, but she shook off the assistant arm as soon as she could. Her limbs ached, but she reminded herself that she was a princess, and an ambassador of Xandria. She must display all the fortitude she could.

The clothes she stood in were those she had been wearing when she had been captured. They were disgustingly filthy. She was glad to discover, though, that she still had her belt and pouches. Her secret armoury was safe. Her head spun and her empty stomach bewailed its condition in waves of paradoxical nausea, but she ignored all that. She stood straight, so that she could look Jume Metra in the eye, and said: 'What now?'

She had to imagine the warrior woman's grudging admiration; Metra's doggedly inexpressive features gave no sign of it. The warrior pointed to one of the shadowy piles. 'The packs we took from your horses are there,' she said. 'Dress yourself in clean clothes.'

'I need cold water to drink and warm water to wash in,' Lucrezia said, 'and food to eat. How long is it since I was stung?'

Metra made a brusque sign to her two companions, who must have been standing by in expectation of such requests; neither had to take more than half a dozen steps. One fetched a broad bowl, the other a drinking-flask and a plate. The water in the bowl was barely lukewarm; the drinking-flask contained a liquid as syrupy in viscosity as it was in taste; the stuff on the plate wasn't bread.

Metra turned on her heel and left. The other women stayed to help as Lucezia peeled off her dirty clothes. Lucrezia had to accept the help which they offered; she barely had the strength to sort through the packs.

It was one of the workers who said: 'Thirteen days have passed since they found you in the forest. The warriors brought you as speedily as they could. There isn't much time. We must quit the nest, and soon.'

Lucrezia peered at the woman wonderingly, wishing that she could see her more clearly.

'You're human,' she said, as if it were a marvel. 'You speak as a human addressing a fellow-human.'

'Don't be afraid,' the second worker said. 'We mean you no harm.'

Lucrezia touched the wound at her neck, where the dragomite had stabbed her. It was almost healed. It wasn't unduly sensitive to her touch, but she could feel a scar.

'What was that thing which stung me?' she asked. 'It wasn't a warrior or a worker?'

'It was a drone,' the first worker told her.

'It was in command of the warriors,' Lucrezia said, carefully not framing the guess as a question. 'It was the drone, not the warriors, who decided that I should be brought here.' In the meantime, she rummaged in the packs which had been taken from Hyry Keshvara's donkeys, searching for something to wear which would not look too absurd. Hyry Keshvara had owned no clothes that were suitable for a princess to wear when confronting a queen, nor was there anything in her luggage which qualified as a good fit.

'Drones are subject to the queen,' the second worker said. 'We are all the children of the queen. We are all of one mind here.'

Lucrezia hesitated briefly over the choice, but there was little scope for indecision. Given that she had no alternative but to seem austere, she elected to be uncompromising about it. She picked out Hyry's plainest shirt and a severely functional but loosely fitting jacket to wear over it. She could only find one skirt, and that was too long, but it offered a better option than trousers whose legs would be too long.

'Would that be the mound-queen?' she asked, trying to recall exactly what Jume Metra had said to her in the forest. 'Or do you mean the dragomite queen?'

'We are all of one mind here,' the worker repeated. 'The mound-queen is the voice of the dragomite queen.'

Was that what Metra had said? Lucrezia struggled to remember, wishing that the sin of forgetfulness were not so very easy to commit. She transferred her belt, with all its accoutrements, and the few ornaments she had been wearing. She had managed to wash the worst of the dirt out of her hair with the same soap she had used on her body, but it was still in poor condition and there was no way to dry it, so she tied it back.

'All right,' she said, when she felt that she was as presentable as she could be, in the circumstances. 'I'm ready. What now?'

'Come this way,' the second worker said. 'Don't be afraid. The queen will explain everything.'

Lucrezia didn't bother to ask which queen they were talking about. After all, everyone was all of one mind here. The voice of one, it seemed, was the voice of all. And yet, they were human – even Jume Metra, who evidently believed that the status of warrior excused every discourtesy. *My father's ministers always said that the game of diplomacy was difficult*, she reminded herself. She tried not to think too hard about where she was and what her chances were of ever seeing the sky again. She had been told not to be afraid, and she was doing her best to take the advice.

The journey to the mound-queen's throne room was a short one – no more than two hundred steps, although the route was full of twists and turns. They had brought her to the very threshold of her destination. That was convenient, given that she ached so badly in every limb, but she didn't doubt that they had done it to save the queen's impatience rather than for her benefit.

The workers led her into a much larger chamber than the one where she had awakened. Now that her eyes had grown more accustomed to the peculiar light the space seemed rather dimly lit, because its glowing ceiling was so high and the light of its walls was interrupted by a crowd of onlookers. Metra was there, and a dozen other warriors. The workers who had brought her pushed her forward, but they stepped back to join the warriors by the wall.

The mound-queen had a throne of sorts. It was by no means as grand as the monarch of Xandria's ceremonial seat but it was the only chair in the chamber, just as Belin's was, and it too was raised upon a dais so that its seated occupant could look down upon the heads of her standing subjects. Like Belin, the queen made up for the ordinariness of her features with the ornamentation of her dress; she wore a helmet, like Metra's, but much more so: a surreal impression of a dragomite's head, with 'antennae' and 'palps'. Her court, like Belin's, included the unhuman as well as the human, but where the Xandrian king had guardian giants the mound-queen had dragomites: two of them, both of the same relatively small and deceptively meek kind as the one which had stung her. They were standing on their four hind legs to either side of the throne, with their heads raised high above the queen's.

The queen was very fat. It was impossible to tell how old she might be, but she wasn't young. She was golden, but very pale. Her throne and its supportive dais seemed to be growing out of the floor of the chamber and she somehow gave the impression of growing out of the throne: it was as if the whole ensemble were some kind of weird unearthly excrescence.

Lucrezia was decidedly unsettled by the sight of the mound-queen, even though there were so many similarities between this occasion and her audiences with her father that she felt she ought to have been able to laugh. It would have been easy enough to see this display as an exercise in tawdry and ineffectual imitation, if only the two patient dragomites had not been there, with their 'hands' pressed together. She wondered whether one of them was the one which had stung her – and if so, which. They seemed absolutely identical, mirror-images of one another. Their presence here, whether dominant or subordinate, implied that the mound-queen did indeed have real power, of a kind which even Belin of Xandria could not command.

'Your name is Lucrezia,' the mound-queen said, without undue ceremony. 'You are from the place called Xandria, in the far north. Are you high-born among your people?'

'Yes I am,' Lucrezia answered warily.

'You were a prisoner of the river men. Our warriors rescued you.'

'Did they rescue me?' the princess answered, trying not to sound accusing. 'It seemed to me that they merely took possession of me. The Eblans wouldn't have hurt me.'

'Perhaps you do not understand what manner of men the river people are,' the queen said sharply, leaning forward slightly. 'Perhaps they told you that they live in cities, and told you that they were *civilised*. They are savages, who hate all other human beings. They fight incessantly among themselves, and they kill dragomites whenever they see them. They kill *us* whenever they see us – if they can. They attacked our workers when they passed by our mound. It seems that the pale people who live in the purple forest are no different.'

And what of your own warriors? Lucrezia thought. *All I have seen of their conduct has been naked brutality.*

'The river people told me that their intentions were peaceful,' she said aloud. 'They too were mortally afraid of the forest people, but they declared themselves anxious to make friendly contact with Xandria. The darklanders are usually peaceful too – but they're mortally afraid of dragomites, and when they saw that your people were allied with dragomite invaders they couldn't help jumping to the conclusion that they were being threatened by strange enemies. Had your emissaries approached them more carefully they'd have been made welcome.' She was not certain that this was true, but it seemed the most diplomatic line to follow.

The mound-queen was uninterested in open debate. 'How many queens has Xandria?' she asked abruptly.

'By tradition,' Lucrezia answered, 'thirty-and-one. But that leaves out of account the petty queens of the Thousand Isles.'

'The Corridors of Power,' the mound-queen said, 'had eighty sister-queens, and every queen had a hundred thousand daughters and more. Every worker and every warrior in the quiet nests had a million sisters to share her quietness.'

Lucrezia noted her use of the past tense, but thought it best to make no direct comment on it. 'Your daughters and your sisters have suffered dire misfortune,' she observed. 'It gives me no pleasure to learn of it, I assure you. I'm not your enemy.'

'We have many enemies,' the queen said, 'but we do not count you one of them. You shall help us. You shall be one of us. Perhaps you shall be our salvation.'

Lucrezia would have been happier had these observations been phrased as questions rather than as statements, but she didn't feel that the time was ripe for contradiction. 'How might I do that?' she asked.

'We have not forgotten Xandria,' the mound-queen said. 'We know that there is a land beyond the forest – a good land, flat and empty. The plague from the south has destroyed everything, and the Corridors of Power are all but empty. Nest-wars have reduced our strength, but there are nests in the north which still have far more warriors than they can feed. They cannot go into the forest, so they will come south. What little remains they will claim, and we can no longer resist them. But we remember Xandria, and we understand what the blind queens cannot. We understand that the forest is a barrier and not a boundary, and that safety lies on its further side. We are not blind; we can see the way to a new beginning. When you are one with us you shall guide us to Xandria, where the hills shall rise again from the empty plain, and the Corridors of Power shall be renewed.'

'The plains north of the forest aren't empty,' Lucrezia said, fighting to remain calm although she understood perfectly well what the mound-queen was saying to her. 'People live there – as many as the land can accommodate. I'm not sure that you understand what I meant when I said that Xandria has thirty-and-one queens. It has only one king, but he is the ruler of five million people. The cities of the north are metal-rich and they have huge armies. You can't just march through the forest and start erecting dragomite mounds on the northern plain. The people whose land you try to take will resist you – and their neighbours won't be slow to help.'

'You shall speak for us,' the mound-queen said. 'We shall not come as invaders, but as guests. We shall not come as enemies, but as friends.'

It won't be easy to persuade the people of Khalorn to see things that way, Lucrezia thought sourly. *It would be no less difficult to stand before Belin's throne to tell him that he must welcome dragomites into his realm than it is to stand here to tell you that he will not.*

'You would be better to go south,' she said.

'The plague came from the south,' the mound-queen replied. 'There are huge marshlands there, which are difficult to cross.'

'Xandria will not welcome you, majesty,' Lucrezia said, feeling that she had little alternative but to make that clear. 'If you need a new home, you had better look to the south. If the plague is like the epidemics which sometimes sweep through the nations of the north, it may well be safer to go where it has already done its worst and passed by than to flee before it. Whether or not the forest can serve as a barrier, there is a danger that you will carry its seeds with you to the northern lands.'

'You shall be our guide,' the mound-queen told her stubbornly. 'We shall have horses and donkeys, and two carts. Your sisters will also be united with us. There is little time. You shall be a queen in your own land, daughter.'

There was a moment when Lucrezia couldn't quite work this out, although she was quite certain that she didn't want to be one of the mound-women, even if it meant becoming a queen. It was the second sentence which puzzled her.

'What carts?' she asked guardedly. 'I had only horses and donkeys when your warriors captured me.'

'We shall have many more,' the mound-queen said. 'The greater number of the drones must be eliminated, but there are three of your sisters numbered in the company, now that the giant has rejoined them.'

Lucrezia was still confused. 'Dhalla?' she said uncertainly. 'Has Dhalla come searching for me? She's with Fraxinus, isn't she? You're talking about Fraxinus's caravan. You're going to kill them all! You mustn't do that!'

'Not all,' the mound-queen said serenely. 'Your sisters shall be one with us, and shall keep two drones, as custom permits.'

'No!' Lucrezia objected. 'You mustn't do that. It's a terrible mistake. If you need help – and I believe you do – you mustn't kill Fraxinus and his men. They're the only ones really capable of helping you. If you make me one of you – whatever that might mean – I'll cease to be of any use to you. You're going about this entirely the wrong way. If you want help, you must come to us as one human to another, to make a proper alliance. You can't just *take us over*. You can't just *absorb* us into the nest. If you do that, you're doomed. Believe me – I know what's north of the forest, and you don't. I'm the one who understands this situation, not you. If you try to go north, whether you have horses and wagons or not, you'll have to run the gauntlet of the dragomite nests which you seem to count as enemies, then the darklanders, and then the armed might of Xandria. You'll all die – every last one of you. You need Carus Fraxinus, and Aulakh Phar. You need their knowledge, their understanding. They'll be more use to you than I am. If you stick to the path you've chosen, you're finished. You have to think in a different way now – a new way. Don't kill the people in the caravan – join forces with them! Accept them as friends.'

The mound-queen paused for thought. It was the first sign she had given that this really was a conversation, an exchange of ideas. After a little while she said: 'There are forest men with them – men who hate and fear us, by your own admission. Men who would try to kill us on sight.'

'They never knew that it was possible for men and dragomites to live harmoniously together,' Lucrezia said swiftly. 'Now that they know it, their attitude might change – but only if you will condescend to meet them face to face and prove to them that their fears are groundless.' *Except, of course*, she reminded herself, *that their fears aren't groundless at all, given your present intentions*.

The old woman slumped, relaxing into the frame of her tawdry throne. It seemed to shift slightly around her, welcoming her awkward bulk into its comforting embrace. There was a speculative gleam in the mound-queen's eye, but there was a cold smile playing about her lips which Lucrezia did not like at all. It was altogether too human for her liking. When Belin wore a smile like that, it boded ill for whoever happened to be in his thoughts.

'Don't act hastily, I beg of you,' Lucrezia said. 'We must talk at

389

length. You must understand what the world beyond the hills is like, for I fear that although you remember Xandria you have forgotten far too much.'

'There is no time,' the mound-queen said.

'You must make time,' Lucrezia insisted. 'I will tell you everything I can, but there are people with those wagons far wiser than I, far better able to help you than I. Go to them, I beg you. Hear what they have to say.'

'We cannot do that,' the mound-queen said. 'They would have to come here. Do you think they would do that, willingly?'

'Yes I do,' Lucrezia said quickly – knowing that it might prove to be a reckless promise. 'If you ask them in the right way, they will come. If you will let me go to them, I can bring them here. Let me do that, I beg you.'

The mound-queen seemed to be giving this due consideration, but after thirty seconds or so had passed she shook her head.

'We would prefer to send our own ambassadors,' she said, 'but we thank you for your counsel. We shall talk at greater length. There is more we need to know before we act.'

Lucrezia breathed a deep sigh of relief, although she knew that the victory she had won was a small one. The queen signalled to Jume Metra as she spoke – a casual, cursory signal which presumably confirmed an instruction given long before. Metra stepped forward and took the princess's arm. Lucrezia looked up at the faces of the dragomites which flanked the throne – at their huge, staring eyes. Their steady gaze stirred up a horrid memory, and made her shiver. *These creatures may seem human*, she thought, *but they live among dragomites, and I still cannot tell for sure whether they are masters, servants or equal partners. Have I said and promised far too much?*

She could not tell.

9

THE HUE AND cry which had spread through the camp like wildfire was slow to die down, although the dragomite warriors kept their distance. Carus Fraxinus was quick to get the column under way again, but no one was surprised when the warriors began to move with it, matching its pace. Jacom quickly came to the conclusion that Andris Myrasol had been right, and that they were in fact being herded. He rode to the big wagon to suggest to Fraxinus that it might be better not to yield to such pressure.

'What do you suggest we do, captain?' Fraxinus retorted, obviously having given the matter much thought. 'Have you counted them? Have you assessed the strength of those jaws? Would you rather be obstinate and challenge them to attack us, even though we have not the slightest desire to stay where we are? If we have to fight, let's do it when they try to bar our way and hold us back. We might stand a slender chance of breaking through their line and running southwards with all the speed we can muster; we stand none at all in a pitched battle.'

It was all true, and Jacom didn't try to argue. He dropped back, and took care to study the shadowy forms which prowled around and behind them. It was obvious that they would be difficult to repel if they chose to attack. A line of cavalry bristling with half-pikes used as lances might cause them some confusion, but if it came to a charge the dragomites would surely burst through. Men with spears and swords fighting from the wagons might inflict a good deal of damage on warriors swarming around them, but they couldn't hold out for long.

Fraxinus was right – the only chance the members of the expedition had of escaping the dragomites now that they were so close was to ride like the wind, and not stop until their pursuers were far behind. That would mean abandoning the wagons, and the donkeys, and almost all of their supplies. Those who escaped – and not everyone would – would be left with what they could carry, and nothing more.

No one promised him anything better, Jacom thought. *He learned that it might be possible to cross these hills, but no one guaranteed that he wouldn't meet dragomites, or that he could walk his carts and a donkey-train across as though it were a well-worn highway.* But he could take little or no pleasure in the thought that Fraxinus, like Jacom and Checuti and Princess Lucrezia, had bitten off more than he could chew.

It was oddly comforting to know that he was no longer entitled or expected to shout orders to his men. They had changed allegiance, and must look to someone else for guidance now. His only responsibility was to himself. Given that his was one of the better horses, and that he had very little in the way of luggage except for his sword, he would be as well placed as anyone if and when the time came to make a bolt for it. There would be no reason for him to waste a single backward glance . . . except, of course, that poor Koraismi had only sat on a horse three or four times since Jacom had undertaken to teach him to ride, and might be easy prey for those massive jaws.

The caravan moved on, and the dragomites followed. Another horse fell into step with his own and he looked around. His mouth curled into a reflexive sneer as he saw that it was Checuti. Andris Myrasol and Merel Zabio were close behind him – close enough to hear anything that was said.

'I ask you again to make a truce with us,' Checuti said. 'Surely this is a common enemy fearsome enough to make us allies.'

'What point would there be in that?' Jacom answered. 'Have you not heard? The guard is disbanded, and we're all equals in the face of disaster. If they attack, it'll be every man for himself.'

'If you think like that we're lost,' Checuti answered. 'Our only chance is to work together, to formulate a plan.'

'A plan!' Jacom laughed derisively.

'I think they can be disabled,' Myrasol said, speaking loudly to make sure that he could be heard. 'The problem is, it requires a simultaneous attack from two sides. They can only turn their heads one way at a time. If one man draws their attention, another can get in close enough to hurt them. They're heavily armoured about the head and neck, but their legs are jointed awkwardly. They can stand on the back four and rear up, but if their hindmost legs are crippled they're in trouble. The horses can out-manoeuvre them, but only if we fight in tight-knit groups. It's our only chance. There's no point in waiting for them to attack – we have to carry the fight to them, and soon.'

'What does Fraxinus say?' Jacom asked.

Checuti leaned over, to speak more confidentially. 'Fraxinus be damned,' he said. 'There's only a dozen men who count in that kind of fight. What do Captain Cerri and his sergeant say?'

'I can't speak for Purkin and his men,' Jacom replied, stressing the word *his* very faintly. 'But Jacom Cerri says that he's not about to take orders from a thief and a vagabond prince.'

Checuti scowled before turning in the saddle to look back at his companions. He shrugged his shoulders, as if to say *I tried*.

'No one's trying to give you orders, captain,' the amber called out impatiently. 'We're just trying to save your rotten life, and ours with it. Look up there, man – that's *death* stalking us! It's time to put your resentments aside, no matter what burden they've built up to.'

Jacom had an uncomfortable feeling that the amber was right. He wished that he'd been the one to think of a plan – however hazardous or optimistic – so that he could have gone to them, and demanded that they submit to his command. He couldn't turn around now, having lost everything he ever had or desired, to join forces with petty thieves. It was too much to ask of any man – even a man who rode in the shadow of unearthly death.

'Go make your peace with Purkin,' he said bitterly – feeling uncomfortably like a fool. 'Make your plans with a man of your own kind.'

Checuti and his companions fell back. The dragomites marched on, like soldiers on parade-drill. That was exactly what they were, Jacom realised. They were in strict military formation, awaiting orders – but from whom?

Phar's salve might still keep us safe, Jacom thought, clutching at straws. *Perhaps they can't come any closer than they are while we're wearing Phar's salve.*

The big wagon, which was leading the column, ground to a halt.

Jacom was still so close behind it that the momentum of his horse carried him past it, and he had to rein in sharply. So did Kirn, who had been riding on the far side of the wagon. The second wagon stopped in its turn. So did the dragomites. Six human figures stood in the path of the column, less than thirty mets away. They wore no armour and carried no weapons, but Jacom was more inclined to take that as an insult than a reassurance. So far as could be judged from their beardless faces they were all women.

'The warriors will not attack you,' one of the women called out. 'We mean you no harm.'

Why, then, are the warriors here at all? Jacom thought – but he said nothing. He looked around at Fraxinus, who was standing up on the bench in front of the wagon. Ereleth had climbed out to stand beside him.

'We are not here to fight,' said the dragomite-woman. 'We too are warriors, but we come unarmed, as a token of good faith. The mound-queen would like to talk with you. There are matters of importance to be decided, and time is short.'

Jacom was surprised – but only momentarily – when the reply that came swiftly back was: 'My name is Ereleth, queen of Xandria.' When he turned round he could see the frown on Fraxinus's face, but it was plain enough that the trader had been pre-empted, and dared not begin an argument now as to who might have the right to speak for the company.

The mound-woman, after a moment's hesitation, said: 'We greet you, queen of Xandria. Will you come to meet our own queen?'

'Your queen would be very welcome to come to us,' Ereleth replied, with an abundance of false courtesy. 'We would be honoured to receive her, and to talk with her.'

'That is impossible,' the other replied flatly. 'We beg you to come into the Corridors of Power. No harm will befall you there, so long as the dragomite queen maintains her reign. We promise you that. Since you are a queen, you may bring as many daughters as you wish, and your two drones. We promise you safe conduct, but you must come with us now. Time is pressing.'

Indeed it is, Jacom thought. *The end of the world is nigh – I can believe it now.*

'Is Princess Lucrezia in your care?' Ereleth asked. 'Is she safe and well?'

'One called Lucrezia is with the queen,' the mound-woman replied curtly. 'She is safe. You will see her, if you come. The queen will hear what you have to say.'

'Very kind of her,' muttered a female voice from a position close behind Jacom. Merel Zabio, her cousin and Checuti had all moved up to his shoulder again.

'I shall be honoured and delighted to pay our respects to your queen,' said Ereleth silkily. She must have known that she had little enough choice in the matter, having decided to appoint herself spokeswoman and declare herself a queen. 'I shall bring but one sister, and two drones.'

'What's a drone?' Merel asked. The question was addressed to Myrasol, but Jacom was too quick for him.

'Drones are their males,' he said. 'As in a beehive, they presumably keep a few for breeding purposes. She means that she'll take Dhalla and two men with her.'

'*Chaos and corruption!*' Myrasol murmured. The vehemence of the curse surprised Jacom for a moment, until he realised the way the amber's train of thought must be running. The next thing the big man said was: 'You're not coming. Even if Ereleth asks you – even if she tries to order you – you're not *coming*.' He was speaking to his cousin.

'Where you go,' Merel Zabio promptly replied, 'I go. Who else is going to look after you in there?'

It must be a good feeling, Jacom thought, to have a lover as brave and as determined as that. He presumed that Myrasol thought the same, although propriety naturally demanded an ungracious and ungrateful response to any such reckless offer.

'Andris Myrasol!' Ereleth called out. 'Checuti! To me, now.'

How ironic it is, Jacom thought, *that although she really is the queen of Xandria, there are only two drones in the entire company who'd answer to her command – and certainly not out of loyalty.* He noticed that she had not called out for Merel Zabio – but that Merel went along with Andris anyhow. He wondered whether the queen might order her away again, given that she could hardly reckon her a good ally, but Ereleth said nothing. Perhaps she didn't care to reveal to the waiting warrior-women that her authority was so fragile.

Jacom studied the huge head of the dragomite warrior which

stood alongside his station, twenty mets away. He imagined thrusting with his sword at the monstrous eyes, wondering if the creature could use its whip-like antennae to parry or whether it would have to meet a blade with its heavy jaw. Surely the jaw could not move as quickly as a trained fencer – but would it have to, since it seemed so massively solid? If the monster reared up, it could lift its eye beyond the reach of a sword-thrust. Would the part of its underbelly thus exposed be vulnerable to a steel blade, or would the point simply bounce off? The legs must be vulnerable, if only at the joints – but how many would have to be crippled before the creature lost mobility, and what would happen to a man who got close enough – and *stayed* close enough – to deliver more than one disabling blow?

The great head moved forward very slightly while he watched, as though nodding in contemptuous acknowledgement of his speculative stare. A man couldn't win such a contest, Jacom decided. Two men might stand a reasonable chance of hurting a single dragomite warrior, if they worked together as Myrasol had suggested, but the odds would still be stacked against them if the warriors attacked in force. How badly had the dragomites and their human allies suffered, he wondered, as a result of the blight? Might they be so reduced in strength that they dared not risk the loss of a single warrior?

While these thoughts were going through his head, Jacom had urged his horse forward a step or two, without quite realising why. It was as much of a surprise to him as it must have been to Myrasol and Checuti when he heard himself say: 'Wait! I'll go with you. Let Myrasol and his cousin stay behind.'

He could imagine that every pair of eyes in that column must have turned on him then, but he could only see Ereleth's, and her expression was thunderous. She didn't want the mound-women to think that her authority could be challenged, and she didn't want him to think it either. For a moment, he thought she was going to say no – but then she smiled.

'Thank you, captain,' she said. 'But I'll take Myrasol with you, if you don't mind – and his little cousin too. We have to keep up appearances, don't we?' She gave him no time to say anything in response before continuing. 'Never fear, Checuti. We'll return long before the worm's hungry daughters begin to peel away your fat. You'll have your own chance to be a hero – I promise you that.'

'I only asked for a truce, captain,' Checuti murmured, in a tone too low for anyone but Jacom to hear. 'I didn't ask you to throw yourself on your sword to save me from a fate worse than death.'

I didn't do it for you, Jacom thought. *I didn't even do it for Myrasol or the girl. I did it for me. I did it because it's my last chance to be brave, or to be anything at all. I did it because I'm stark raving mad.*

In the meantime, he urged his horse forward a few more paces and then dismounted. Andris Myrasol and Merel Zabio followed him. Dhalla helped Ereleth down from the wagon and then came to join them, carrying her heavy spear.

Andris Myrasol didn't look quite so big next to Dhalla – and Merel Zabio looked positively tiny, in spite of the fact that the old queen was even tinier. *And I'm in the middle*, Jacom thought. *Neither one thing nor another.*

When they moved off into the starlit night, the dragomite warriors stayed where they were, keeping watch over the caravan. Jacom didn't doubt, though, that there would be more than enough dragomites inside the mound into which they had consented to be taken.

ANDRIS WAS INITIALLY surprised by the dimensions of the tunnel into which he and the others were led when they entered the dragomite mound. Because the dragomites themselves were so big he had expected the tunnels to be wide and high, but in fact they seemed unreasonably low and narrow. He had to duck his head in order to pass along it, and there was insufficient room for Merel to walk comfortably beside him, as both he and she would have wished. It was plain that the dragomites never reared up while they were in the outermost tunnels of their mounds, and never had to pass one another. He concluded that the monsters must employ distinct entrance and exit routes.

There was considerable difficulty with visibility here. The walls were streaked with some kind of light-emitting substance but its growth was meagre and intermittent. Fortunately, the downward-sloping floor was even and the gradient gentle. The slightly curved walls were very smooth. When Andris placed a hand on a wall to steady himself – rather gingerly, lest he injure the light-producing organisms which grew there – he discovered that it was warm. The further into the mound they went, the warmer the walls became. The humidity of the air also increased by degrees.

As they marched through the dark tunnel in single file there was little or no conversation. The sound of Ereleth's voice floated back to Andris once or twice, but her questions went unanswered. He had one of the mound-women in front of him; she never looked back, and he made no attempt to communicate with her. Merel was directly behind him, but she was subdued, perhaps anxious about his reaction to her defiance of his instruction to stay behind. With the best will in the world, he could not be glad that she had insisted – he would far rather have had himself alone to worry about – but he knew better than to freeze up sulkily now that her presence was an accomplished fact. Three or four times he turned around to whisper comments about their winding course and the depth to which they were descending.

They had come into the mound on a hillside, but Andris judged that they must now be far below the level of the gully in which the caravan had come to rest. They frequently passed branching side-passages, but these were usually empty as far as the eye could see. The first time he caught sight of the head of a dragomite worker his heart leapt into his mouth, but it made no move towards him; it was waiting patiently for the humans to go by. The second time it happened he reminded himself sternly that in a dragomite nest one could hardly expect to avoid meeting dragomites. This reminder served its initial purpose well enough, but it didn't prepare him for the sights that greeted his eyes once the tunnels through which they passed had broadened out, giving them periodic access to larger chambers.

Here there were dragomites and their parts in great profusion, but all but a few were, indeed, in parts – and all but a few of those which remained whole were dead. The walls to either side of the procession were dark, not because no light-providing fungus grew there but simply because the stripped-down exoskeletons of workers and warriors were heaped up there in such profusion. In the largest chambers of all, the piles were even higher, infinitely more macabre as they bathed in the light of vaulted ceilings. There were heaps of human bones too, including skulls by the hundred – many of them not full-grown.

It was possible for the humans to walk two abreast in this region – intermittently at least – and there was plenty for them to talk about, although their escorts still remained stubbornly silent. Merel fell into step with Andris as often as she could, and Jacom Cerri took the opportunity to move up behind them to a position from which he could attach himself – albeit loosely – to the thread of their discourse.

'Is this their charnel-house?' Merel asked Andris. 'Are we being treated to a tour of their cemetery?'

'They are prudent folk at the best of times, so Phar says,' the captain put in. 'They cannibalise their own, for the meat of their flesh and the materials of their exoskeletons. I presume they treat their human recruits in like fashion.'

Phar had said the same to Andris, but he was never sure how much of what was rumoured about these creatures was mere superstition. He noticed, though, that in spite of the warmth and moistness of the air the stink of decay was not particularly pronounced. Indeed, the air seemed cleaner than the air he had been breathing for the last few days on the exposed surface of the dragomites' underworld, which reeked of rotting vegetation.

'This plague must have overwhelmed their capacity to deal with the dead,' Andris said. 'They remain slaves to the habit of storing chitin and bone, but they have fallen far behind in the work of recycling their materials. Did they starve, do you think? Has the blighting of their fields wiped out such legions of workers that there is food for queens and warriors alone?'

'Look there, and there,' said Cerri, pointing to empty eyeless skulls which showed unmistakable signs of battery and breakage. 'According to Phar, dragomite nests fight fierce wars against one another even when resources are plentiful. What awful conflicts shortage must precipitate! Before the blight came, every slope of these hills must have been swarming with live dragomites tending their unearthly crops.'

There was such fascination in the soldier's voice that Andris wondered briefly whether he really had been enthusiastic to see the inside of a dragomite nest when he volunteered to take the place of one of Ereleth's victims – but it was easier to believe that he was talking so earnestly now to cover up his confusion and his fear. Andris had every sympathy with that.

'Have the humans adopted the same cannibal habits as their allies, do you think?' Merel asked. 'Do they think of us as meat, perhaps?'

'If they too have been involved in fierce battles for survival, that massacre they carried out in the forest becomes more understandable,' the captain said sombrely.

'I doubt that the making of treaties comes naturally to them,' Andris said. 'This invitation which they have extended to us might well be a new departure for them. Let's hope that they have turned a significant corner in their history.'

'If this body-armour can be worked by metal tools,' Cerri mused, 'it might be a useful resource. It can hardly be incorruptible, but if they can trade it while it remains fresh . . . can that be why they have decided to talk to us?' It was clear from his voice that he thought it unlikely; he was still talking for the sake of talking.

'I can't imagine what they want from us,' Merel replied acidly, 'but I doubt if Fraxinus would sell them what metal he has for a cargo of gargantuan insect-parts.'

'I think they have taken some care to show us that they could take our metal very easily,' Andris put in. 'Whatever the mound-queen wishes to say to us, it will not involve any commonplace haggling. I fear . . .'

He broke off as they reached a new place, where the winding corridor was flanked on either side by a series of short, blind tunnels and near-spherical cells. The vast majority were unoccupied, and most were very badly lit, but there were a few in which small groups of human women or dragomites were at work with many kinds of tools. Some were spinning cloth or sewing clothes, others shaping bowls and implements. Here, for the first time, they saw live human children – all girls, to judge by superficial appearances – and here too they saw several new kinds of dragomites. Some, Andris assumed, must simply be immature workers of the kind frequently seen on the external slopes, but others were presumably specialist artificers of various kinds whose labour was confined to the nests and which never had cause to look upon the light of day. Certainly their eyes were large and prominent, and their limbs were adapted for manipulation rather than motion. Some, he suspected, never moved from the situations in which they had been placed, their bodies resting like huge rounded pots while their spidery limbs reached out to perform various tasks upon materials ferried back and forth by general-purpose workers or humans. Had all the cells been occupied, Andris realised, there would have been many thousands of individuals at work here instead of a hundred or so.

The air was full of new odours, all of them strange and some rather unpleasant – but after trekking so far across the rotting hills Andris did not find them significantly uncomfortable. Ereleth must have paused to look around, for the procession came to a momentary halt – but the mound-women must have hurried her onwards. The visitors were given no opportunity to make a detailed study of the chambers they passed by; they had to make do with a series of brief glimpses, perpetually interrupted by the jostlings they were forced to undergo as the inhabitants of the sprawling factory tried to carry on their business regardless of the awkward presence of strangers.

Andris soon abandoned any attempt to count the many different kinds of labour in which the humans and dragomites were engaged, and had to accept that many of their endeavours were unidentifiable. It was easy enough to see what those who were working with saws and mortars were doing, and those who were finishing weapons, bottles and jars, but many were working with more mysterious agents. He looked for evidence of the customary technologies of human towns – the pastes used for dissolving or cementing stone, metal and glass, and so on – but the conditions were so strange that it was very difficult to estimate the degree to which the lore of the mound-people and their alien co-workers overlapped the lore of more familiar tribes.

Andris did, however, observe two striking differences which made the activity of the mound-people different from all the other human cultures he had encountered in his travels. Firstly, they worked entirely without the aid of fire; he saw no sign whatsoever of cooking or smithing. Secondly, they were remarkably parsimonious in their use of speech; although they did talk to one another they seemed to do so in painstakingly utilitarian fashion. There was no evidence of any idle chatter, nothing resembling gossip. They were not incurious about the strangers filing through their workplace – hardly anyone failed to look up to watch them pass – but they never seemed to turn to one another to say: 'Look at the giant!' or 'What strange clothing they wear!' or 'Isn't that one pale!' or any of the thousand other things that any other human crowd would have wanted to jabber about.

'Do you suppose they murder all their male children?' Cerri asked. 'Or do they have some trick which assures that ninety-nine births in a hundred are girls?'

'Perhaps the mound-women only give birth to girls, as giants do,' Andris said. 'But the fact that they called us drones suggests that they have males somewhere. If two is the number which they naturally associate with a queen, perhaps two is all they have.'

'If one queen is enough,' Merel commented, 'then one drone

ought to suffice – but if all the mound-women can bear children, two would surely be inadequate.'

'I've met men who'd be glad to volunteer, were the latter the case,' Cerri observed drily.

It was a very feeble joke, but Andris recognised that there was a certain courage in being able to make any jokes at all in such gloomy and alien surroundings. 'They're not nearly pretty enough,' he responded. 'And the fact that they talk so little doesn't necessary imply that they're not inclined to shrewishness. No sane man would ever volunteer to serve as stallion to such a herd as this.'

'Some of these captive dragomites have such clever hands I wonder they need human assistants at all,' Merel said, pointedly changing the subject. 'I can't see a single human doing anything that a dragomite couldn't do as well or better.'

Andris looked for evidence to contradict this allegation, but could find no certain falsification before they passed yet again into a narrower and gloomier corridor which wound so tightly around and so steeply down that it reminded Andris of a spiral stair. There were fewer side-branches here, and when it delivered them into another chamber of some considerable dimensions he thought at first that it might be completely sealed. He realised quickly enough, however, that here were doors: a phenomenon he had not knowingly encountered before in the dragomites' realm.

The doors were not hinged, like those human used; they were like vertically set mouths or dragomites' eyelids or – he couldn't help making the comparison, although it embarrassed him to think of it – women's sexual parts. In response to some signal which he could not detect, lenticular slits opened up in the walls to allow the newcomers to pass through. The whole party passed through four such apertures, each of which closed behind them.

Now, Andris thought, *we are most certainly prisoners, and helpless ones, closed off from the outside world by barriers we cannot break*. He knew, though, that it was absurd to think that they had not been prisoners until such solid barriers had been placed across their exit route. If nothing else, they were utterly and hopelessly lost; they had not the slightest chance of remembering the route they had followed had they been required to retrace their steps.

The corridor through which they now moved was the warmest so far, and Andris found himself sweating freely. The air itself seemed wet and vaporously hazy, and the odours it carried, though less complicated than those in the factory-tunnels, were somehow more cloying. The walls were still as firm to the touch as they had been higher up, but they were made of some exoskeletal substance very similar to that with which the dragomites were armoured, and they were decorated with spirals and whorls very similar to those which ornamented certain parts of the dragomites' own bodies. The patches of luminous fungus were much more precisely arranged here, in a pattern which might have been perfectly regular had it not been for the fact that some were missing and others broken. Andris had wondered before whether the gloom had been unnaturally deepened by the effect of disease upon the light-producing organisms; now he became certain of it. The blight which had devastated the surfaces of the mounds had also penetrated their most intimate depths.

The procession stopped again, its ranks closing up in spite of the relative narrowness of the tunnel. The mound-woman who had been walking in front of Andris all this time abruptly turned and said: 'Drones are to be quartered here.'

Where? Andris thought, just as another aperture gaped open in the wall, in response to some invisible stimulus. The mound-woman indicated that he should step through it, but he couldn't quite bring himself to do so now that there was no one to give him a lead. It seemed too much like stepping into the living maw of some avid monster. Attention was deflected from his own hesitation, however, by Merel's protesting voice. 'You can't separate us!' she said. 'I'm staying with Andris.'

'No,' the mound-woman said flatly. 'Drones here. Warriors have separate quarters. It is the way. No harm will come to you.'

'We don't operate like that,' Merel said pugnaciously. 'We don't have drones and warriors and a dozen different kinds of workers. We just have men and women, sometimes coupled together. Andris and I are together. Captain Cerri can share with the giant.'

'Thank you,' muttered the soldier – but he made no protest of his own.

'Do as she says, both of you!' The command came from Ereleth, who had elbowed her way back from the front of the column. She fixed Merel with a stern gaze and added: 'You weren't asked to come, girl, but now you're here you'll do as you're told.'

'It's all right,' Andris assured his cousin. 'If they meant to do us harm they'd have done it long ago. While we're here, I guess the captain and I are drones – and you're a warrior.'

When he said all that, it became much easier for him to step through the unwelcoming threshold. Cerri followed him meekly through. The 'lips' closed behind the soldier, sealing the two of them into an elliptical space which was some two and a half mets high and broad, and four long.

The light was dim but tolerable. There were two parallel ledges which were ominously reminscent of pallets in a cell. Opposite the point where they had come in was another ledge, set much higher, bearing two bowls and spoons. Beneath it there was a dark hole set at an angle, at a height adapted for a normally-sized man to lean against in a half-sitting position.

'I hope that's what it looks like,' Andris said. 'I really should have gone before we set out.' He peered into the hole uncertainly for a moment or two before shrugging his shoulders and getting on with it. The sound of the urine hitting the wall of the conduit must have brought on a similar urge in his companion, who was quick to follow as soon as he had finished and moved aside.

'Isn't it uncanny,' Andris observed, 'how prison cells always look like prison cells no matter where you are. Even in this rotting underworld, where the people think they're ants, the facilities are the same as they always are. I expect the hole has to be set at a different angle in a warrior's cell, though. That one's definitely just for drones. I'm sure I can feel Ereleth's worm wriggling around in my entrails. Do you suppose we'll get fed soon?' Now *he* was talking for the sake of talking, to stave off full awareness of the awfulness of their predicament.

'A drink would be welcome,' the captain replied, taking over readily enough. 'Even that disgusting firewater the darklanders brẽw. I have a feeling that we're superfluous to this whole business. I suspect that drones might not get involved in serious discussions here. Perhaps we're only here to make Ereleth seem more of a queen than she actually is.'

'That's fine by me,' Andris said, sitting down on the ledge where he was presumably supposed to sleep, 'provided that she can

405

handle matters to her own satisfaction. If she can get the princess back, she just might decide to poison this damned worm. Checuti must be sweating, up there with all those warriors, not knowing whether Ereleth will ever come back. In a way, it'll be worse for him than for us. You weren't really doing anyone a favour, you know, when you put your hand up that way. Not that I don't appreciate the attempt, mind – but it really was a wild move.'

'Maybe waiting up above *would* be worse,' Cerri said defensively. 'Maybe I was just being selfish.' He didn't sound as if he meant it, and he certainly didn't expect to be believed.

'Except that you don't have a worm which needs regular doses of contraceptive from Ereleth,' Andris pointed out. 'If you were up above you wouldn't necessarily give a damn whether Ereleth or I ever came up again – and you'd have a chance of evading the warriors even if they did attack, simply because a horse can outrun a dragomite. What's the betting that your sergeant and the other guardsmen are making contingency plans right now?'

'He's not *my* sergeant any more,' Cerri replied distantly. He was pretending to be past caring but Andris wasn't fooled. 'Don't imagine that the fact that I'm down here will make any . . .'

The soldier's voice trailed off as his attention was caught by something. Andris followed the direction of his stare to the wall above the shelf on which the bowls were set. The substance of the wall was moving and changing. It was as if the wall grew two lumpen breasts with grotesque teats, which promptly began to dribble something milky into the two bowls.

Cerri made a disgusted sound. 'That's *gross*,' he said. 'Can you eat that stuff, after watching *that*?'

'Actually,' Andris said, 'I'm too hungry to be squeamish. After all the unearthly stuff we ate in the darklands and some of the horrors in Fraxinus's not very rotproof jars I'm really not that particular.'

As the wall regained its normal smoothness he went over and picked up the bowl. The 'milk' was creamy and warm, and had the nicest odour he had encountered in many a tenday. He raised it cautiously to his lips, tipped the bowl, and took a cautious sip.

It tasted wonderful.

'I'll have yours if you don't want it,' he told Cerri – but once the captain had tasted the stuff he was in no mood to give it up. When the bowls were empty they were quick to replace them, but the teats had vanished into the wall again.

'That was the best prison food I ever tasted,' Andris said regretfully. 'Considering what they charged for that slop in Belin's citadel, I'd say it was worth at least . . .'

He stopped abruptly as the captain's restless gaze was caught and held yet again, this time by something behind his own head. Even before he moved from the ledge, Andris knew that the wall was opening up behind him, forming yet another vertically-lipped mouth, and he felt a sudden pang of fear at the thought of being *swallowed* and *devoured*.

He threw himself over to Cerri's side of the room, twisting his awkwardly huge body as he did so, to see what horror was coming through the hole. His undisciplined imagination was already forming a picture of jagged rot-yellowed teeth and an avid, sticky, forked tongue . . .

But what he actually saw was far worse than that.

11

LUCREZIA HUGGED ERELETH with all the passionate relief of one who has just been visited by an unexpected miracle. Although the princess was entitled by rank to treat her thus, Ereleth did not react with unalloyed pleasure and took care to escape the embrace as soon as possible.

'Hardly quarters befitting a queen,' the old woman remarked, looking around the narrow cell, at its ill-defined ledges and its strange decorations. The door-slit had closed behind her, and that wall now appeared as seamless as the others.

'They're the best I've had in some considerable time,' Lucrezia assured her mentor. 'If you've travelled more comfortably you've been fortunate. But that doesn't matter – I was never so glad to see anyone in my life! Have you really come all the way from Xandria in search of me? You were brave enough to come into the Dragomite Hills . . . even into the heart of the nest!' She did not add *I would never have suspected that you were capable of such affection* in case it sounded faintly insulting, although it was perfectly true.

'On the other hand,' Ereleth said, with a sigh, 'I don't suppose the mound-queen's quarters are any more salubrious. These people have the concept of royalty, but they interpret it after their own eccentric fashion.'

'Oh, I don't know,' Lucrezia said, deflated by Ereleth's failure to acknowledge anything she said. Resentment encouraged her to pretend an understanding of which she was far from confident. 'The politics of this place don't seem to be all that strange, save for the total absence of human males.'

'I fear they might be stranger than you imagine,' Ereleth said, sitting down on one of the sleeping-ledges and brushing dirt from her sleeve. 'In fact, I suspect they might be stranger than the queen herself imagines, if my brief interview with her just now provided an accurate display of her intelligence.'

Lucrezia felt a stab of envy at the revelation that Ereleth had seen the mound-queen in her absence. Was she to be ignored now that Ereleth was here? Or was it simply that the mound-queen had wanted to question Ereleth before she had a chance to discover what Lucrezia had already told her?

'She intended to kill Fraxinus and all his men,' Lucrezia said. 'To prevent her doing that I had to promise that we would help her – and that we would be far more valuable to her as partners in a contract than as captives working under threat.'

'So I gathered,' said Ereleth negligently. 'Her reaction to the evil circumstances which have overtaken the nest is, I think, as instinctive as the response of the dragomite workers. She doesn't understand what's happening, and seems unable to think of anything but formulating a plan which might allow the nest to be transplanted to a safe place. She's desperate, but she's also desperately uncertain. Even if this blight isn't the beginning of the end of the world her instincts may be sadly misdirected. If, on the other hand, this *is* one of the crises which the secret commandments anticipate, her schemes are utterly futile.'

It was by no means the first time Lucrezia had heard Ereleth talk in this teasingly enigmatic fashion, but it seemed utterly inappropriate to the present circumstances. It would have been pleasant had Ereleth been openly glad to see her – or, at the very least, more appreciative of her own gladness. Perhaps, she thought, the queen was mortally afraid but did not care to show it. Some people, she knew, did become excessively business-like as a defence against fear – if one could call being irritatingly mysterious 'business-like'. Lucrezia had always resented Ereleth's tendency to allude to a secret wisdom which she allegedly possessed but would not share. The princess had to remind herself now that she had every possible reason to thank her teacher and would-be rescuer, and to be tolerant of her mannerisms.

'What have you said to the corpulent queen?' she asked, that being the most neutral question she could think of.

'Very little, so far,' Ereleth replied. 'There's no need to be afraid, child – I reasoned out what you must have said to her, and was careful not to contradict it. It should be easy enough to persuade her that she needs us; she's half-persuaded herself of that already.'

'The problem is,' Lucrezia put in, 'that she's so thoroughly persuaded of it that she kept talking about my becoming one with them. I don't know what that means, but I don't like the sound of it.'

'Nor I,' Ereleth conceded. 'Do you have any idea, perchance, why she is attended by two *dragomite* drones? The warriors who came to the surface seemed to expect that I would bring two drones with me when I declared myself a queen, and they accepted humans readily enough.'

'I've seen no human males here,' Lucrezia said. 'Who came with you? Fraxinus and Phar?'

'Andris Myrasol and Captain Cerri,' Ereleth informed her, as though it were the most natural thing in the world.

'The mapmaker and the guard-captain? What in the world . . . ?'

'It would take too long to explain. You must be careful of the captain – your father exiled him and all his men from Xandria until he could bring you back. His men have gone over to Fraxinus, but they might be tempted back again. You need have no fear of the amber, though; he knows what you intended to do with him; but he's not in a position to bear grudges and he won't interfere with our purpose.'

'What is our purpose, exactly?' Lucrezia asked uneasily. She didn't quite understand what Ereleth meant about the guard-captain. 'To return to Xandria?'

'Certainly not,' Ereleth said. 'Unfortunately, the mound-queen does seem to want to go north, to some desolate corner of the provinces. You advised her against it, I believe – that was quick thinking.'

'It was also good advice,' Lucrezia said, to demonstrate that she wasn't a fool. 'She wants to begin raising a new range of Dragomite Hills, but her chances of doing that within the bounds of the empire would be very slim. Even if I didn't have other very good reasons for wanting her to go elsewhere, I'd still have counselled her against trying it.'

'Very true, daughter,' said Ereleth. She was probably being sincere, but it still sounded sarcastic to Lucrezia's sensitive ear. 'Belin would never tolerate dragomites establishing a niche even in the most distant and desolate region of his precious empire, of course; he'd see it, rightly, as the thin end of a very nasty wedge. That's hardly relevant to our present predicament, though. The question is, how do we convince her that she ought to go west instead?'

'Don't you mean south?' Lucrezia asked.

'To begin with,' Ereleth conceded. 'But once we're out of the hills, we ought to go west or south-west. There are serpents in the Grey Waste, and there's a place on Myrasol's map called Serpent's Lair; our first destination must be one or the other, no matter what Fraxinus thinks best. Unlike the amber and the fat thief, he's not committed to obey me for the moment, but I'll have time to repair that difficulty if only I can get us out of the mess we're in right now.'

'Are you sure, house-mother, that my objectives coincide with yours?' Lucrezia could no longer leave the question unvoiced. 'I know that you've come a very long way to find me, but . . .' She trailed off, realising that it sounded horribly ungrateful.

Ereleth smiled crookedly. Her thin face looked decidedly eerie in the wan light: like the face of a phantom.

'What *are* your objectives, daughter?' she asked softly. 'Checuti told me what you said to him, of course . . . but all that seemed a little vague, and Keshvara's dead now. What would you do now, if you had a choice?' Her tone was calculated to inform Lucrezia that she did not have a choice, and not merely because she was a prisoner of the mound-queen, but it was not a rhetorical question. Ereleth's eyes were fixed upon her face with avid curiosity.

'If I could,' Lucrezia said, 'I'd join Carus Fraxinus. I'd do what Hyry Keshvara intended to do – find a way, if one exists, to the Pool of Life and Chimera's Cradle.'

'Why?'

'Why not?' said Lucrezia defensively.

'That's no answer. I ask you again: *why?*'

'I'm not going back to Xandria, let alone to Shaminzara,' Lucrezia said calmly. 'That's not the kind of life I want. I could never have been happy following that kind of path through life, even if none of this had ever happened. Now . . . well, I've had a terrible time these last few tendays, with hardly a moment's comfort or solace, but it feels . . .' She groped for words, but couldn't find them.

'You don't know why,' Ereleth said, but not with the air of one triumphantly winning an argument. 'You can't. But you're right. You could never have been happy within Belin's scheme of things. You have Serpent's blood, which would always have been restless in your veins. In a crisis – *any* kind of crisis – it becomes more restless still. Everything that has happened since Hyry Keshvara brought those seeds to you has intensified that restlessness. You're not alone, daughter. I don't have the alien blood in my veins, but I do have custody of certain secret commandments. Even people who have neither aren't entirely immune from the effects of this strangely pregnant sense of disaster, this notion that the world we know is undergoing some kind of metamorphosis. It's in us all to some degree, you see. It's written in our flesh. It leads many to destruction, and always will, but some of us find the right balance of desire and wisdom, impulse and control. You and I, princess, with proper assistance from others – witting or unwitting – might be able to do what this awkward legacy was intended to impel us to do.'

'And what,' said Lucrezia patiently, 'is that?'

'According to the commandments handed down to me,' Ereleth told her, 'we must find a Serpent. Not just any Serpent, but a Serpent with . . . well, they certainly don't call it *human blood*, for they had it long before we did, but they can hardly call it *Serpent's blood* either, for fear of confusion. A Serpent with some special magic incarnate in its flesh, usually dormant but ever ready to be expressed when the times are ripe. The Serpents have their own lore, you see, and their own secrets. They have lived in the world far longer than humans, and were adapted to its ways by a long process of evolution – millions of years, according to the lore, although the figure might not be literally meant.

'The forefathers learned certain lessons from the pattern of the Serpents' adaptation, which they built into the scheme of *Genesys*. Whether they had learned those lessons well enough, or applied them with adequate skill they could not know. The secret commandments aren't prophecies, and they make no promises; they offer hope rather than certainty, beginnings rather than ends.

'When we've found the right kind of Serpent, we must find the right kind of Salamander. Then, *and only then*, we shall have what we need in order to go – or to *return*, as the secret commandments insist on putting it – to the Pool of Life.'

412

'And what then?' Lucrezia asked sceptically. *All this is myth,* she reminded heself. *Ereleth knows well enough that the fringes of the lore have accumulated all manner of quaint fantasies. If she believes in her secret commandments, it is because they're the only thing she owns which allows her to think of herself as a superior being, a true queen of witches. Her belief is no evidence of their truthfulness.*

'Then it begins,' Ereleth told her. 'I told you – we aren't dealing with prophecies or promises. *There is no destiny. The future cannot be foreknown, but the human mind is pregnant with many designs, some of which can be realised if only the necessary instruments can be devised and forged.* What we have to do with, you and I, is the devising and forging of instruments.'

Lucrezia recognised the saying Ereleth had quoted. It was sometimes bandied about the corridors of Belin's citadel, and had been a favourite of more than one of his ministers. The design which preoccupied *them* was, of course, Belin's empire – the impossible empire, as they liked to call it, boasting of their ability to do what had never been done before. When they spoke of *necessary instruments* they meant treaties and terms of trade, methods of transportation and building . . . and, of course, the thirty-and-one queens of Xandria and their plethora of royal children. Ereleth evidently had a very different context in mind; but she too thought of people – including herself – as instruments.

Lucrezia wasn't sure that she liked the idea of being a mere instrument; she had always wanted to be something more than that. She hadn't had the least desire to be an instrument of Belin's empire, and she couldn't see that there was any greater merit in being an instrument of Ereleth's secret commandments – or of her own Serpent's blood.

My restlessness is my own, she thought, seizing the idea as firmly as she could. *Whatever there is in my flesh to give it birth, it is my own. I am its master, not its slave. I have no need of secret commandments to tell me what I am or where I must go.* Hyry Keshvara would have agreed with her wholeheartedly – of that she felt certain.

To Ereleth, she said only: 'I see.' It was, at best, a half-truth – but at least she now knew, at long last, what Ereleth's secret commandments instructed her to do, and why the witch-queen had always taken a special interest in her.

'If the amber's map is to be trusted,' Ereleth said, 'there are Serpents and Salamanders to be found south of the marshes. There is safety in numbers, and Fraxinus is a tolerably clever man as well as a leader who commands respect from his followers. He'll be very useful to us, if we can keep him and bind him to our will. The question which faces us immediately, however, is how soon we can extricate ourselves from the clutches of the mound-queen. We must strike some kind of bargain with her, even if we mean to break it. We must offer her some seeming guarantee of our good faith. We must decide now what we shall say to her when we see her again – which will be soon enough, for she insists that time is pressing. She could hardly refuse me permission to see you and make sure that you were well, but she is impatient to come to some decision as to what can and might be done for her people and for the dragomites whose nest they share.

'She is under great pressure, I think, from her dragomite allies, although I can't make any judgment as to her exact relationship to them. The nest is in a parlous state, and I can only presume that it might be invaded at any moment by warriors from another nest. The internecine wars in which the dragomites are now engaged are wars of extermination – that's surely why the queen is so desperate.'

'If that's so,' Lucrezia pointed out, 'we too have every reason to want to be out of here as soon as possible. Perhaps we should promise her anything at all, simply to start things moving. Even if we had to go back to the forest before we can resume our own course . . . if the worst came to the worst, perhaps we ought to agree to that, as a way of buying time.'

'Perhaps,' Ereleth agreed. 'But I fear that we'll have to be cleverer than that if we're to persuade her to trust us. If we knew more about her relationship with the dragomite queen, we might be better able to devise a seductive offer.' She looked around the cell as she spoke, as if she were looking to the bare walls for inspiration.

'I've seen no dragomite queen,' Lucrezia said. 'But Jume Metra did refer to one, saying that the mound-queen was her voice. The mound-people don't seem to be slaves of the dragomites, but neither are they masters who keep dragomites as men of our kind keep cattle. I can't fathom the exact nature of their relationship with the monsters, and they're very unenthusiastic to explain it. How closely does their own political organisation match that of the dragomites, do you think? Hyry told me that the dragomite queens are mothers of every worker and warrior in the nest, but that surely can't be true of the mound-queen – can it?'

'No,' said Ereleth, 'It surely can't. But it would be useful to know, I think, exactly who and what we're dealing with if we do make a pact with the queen. Queens can be mere instruments, as you and I know very well, and if there is another power behind her throne ... we must be mightily clever, daughter, as well as mightily brave, if we're to come through this ordeal. Perhaps I should have brought Fraxinus instead of that doltish amber – but he might not have agreed to come, and there was no time for elaborate discussion. The responsibility is ours, and ours alone.'

Which is cause for satisfaction, in its way, Lucrezia thought. *Isn't that exactly why I ran away when I had the chance? I wanted responsibility, as well as adventure – and now I have them both, in the fullest possible measure.*

The wall which had opened to let Ereleth into the cell opened again now, to reveal Jume Metra. Dhalla was behind her, and Lucrezia's heart leapt again at the thought of having so many friends who were prepared to risk any and all hazards to be near her.

'There is no time,' said Metra, yet again. 'The carriers are almost ready, and we dare not let them linger in the nest. Whatever you have to say to the mound-queen, you must say it now, and quickly.'

'We're ready,' Ereleth said, effortlessly matching the mound-woman's colourless tone.

Lucrezia could only hope that it would somehow become true by virtue of having been said.

12

JACOM PLODDED ALONG in the wake of his new guide, wondering why his legs hadn't turned to water. In fact, he felt quite numb; even when he touched the place where the tacktick had left the greater part of its filthy head buried in his flesh he couldn't conjure up any fierce pain.

There's something in this steamy air, he thought. *Something that saps the will and the imagination. Will I become a mere machine of flesh, like those stupid women, if I stay here long enough?*

He had no more idea now of what the thing in front of him might be than when it had first stuck its weirdly shining head into his cell through an aperture in the dividing wall, but the intensity of that first shock had dwindled almost to nothing. At first he had wondered whether the creature might be some strange chimera compounded out of man and dragomite, with a generous measure of firefly added in, but now he conceded that it was utterly alien, its nature beyond the reach of any theory he could devise.

It was two-legged and two-armed and it walked upright, but its gait was very strange and quite unhuman. It was extraordinarily thin – all skin and bone, with hardly any flesh to muscle its long limbs. Its feet were broad but shallow pads, with a circular halo of toes connected by rubbery webs, while its 'hands' were bunches of slim tentacles, like the clusters which sprouted from the backs of the larger flowerworms. Its skin was very smooth and luminously dappled in various shades of grey – markings which were strangely changeable. It was not merely that the patches grew darker and lighter, but that their pattern changed constantly. The flesh of its head was hardened as if by an exoskeleton. Its eyes were large, with twin lids that narrowed to vertical slits. Feathery antennae like a dragomite's extended from its forehead, but its mouth was not in the least like a dragomite's; it had lips like a human's and a tongue like a human's but – so far as Jacom could see – it had no teeth at all.

'Are you a Serpent, or a Salamander?' Myrasol had asked, when first it had asked them to accompany it into the dark corridor.

'Come with me,' it had replied, lingering over the *th* sound the way a human with a lisp might have done.

'Come with me,' was its invariable reply to all questions, sometimes repeated over and over in a curiously pathetic way, almost as if it regretted the necessity of asking. Jacom had arrived eventually at the conclusion that it was not an intelligent being at all, merely one which could be schooled to carry messages. If so, then it presumably wasn't a Serpent or a Salamander. Perhaps humans were not the only other species able to form close relationships with dragomites – and perhaps some others had been so long associated that they no longer existed outside the nests of their hosts.

He and Myrasol had consented to follow the creature because there seemed to be no alternative. It would have been ridiculous to start a discussion between themselves as to whether the warrior-women knew that they were being removed, and whether they might object if they found out. Jacom was all too well aware of the fact that he was a helpless cork on the sea of fate, ready victim of the slightest eddy of fortune. If walls opened up and monsters beckoned, saying 'Come with me' in a reasonably polite fashion, what reason or authority did he have to refuse? He was already deep in the bowels of an alien landscape, where he might be seized, crushed, killed and eaten at any moment. What possible virtue was there in resistance? In any case, given their recent treatment by members of their own species what reason had he or the big amber to fear the enmity of mere monsters?

The tunnel along which the creature led them would have been utterly dark had it not been for the light radiated by the creature itself, and that light was hardly bright enough to illuminate the walls. All Jacom knew of these surroundings was that the walls were warm to the touch, and noticeably softer than the walls of the corridors through which he had earlier been led. The lacuna which contained them seemed to be opening in front of their living beacon and closing again behind them as they passed. It was as though they were carrying a tiny air-bubble with them as they tramped through the fleshy bedrock of the Dragomite Hills – but the moist air remained breathable enough.

'How much further?' growled Myrasol, who was bringing up the rear, when they had been moving for fifteen minutes or so. Jacom relayed the question forwards, but their guide didn't deign to turn around as it answered 'Come with me.'

'As long as it takes,' he said, voicing the inference he had picked up.

'It can hardly know or care that I'm bound to Ereleth by the threat of early death,' the amber said, with a sigh. 'So I suppose there is no point in trying to persuade it that I'm not free to wander wherever the whim might take it, even to the remotest depths of the world.'

'Probably not,' Jacom agreed.

'On the other hand,' Myrasol said, 'the mound-women are convinced that time is pressing, and it might well share their anxiety. Perhaps it is taking us to the *true* queen of this dark empire: the *dragomite* queen.'

'Come with me,' said the luminous one, without turning its head.

'Be patient,' Jacom said, trying hard to make light of it all with a cavalier attitude and an ironic tone. 'All will doubtless be explained in the fullness of time.' He did not believe it; he had lost faith in the explicability of the world.

Their patience was not tested to an unreasonable limit; soon afterwards they came into a different system of caverns, which were unmistakably permanent. Jacom was aware of new spaces to either side of him, and less featureless walls, but the gloom was intense and it was difficult to see anything except for their strange guide. Such streaks of light-broadcasting fungus as there were in these caves seemed distant and sickly. The floor was uneven here, and their route became very indirect. For the first time since they had come into the underworld they encountered abrupt corners.

Jacom perceived, though not without difficulty, that the walls of these tunnels were neither smooth nor plain, but had complex sets of chambers let into them at regular intervals. The apertures were arranged in vertical rows of four; each one was broad enough for a man – even a man of Andris Myrasol's bulk – to crawl through.

Jacom tried to see what might be inside, but their summoner hardly ever paused. Although he had the poorer view, by virtue of being in rear, it was Myrasol who ventured a hypothesis as to their nature.

'I think they're egg-chambers,' he said, 'but all but a few of them are empty.'

They were not all empty, but if the stink was anything to go by, most of those which weren't no longer contained healthy eggs. Jacom avoided the ones which reeked of decay, but he put his hand briefly into several of the apertures as he passed by, until he felt the surface of a smooth and rounded object. It had a waxy quality about it, and he concluded that Myrasol might be right.

There were dragomite workers hereabouts; Jacom could hear them moving, and occasionally caught a glimpse of reflective eyes in a side passage, but the creatures made no move to interrupt the progress of the guide.

'If this is where her eggs are stored,' Myrasol said, 'we might indeed hope to see the dragomite queen herself, in all her glory. Perhaps that *is* where we are being taken.'

Curiosity as an antidote to fear, Jacom thought – but the judgment was too harsh. How could one not be curious? He could hardly claim that he was witness to sights that no human eyes had ever seen before, but he was certain that no Xandrian had ever seen them. If ever he were fortunate enough to return to his father's estate, he would have such tales to tell that . . .

Given his luck, he realised, no one would believe a word of it.

'What a monster she must be,' he said, in answer to Myrasol's speculation.

'It will be a rare privilege to have an audience with her,' Myrasol said, stoutly maintaining his determination to treat this nightmare lightly, 'but we will need a better interpreter than our palely lit friend if we're to make much sense of what she has to say.'

How brave we are! Jacom thought. *True courage is not the capacity to lay about oneself with a sword until bloody corpses pile up about one's feet – the frenzy of terror-stricken panic suffices for that. True courage is to be meekly led into the deepest heart of a nightmare, remaining calm the while.*

He *was* calm, but he wasn't sure that it was courage made him so. If he was wrong about there being some tranquilliser adrift in the cloudy air, the likelihood was that he and the amber had simply exhausted their resources of anxiety.

When Phar had told him all that he knew and suspected about dragomites, Jacom had imagined the dragomite queen to be a worker writ enormously large – with a vastly distended abdomen. Having some slight familiarity with the life of honey-bees he had assumed that she would lie in state in the very heart of her hive while her loyal workers fed her constantly. Now, he imagined being taken to stand before her huge head, to be inspected by the biggest and blackest eyes in the world. When they entered a broader tunnel slightly less gloomy than the rest he thought such a meeting might be imminent, and that expectation inhibited and delayed his understanding of what he actually saw.

They passed into a corridor which seemed to be lined with huge bulbous warts, some projecting at right-angles, others hanging limply down. Some were distended and some were not; many gave the appearance of being shrivelled. Jacom did not immediately realise that the puckered mass at the tip of each one was a huge closed sphincter. There were at least forty of them, perhaps more.

He did not begin to guess what they might be until he saw one of the sphincters gaping wide, discharging – with difficulty – an elliptical object the size of a man's torso. At first he assumed that some kind of excretion process was under way, but that seemed too absurd.

'What *is* that?' Myrasol asked, crowding close to peer over his shoulder and share the benefit of the light cast by their luminous guide.

The question triggered the answer. 'It's an egg,' Jacom said.

He stopped dead as he said it, but quickly had to hurry on, partly because their guide hadn't hesitated and partly because he realised that a dragomite worker was behind Myrasol, impatient for them to move on. He looked wildly about him, although it was now too dark to see anything.

'Filth and corruption!' Myrasol said, in an awed tone. 'You're right. Don't you see, captain – *the very walls are alive!* We're not being taken to *see* the dragomite queen, *we're inside her!* She's built into the structure of the mound!'

Jacom felt sure that the amber was right. The bulbous organs which they had passed by, he realised, must function in much the same way as the 'teats' which had formed in the wall of the cell to discharge 'milk'. These caves were the ovaries of the dragomite queen, pumping out eggs by the score – or perhaps, when all was well, by the hundred. As each egg fell a dragomite worker was presumably supposed to come forward to take it and carry it away. It seemed, though, that egg production had slowed dramatically – and many of the chambers where eggs were stored were empty or possessed by decay. But how were the eggs fertilised?

'Is this how Ereleth's worm would feel, if it were sentient?' Myrasol whispered. 'This whole place is alive. We're strolling through the guts of a creature the size of Xandria's citadel – a creature whose myriad daughters move constantly back and forth between the world and the womb from which they sprang. The dragomite queen *is* the nest, the surface of the mound is just her outer tegument, her exoskeleton. The blight is in her as well as on her – it's sinking into the very core of her being. How long has she lived, do you suppose? How long might she have lived, had the blight not come?'

Again, Jacom judged that Myrasol had guessed correctly. The blight which had come to the Dragomite Hills was no mere crop failure. The threat which it posed was much more profound.

'Come with me,' urged their attendant phantom, hurrying them on into the gloom.

What, Jacom wondered, could possibly lie at the far end of this procreative corridor, beyond the womb of the dragomite queen – a womb within a tomb, if Myrasol's intuition could be trusted. He stepped forward more rapidly in reflexive obedience to the summons.

They soon emerged into another cave, not quite as gloomy as the ones through which they had passed.

'Here,' said the phantom.

It stood still at last, and immediately began to fade. The light within its skin died away to complete darkness, explaining by its absence how bright it had been. Perhaps the fungus growing on the ceiling and walls of the cave grew brighter in response, or perhaps it was simply that Jacom's eyes adapted to the gloom, but their destination revealed itself to him by slow degrees.

The floor was very uneven, pitted with craters with raised rims, which cradled what Jacom was immediately able to see as eggs – but these eggs gave the impression of having been generated where they lay, and of still being connected to the flesh which cradled them. Unlike the dragomites' eggs, which had been grey-white and opaque, these were red-veined and almost translucent . . . and they were watched over by guardians far stranger than dragomite workers.

Here, the faintly luminous walls had eyes – and mouths, and ears . . . and even, occasionally, limbs, or at least the bare outlines of them.

It was as if half a hundred living beings had been filleted, and their boneless flesh spread out upon the inner surface of the cavern, as some preserve might be spread on a slice of bread . . . or as if their flesh had been half-consumed by the flesh which lay behind and beyond it, to form a horrible mosaic.

Jacom had no doubt that some of the eyes could see, and that they were staring at him. Perhaps they could all see – or would have been able to, had disease not struck so many blind.

He had no notion of what this place should have looked like had the queen which contained it been healthy, but he was convinced that this was a nightmare in reduced circumstances. The processes of corruption which had attacked it seemed palpable in the humid air and in every apparition decking the walls. It made no difference where he looked: there were faces in distress – dying faces.

He did not doubt, either, that the faces in the walls had brains behind them, contained within the flesh of the dragomite hive – within the flesh of the dragomite queen. It took him a little while, though, to take hold of the notion that those brains were brains of a human kind, and that the summoner which had brought them here might also be a kind of human in spite of all its alien embellishments. And yet, all of this was part of the body of the dragomite queen; everything which presently surrounded them was bedded in her flesh, and must be part of her.

These eggs, Jacom saw, were not really eggs at all, but wombs: amniotic sacs nourished by maternal blood which flowed in unearthly veins. This was where the dragomite queen gave birth to her human commensals, parodying human birth.

Jacom was dumbstruck, with amazement and with horror.

'Something like this is what the princess intended for me,'

Myrasol murmured in his ear. 'Checuti told me that Keshvara brought her some vile bush from far beyond the darklands, whose seed she wanted to plant in my flesh, so that I too would become a chimera, human and unearthly flesh combined into some vile collective. These mound-women may look human enough, but they aren't really human at all. They're just another kind of dragomite!'

Jacom shook his head, although the movement must have been hardly visible to his companion. He wasn't sure how much denial there was in the gesture and how much simple wonderment. He had the strangest feeling that perhaps he ought to have expected this, having seen and felt signs enough since they first came into the mound, and that his astonishment was very stupid.

'Come here,' said a voice, which was not the voice of their guide. 'Come here, to me.'

13

A
FTER SO MANY days of hectic travelling, Checuti found a
whole day's idleness surprisingly difficult to bear. It would not
have been so bad had the caravan stopped in a pleasant location –
preferably somewhere which had supplies of food and water close
at hand – but the middle of the Dragomite Hills was quite the most
unpleasant spot he could imagine, and the everpresence of the
warriors was discomfiting in the extreme. They no longer stood as
ominously still as statues, and were in fact continually wandering
back and forth from the interior of the mound in whose shadow
the caravan had come to rest, but there were always eight or ten
nearby, within what he could not help but think of as 'striking
distance'. There was another group much higher on the mound,
around and about one of its several peaks; they too were
constantly being changed as others relieved them of their
mysterious duty.

'This is a bad situation,' Checuti said to the little monkey which
sat, timid and dispirited, upon his left shoulder. The pet had stuck
to him through thick and thin, but it had liked the forest – which
was its natural habitat – far better than this desolate place. 'In a
way, it would be better to be down there in the mound, where
Ereleth would at least be close at hand. That way, if some terrible
accident should overcome her, I could race to her side – just in case
she wanted to reach into her belt and pull out the poison which
would destroy the worm inside me, thus proving herself capable of
one last magnanimous gesture.'

The monkey chattered half-heartedly. It was, Checuti
supposed, as shrewd an observation as was possible in response to
such arrant nonsense.

Aulakh Phar called out to him then, asking him to hand over a
drill-bit and a gouge because his hands were full and he was at a

delicate stage in his work. The aged physician was replacing the rotten spokes in one of the wheels from the smaller wagon.

'You're completely crazy,' Checuti opined, having answered the request. 'Of all the times to take a wheel off the wagon, this is the worst imaginable. What if we have to make a run for it?'

'If we have to make a run for it,' Phar pointed out, 'we need to be absolutely sure that none of the wheels is going to shatter. We're not going anywhere until Ereleth comes back.'

'Aren't we? Maybe you haven't noticed the sergeant and his band of cut-throats whispering away like washerwomen. Their horses are saddled and their saddle-bags are fully loaded. One sign of aggression from those six-legged monstrosities and they'll be off. They won't even bother to look back to see whether you're following. Anyway, we can't stay here much longer. We've no guarantee that it'll rain again and our supplies of fresh water will soon get dangerously low.'

'This sort of maintenance needs doing,' Phar insisted stubbornly. 'We've hardly been able to do patch-work during the short stops we've been making at midday and midnight. Frankly, I wouldn't blame the guardsmen if they did try to make a run for it – nor our men if they decided to go with them. But Fraxinus won't go without Ereleth and the others – and you can't.'

'Fraxinus doesn't even like Ereleth.'

'That's not the point. Fraxinus has old-fashioned ideas about loyalty. Anyway, he's incurably curious – maybe far too curious for his own good. He wants to know what in the world is going on. If we do propose to open a trade-route across these hills, it would be very useful to know. If we'd been able to deal with the mound-people before, our ancestors might have established a highway here a thousand years ago.'

'I can't believe that,' Checuti told him.

Phar shrugged. It was patently obvious that he couldn't either. Perhaps the repair-work he was doing really was urgent – or perhaps he desperately needed something to occupy his hands and his mind. Checuti could sympathise with that, to a degree. There was something distinctly unsatisfying about wandering back and forth in plain sight of the huge-jawed dragomite warriors.

'Is it my imagination,' Checuti asked, 'or are those dragomites nervous? The ones way up the slope are lookouts, aren't they? What do you suppose they're looking out for?'

'More dragomites,' Phar said. 'What else is there? My guess is that the nest's been so badly hit by the blight that there aren't enough warriors left to defend the queen. Maybe there used to be dozens of other nests in which humans and dragomites worked in association, and maybe they really were the Corridors of Power around here. Now, their empire's about to fall, and they're expecting the barbarians any minute. They didn't invite Ereleth down there for tea and cakes – they want our help. My guess is that they want us to help carry away a batch of eggs, so that they can start over.'

'Why would they need us?' Checuti asked uneasily.

'Probably the same reason we needed Andris Myrasol,' Phar said. 'They don't have any idea what's beyond the horizon.'

'There must be more to it than that,' Checuti said.

'Your guess is as good as mine,' the old man muttered, lowering his head over the wheel. 'Maybe better. You're the criminal mastermind – I'm just an old fool with itchy feet.'

'Another hundred days might have made all the difference,' Checuti said, not without a trace of vindictiveness. 'By then, there might not be a living dragomite to be seen. If Fraxinus hadn't been in such a reckless rush . . .'

'If you hadn't been stupid enough to stick your nose into our affairs,' Phar retorted, 'you'd be living it up in the wilds of Khalorn. Don't start lecturing *us* about recklessness. I suppose I was infected, without quite realising it, by all that darklander agitation – all that stuff about the end of the world. Even though I didn't believe it, it did serve to communicate a certain sense of urgency.'

'Yes,' said Checuti reflectively. 'It did, didn't it?'

Phar showed no further sign of requiring his help, so Checuti strolled away from the wagon, moving back towards the rear end of the column. The southward-sloping gully in which they were situated extended behind them due north, and its narrow opening encapsulated a surprisingly good view of the hills they had already negotiated. From fifty mets away at the top of the slope, he judged, it would probably be possible to look over the route they had followed. The dragomite warriors were all on the slopes to either side, so there was no particularly powerful disincentive against his wandering back up the slope, so he did.

He had not quite realised how high they were until he reached the mouth of the canyon, which did indeed provide a good view over the northerly hills. The mounds to either side of him now, he realised, were the tallest in the range – or, at least, this part of it.

He scanned the horizon for signs of movement. Then he looked back at the caravan and the steep slope which Ereleth and her companions had ascended the night before, with their escort of human warriors. The entrance which they had used in order to go into the mound was still guarded by two dragomite warriors. On impulse, he begun to climb himself, up the less sheer of the two slopes which enclosed the maw of the gully. He climbed to the nearest of the unguarded tunnels let into the mound and peered into the darkness. There was no sign of anything moving within. He continued upwards, using his hands to help him when the slope became too sheer. He had to be careful not to slip; the rotten vegetable matter was very slick in places.

He paused on a ledge to look back at the column, which suddenly seemed ridiculously small.

What is it, after all? he thought. *Two wagons, three ragged tents linked by an extremely untidy trail of assorted debris, plus thirty horses, a dozen donkeys and a mere handful of men . . . well, three and a half handfuls of men, to be pedantic. Not an army, anyhow – not a force with which to take arms against a whole world. What real chance have they of crossing a thousand kims of unknown and dangerous territory, to reach the Navel of the World? And what could they possibly find there that might be worth the trip?*

Checuti noticed that one of the guardsmen, who was pretending to be on sentry duty, was staring at him suspiciously. It was as if the man thought that he were trying to sneak away and make a run for it.

Dolt! Checuti thought. *I'm the one and only person who needs Ereleth to come out of that nest alive and well. Never mind watching me – watch that sergeant of yours! He'd sell the lot of you for a handful of beans and a chance to eat them. I used to look after my men far better than any leader you've ever followed.*

He looked up again, wondering if he could go all the way to the peak of the mound – but half a dozen dragomite warriors were there already, and he wasn't about to compete with them for a mere position of pride. They were in a state of high agitation, dancing back and forth with astonishing agility considering that they were so precariously perched on such a precipitous slope.

While he watched, they all began a helter-skelter descent, vanishing within seconds into the first tunnels they reached.

Desertion! he thought. *They've had enough – they can't stand the sunlight.* Then he realised how ridiculous the thought was, and how stupid he was for wasting time with it. Slowly – knowing what he would see – he turned sideways to look northwards again, at the route which they had followed in coming here.

'Oh filth,' he murmured in the monkey's ear, pronouncing the expletive with inappropriate gentleness.

The hills to the north, on either side of the track which they had followed in order to get to where they were now, were alive with dragomite warriors – not thousands, perhaps, but certainly hundreds. Far too many, at any rate. *Far* too many. They seemed to be heading directly for the spot on which Checuti stood, although that was probably an illusion of perspective. Almost certainly, apprehension assured him, their target was something else – not him, not the caravan. He looked back down at the wagons and the tents, which seemed even tinier now. The smaller wagon was still balanced on three wheels and a stack of boxes while Phar slotted the replacement spokes into place.

He started running, bounding down the slope with huge, reckless strides. He said nothing, but the shouting had already started. The sentry had readily deduced that something was wrong and had run to a vantage-point where he could see enough of the northward hills to know what was afoot. He was ready for it – all the ex-guardsmen were ready for it. Their cries echoed from the slopes to either side, back and forth in mad reiteration.

'Mount up – up – up!'

'To horse – horse – horse!'

'Ride south as fast as you can – can – can!'

'Leave the wagons! Leave everything – thing – thing!'

'Dragomites – mites – mites!'

The ex-guardsmen were mortally afraid of dragomites. They ran for their horses in flat panic, and the other goldens ran with them, except for Phar. Fraxinus was still invisible inside the big

428

wagon. Two adult darklanders were the only ones who stood their ground – they were looking for Fraxinus, valuing his guidance even over their own instinctive fears.

As Checuti ran back to the column, in amongst the horses, Fraxinus emerged from the big wagon, looking wildly about: at the detached wheel which Phar still held in his hands; at the madly running men; at the darklanders.

'The dragomites are coming!' Sergeant Purkin yelled to Fraxinus. 'Far too many to fight.'

Checuti was no more than twenty mets from Fraxinus when he stumbled and fell. Fortunately, he knew well enough how to fall; it was a useful skill for a thief to have. The monkey leapt from his shoulder with artful agility. Checuti's reflexes bade him roll with the fall and he did, using the remaining impetus to draw himself upright again, but he cursed the excess weight about his midriff. He staggered in a most ungainly fashion, but kept to his feet.

'We have no choice, man!' Purkin was shouting to Fraxinus, by way of justification rather than exhortation. 'We must ride or die!'

Fraxinus looked away from the sergeant. He looked, in fact, directly at Checuti – and Checuti felt a perverse thrill of pride at the thought that such a man should look to him for advice in a crisis like this.

'It's true!' he called out, thrusting out his arm to point in the direction from which danger was coming. 'They're attacking the mound. Go to the wagons – prepare to stand them off with swords and spears!'

He sincerely believed that this was sensible advice, but hardly anyone was disposed to take it. He was in amongst the scattering horses now, and the crowd swallowed him up. He found the darklander boy Koraismi running by his side, and urged him on – but Uluru or not, darklander or not, Koraismi was in no mood to do as Checuti directed. Although the lad had been unable to ride when he joined the expedition, Jacom Cerri had taught him the rudiments of it, and now he had only one thought in his young mind: to get away. Almost everyone else had the same idea.

The horses didn't take kindly to being charged in this unruly fashion, but most were already saddled and loaded. Those which were not, and which resisted, were immediately let alone in favour of more docile companions. The guardsmen who had mounted first were pointing at the mouth of the canyon, where huge-jawed warriors were already visible, pouring over the ridges in awful profusion.

We'll lose everything! Checuti thought, as he tried to fight his way through to the nearer wagon, intent on following his own advice.

Koraismi was trying desperately to haul himself up on the back of a ready-saddled horse, but could not do it. Unthinkingly, Checuti stopped and turned. He grabbed the boy about the waist and lifted him bodily into the saddle.

'Go!' he shouted.

It was the horse, not the boy, which obeyed him. The boy clung to the rein for dear life as the animal hurled itself forwards, away from the charging dragomites. All the horses which remained unsaddled joined the rush to escape, and the donkeys too. The whole lot were running in the same direction, like the herd animals they were, and there was nothing now to stop Checuti running to Phar's wagon. The two adult darklanders were already climbing up alongside Phar, and one reached down to lend a hand to another boy, no older than Koraismi. Fraxinus was climbing up on the same wagon, leaving his own to look after itself.

Checuti knew as he jumped up behind the trader that five men and a boy could hardly be expected to stave off a whole horde of creatures like the ones which were now thronging the canyon, even with the advantage of the wagon's height and the protective shelter of its wooden sides, but it was the only defence they had. The dragomites were too big, and their enormous heads too heavily armoured, to be long inconvenienced by the wooden palisades, but any barrier was better than none at all.

Phar was passing out the guardsmen's half-pikes, which had been stored here, but Checuti knew that he was not strong enough to wield one effectively and could not believe that Phar, Fraxinus and the boy could make any better use of such weapons. He took one anyway, but he knew that if they were to be seriously involved in the beginning battle, their part would be over in minutes. If the mounted guardsmen boldly joined in, trying to cripple the dragomites according to the method Andris Myrasol had worked out, the defenders on the wagon might stand some sort of chance even in a pitched battle – but he knew that the men who had run for the horses had no such intention in mind.

As Checuti stood shoulder to shoulder with Fraxinus and one of the darklanders, he had no alternative but to cling hard to his initial – and entirely rational – conviction that whatever appearances might suggest, the attackers were not aiming for the wagons at all: their target was the nest. The only problem with that thesis was that the attacking warriors might not be able to discriminate between the mound-people, who were presumably their enemies, and other humans, who were not.

For a few moments, it seemed that they were not inclined to make any such discrimination. The warrior host swarmed about the disabled wagon, reaching up with their massive jaws to snap at its defenders, utterly unintimidated by the pike-heads that were thrust at them. Some reared up on their hind legs, so that their mighty heads towered above the little group of defenders, and as Checuti stared up into the narrow slits of darkness which showed through their almost-closed eyelids he was convinced that he was looking into the face of death.

He thrust the half-pike out defiantly, aiming for those eye-slits, but the head was caught by two massive jaws, which abruptly snatched it out of his hands and hurled it contemptuously aside. He could not help but raise his arms reflexively, but the thought uppermost in his mind was that it was best to die suddenly than to suffer long-drawn-out agonies, and that this was not the worst of ways to die.

A lunging jaw knocked him sprawling on to his back, and he decided to exercise what little freedom of choice he had left and lie still, waiting to be crushed or cut in two.

He lay with his eyes shut for several seconds . . . and then several more . . . and then a minute.

He felt his arm gripped, but not by a dragomite warrior's jaws. He was helped to his feet again – and when he found the strength of mind to open his eyes he found that he was looking at Carus Fraximus. No dragomite warriors were looming over the wagon now; they were swarming up the slopes to either side, letting the wagon and its defenders alone.

He should have felt relief, and gratitude, but in fact he felt a perfect fool. He felt that his instincts had let him down, and made a coward of him in a horribly clownish way. Hope and rationality had, after all, triumphed over confusion and despair.

The warriors were disappearing now, as if by magic. They had spread out to use every one of the holes let into the mound. They were pouring into the interior of the hill in their tens and their hundreds.

'Nest-war,' said the darklander beside him, in a tone that was almost laconic. Checuti knew well enough that all darklanders were past masters of the underrated art of being wise after the event, but the savage's apparent composure astonished him nevertheless. He was pervesely glad to see, though, that the other adult darklander and the boy were still petrified by fear, unable as yet to start talking about the great victory they had just won.

Ereleth is inside that mound, he thought, in a peculiarly cold fashion. *So is Andris Myrasol, and that poor cousin of his. They're as good as dead – every last one of them, including the princess. So am I. All I've won is a slow death instead of a quick one. What have I to be glad about?*

'Look!' Fraxinus said, dropping the half-pike with which he had tried to ward off the warrior dragomites.

Almost all the warriors had disappeared into the mound by now, but there were others coming in their wake which had now reached the lip of the gully. These were not warriors, but workers – and a few which were neither workers nor warriors. There were others with them, who were not even dragomites.

'See,' said the darklander who had spoken before, in the same irritatingly airy way. 'Our kinsmen said as much. Humans do ride dragomites – and Serpents too.'

Checuti saw that he was absolutely right. There *was* a human riding one of the worker dragomites, and that was not the only dragomite which had a rider. In normal circumstances he would have paid more attention to the rider which was not a human being, but there was something about the lone human which caught and held his stare. He could see that she was neither coloured nor dressed like the mound-women he had seen the previous night, but he had to shield his eyes and squint as he attempted to make out the cast of her features.

He turned to Fraxinus wonderingly, and said, 'I think I know that woman. I know it seems absurd, but I'm sure I've seen her somewhere before.'

'So have I,' Fraxinus said. His voice was dry but he had the grace to sound astonished. 'But I never thought to see her again, or in such strange company. It's Hyry Keshvara.'

14

WHAT HAPPENS WHEN *a child is due to be born?* Andris was thinking as he looked around, unsure which direction the voice had come from. *Does the process take sixteen tendays, as with the unborn children of Ferentina and Xandria? Is our luminous friend a midwife? Do the walls grow teats to suckle infants as well as to feed prisoners? There must be a nursery somewhere nearby . . .*

'Here,' said the voice again. He scanned the walls, wondering which of the obscene mouths might have opened.

'There,' said Cerri, taking his arm and moving him so that he could see. The cave had many columns and coverts, and the relevant alcove had been screened from his roaming eye.

He saw what Cerri was pointing at, and understood why the person they had been brought to meet had not come forward to greet them. Not all of those who were gathered in this obscene place were spread thinly about the walls, but all were captives nevertheless, irrevocably joined in a union with the dragomite queen which was surely too intimate by far. He had to reassure himself that he and the captain had not been brought here to meet a similar fate. Whatever the mound-people wanted of Ereleth and her companions, it was not to add their flesh to this mad riot – this diseased and dying riot.

The person who had spoken had a head and a torso and two arms, but he – Andris thought it was a *he*, although there was no conclusive proof – had no distinct body-parts at all below the waist. He sprouted from the folded flesh that was layered upon this inner surface of the dragomite queen like some kind of appalling flower sprouting from bindweed covering a wall. He was not alone, but his companion was slumped down, seemingly dead.

Wilted, Andris thought. *Rotting on the stem*. He could not put out of his mind the thought that Princess Lucrezia had possessed a seed which was capable of doing to a healthy man what the dragomite queen had done to these, her human-seeming lovers.

The two half-men were bald and ugly, but had their lower extensions been hidden by some discreet curtain they could have passed for human readily enough. Even the one which was unmistakably alive and wide awake seemed listless, as he stared at Andris and Checuti in a disconcertingly blank fashion.

'Come closer,' the half-man said eventually. The voice was deep but whispery.

Andris obeyed, but Jacom Cerri hung back. In such poor light, Andris knew, they must seem little more than shadows to their summoner, but the half-man's eyes were big and their pupils must have been fully distended.

'A pair of drones,' the whispery voice opined. 'Human males, from the purple forest, or beyond. I never thought to see such a sight. I greet you – brothers.' There was a croak in the voice now, as though it required a considerable effort for the half-man to speak at all.

'Brothers?' Cerri repeated, as though the word had suddenly become loathsome to him. Andris, by contrast, felt that he knew all about the limits and petty treasons of brotherly love – the term was no insult to him.

'From far beyond the forest,' Andris said, determined to be calm. He, after all, had legs. He had more right to be in control here than anyone else he could see.

'I thought so,' said the half-man.

'Do you receive news of the world, even here?' Andris asked. 'Have you maps?'

'We are brothers,' the chimera insisted, evidently thinking that there were more important matters to address than the extent of his knowledge of the world without. 'You must understand that, if you can.'

We must understand everything, if we can, Andris thought. *Is that not what Fraxinus would say? What else is there for us to win but understanding – provided, of course, that we can stay alive?* 'I am Andris Myrasol,' he said aloud, speaking with awkward formality, 'I was once a prince in Ferentina, but I am an unwilling

435

servant now. This is Captain Jacom Cerri of King Belin's guard – a soldier of the greatest empire in the world.'

'We have little need of names here,' the half-man said unapologetically, 'but you may call me Seth if you wish. I am a drone, consort of the dragomite queen, but my forefathers were yours; my ancestors walked on the surface of the world, as you do. Come closer.'

It was Andris who obeyed this instruction. The half-man reached out a bony hand to him. It was trembling. Andris reached out and took it in his own, bearing its weight as the half-man's arm sagged. Their grip was not a conventional hand-shake, thumb to thumb, but a reversed clasp which allowed Andris to lift the other's hand and bring it close to his chest in a reassuring embrace, and this he did. It didn't seem so very brave, given that the other man was in no position to hurt him.

He was very close to the half-man now. He towered above the other as he towered above almost all of his fellows.

'Thank you, brother,' the half-man said.

Why am I doing this? Andris thought. *How am I able to do it? Have my wilder dreams prepared me for such gestures?*

'We had no idea that humans lived with dragomites,' Andris said. 'We could not possibly have guessed that *this* was the manner of their partnership.'

'No,' said the half-man, as Andris stepped back, releasing the feeble hand. 'How could you? But we are human still. You must understand that. The warriors may have told you that we are all of one mind here, but it is not so. They do not understand. We are not all of one mind, nor all of one body, no matter how things may appear. I am a man, Andris. We are brothers in blood and brain.'

'He calls us brothers because he wishes to make claims upon us,' Cerri said, with cold, implacable fear in his tone. 'He intends to invoke the responsibilities of brotherhood. Find out what he wants before you call him brother in return.'

Andris turned on the captain, unaccountably angered by the rudeness of this cynical interjection, but Seth uttered a thin laugh.

'He's right, Brother Andris,' he croaked. 'He sees immediately what I am about – what further proof of kinship do you need? He puts himself in my place, recognises my nature and my need. Who could doubt, now, that we are all brothers here?'

'What do you want?' Cerri countered harshly.

'What do *you* want, Brother Jacom?' the half-man retorted resentfully. 'Firstly, not to die. Secondly, to live well. Thirdly, to live long. Do I not read you aright? Am I not your brother in spirit and soul? Are we not *all of one mind*, in these respects at least?'

'I'm no deist, to believe in spirit and soul,' Cerri retorted grimly. 'I believe in flesh, and flesh alone. All flesh has desires such as those. Were you the voice of the dragomite queen, you'd say the same.'

'Oh no,' the half-man said. 'I know far more than you about that. Your own queen has already heard what *that* voice has to say, and will hear far more. The dragomite queen is an altruist through and through; self-sacrifice is bred in every fibre of her being, for she is the ultimate mother and knows no will but motherhood. Were she not so vast and so imperious she'd be better called a slave than a queen. Her only desire is the survival of the nest – she cares not a whit for her own flesh, which has long since outgrown any capacity for self-awareness or self-protection. She will die content, but I cannot. I am a drone, like you. I am mind and memory, lore and lust. I am your brother, whether you will say so or not. All men are brothers, who have the forefathers in common.'

'In Ferentina,' Andris said whimsically, 'brothers are often the deadliest of enemies, becoming murderous in matters of inheritance. I've learned not to rely too much on the obligations of brotherhood. Perhaps you should tell us why you sent a messenger to bring us here. I fear that we're not in command of our fellows. We too have a queen of sorts, who has a giant warrior with a mighty spear to protect her from usurpers. I doubt that we're in a position to rescue you from the corruption which is evident hereabouts – nor are you, it seems, in any position to be rescued.'

'Not true,' replied the half-man, with a wry smile. 'As you might have observed, certain affairs of the flesh work differently here. You have privileges I have not . . . but I have privileges of which you have never dreamed. Are you a gambling man, Brother Andris?'

Andris imagined that he heard the voice of Checuti smothering a wry laugh. 'Only for money,' he replied. 'Never with my life.'

'Will you venture a certain inconvenience against vague

promises?' the half-man asked. His voice was growing feebler by degrees, and his eyelids were drooping now. His thin arms dangled heavily, the fingers twitching. 'I would not ask so much were the situation not desperate, but I swear that you'll be amply repaid, when circumstances permit.'

'What inconvenience?' Andris asked. 'What promises?'

'I want you to carry me out of here,' the half-man said bluntly. 'I want you to carry me out and keep me with you – hidden if necessary but not too tightly wrapped, for I shall still need a little air to redden my blood. I want you to nourish me as best you can, with drops of sweet liquid squeezed into my mouth. I want you to keep faith with me even if I seem to be past recovery, until the flesh falls away from the bones of my skull. I want you to make what efforts you can to make me whole again, if and when you can find a way, and I want you to try as best you can to find a way. I hope with all my heart that all this will not prove too heavy an investment. In return, I promise that if ever you can rouse me from my sleep you shall have all the benefit of my wisdom. I must warn you, because I am a fair man, that you might have to go to Chimera's Cradle itself in order to recover that wisdom – but if the world's crisis is indeed come, you will need me soon and you will probably find the means to do it much closer to home. Will you do it, Brother Andris? Tell me quickly, for there is little time to spare.'

What is all this? Andris wondered. *It must be a dream. I must have fallen asleep when I drunk that drugged milk which oozed from the wall in my cell. This is a product of my own imagination: my deepest fears, my most profound resentments. But if that is what it is, why should I be frightened? All being well, I should awake from it – and if the worst comes to the worst, should I not count myself a lucky man to die in my sleep, without pain or ignominy or sensible awareness of the end?*

'I cannot see how it might be managed,' he said aloud, 'but I shall be happy to try. Why should I not, *Brother Seth*?'

The long, thin arms twitched again, but then became still. If the half-man had been trying to raise them, he no longer had the strength to do it. His face was contorted, but there seemed to be more anger than anguish in the grimace.

'You . . . will have to help me . . . brother,' he whispered. 'Take my head in your hands, if you please.'

Knowing perfectly well what was about to happen – for was this not a dream of his own invention, incapable of producing any authentic surprise? – Andris took the frail bald head in his huge hands. He did not have to twist or pull. The eyes closed, the mouth fell silent, and a fissure opened up in the throat in exactly the same way that a fissure had been opened up in the wall of their cell when the dream began, save that this parting was horizontal instead of vertical.

'Andris,' said Jacom Cerri, coming forward to join him at last, and deigning to use his given name. 'Don't . . .'

He was too late. He might have been a captain once, but he was a mere bystander now, with no possible claim on the friendship or loyalty of a man he had dishonestly wronged.

Andris moved his own body, protectively, to screen the now-agonised expression of his unfortunate kinsman from Cerri's intolerant gaze. As he was gradually decapitated by the force of his own will, the half-man's features became calm again. His eyes eventually closed, as his unconscious head fell into Andris's tender care.

No man – certainly not his own brothers – had ever placed such faith in him before. It didn't trouble him in the least that all he had received as a price for his solicitude was a very vague promise. Wasn't that the way men were supposed to treat with one another: with courage, with honour, and with trust?

439

15

LUCREZIA AND ERELETH faced the mound-queen together. Dhalla stood impassively on guard behind them, standing rigidly to attention with her spear in her hand, but that appearance was let down by the much tinier figure of Merel Zabio, who stood beside her in a calculatedly negligent slouch.

The mound-queen's massive bulk was slumped awkwardly upon her remarkable throne, which seemed to have enfolded her even more tightly than before, as if it were a protective calyx folding in upon a flower as dusk fell. The two dragomite drones which flanked the throne to either side were agitated: their antennae bobbed and vibrated, and their front feet – upraised as if they were hands – were busy signing to the human workers and warriors who were constantly appearing and disappearing.

'There is no time to spare,' the mound-queen said. 'The dragomite queen is dying, and the nest with her. The subject nests are already dead, and all their nearer neighbours, but the race to occupy the Corridors of Power is begun and the invaders will come soon enough. An empire is falling. You understand what that means, I think.'

'We understand,' Ereleth agreed.

Perhaps we do, Lucrezia thought. *If Xandria's centre fell – if the city wall broke and the citadel crumbled – the fringes of the empire would simply fall apart, becoming independent states again. Would-be conquerors would rush inwards from all directions, vying for the privilege of taking the centre, the heart from which a new empire might grow. However bizarre this empire of men and dragomites is, its Corridors of Power must likewise have a heart . . . and when the heart fails, chaos comes with a headlong rush.*

'We could take your wagons and your horses,' the mound-queen said. 'We could kill you all, if we were inclined to do so.

That is not what we desire or intend. We shall take you safely through the hills, guarding you against the warriors of other nests, if you will help us thereafter. We will need to carry a number of eggs, and certain other materials, which are not your concern.'

'We agree to that,' Ereleth said promptly, 'but we must go south and not north. We could not guarantee your safety in the Forest of Absolute Night.'

'Could you guarantee our safety in the Soursweet Marshes?' the mound-queen demanded impatiently. 'They extend at least as far as the forest, and they are no less dangerous. We can no longer afford to care which way we go, as long as we go – but we need more from you than promises which you might break at the first opportunity.'

Now we get to the heart of it, Lucrezia thought.

'How much more?' Ereleth asked, without beating about the bush.

'One of you, at least, must become one with us.'

Ereleth had been forewarned of this, and she had a reaction ready. She half-turned, and flicked a casual finger in the direction of Merel Zabio. 'Take her,' she said. 'She's yours to do with as you will.'

Lucrezia watched the thief's expression as it grew incredulous, and then thunderous – but she was not surprised when the mound-queen said: 'No. We need a high-born. We need a queen. It would be wise, perhaps, to have a princess too.'

Ereleth showed commendable resilience in the face of this statement. 'That is not acceptable to us,' she said. 'We will not bargain with you on such terms as those.'

'You are not in a position to make bargains,' the mound-queen said. 'The price set upon your lives is that you must do everything in your power to help the nest. You are a queen among your own people, but you can only be a servant here.'

'What exactly do you mean,' Ereleth was quick to counter, 'when you say that I must become one with you? What are you proposing to do to me?'

'You need not be afraid,' the mound-queen said – although Lucrezia had never heard such a hollow assurance. 'We offer you long life and renewed strength. We offer you a chance to be more than you are, more than you could ever have hoped to become.'

This is bizarre, Lucrezia thought. *They have the power to do exactly as they wish. Why do they need our consent?* It was clear, however, that the mound-queen not only felt that she needed Ereleth's consent, but that she expected to get it. The only compromise which had been offered related to the inclusion or exclusion of Lucrezia. The princess wondered whether her mentor loved her well enough not to turn around and say 'If you need a high-born, take her, but let me alone.'

What Ereleth actually said was: 'I ask again, what exactly do you propose to do to me?'

'The dragomite queen will give you armour to wear,' the mound-queen said. 'Living armour. We shall work together, you and I. We shall speak with one voice, and we shall be of one mind . . . but you should not be afraid, for we shall take the greatest care to conserve every vestige of your lore and your wit. You shall be Ama-Ereleth, just as I am Ama-Metra. We have lost too many sisters to the plague, but we shall surely find more. In the fullness of time, we shall surely find more.'

Lucrezia's hand went to her belt, and she began untying the knot securing one of her pouches. She felt that it was time to make her weapons ready – but Ereleth's hands were still resolutely folded.

'If you do this,' Ereleth said calmly, 'my people would no longer regard me as a queen. They would no longer follow my orders. They would regard me as an alien, to be killed. If you want my help – and I still offer it – you must let me be what I am. There is no alternative. If you need a hostage I will give you the girl, but the mere fact of my offering her to you is proof that she is of very little use. If you try to do what you have threatened, you will prove yourself an enemy, and you will be treated as one by all my people. If you try to make me one of you, you will throw away your only chance to obtain the help you need.'

The mound-queen stared at her captives, with resentment seething in her darkly rimmed eyes. *She is human*, Lucrezia thought, *but not quite human enough.*

The dragomite drones were waving their antennae so rapidly that they were mere blurs. The human workers and warriors who came and went continually back and forth through the chamber were moving very swiftly, with panic in their expressions. Lucrezia judged that there really was no time, and that the mound-queen must decide now whether to make good her threat or whether to capitulate.

'I can save you,' Ereleth said boldly – evidently feeling that there was no need to be parsimonious with her promises. 'I can force Carus Fraxinus and Aulakh Phar to help to find a home for the nest, and I will – but it is you who are in no position to make bargains. If you do anything to injure or displease me, you will die. The dragomite queen will die. The *nest* will die.'

They cannot believe it, Lucrezia thought. *But have they any recourse at all save to take the risk? They dare not seize her and claim her. They dare not take the risk that she is right. They have to accept what she says, for there is no time left for prevarication.*

'What Ereleth says is true,' she said aloud, speaking as boldly as her mentor. 'You need us, if you are to have any real chance of building a new nest elsewhere in the world, and it is our knowledge you need, not our status. You do not need Ereleth because she is a queen, but because she is wise – and that is why you need Carus Fraxinus and Aulakh Phar too, and Andris Myrasol. How you have conserved your own lore I don't know, but we have divided ours between us, and we make use of it by joining together by agreement, free and yet united. If we are to be of use to you, those are the only terms we can offer, the only terms on which our help can be bought.' She was aware, in saying this, that it would sound hideously ironic to Merel Zabio, who knew only too well what terms Ereleth had offered her cousin and her friend the thief – but the girl knew better than to object here and now; no matter what resentments she might be harbouring, she wanted to get out of here.

The mound-queen didn't turn her head to look at the dragomite drones, but their antennae dipped to touch her about the head and shoulders, and there must have been some meaning in the signal. Lucrezia looked around the walls of the vaulted throne room. Was it her imagination, or had the light grown fainter? Was the odorous air more deeply tainted with the reek of decay? Had the throne itself changed its shape, so as to sag a little to one side?

The drones moved forward slightly as human workers came to them, signalling frantically. This time, one of them turned to face the queen and to demand her attention. She sat up straight, scowling. Jume Metra came to stand before the throne too, reaching up to touch the 'hand' of the drone.

'Your drones are no longer in their lodgings,' Jume Metra said, turning again to face Ereleth.

'Do you imagine that I'm responsible for that?' Ereleth asked. 'You must look to your own people for an explanation.'

Even in a dragomite hive, Lucrezia thought, with a thrill of wry amusement, *the right hand of authority does not always know what the left is doing. How reassuring that is! There is disorder wherever humans are, even when they form alliances with dragomites.* She became aware, though, that Merel Zabio had reacted to this news with evident dismay.

The mound-queen looked around again, first at one drone and then the other. 'There is no time at all,' she said, her capacious flesh shaking as if it had been seized by a sudden agony of dread. 'You must flee as best you can. The queen still lives, but the scavengers have come ahead of time, to feed upon her living flesh. Take them, daughters! Save them if you can, and accept whatever help they will condescend to give us. Go! *Go!*'

Jume Metra had hesitated, but now the message got through. She seized Ereleth by the arm, saying 'Come!' and pointing to one of the tunnels leading out of the throne room. The two drones were already moving towards another, and there were workers running this way and that in what seemed to Lucrezia to be utter confusion.

It was Dhalla who came to the princess, saying 'Quickly, highness!' as she offered a helping hand. The princess immediately moved to go with her, following Ereleth – but Merel Zabio grabbed her left arm and held her back.

'Wait!' the girl said anxiously. 'What about Andris? You can't leave him here.'

'That's none of my concern,' Lucrezia said, trying to struggle free – but the girl would not let go, and in spite of her slenderness she was considerably stronger in the arm than the princess. Lucrezia felt a flood of anger, and lashed out with her sharpened fingernails. She felt slightly ashamed of herself as she did so, not because she feared to hurt the girl but because she could not help wishing that she had had time to anoint her nails with some deadly poison.

The gesture was wasted. Merel Zabio ducked away from the thrust, and would doubtless have continued to hold on had she

444

been allowed to do so. She wasn't. Dhalla, who was far more powerful than she was, reached out a long arm in an insultingly casual fashion and slapped her backhandedly across the face. The blow knocked the girl off her feet, and she let go of Lucrezia's arm as she fell backwards in an untidy heap, seemingly unconscious.

'Run, highness!' the giant said, pointing to the tunnel into which Metra and Ereleth had already disappeared.

Lucrezia wanted to run, but she didn't look towards the tunnel or at Dhalla's anxious face, because her attention had been caught by the sight of the mound-queen, still sitting on her foolish throne. *She* had not begun to run, nor even to raise herself up from her station. The agony of her dread had passed as quickly as it had come, and she was very still now … almost lifeless. The expression on her face spoke of defeat and despair. Whatever she had hoped to save of the nest – and might still hope to save – it was not her own flesh or her own mind. She saw Lucrezia staring at her, but she hardly seemed to have the strength of will to respond. She said nothing, and her gaze fell, as if she could no longer meet the eyes of a truly human being. She was looking in the direction of Merel Zabio's fallen body, but she was not looking *at* it. It was as if she had no capacity left to be interested in such a petty tragedy.

The chamber was almost empty now; even the drones had gone – but the mound-queen remained where she was.

She can't get up! Lucrezia thought. *She really is bound to her throne, like a flower in its cup. Her flesh is fused with alien flesh, like the armour she promised Ereleth. She's not human at all. She's a chimera!*

'Princess!' cried Dhalla, reaching out as if to seize her and carry her away by force – but it was too late. In one of the openings beyond the throne the head of a dragomite warrior appeared. There was red blood on its jaws, and Lucrezia was in no doubt that it was human blood.

The mound-queen screamed as the thing came forward, with appalling speed, avidly reaching out for her with its awful bloody jaws.

Dhalla grabbed Lucrezia then, and hauled her back – but not to bundle her into the tunnel into which Metra and Ereleth had gone. Perhaps they could have reached it, provided that the warrior had concentrated its attention solely on the helpless mound-queen, but

Dhalla wasn't prepared to turn her back and take that chance. Bracing her hugely muscled legs, she threw back her right arm to its fullest extent and hurled her spear with all the might of which she was capable.

It flew through the air with awesome velocity, and struck the dragomite between its great black eyes.

No ordinary arm could have hurled the weapon with force enough to penetrate a warrior dragomite's armoured skull, but Dhalla's was no ordinary arm. The spear smashed through the chitin and embedded a full met of its shaft in the softer flesh beyond.

Any earthly creature would have fallen dead on the instant, its brain ruined – but the dragomite wasn't an earthly creature, and it didn't fall. It did, however, turn away from the mound-queen who had been its first intended target.

Instead, it came scuttling over Merel Zabio's supine form – heading straight for Dhalla, and for the princess who was cradled once again in the giant's protective arm.

16

'COME WITH ME!' said the guide which had brought Jacom and Myrasol to the lodging-place of the human drones. Its voice was plaintive and the patterns of its luminous skin had begun to change with startling rapidity. Jacom didn't like the look of it – and he didn't like the look of Myrasol either. The big amber seemed to have gone into a kind of trance; he was standing there staring at the severed head which he held in his capacious hands as if it were a football.

'I think it's getting anxious,' Jacom said, hoping to bring his companion back to reality. 'There's a definite note of urgency in its voice.'

Myrasol continued to stare down at the head. Its eyes had fallen closed, and the expression on its face was curiously peaceful, as if the promise he had made to the intelligence which had animated it had provided a desperately desired reassurance.

'Come *on*,' Jacom urged, tugging at his sleeve. 'For Goran's sake let's get out of here!'

The amber allowed his legs to be urged into action by Jacom's insistence, but he hardly seemed conscious of making his exit from the grotesque chamber whose walls were plastered with living human flesh – or, to be strictly accurate, with *dying* human flesh. Nor did Jacom pause or turn aside for any more detailed examination of the dragomite queen's inert birth-canals; he couldn't wait to be gone from there now that their guide seemed anxious to take them.

In the gloomy but more spacious cave byond the chamber of horrors there was a great deal of activity. Dragomite workers were running this way and that, many of them bearing bundles of eggs which had been glued to their backs in transparent encasements, like the spawn of enormous toads. The luminous humanoid had to duck and dodge as it weaved its way between these hurrying workers; Jacom had little difficulty doing likewise but his dazed companion was much clumsier.

The vertical slit which eventually opened up in one of the smoother walls, in response to their guide's impatient urging, was one of many. The burdened workers were exiting in like fashion, although others were still entering in order to receive their own quotas of eggs.

'They're abandoning the nest,' said Myrasol faintly, as he finally looked up from his contemplation of his own egg-like burden. 'Why? What's happening?'

'I don't know,' Jacom said, still pulling hard on his companion's sleeve, although he had neither the stature nor the musculature to impose his will on a man so much bigger than himself, 'but one way or another, this place is falling apart. Let's just get out of here, shall we?'

Myrasol began to move a little faster, encouraging their guide to scuttle even more rapidly. As soon as they were in the newly opened tunnel they began to climb steeply, and for a moment or two Jacom felt relief at the thought that they were heading for the surface and the sunlight with all possible haste – but only for a moment or two. Myrasol had no sooner started moving at a sensible pace than he stopped abruptly, and said: 'What about Merel?'

Jacom turned, but the luminous creature hurried on, leaving them in near-darkness.

'She'll be taken care of,' Jacom said, with sudden anger in his voice. 'Come on, damn you!' He didn't know whether it was true or not, and he didn't care. He just wanted to get out – but he couldn't abandon Myrasol. That wasn't because of any bond of friendship that had sprung magically into being between them: it was a simple desire not to be left alone with the thing that had been sent to fetch them and now seemed intent on getting them out.

Myrasol took the head into his left hand, gripping it by the bald pate, so as to set his right arm free. 'No,' he said stubbornly. 'I don't trust Ereleth or the giant, and I certainly don't trust the dragomites. I want Merel with me – and if that animated lantern wants *this* carried out of the nest it'll have to take me to Merel first.'

It was by no means obvious, of course, that the 'animated lantern' was intelligent enough to know what was happening – but it did seem to care. When it realised that its followers had stopped it came back, still bleating 'Come with me! Come with me!'

'Take me to my cousin,' the amber instructed the creature. 'The girl who was brought down here with me. Not the old woman, nor the giant – the young woman. You have to take me to her.'

'Don't be stupid,' Jacom said exasperatedly. 'It can't understand you.'

'Take us back to the cells,' Myrasol said, staring into the guide's saucer-like eyes. 'Merel was put into one too. When we have her, we can go on.'

Jacom reached out then, trying to take the disembodied head from Andris's hand, but there was no way he could do that without the amber's consent.

'You had your chance when he asked for help,' Myrasol said grimly. 'No brotherly love, no ticket to the earthly paradise. If I weren't the sort of person who cared about my cousin, I wouldn't be the sort of person *he'd* want looking after him, would I? Merel risked her neck to get me out of Belin's citadel, where *you* put me, and I won't leave her fate to chance.'

'Come with me!' screeched the guide, waving its tentacled hands in a mad pantomime of concession. 'Come with me!'

When it set off again, Myrasol followed, and Jacom fell into step behind him. He soon observed that they were no longer climbing steeply, but moving more or less horizontally through that part of the dragomite hive which was alive, but he didn't know whether he ought to be glad about that or terrified. No more than a few minutes passed before they were disgorged into one of the permanent corridors where the air was a little fresher and cooler and the lighted walls a fraction brighter. The tunnel was deserted; they met no workers coming in the opposite direction, nor did they glimpse any in the branching tunnels.

After several more minutes the tunnel widened out again, letting them into the complex of chambers to which they had been brought by the human warriors. These chambers were by no means deserted, by humans or by dragomites, and their guide was forced yet again to duck and dodge as it hurried forward.

Although human warriors and workers were milling in every

449

direction it quickly became obvious to Jacom that he and his companions were moving against the main tide. He was about to renew his complaint, but Myrasol was in no mood to listen, and he changed his mind when he suddenly caught sight of someone he knew.

'Look!' he said excitedly. 'It's Ereleth! The giant and your cousin must be with her!'

The nascent elation died in Jacom's heart, though, as he perceived that Ereleth's companions were all mound-women. Even so, both men turned aside to go after her, although their guide continued the way it had been going.

'Ereleth!' Jacom shouted after her. The mound-woman who was leading her tried to prevent her pausing, but the queen brushed her off impatiently.

'Where's Merel?' Myrasol asked bluntly. 'Is she safe?'

Ereleth's initial surprise at seeing them turned to shock as she realised what Myrasol was carrying. The witch-queen stared at the head as if she expected to recognise the face – and made no answer to the question which Andris had put to her.

'Tell him, for Goran's sake,' said Jacom. 'It's not what you think!'

'Whose head is that?' Ereleth demanded – but she was looking about her as she said it, as if surprised to find that there were no humans with her except mound-women.

'My brother's,' Andris retorted. 'But it's my cousin I want now. Have you seen her?'

'Come with us,' Ereleth said, belatedly. 'You must come with us. The nest . . .' She broke off as she caught sight of the luminous creature, which had fought its way back once again to regain contact with its troublesome charges. Her eyes grew wide with fear and fascination – but the fascination was already outweighing the fear.

Myrasol was staring angrily at Ereleth, perhaps having caught an expression in her eye which suggested to him that she *had* seen Merel Zabio, and knew exactly where she was. Deliberately, the amber raised his left arm and extended it towards her, showing her what it was that he carried. 'Tell me where she is,' he said, injecting all the venom he could muster into the command. 'Tell me, you murderous bitch, or I'll . . .'

It was his turn to be interrupted as this display overrode Ereleth's fascination with the humanoid monster and recalled her presence of mind. She drew herself up to her full height, in a queenly manner.

'Your cousin's back there,' she said flatly, pointing along the corridor. 'We were all in the mound-queen's throne room.' For a moment, it seemed as if she might go back herself, but the warrior women with her were trying to force her in the opposite direction.

'If you've hurt her . . .' Myrasol began – but Jacom cut him off in peremptory fashion.

'Come on,' he said. 'If you must . . .'

Myrasol rounded on him. 'Go with *her!*' he snapped. 'Do your duty, captain – and get out while you can!'

I ought to do exactly that, Jacom thought, *but he means it as an insult, not as a kindness.*

'Come with me!' bleated the guide – and Myrasol went. Jacom hesitated for a moment, but Ereleth was already hurrying away, and her solicitous attendants didn't seem to care about him at all. He was jostled by a dragomite worker for whose massive bulk he had perforce to make room, and the contact seemed – oddly enough – to steady his fevered emotions.

Dragomites no longer bothered him, he realised; he had grown accustomed to their nearness within hours, much as he had long since grown accustomed to the nearness of horses. There was nothing in their unearthliness to disturb him now.

He raced after Myrasol, and eventually caught up with him in spite of the fact that he had not the other's massive stride.

'You should have gone with Ereleth,' the amber said, without breaking stride. 'She's headed for the surface – or for safety, at any rate.'

'I know,' Jacom replied, panting hard between phrases. 'But I'm with *you*, brother. This time, I'll not leave you to your fate. I owe you that.'

He observed, bitterly, that Myrasol didn't thank him for this recklessness.

As they had run through the tunnels the way had become clearer and clearer. It was noticeable now that every other living thing they saw was headed in the opposite direction. The luminous creature seemed rather drab in these lighted corridors, and its skin had darkened considerably. It still seemed pathetically thin and frail, and Jacom felt a surge of admiration for its steadfastness – exactly the kind of surge which Andris Myrasol ought to have felt when Jacom came after him.

Can the world be such a terrible place, he thought, *when it can play host to three such fools as we?*

They came into the throne room then, where the guide darted to one side. Jacom's eye was immediately caught by the fallen form of a young woman who was being trampled beneath the feet of an angry dragomite – but it was plain to see that the dragomite hadn't the slightest interest in her. The shaft of a spear was jutting out of its forehead, like the horn of a unicorn, and it was charging full tilt at the person who had had the temerity to put it there: the giant, Dhalla. Meanwhile, the latter was busy placing Princess Lucrezia against the wall of the cave, and the fat woman who was sitting on the throne seemed to be struggling to get to her feet.

Jacom stopped dead in his tracks. Myrasol thrust the severed head into his hands, saying: 'Look after this.' While he was still looking down at it, petrified by disgust, the big amber bounded forward, dodging around the dragomite's jaws.

It was perfectly clear to Jacom that Myrasol's only purpose was to reach his cousin and pluck her from the floor – but it wasn't clear to the dragomite. The monster turned its huge head reflexively, and reached out for the amber's hurrying figure. It might have got him, too, had he been slightly less nimble, but he was not in any sort of trance now and he danced clear of the sideways thrust.

Until it turned its head the dragomite had not seemed to be in the least inconvenienced by the spear in its head, but the lateral movement was a bad error of judgment. The weight of the spear dragged the head down and the blunt end of the spear scraped the ground. The friction must have forced the broad head of the weapon sideways within the wound, and that must have done some damage, for the enormous creature was seized by a sudden convulsion. It lost control of its legs, and slumped to the floor, thrashing its limbs madly but impotently.

Myrasol picked Merel Zabio up as if she weighed nothing at all, and leapt to the wall of the chamber, where he ended up side by side with Princess Lucrezia.

The woman on the throne managed to come to her feet then, and she stepped forward a pace. Her legs, though stout, weren't able to support her, and she had to lean back on her equally stout arms while her bloated hands rested on the arms of her crude throne. Jacom saw her face change as she realised that she couldn't walk, but her expression was indecipherable.

'No time at all,' the mound-queen said, to no one in particular.

It was only then that Jacom noticed the blood gushing on to the floor in front of the throne, where the woman stood. He couldn't see the wound from which it was flowing, and didn't want to – but the mound-queen continued to stand up. It reminded him of the way Ereleth had gathered herself together in the tunnel, when she had remembered that she was a queen. He realised that she was looking at the head cradled in his hands. Her expression was still unreadable.

'He will tell you nothing but lies,' she said venomously. 'We are no kin to creatures like you. We never needed you. The nest can look after its own.' Having said that, she fell forward, to lie prone in the lake of her blood, struggling impotently to rise again. Jacom could now see the gaping holes in her clothing, where she had had to tear herself free from the throne with whose alien flesh hers had been intimately joined.

'Come with me!' begged their guide plaintively, already moving back towards the entrance through which they had just come – but no sooner had it reached the narrow mouth of the tunnel than a huge head was thrust through it: the head of another dragomite warrior.

The massive jaws of the warrior snapped shut about the humanoid creature's midriff, slicing it in two. As the upper part of the body fell, the creature shrieked.

The astonishingly loud and agonising call echoed from the walls and ceiling of the chamber, multiplying into a ghastly chorus. The ugly head ducked briefly as the jaws flicked the two halves of the skeletal form to one side, and then the rest of the monster hove into view as it scuttled forward.

Jacom was nearer to the monster than anyone else, far too close for his own comfort. He hurled himself forward, sprinting for the narrowest of all the tunnels which offered exits from the throne room – but before he reached it that gap too was filled to capacity by the frightful head of a warrior dragomite.

Jacom stopped as abruptly as he could, and threw himself sideways, to the place where Andris, the unconscious Merel and the princess were already huddled tightly together.

Oh filth, he thought, with surprisingly little vehemence. *Wrong again. I should have gone with Ereleth after all.*

The twin warriors were converging upon them now, from opposite directions. There was, as the mound-queen had shrewdly observed, no time at all for the formulation of any kind of plan.

17

As the two dragomite warrors converged, one of them skirting the still-thrashing body of the other which had been killed by Dhalla's spear, Lucrezia pressed herself back against the wall of the cavern, wishing that it might swallow her up. The big amber laid his unconscious cousin down in the angle where the floor met the wall, and knelt over her, shielding her with his body as he tried to revive her.

The young captain scrambled to her side. He was carrying a human head, but he had to put it down while he tried to wrestle the sword from his belt because it was too large for him to hold one-handed. While she looked down at the head, trying to figure out whose it was, he pulled her towards him urgently. She resisted; she had not the slightest confidence in his ability to rescue her. She was looking to Dhalla for that, on the grounds that Dhalla was the only one here who had demonstrated that she was capable of killing a dragomite.

The captain didn't understand why she was pulling away, and he kept pulling too. Dhalla was on the other side of the throne, moving behind one of the warriors, with the obvious intention of recovering her spear. Lucrezia tried to shake off the captain's insistent hand, pressing herself harder and harder against the lukewarm wall.

Had either of the dragomite warriors turned its head towards them it could have been upon them within a couple of seconds, slashing at them with its awful jaws – but neither of them did. Their black eyes were fixed on one another.

Lucrezia tried even harder to pull away from Jacom Cerri, wishing that there were a space behind her into which she could move away from him – and suddenly, there *was* such a space. There was a tunnel mouth where none had been before: a narrow portal which had opened up like a pair of vertical lips. She was pulling so hard that she fell into it as soon as it opened – and the young captain was holding on so firmly that he too was pulled over. He fell on top of her, but he released his grip then and she was able to scramble away. For a second or two the aperture through which they had tumbled remained open, so that the wan light of the throne room spilled through it – but then it closed. The mouth had swallowed them, and the darkness was absolute.

Lucrezia would not have been in the least surprised had the walls to either side of them closed in, crushing them both to digestible pulp, but they didn't. The bubble of air which had been trapped with them became warmer and more humid, but she didn't choke.

'It's all right, highness,' the captain whispered. 'I've been through this before. Last time, the dragomite queen sent a lantern to guide us, but you saw it broken a few minutes ago. We'll have to make our way by feel, until she can bring us to a lighted tunnel.'

'She?' Lucrezia echoed, quite unable to follow the sense of the argument.

'I'll lead the way, highness,' Cerri said, pushing past her as she said it. 'Take hold of the hem of my skirt and don't let go.'

He grabbed her hand and guided it to the edge of the coarse cloth which made up the lower part of his uniform. He wasted no time in moving off thereafter. She could hear the sound his hand made as he trailed it along the wall. *How can he be so calm?* she thought. *How can he know intuitively what to do?*

'My father sent you to fetch me home,' she said, repeating what Ereleth had told her as she began to walk behind him, heading into the dark abyss.

'He did,' the captain replied. 'But rumour has it that you don't want to go.'

'No,' she said faintly. 'I don't. But if . . .'

He interrupted her rudely. At any other time, it would have been an unforgivable failure of politeness, but she realised that he must have guessed what she was about to say, and that his reply was both chivalrous and magnanimous.

'If we get out of this alive, highness,' he said, 'I'll commit myself to your service. I'll go wherever you want to go: to the Navel of the World or the north pole, if necessary.'

Lucrezia made no immediate reply to this. It was, she realised, an offer made under dire stress, of which he might repent if he ever had the opportunity. The course they were following took them up a considerable gradient, but she was sure that they were not moving in a straight line. If they were headed for the surface they were taking a circuitous route.

'Why?' she said eventually, in a very different manner. 'Why did the tunnel open up for us? Why should the dragomite queen save us from her own warriors?'

'I don't know, highness,' Cerri replied, as he moved relentlessly forwards and upwards. 'Your guess is as good as mine. It might have something to do with that head which Myrasol has. We were taken out of our cell in order to find and fetch it, but I can't begin to comprehend the balance of power here. It called us *brother* and offered to serve as an oracle if we would only take it away. It seemed to be at odds with the mound-queen and her human warriors – but not, perhaps, with the dragomite queen. I fear that I can't even begin to fathom such mysteries – and I don't have the head with me now, for I set it down back there when I drew my sword, so it may be that it has nothing to do with this opportunity to escape – if it is, indeed, an opportunity . . .'

If it has nothing to do with the head, Lucrezia thought, *it might be for my benefit, for the sake of the challenges I laid out, the promises I made. The dragomite queen has a mind, and the mound-queen was her ears as well as her voice. She is saving us because we did indeed persuade her that she needs us desperately, because we are the only chance she has left to save . . . herself?*

'Not *herself*,' she murmured aloud. 'Her children. Her *chimerical* children. She thinks them uniquely precious, as all mothers do.'

'Highness?' the captain said uncertainly.

Lucrezia opened her mouth to give him a fuller account of her hypothesis, but she was breathing too hard. Long inertia had exacted a severe toll on her strength. The muscles of her legs would have had difficulty coping with the uphill course even at the best of times; at present they were simply not up to the task.

Her guide realised that she was exhausted, and stopped. She was aware of his fumbling as he tried to re-sheathe his sword. Did he intend to pick her up and carry her?

457

'Keep moving!' she gasped, intending it as a command. 'And keep your sword in your hand.'

He obeyed her, but he didn't climb as quickly as he had before.

Within minutes the darkness opened up before them to let in what seemed at first to be a veritable flood of light. In fact, though, the corridor into which they were discharged was very dimly lit. The air seemed cooler and fresher, though, and Lucrezia was grateful for any light at all. She was able to look her companion in the eye at last. She had seen him before, but only in the distance, and never as dirty.

'Thank you, captain,' she said.

'Don't thank me yet,' he said, with a calculated grimness which was almost pompous. 'The dragomite queen brought us here, but now we have to make up our own minds which way to go, and the open air is still a long way off.'

Lucrezia looked hesitantly to her left and her right, but it seemed obvious enough which direction they should take. The corridor was not level, and they were upward-bound. She pointed. He nodded agreement, and set off again. She had no need to hold on to his skirt now.

Within minutes they came to an intersection where a chain of dragomite workers was trekking from left to right, following an uphill gradient. They shrank back, but the workers made no aggressive move towards them and the procession soon passed.

'Do we follow them?' the captain asked.

'Yes,' she said, judging that they too must be trying to escape, and hoping that they knew the best route. 'Stay close behind them, if you can. If they belong to this nest, there's no need to fear them.'

He obeyed her without question, as a good guard-captain was honour-bound to do.

She began to wonder whether she had made the right choice when they came into a much larger open space, which must have been used in better times as some kind of food store, where 'crops' harvested from the slopes had been brought for sorting, processing and redistribution. Far the greater number of the remaining stockpiles were mere rotten heaps, but there were still a few stacks which had not been spoiled. The column of workers she and Jacom had followed were evidently involved in the task of collecting the useful foodstuffs for removal – which might have suited their own purpose very well, had it not been for the obvious fact that these workers had come too late. As the workers advanced – moving past hundreds of empty exoskeletons which were the relics of their dead sisters – the tunnels through which they would presumably have made their exits were already discharging warriors which fell upon them with awesome ferocity.

Some of the workers attempted to flee, but no matter which way they turned they could not find an escape-route. Others attempted to fight, meeting the gigantic jaws of the warriors with their own feebler ones, rearing up on their four back legs so as to use the front ones as if they were arms. Some actually took up crude weapons of one kind of another with which to thrust and stab.

Lucrezia looked behind her into the mouth of the tunnel from which they had come, but there was no longer room for them to move back into it. Lucrezia wanted to shout a warning to the creatures which were coming through it one by one, to tell the whole procession to turn about and go back, but she knew how futile such a gesture would be. As Lucrezia and Jacom moved sideways out of their way, the workers kept coming forward, one after another, delivering themselves into a trap from which none would escape.

The captain politely pushed her back so that she was stationed against a wall. He took up a position in front of her, ready to mount what defence he could, if and when it should become necessary.

There seemed to be no immediate danger, although more and more warriors were spilling into the cavern. They soon outnumbered the workers, so that they had little difficulty in cornering and slaughtering their adversaries, and that was the work to which they devoted themselves; if any of them saw the captain and the princess the sight did not distract them in the least. The two humans had nothing to do but watch the carnage.

The workers were by no means impotent to hurt the warriors; when it came to 'hand-to-hand' combat the workers were only a little weaker and considerably more dexterous. They could land telling blows, and had they had more room to manoeuvre they might have been able to give a better account of themselves – but the cavern was too cramped and too crowded, and the warriors had those murderous jaws, whose outer edges operated like massive clubs and whose inner edges could be brought together like huge pairs of shears, slicing through limbs or palps and sometimes cracking skulls like eggshells. Without warrior sisters to defend them the workers could only delay their own destruction. The battle was lost from the moment it was joined, but still it had to be fought and finished.

The ichor of the dragomites, Lucrezia saw, was not so very different in colour from human blood. Its odour, though not identical to the reek of human blood, was sufficiently similar to imply a kind of kinship.

What would a dragomite spectator think, Lucrezia wondered, if she had stood on one of Xandria's quays, watching an army trying to scale the wall of the citadel? That too would have seemed like slaughter, the only exception being that it was the slaughterers who were penned in, while the slaughtered had only to give up and retreat. Perhaps the dragomite would have understood the madness of it better than a human observer, for the dragomite would know what irresistible compulsion there is in certain kinds of instinct and certain kinds of command.

It was not as horrible a sight as she might have imagined. It was, in fact, rather fascinating. Although she had lost her initial horror of dragomites and had even begun to cultivate a certain perverse empathy with their kind she was not yet capable of pitying their destruction. As she watched the titans struggling, one to one or in groups where several warriors would tear apart a single worker, they seemed entirely mechanical. They could not scream, and did not offer any evidence convincing to human eyes that they felt pain or anguish.

Lucrezia suddenly became aware that no more workers were pouring out of the tunnel-mouth beside her. The rearmost member of the column had come forward to meet her ugly destiny. She stepped forward to tap the captain on the shoulder and bring this fact to his notice. Cerri nodded, both to confirm that he understood and to indicate that the princess should lead the way while he guarded against the possibility of pursuit.

The princess moved into the tunnel, walking as quickly as she could. Her legs were painfully weak but she concentrated her attention on striding without the least trace of a limp. She went forward boldly, determined not to falter until she could not take another step — but it never came to that. She had gone less than fifty paces before she met a dragomite coming the other way.

This one was not a worker. This one was a warrior.

Lucrezia had no way of knowing whether it was one of the nest's defenders hurrying to the relief of its sisters or yet another attacker hastening to take part in the massacre, but she had no reason to suppose that it would make a great difference to the monster's reaction to finding her in its path. She stopped, and tried to meet the dragomite's stare with all the courage that her own pathetically tiny eyes could contain.

Cerri moved awkwardly past her, and raised his steel blade, as though he too were a warrior dragomite, stunted and crippled in the body but equipped nevertheless with a single fearsome jaw.

The warrior had paused too, but confrontation with a sword-blade was enough to provoke it to action. It darted forward with alarming alacrity, and used its jaws with astonishing precision to pluck the sword clean out of the captain's grip. He had aimed his own thrust for the eye, but it never landed. As soon as he was disarmed the monster struck at him with one of its antennae, which lashed out like a whip to swipe him about the forehead. He staggered sideways and slumped against the tunnel wall, dazed but not unconscious.

Amazingly, and with truly heroic stupidity, the young man used his arms to thrust himself away from the wall, so that he lurched back into the path of the dragomite, placing himself directly between the princess and those horrid jaws. He spread his arms wide as though to make a barrier.

It seemed to Lucrezia to be a noble gesture, however futile.

The dragomite reached out its ugly head, and picked the soldier up in its jaws. Lucrezia didn't doubt that it could have cut the man in two now that it had seized him, but it didn't. Instead, it held him off the ground for a moment or two, and then simply *set him down again*, placing him carefully to one side.

She's on our side! Lucrezia thought. *She's one of us!* Even so, she backed away reflexively, and kept on backing up, without once daring to look behind her. The warrior followed her, matching its paces so exactly to hers that its staring eyes remained precisely the same distance from her own. She could hardly bear the awful scrutiny of that black stare, and when her legs gave out it was as if the eyes had hypnotised her and commanded her to fall. So extreme was the treason of her body that she fell very heavily, barely able to use her arms to cushion the impact. She felt sick and dizzy, but she fought desperately to retain consciousness.

Her eyes filled with tears and she lost sight of everything. When she felt the touch of something on her body she couldn't connect the sensation to anything visible, and for an agonisingly long moment she was convinced that it was the touch of a dragomite warrior's jaw.

Then, with a sudden shock of relief, she realised that she could feel *fingers* trying to grip her waist, *hands* trying to help her to her feet. She knew that it couldn't be Jacom Cerri, because the dragomite had moved smoothly past him, so she spoke the first name that came into her head, which was: 'Ereleth!'

Then her eyes cleared slightly, and a head loomed into view. She was so disorientated that she didn't know whether she was standing or lying down, or which way was up, but she could see all too clearly that the head didn't belong to Ereleth, nor to any other human being.

She tried to scream, but couldn't.

'Iss ssafe now, prinssess,' said a quaintly unhuman voice, struggling with the pronunciation of words which were evidently ill-fitted to its vocal apparatus. 'Iss ssafe. Iss very, very good.'

18

Andris had only one thought in his head as the two warriors closed in on one another, and that was to discover some slight chance of survival for Merel. When he saw the wall open to swallow Princess Lucrezia and Jacom Cerri he tried to follow them – but the wall closed behind them, seamlessly, before he had a chance to execute his plan.

The story of my life, he thought bitterly. *At the critical moment, magic doorways open up for princesses and soldiers, but never for ex-princes and soldiers of fortune.*

Carefully, he laid Merel down on the ground, shielding her body as best he could without actually resting his weight upon her. She still hadn't stirred, but he knew that her heart was beating because he had felt it when he picked her up. He reached out to pick up the disembodied head which Jacom Cerri had abandoned, and looked over his shoulder to see what was happening in the middle of the cave.

The two warriors drove hard at one another and their hugely-jawed heads clashed brutally above the mound-queen's recumbent form. The jaws locked together like the antlers of rutting stags fighting over a harem of hinds, and the warriors twisted their armoured necks fiercely as if they were trying to turn one another over. Although they made constant adjustments to their position they hardly moved from where they were, each one reluctant to yield a met of ground.

Over to the left, where the first warrior had fallen, the giant was still trying to recover her spear. She was having difficulty because the warrior was not yet inert, and she did not want to be struck by a thrashing leg or caught by one or other of the jaws by virtue of a convulsive movement of the dragomite's head.

Andris had once watched a battle for the dominance of a herd of deer fought by two antlered stags. The contest had been fierce and violent but he had been conscious of a certain reserve, as if the combatants had known that what they were involved in was a test of strength in which defeat might be conceded at any time without further injury being inflicted. It was apparent to him from the outset that this fight was different. This was to the death, and could have no other possible outcome.

Braced by all six of their legs, each fully determined not to retreat, the two warriors clubbed and stabbed at one another with their massive jaws, actually striking shards of chitin off the leading edges. The two heads were moving so quickly that several heavy blows were being struck in every second, yet neither one flinched. A severed antenna fell, still writhing, from the head of the nearer warrior. Its impetus carried it close to where Andris knelt, and he flicked it away with his booted foot, as if it were a snake about to sink its fangs into his fleshy calf.

He became conscious that Merel was stirring beneath him and immediately reached out to her. As if seized by a sudden claustrophobia she began to struggle against his solicitous hand, and he soothed her as best he could.

'It's all right,' he hissed. 'It's me – Andris.'

'Andris?' she said, ceasing to struggle the moment she heard the name. 'What the . . .'

He saw her eyes widen as she saw what he held in his free hand, and widen again as she looked past him to see what was happening beyond his protective shoulder. She sat up abruptly.

'It's all right!' he said, painfully aware of the absurdity of the reassurance. 'Can you get to the tunnel-mouth?'

She didn't reply, but she put her hand to her dizzy head. She didn't close her eyes, because she didn't dare. He half-turned to follow her gaze. The chitinous jaws of the warrior dragomites were still hacking at one another and at the armoured heads behind, making an appalling rattling sound. One of the monsters must have sustained a serious injury because red ichor was jetting in ragged spurts from one of the clashing heads. Andris could see it falling like rain into the still-widening pool of blood in which the mound-queen's body lay. He supposed that the mound-queen must have life in her yet, else her heart could not continue to pump the blood out of her body, but her prostrate form had been buffeted several times by the fighting dragomites and it was obvious from the awkward angles at which her limbs now lay that her long bones had been broken. The dragomites' ichor seemed to mingle and mix readily enough with her human blood – a fact which could no longer surprise Andris.

Suddenly, the uninjured dragomite shifted its position, scuttling round as if to catch its opponent off guard – but the move was a desperate reflex rather than a cunning stratagem, and Andris saw almost immediately what had occasioned it. A third dragomite had entered the chamber, enthusiastic to dive headlong into the fray.

It's all over now! he thought. Whichever of the fighting dragomites had received the support of a nest-mate would now be certain to win. In this kind of fighting, two heads were far better than one.

For a few seconds the dragomite which had been winning the contest only moments before danced upon its six limbs, hurling itself this way and that to avoid being cornered by two sets of jaws, but every instinctive move met an equally instinctive counter-move, and it required less than a minute for the two warriors working in concert to position themselves diagonally to either side of their opponent, and then to move in for the kill. The fact that one of them was hurt made little or no difference. The eyes of the lone fighter were savagely pulped and the hinges of its jaws disabled. It was then an easy matter for the victors to finish their work, cutting and slicing at the limbs and body-joints of their erstwhile opponent.

Andris was glad to see that Dhalla had recovered her spear, but not so happy to see her warily working her way towards the nearest portal. It seemed that she had no intention of trying to help him. He felt an impulse to call out, begging for aid, but something stopped him: pride, perhaps, or simple stubbornness. She had saved his life once already, but only because Ereleth was in danger too, and because he was Ereleth's creature.

She reached the dark tunnel-mouth, and took one step into it – but then she looked behind her, and caught his eye. She gazed at him – quite coldly, it seemed – and then she turned back. Instead of disappearing into the tunnel she continued to circle the room until she reached their station. Then she swung around to watch with

Andris as the execution of the warrior dragomite was completed. It had almost ceased to thrash and twist.

The two surviving warriors – one of them injured but the other quite unhurt – slowly turned to face the little group huddling by the wall. Andris came to his feet, although he used his free hand to force Merel to remain on her knees. The giant took a large knife from her belt and stiffly held it out to him. It was no sort of weapon for use against such adversaries as these, but he took it and was grateful. She hefted the spear, ready to hurl it at the uninjured warrior.

The two warriors were standing still – or almost still, for their antennae were moving very rapidly, vibrating madly as they bobbed and twitched.

'Stay exactly where you are,' said a hoarse voice. 'A little of my blood is on your clothes, and you had best be careful.'

Andris froze. He looked at the broken body of the mound-queen, which had been flipped on to its back by the conflict which had raged above her. The legs still lay at crazy angles, but the head had lifted slightly from the lake of blood and ichor. Her eyes were open. Andris was less surprised than he would have been had he not held the head of one of her drones in his left hand.

'Are they yours, then?' Andris whispered, meaning the two warriors.

'Not *hers*,' the mound-queen replied, speaking faintly but more easily than could have been expected, given that she had been so comprehensively trampled after tearing herself free from the throne. 'Conquerors, if they've come so far so quickly. Such warriors as the nest has left will be covering the retreat of the egg-bearers. Nothing left down here counts for anything, now, but if you can keep quite still until the drones come . . .'

So far as Andris was concerned, the most revealing word in this speech was *hers*, where he might have expected *ours*. If 'hers' meant 'the dragomite queen's' – and what else could it mean? – then the mound-queen was no longer the voice of another. This was her own voice. *We are not all of one mind*, Seth had told him, *nor all of one body, no matter how things may appear*. Although the mound-people had little use for names, they did have names. No matter how intimately bound together the flesh and the thoughts of these chimeras were, they had not fused into a seamless whole. They were capable of difference, of conflict, of confusion . . . perhaps, as they stared death in the face, of hysteria, of the kind of surrender to the irrational that had stopped Dhalla from taking her opportunity to escape and brought her to stand beside a man she could not love or admire.

'What's happening?' Merel asked breathlessly.

'I wish I knew,' Andris whispered.

'They're following instructions,' Dhalla said, meaning the dragomites. 'They've been told, somehow, not to attack us. They have very little mind, but they'll obey, if we don't provoke them.'

It seemed to Andris that this was a clever guess. It made sense of the warriors' patient inaction – but whose 'instructions' were they following?

'The giant's right,' whispered the stricken mound-queen, 'but they're uncertain, their instincts confused. Bide your time. The drones will come as quickly as they can, with their own egg-bearers – and perhaps their own mound-queen, although I had not thought it possible.'

She stopped abruptly as one of the warriors – the injured one – turned its head in her direction. She was all but dead, but she was capable of fear. Within a few seconds, though, she began again. 'We did not know how much we needed one another,' she said, her voice becoming even fainter. 'Guard my daughters well, if they will let you – and my brother too. Be still, and all will be well. If you value your life, *be still*.' Her head sank back then, into the sticky mess which flooded the floor. Andris had seen too many wonders to be certain that she would not rally again, but the battered and unreasonably fleshy body looked as dead as dead could be.

'What's happening here?' Merel whispered plaintively. 'For Goran's sake *tell me what's happening*.'

'The nest-war's over,' Andris said, 'but something else has happened – *is happening*. The new tenants of the Corridors of Power aren't quite what the mound-queen or her drones expected, and they don't want us dead.'

'Thanks,' said Merel faintly. 'Now I understand everything.'

'Ereleth will understand,' said Dhalla confidently.

Is that supposed to reassure us? Andris wondered.

Silence fell, and remained for several minutes – but the constant stare of the warrior dragomites was too oppressive to bear, and Andris felt that the three of them were engaged in a tacit contest to see who would break first. It was Merel.

'I'm not sorry I came,' she said. 'I want you to know that, Andris. I'd rather be with you than up there, waiting for news of you. Whether we get out of this or not . . .'

She sounded embarrassed – probably, Andris guessed, because Dhalla's inhibiting presence made it difficult for her to express her feelings.

'I understand,' he said. 'And I hope you'll understand when I say I'd rather you were five hundred kims away from this whole mess, somewhere safe. For myself, I'm very glad I met you – but in a way I'd far rather you'd never got my message. I'd rather be feeding a thornbush with my living blood, if that would mean that you'd be safe . . .'

Dhalla refrained from adding to this sentimental exchange. The next voice Andris heard was female, but it wasn't hers. It came from some distance away, within the mouth of one of the many tunnels. The speaker was not yet visible. 'Is this it?' it asked.

'Ssiss iss it, prinssess,' answered another voice, whose like he had certainly never heard.

Princess Lucrezia stepped into the chamber, and stopped abruptly as she caught sight of the waiting dragomites. One of her companions came on ahead of her. Andris had never seen a Serpent, but he had heard descriptions of them, and knew that this was one. Her other companion – Jacom Cerri – hung back.

'Dhalla!' the princess said, jolted into movement again by the sight of the giant. 'Are you all right?'

'Iss all finisshed now,' the Serpent said, looking straight at Andris and the severed head. 'Iss all ssafe.'

Andris relaxed, not knowing until he did so how rigid his determination not to move had made him. He moved Seth's head to a more comfortable position and handed Dhalla's knife back to her.

'Thanks,' he said.

'It was always rumoured that she had Serpent's blood,' Merel murmured. 'It's always the wildest rumours that turn out to be true.'

'Name iss Mossassor,' said the Serpent earnestly, still addressing itself to Andris. 'Am ssearsshing for garden, ass iss prinssess, ass iss Kesshvara. All ssearssh for garden togesser, now. All friendss. Iss good. Iss very, very good.'

Andris glanced at the two waiting warriors, neither of which had made a hostile move. He concluded that there was some truth in what the darklanders believed. Serpents evidently could control dragomites. Just now, he was profoundly glad of the fact.

'It's all right,' Princess Lucrezia assured them. 'Mossassor can secrete stuff through his skin that's far more powerful and far more versatile than the stuff Aulakh Phar gave you to put on your foreheads. Serpents and dragomites are kindred species, you see – after a fashion. They have a sort of non-aggression pact, which goes back a million years and more. In times of crisis, things change inside some of them – and inside some of us too. We aren't consciously aware of the triggers or the effects, but they're there. That's part of what it means to have Serpent's blood – or Salamander's fire.'

'Iss true,' the Serpent added, as if it were desperately anxious to establish that its word could be trusted. 'Hass ssaved you all. Musst all look for garden, with prinssess with Serpent'ss blood. Iss very, very important. In flessh – all flessh. Musst not war, musst be on ssame sside, elsse all losst. Iss very, very important.'

'Just like the darklanders,' Merel muttered, although Andris couldn't quite see why she sounded so aggrieved about it. 'He thinks it's the end of the rotting world.'

'Yess,' answered Mossassor gravely. 'Iss essactly ssat. End . . . and beginning. You musst all help – all. Isst debt, you ssee. Iss debt you owe uss. We ssave you for ssiss. Not eassy, but we musst.'

Andris remembered the blind story-teller in the Wayfaring Tree, and wished that he had listened more closely to the legend that the man had tried so earnestly to relate – especially the part about the forefathers making a deal with Serpents, offering promises that could not be fulfilled for a very long time. *It seems that I'm accumulating quite a stock of bizarre debts*, he thought, still cradling his adopted brother in the crook of his left arm. *But that's not bad. A man with obligations has directions in his life – and that's something I haven't had for a long time*. He put his right arm across Merel's shoulders, and drew himself up to the full extent of his height as though he were ready, willing and able to take arms against the whole world on behalf of those who needed him.

'All right,' he said, to no one in particular. 'Why not? It suits me. All friends, all searching for the garden together. What have I got to lose? I was proud once, but not any more. I'll work for Fraxinus, for Ereleth, for the Serpent king or the dragomite queen. I'll draw maps for anyone.'

'No Sserpent king,' said Mossassor, in a curiously earnest fashion. 'Iss only uss. Iss good, iss good.'

Andris stepped forward then, and walked towards the warrior dragomites. They watched him quite impassively. For once, even their antennae were still. He stopped by the body of the mound-queen, and knelt down beside her. She was, as he had supposed, quite dead.

He looked over his shoulder at the Serpent, which had turned to watch him.

'Not quite a bloodless victory,' he observed. In spite of what he had said to the Serpent he was not too proud to be smugly satisfied with his awesome self-possession. Although he had not struck a single blow in anger against any man or dragomite, he felt like a hero, and he felt that he was entitled to feel like a hero.

'Iss not way ssingss work,' the Serpent replied. It was impossible to tell whether it was sorrowful or not. 'No promissess. Many dangerss, more blood . . . but all on ssame sside, yess?'

'Yes,' said the princess – who was, after all, the highest-born among them. 'From now on, we're all on the same side.'

470

19

CHECUTI SAT CROSS-LEGGED on the ground, leaning back against the newly repaired wheel of the small wagon, carefully polishing his sword. Technically, of course, it was the property of the king's guard, but in the circumstances he felt perfectly entitled to appropriate it, on the grounds that no one had a better claim to it. While he polished away – taking great care over the job, as the sword was now his most valuable asset – he tried to figure out how long his meagre supply of anti-lustrust salve would last. The result of the calculation was far from satisfactory, and he resolved to steal some more.

His faithful monkey had retreated under the wagon to avoid the sun. When Checuti had begun his work he had been in the shade himself, but the sun was now at its zenith and the precious shadow had melted away. He knew that it was going to be a long, hot afternoon, but he was determined to make the best of it in case it turned out to be his last. Living on the edge of extinction gave an uncommonly sharp edge to life.

It was most unfortunate, he mused, that he had been drafted into this business without having time to prepare proper plans – but if he did manage to survive, it might not turn out so badly. Perhaps it was good for a man to be forced to return to square one occasionally, to ensure that he retained all his skills. At present, he was as poor as poor could be, but a man with his talent for acquisition surely need not remain so for long.

He was mildly surprised by his own light-headedness and perverse optimism. It must, he concluded, be the effect of having stared death in the face and watched it turn aside in the nick of time – either that or sunstroke.

A shadow fell across his work and he looked up. It was the female dragomite-rider and heroine of the hour, Hyry Keshvara.

'Hello, Checuti,' she said. There was a strange note of satisfaction in her voice, presumably occasioned by finding him in such reduced circumstances.

'I'm glad to see that the rumours of your death were exaggerated,' Checuti said equably. 'Is the grand conference over?'

'It's hardly begun,' the trader said, leaning against the side of the wagon. 'Fraxinus won't get much out of Ssifuss. Mossassor is the one who thinks it knows what it's doing.'

'And does it?' Checuti asked.

'Maybe. It knows a lot more than I do, or thinks it does, but Ssifuss is more than a little sceptical. I think it sees itself as a benevolent restraining influence, although it strikes me as being more than a trifle churlish. It and Fraxinus are busy discussing paedogenesis. Do you know what paedogenesis is, Checuti?'

'No,' Checuti said.

'Neither did I. Even Fraxinus had never heard the word, but Aulakh Phar explained it. Now we all know what it means, and we only have to figure out exactly how it applies to what we're doing, if it applies at all. Ssifus isn't sure, so how can we be?'

Checuti continued polishing the sword-blade. He felt a slight tug at his sleeve as the monkey leaned out from beneath the wagon to see what was going on. After taking a brief look at Keshvara the monkey disappeared again. *She's not that bad*, Checuti observed silently. *Not bad at all, considering the competition.*

Keshvara abruptly changed the subject. 'After you foisted the princess on to me, you sent men to follow us, didn't you? To make sure that we went south instead of going back to Xandria.'

'Just for a day or two,' Checuti agreed.

'Shortly before we reached the forest, four men attacked us. Were they your men?'

Checuti looked up at her, squinting against the midday light. 'No,' he said. 'My men were instructed not to harm you.'

'Did they come back?'

'Yes.'

Keshvara thought about it for a moment or two, then nodded her head to signal that she believed him. He took it as a compliment. He was, in fact, telling the truth – but such was his reputation that two people out of three wouldn't have believed him.

472

'What happened to the four men who attacked you?' he asked curiously.

'I killed two of them,' Keshvara said blandly. 'The princess killed the other two. But if you hadn't forced me to take the princess with me, I'd never have been attacked at all . . . and I wouldn't have been up that rotting tree at that rotting ford, sticking my stupid hand into the nasty bit of that rotting flowerworm.'

'And you wouldn't have met up with your Serpent friends, and you wouldn't have come riding out of nowhere on the back of a dragomite to save my worthless life, at least for a day or two,' Checuti finished for her. 'And I would never have got mixed up with Ereleth in the first place, and . . . what do you want, an apology?'

'It'd be a start,' Keshvara said.

'All right,' he replied, with a shrug of his shoulders. 'I'm sorry. I should have let Burdam strangle the little bitch. OK?'

She shook her head wearily. What had she expected?

'So what's paedogenesis?' he asked. 'And why is Fraxinus so excited about it?'

She sat down beside him, screening her eyes from the sun as she looked up at the deserted slopes of the dragomite mound. Like everyone else who couldn't sleep, even though it was midday, she was waiting anxiously to see who would come out and who wouldn't – but not quite as anxiously as he was.

'According to Phar,' she said, 'there are certain kinds of darkland flies whose maggots live on rotting wood.'

'That's maggots for you,' Checuti remarked bitterly, 'no taste at all.'

'The thing is,' she said, 'that rotting wood doesn't last very long in these parts, because there are half a hundred things avid to devour every fallen log. So the flies have a neat trick which enables them to make the most of their opportunities. When a clutch of eggs hatches inside a rotten log, the maggots get busy, eating like crazy, and while the rotting log lasts they don't actually bother going through their full life-cycle – which would normally involve turning into pupae for a while and then hatching out into real flies. The maggots breed as maggots, and lay eggs of their own, which produce more and more maggots. That way, they can crowd out

473

most of their competitors. It isn't until the rotting log's nearly finished that they revert to doing things the way most other flies do, pupating by the thousand and lying dormant for a while, until they produce a whole flock of adults – which promptly mate like crazy and then fly off in every direction, in search of juicy trees hovering on the very edge of terminal decay. Paedogenesis means *breeding young*, or words to that effect. That's what the maggots do, you see, just so long as everything is going well and the good things of maggoty life are in abundant supply.'

'Very clever,' Checuti said. 'So what?'

'Mossassor reckons that the forefathers made some creatures with a similar lifestyle, only much more so. Don't ask me how, but even Ssifuss agrees that designing and making living things is what the legendary *Genesys* business was all about. The people of the ship were our ancestors, but they didn't just *give birth* to us the way we give birth to our children. They *designed* us, and they designed and made a million other things as well. Every species, in fact, that we call "earthly" – or their ancestors, at least. Pigs, horses, dredgers, gnarlytrees . . . and countless tinier things. Including things that live *on* us and things that live *in* us.'

'Why would they do that?'

'Because it was the only way, apparently, that we could live in the world at all. According to Mossassor – and the lore, according to Fraxinus's reading of it – they couldn't have done it without borrowing some stuff from Serpents and Salamanders. Don't ask me what they borrowed, or why they had to, or what they did with it, but let's accept for the sake of argument that they did. Well, some of the things they made – some of the most important things they made – were paedogenetic. Not flies and maggots, you understand – much smaller and subtler things than that.

'For generation after generation, these things breed while remaining immature in some crucial sense . . . but from time to time, they respond to some kind of environmental signal and they go into a wholly different reproductive mode. All of a sudden, after hundreds of generations – maybe thousands – they start . . . well, whatever their equivalent of pupating is. They start producing something new, something different. And because they're inside us – inside some of us, at least – they start affecting us differently. They start fouling up the way we normally behave.

'That's what Mossassor says, anyway. That's what it thinks we mean when we say someone has Serpent blood. It thinks they have something inside of them which can suddenly flip into a whole new way of being . . . and flip them, too. It's not just people who have Serpent's blood, though . . . potentially, at least, it's all of us . . . one way or another. Them too – Serpents, I mean. And dragomites. And Salamanders. And . . . well, everything. The whole damn world. For hundreds of generations . . . thousands of years . . . it's all maggots. Then, all of a sudden, it's pupa time . . . and after that, fly time. Not literally, but something like that.

'In short, something very, very weird is happening . . . in our blood, in our heads, and – most of all – in the Pool of Life at the Navel of the World: in Chimera's Cradle.'

Checuti studied her face carefully. 'You believe all that, don't you?' he said. 'Even though this Ssifuss doesn't, you do.'

'Every rotting word,' she agreed. 'I can barely grasp the elements of it, and I certainly don't know what it implies for the world or for me, but I believe it. Mossassor believes it, and Fraxinus is more than halfway to believing it. Ssifuss doesn't *want* to believe it . . . but it's here, isn't it? We're all here.'

'You're saying that something inside of us – some living thing squirming in our guts like that worm Ereleth fed me – brought us here without our even knowing it?'

'In a manner of speaking,' she agreed. 'But then again, it certainly didn't force us. That's not the way it works. We make our own decisions. Maybe there are things in our flesh which aren't, strictly speaking, *us* – and maybe there are ideas in our mind which aren't entirely *our own* – but we're still free. In some essential respect, we're still free. Every time we go to sleep, we become someone else . . . but when we wake up again, we're still *us*. Something like that, anyhow.'

'And all this is supposed to make sense, is it?' Checuti said. 'Or are you telling me in the hope that I'll tell you that it *doesn't* make sense, so that you can forget it?'

'I'm telling you,' she informed him frostily, 'because I thought you'd like to know. I thought you were *entitled* to know, even though you're just a lousy thief who can't be trusted any further than I could throw a feather into a headwind, and who'd probably be doing us all a big favour if you decided to desert, disappear or

475

die. Assuming that Mossassor comes out of that mound, you see, we're all going on together: south, to the marshes and Salamander's Fire and the Silver Thorns, all the way to the Navel of the World. I just thought you'd like to know why, or as much of the why as anyone else knows.'

'I see,' Checuti said. 'Thanks.'

She stared into his eyes, as if she were trying to judge whether he believed her, and whether he cared. He wished that he had an honest answer to show her, but he didn't. The only thing he was sure of was that she meant every word of it.

To stave off the force of that assertive gaze he said: 'It's true that Serpents can control dragomites, then. The darklanders were right about that, too.'

'The Serpents can't exactly *control* the dragomites,' Keshvara told him evenly. 'They didn't lead that army here, no matter what it might have looked like. It's just that they can talk to the dragomites in their own language of odours and vibrations. The dragomites tolerate them – to the extent that if only Mossassor can reach the people trapped in the Corridors of Power it'll be able to protect them from the invaders.'

Checuti considered the implications of the word *tolerate*, on the assumption that it must have been carefully chosen. 'If your Serpent friends can't actually control dragomites,' he said slowly, 'that means they aren't actually controlling the situation as a whole, doesn't it?'

'I'm afraid so,' Keshvara replied. 'But we're not in mortal danger. Mossassor was very certain of that.'

Speak for yourself, Checuti thought. *I've got a worm in my guts which needs Ereleth's tender care to ensure it stays lonely.*

'Not that any of us is actually in control,' he observed aloud. 'Fraxinus and Ereleth both think they're in command of the expedition and they hate one another's guts. Myrasol and I hate Ereleth too, but we have to follow her orders regardless. As for the princess, and that gloomy young captain . . . do you really think we'll meekly follow a Serpent whose own kind think it's probably crazy, when we can't even organise ourselves?'

'We all want the same thing,' Keshvara said. 'Life, preferably long and preferably interesting. It doesn't matter who's in control, as long as we're all headed in the same direction.'

'Not to you, maybe,' he said, choosing to voice the thought this time. 'But Ereleth is in control of me, and I don't like it. The thing that's living inside me certainly isn't leaving me much freedom of choice.'

'No,' she said. 'I guess it isn't. Still – now you know as much as I do. That's something, isn't it?'

She was right, and he couldn't deny it. Even if it turned out to be nonsense, it was the nonsense which was driving their rescuers – the nonsense that had saved their lives, at least for a day or two. He had to know things like that, if he were to bring all his cleverness to bear on his present predicament.

'After all,' she continued, 'we wouldn't want things to be too simple and straightforward, would we? That'd take all the savour out of life, wouldn't it?'

He recognised the quotation, and condescended to smile wryly. 'Thanks for bringing me up to date,' he said. He added: 'I appreciate it,' just to make sure that she understood he wasn't being sarcastic, and then stretched out his right hand.

She took it.

'Funny old world, isn't it?' she remarked, evidently unable to resist the temptation. 'But then, you like it that way, don't you?'

As they sealed their uneasy friendship, Checuti saw Ereleth step out of the mouth of a tunnel on the slope high above them, hiding her eyes from the sudden sunlight. She was flanked by half a dozen mound-women. They all looked down at the waiting horses and wagons.

Ereleth was dirty and dishevelled but somehow – perhaps it was the vivid brightness of the sunlight in which she bathed, and the way she welcomed its dry heat as though it were hers to demand and command – there was no mistaking the fact that she was a queen, of sorts.

477

20

THE OPEN AIR had never felt so good to breathe, and the sight of the sun – although the afternoon was bruisingly bright – had never been so welcome to Andris's eyes. He felt that he had descended into a kind of hell and had emerged again, triumphant simply by virtue of having survived. He felt that he was stronger now than he had ever been, tempered by adversity and by horror.

No one rushed to greet him or to enthuse over his salvation. The only one of their party who received any kind of welcome was the princess; she and the Serpent named Mossassor were the centre of attention. Andris might have commanded more attention by displaying the head of the human drone like some gruesome trophy, but he had taken care to secrete that within his shirt – remaining sensible, of course, of the warning he had been given about wrapping it too tightly.

He returned as quickly as he could to the small wagon, where his personal possessions were stored. Merel and Jacom Cerri went with him. There was no water for bathing but they cleaned themselves as best they could with damp rags and put on clean clothes. Then they found a sealed jar full of biscuits and another of spiced and salted meat, and fed themselves. Then Andris dissolved some sugar in a little fresh water, and dripped it on to the tongue of the disembodied head.

Afterwards, Andris placed the head in a dark corner, where it would be unobtrusive. Merel constantly darted glances at it, as if expecting its eyes to open.

'Can it really survive like that?' she asked. 'It has no lungs to enliven its blood, and no heart to pump the blood through its brain. Surely it requires more than sugared water to sustain itself.'

'It seemed to think that it could live long enough to be united with a new body, if only I could find out how to do it,' Andris said.

'I suppose it has provision of some kind for the enlivening of its blood and the adequate supply of its sleeping brain. It isn't truly human – or, at any rate, not *merely* human. It's a chimera: a fusion of earthly and unearthly flesh. I suspect Dhalla may be a chimera too – and possibly the princess, though she doesn't show it.'

'Perhaps we all are,' Merel suggested, not meaning it.

'Perhaps we are,' Andris said thoughtfully.

'I don't believe that,' Cerri said. 'There was too much nonsense being talked around here even before that damned Serpent added his contribution. We'd be far better off without any of it.'

'We don't have that option, Jacom,' Andris said quietly. He used the captain's given name deliberately, to emphasise the fact that they had made their peace, and could disagree without injuring their new-found and still-awkward amity. The captain contrived a slight smile in recognition of his courtesy. Cerri seemed happier now – as a man who had been through what he had been through had every right to be.

'Did it really call you *brother*, and ask you to find it a new body?' Merel asked.

'It did,' Andris assured her. 'And I accepted the duty. It seemed important – not just to the drone but in some more general sense. All that my actual brothers ever wanted was either to recruit me to their schemes or to stab me in the back. I've no real reason to think that this desperate pretended brother has any nobler intentions, but . . . you've taught me a lesson in kinship, cousin, and I must put it to the test. I don't know how to do what it – what *he* – asked me to do, but I'll surely try. Fraxinus and Phar might be able to advise me – and they'll certainly be interested.'

'The princess was interested,' Merel observed. 'I could see that plainly enough. Perhaps witches have their uses for severed heads, just as they have their uses for broken-legged bodies. I think the Serpent was interested too, although it's hard to tell when a face shows as little expression as that. He's trying very hard to be friends, isn't he? *All on ssame sside, yess?*'

Merel glanced at Jacom as she said this – dutifully pretending, for Andris's sake, that she intended no insult to him. Andris was glad when Cerri smiled again.

'I'm not complaining,' Andris said. 'He – actually, I think the Serpent really is an it – saved our lives down there.'

'We might not have needed saving,' Merel pointed out grimly, 'if that giant hadn't hit me. I'd vow to get even if she wasn't three times my size and five times as nasty.'

'We've got grudges enough to bear,' Andris told her tiredly. 'She didn't mean to hurt you, and she came to take her stand with us when she could have slipped away. Let's just be thankful that Ereleth got out safely – she still holds the key to my continued survival. Finished?'

Merel and Cerri nodded, and Andris gathered up the remains of their meal. He moved to the rear of the wagon to stow the debris in an orderly fashion. Checuti was just about to climb in, and Andris extended a helping hand to him. The thief-master pointed at the slope from which Andris and his companions had earlier descended. 'It's all over,' he said. 'We're on our way.'

Andris followed the direction of the pointing finger, and then looked the other way. Cerri moved to join them and they all looked out, shading their eyes against the sun.

To the right and left of the wagons and the donkey-train, less than fifty mets distant on either flank, two columns of dragomites and mound-women had formed, each with a single warrior in the van. The dragomite workers had clusters of eggs cemented to their backs, encased in translucent masses of hardened slime. From the ridges above, other warriors looked on. To Andris they seemed identical to those whose departure they were supervising, but he knew that they were enemies and conquerors, made gracious in victory only by the diplomatic intervention of the Serpents.

Two darklanders had already taken their stations at the front of the wagon, and they were urging the waiting horses to action.

'Passengers only on this wagon,' Checuti observed drily. 'All the important people are up ahead, planning the future of the world. Fraxinus and Phar, the three Serpents, Ereleth . . . can you imagine how painful it is for one of my abilities to feel excluded?'

'It's not going to be easy to feel included,' Cerri commented. 'The order of things has been turned upside-down. Dragomites march alongside men, Serpents enter into earnest discussion with men as to the meaning of a word I never heard before, and the true significance of Serpent's blood and Salamander's fire. It's difficult to feel that we're really part of something like this.'

'We could be part of it,' Checuti said, 'if only we were invited.

You ought to regret it as much as I do, captain. Your future lies with us, now that your guardsmen have ridden off and will probably never be seen again – taking that boy you befriended with them. You might not like the idea of allying yourself with Serpents and dragomites – not to mention we three diehard rogues – but you have precious few alternatives. Given that you're included, whether you like it or not, wouldn't you rather be fully included?'

Cerri shrugged, with only a slight hint of resentment in his pale eyes.

'I've had enough of quarrelling,' Andris said. 'I'm too tired for this kind of sniping – and so is Jacom.' Again he used the given name deliberately, for Checuti's information.

The thief-master evidently took the inference. 'A thousand pardons!' he said. 'You're brothers in blood, now, are you not? You descended into the underworld as enemies, shared many adventures, and came back fast friends.'

'Yes we did,' Andris agreed flatly. 'Shall I tell you what happened down there? Shall I tell you what you missed because Jacom took your place?'

Checuti held up a placatory hand. 'I'm sorry,' he said, this time sounding as if he meant it. 'Yes, you must tell me what happened, when you have the time and the patience. I had already offered Captain Cerri a truce, if you recall, and I'm more than willing to offer him my hand now. When the order of things turns upside-down, we must be prepared to commit ourselves to strange alliances. I know that.'

'You cannot know how strange,' the captain muttered, as he reached out to touch the thief-master's fingers in belated acknowledgement of their truce. Andris knew that he was referring to the severed head, but felt that it would be best to leave an explanation of that until he had time to give a full and proper account of everything he had done since Checuti had seen him last.

'I wish that hulking oaf Burdam Thrid were here,' Checuti said, trying to bury the awkwardness of the situation with more trivial chatter. 'It would be useful to have someone to lord it over. I've been a plotter and a planner far too long; I've lost the art of being a mere bystander. But you three are better company than Burdam ever was, and although I'm a leader by vocation I can stand being a mere companion for a while.'

'I was born to be a leader of men myself,' Andris observed, 'but I never really tried. I ran away instead. I suppose I'm running still, but I don't feel that I am. Not any more.'

'That's because you think you've found your lady love,' Checuti retorted. 'I suppose you think that puts you one up on everybody else, at least until the fever passes.'

'It does put me one up on everyone else,' Andris said drily, 'unless Fraxinus is carrying on with Keshvara. Somehow, I doubt that.'

'Perhaps Captain Cerri will get together with the princess,' Merel suggested. 'He *is* the best-looking man around.'

Cerri actually blushed at that, and Andris didn't bother to correct her. Checuti waved a hand airily and said: 'Oh no – she needs an older man to take her in hand – someone sophisticated. If only she weren't a witch . . .' He trailed off, and added, in a much quieter tone: 'Talking of witches . . .'

Princess Lucrezia had suddenly appeared within their field of vision, standing to one side as the wagon overtook her. Now she began to walk behind it, looking up at the three figures standing by the backboard.

'May I come up?' she asked.

Andris was surprised that it was framed as a request and not a command. 'Certainly, highness,' he said, promptly enough. He extended his hand yet again. He was sorely tempted to drop her when she grabbed it, all the more so because she was rather less agile than she should have been, and made much heavier work of clambering up and over the backboard than he had expected.

'I suppose I should introduce my companions formally, highness,' said Checuti, defiantly determined to recover the light mood. 'After all, this is your first meeting with them in the real world. You will, of course, remember your humble servant Checuti, prince of thieves – briefly the part-owner of a royal treasury the equal of any in Xandria, and even more briefly the hostage-keeper of your royal person. This is Merel Zabio, an enterprising young pirate of my acquaintance, now – unfortunately – well on her way to becoming a dull wife; this is Captain Jacom Cerri, a loyal but unlucky officer of your father's guard; and this is Andris Myrasol, prince of Ferentina, once imprisoned in your father's jail for a crime he didn't commit and intended by yourself for a fate worse than – and including – death. My friends, this is Princess Lucrezia, witch-princess of the greatest empire in the world – who demanded in right regal fashion, when I happened to kidnap her by accident, that I should do anything I liked with her, except send her home. Did you come to inform us of some momentous decision made at Fraxinus's conference table, highness?'

The princess bore all this tolerantly, and not entirely without amusement. She didn't protest that she already knew Jacom, Andris and Merel well enough, having walked from the depths of the world to its surface in their company.

'I've brought you both a gift,' she said.

Andris was astonished. Even Checuti was not quite equal to the task of remaining calm and flippant – but doubts immediately set in.

'What gift?' Andris asked, sounding surly in spite of himself.

'You know what gift, Prince Myrasol,' she said. She took something from one of the many pouches at her belt, and opened her palm to display what she had. There were two grey lumps. Andris had never been offered anything which looked as unappetising. Nevertheless, he picked up one of the two. Checuti took the other.

'Did Ereleth send you?' Checuti asked warily.

'No she didn't,' Lucrezia replied firmly. 'And that's no mere palliative to keep the worms from reproducing themselves while leaving them alive. It's deadly poison, to them but not to you. You won't like the taste, I fear, and the stuff will give you a frightful pain in the belly for half a day or more, but it *will* set you free.'

'I don't wish to sound ungrateful,' Andris said, staring hard at the object he held between thumb and forefinger, 'and I'm acutely aware of the fact that the purpose for which Ereleth recruited our services has now been fulfilled, but in Ferentina we have a saying: *Never rely on the gratitude of princes.*'

'Xandria,' the princess said, 'is a civilised nation. Its people are honourable . . . and it breeds the greatest cheats and liars in the known world. Ereleth told me what she did, and why. She also said that we might well have further need of you, and that loyal servants might be a very rare and precious asset in days to come. I agreed, as meekly as any loyal pupil of a clever witch-queen. But I owe you both a debt, and I'm here to discharge it.'

483

Andris frowned. 'Would you really have done what Checuti said you intended?' he asked haltingly. 'Would you really have forced me to eat a seed which would have grown in my guts, sprouting thorns inside me and putting forth poisonous flowers from my living flesh?'

'When we're offered the seeds of a miracle,' the princess replied, 'we're understandably anxious to see them flower. Yes, I would have done it, in a fever of curiosity. But what I offer you now is a very different seed, whose produce is longer life for you and the thief, and I hope you might deign to consider it adequate recompense for a hurtful intention which was, after all, never fulfilled. I think we shall all see marvels enough, in the days which lie ahead – and if Hyry's Serpent friend is right, we may all have things growing inside us which have yet to display their flowers and their thorns. The seed which the bronzes sent to Xandria was a summons, of sorts, and it has done its work. I'd rather make my peace with those who will be by my side in days to come than have them hate me.'

'I could swallow this and hate you still,' said Andris wryly. 'Had you thought of that?'

'You might,' agreed the princess. 'But I shall be more comfortable, knowing that I have done what I could to repair the matter. A hard road lies before us, and if I have judged the matter accurately there is far more enmity within our ranks than we can comfortably accommodate. Eat it, please.'

Andris looked down at Merel, who shrugged her shoulders very slightly. It was Checuti who set an example, thrusting the grey stuff into his mouth and chewing. An expression of deep disgust possessed his features, but he swallowed regardless.

Andris did likewise.

It really did taste absolutely foul. He had to fight an instinct to gag and spit it out. The thought that he still had the belly-ache to look forward to was not a pleasant one.

When Checuti had got rid of the taste, as best he could, he said: 'Now we'll never know whether the whole thing was a bluff. We'll never know whether we were played for suckers by a pair of charlatans.'

The princess didn't seem to be offended by his cynicism. 'So far as I can tell,' she said, 'the lore of witchcraft consists in the main of learning to cure sicknesses which one would never encounter were there no witches in the world to inflict them – but the sicknesses are real enough. I have a natural aptitude for such work, it seems. It's said that I have Serpent's blood – and if even Serpents are willing to entertain such a notion, who am I to doubt or deny it? Don't waste your time with hatred, Prince Myrasol. We're in this together, you and I – and we have a long way to go, if your map can be trusted.'

'My map is good,' Andris said. He was glad to find that he wasn't actually going to be sick. He put a protective arm around Merel's shoulder, and felt the pleasant pressure of her body as she moved as close to him as she could. 'If it shows a long, hard road,' he added, 'that's exactly what we face.'

Lucrezia wasn't to be denied the last word – she was, after all, a princess of an empire far greater than tiny Ferentina.

'We'll reach its end eventually,' she said, 'if we can only accept that we're all on the same side.'

Somehow, the words sounded much saner when they weren't pronounced with a Serpent's hiss.